MARKED
FOR DEATH

'Utterly compelling from start to finish, and up there with my top reads
of the year'
— Robert Scragg, author of *What Falls Between the Cracks*

'Thrilling . . . A right proper page turner . . . An edgy, considered and
pitch perfect crime drama with great depth, some engaging twists and
plenty of unexpected moments — I loved it for its fresh feel and utterly
riveting plot. Bring on more is what I say. This is a series I'd like to see
run and run. Highly recommended'
— Liz Loves Books

'A gritty, multi-layered, engaging cleverly constructed thriller . . . a
fast, slick explosive read which will leave you breathless, with a clever
and unexpected twist at the end. If like me you loved *Killer Intent*, then
you're in for a real treat. Cannot recommend this highly enough. This
will undoubtedly be one of the reading hits of 2019'
— AMW Books

Praise for *Killer Intent*:

'A twisty, action-packed conspiracy thriller. Kent knows how to bring the
thrills'
— Mason Cross, author of the Carter Blake series

'A perfectly plotted blockbuster of a book with killer intent'
— Imran Mahmood, author of *You Don't Know Me*

'A must-have read of 2018'
— *Sunday Express*

'A compelling combination of political drama and lethal action.
There are echoes of Michael Dobbs's *House of Cards* but there is more
derring-do in Kent's twisty tale, which has all the makings of a bestseller'
— *Daily Mail*

MARKED FOR DEATH

TONY KENT

Elliott&Thompson

First published 2019 by
Elliott and Thompson Limited
27 John Street
London WC1N 2BX
www.eandtbooks.com

Hardback ISBN: 978-1-78396-392-8
eBook ISBN: 978-1-78396-393-5

9 8 7 6 5 4 3 2 1

A catalogue record for this book is available from the British Library.

Typesetting: Marie Doherty
Printed in the UK by TJ International Ltd

For Victoria and Joseph
You made everything complete

ONE

Phillip Longman was not woken by the sound of breaking glass. That would have required sleep, and sleep was something his elderly body no longer seemed to need.

A metal rail hung from a reinforced section of the ceiling. Longman's frail hands gripped it as tightly as they could. Using all of his strength, he pulled his body upright. The automated mattress followed, designed to support him if that strength gave out. Longman was a proud man. Too proud to be raised by a mechanical bed. Too proud for a panic alarm. But pride could not keep him vertical. The mattress was Longman's concession to his body's decay.

The sound of exertion filled the room. Grunts. Groans. Heavy breaths. In his younger days Longman had been an active man. Even into his sixties his physical fitness had marked him out from his peers. But his sixties were long gone. Now he could barely climb out of bed.

The mattress finally caught up and pressed against Longman's back, taking the brunt of his weight. He released his grip on the metal rail and silence returned to the room.

Longman listened carefully.

The sound had been unmistakable. Shattering glass makes a distinctive noise that even his diminished hearing could pick up. But identifying its source was much harder. Was it the sound of a dropped ashtray? A wine glass? Or of a broken window, smashed to admit the uninvited? Not that one possibility was better or worse than any other. In the otherwise empty house of an eighty-five-year-old widower, every one of them was a concern.

Longman strained to listen. At first there was nothing. At least nothing *he* could hear.

The house was big. Much *too* big now that his wife had passed away and his children had moved on. But Longman had been unable to bring himself to move. To leave the family home of fifty years. He knew it inside out.

And it was that familiarity that made the next sound an unintentional alarm. The creak of the first step on the main staircase.

It was a feature of the house that went back decades. In the daytime – during the housekeeper's working hours – it would be the most natural sound in the world. But when the bedside clock read 3 a.m.? At *that* hour it was terrifying.

The sound of footsteps followed the first creak, but it was drowned out as Longman threw back the duvet and freed his frail legs from its weight. Crippling arthritis forced him to shift his entire body in one movement as he swung his legs from the bed and towards the floor. The pain was excruciating; he had not moved so fast in five years, back when his hips did their job. But he ignored the agony and climbed to his feet, one hand on the solid bedpost for support.

His breathing was out of control, his heart a piston. But Longman pushed himself on, staggering to the walk-in closet in the far corner of the room. For the first time in years he made the distance without a stick or a frame for support. Exhausted, he stumbled as he reached the door. Only his adrenaline kept him upright.

Regaining his balance, Longman gripped the closet door's handle and then paused, holding his breath in an effort to hear. Nothing could stop the thumping pulse that filled his inner ear, nor the fear that his overworking heart would not keep the pace. Still, it was quiet enough to hear the footsteps.

The closet opened easily. Longman transferred his weight from the handle to the frame, in order to let the door pass. Once open he moved inside. Fumbling in the dark, he found the light-switch and pressed it just as the sound of footsteps stopped outside the bedroom.

The light was at first blinding, but Longman's eyes adjusted quickly. The sight that greeted them, however, was not worth the effort. The hope that had been carrying him disappeared in a single breath.

What did I think I'd find? Longman asked himself. *What bloody weapon would have been of use anyway?*

Longman had not heard the door open, but that sixth sense that humans possess – that feeling that tells us when we are not alone – had not diminished with age. The bedroom was no longer empty. Longman knew *that* before he turned to see who had joined him.

'You?' Longman's exclamation was more an accusation than an expression of shock.

It was the eyes. The most soulless Longman had ever seen. He would recognise them anywhere.

'You remember me.'

The reply was a statement, as sinister as the speaker. A predator born and bred.

'Some things one never forgets.' Everything about the man was as Longman remembered. 'And some people.'

A smile formed on the predator's lips, but his pale eyes remained cold. It was a smile of triumph, not happiness.

'True.'

The man moved closer. His pace was slow. Deliberate. A viper finding its range.

'It's good you've kept that mind of yours,' he said. 'Even at your age.'

'What does that matter?'

The old man spoke with defiance. Those pale, merciless eyes had told him his fate. But he would not face it on his knees.

'Oh, it matters.'

For the first time there was life in the voice. A reaction to Longman's own fire. It did not add warmth.

Only inches now separated their bodies as Longman felt a vice-like grip constrict his wrist.

'Because it means you'll feel every second of what's coming.'

TWO

Michael Devlin wiped through the condensation that clung to the bathroom mirror. His reflection stared back at him. Stripped to the waist, a collection of scars dotted his torso. They were remnants of injuries that were rare for men of his so-called 'civilised' profession. Permanent reminders of a life more eventful than he had ever intended.

Michael plunged his hands under the running hot water and threw the pool that grew between them onto his already dripping face. The sting of the heat bit into the scar tissue under his left eyebrow. It was a familiar feeling. Another old wound.

Minutes later he was clean-shaven. A full-head plunge into a basin of ice-cold water ended the process. It was an important morning ritual, shocking him to full consciousness ahead of the day.

With his morning fog shifted, he dried himself and quickly finished getting ready, pulling on a bespoke pin-striped three-piece suit that highlighted his tall, triangular frame.

Michael was not a vain man but he understood the importance of appearance. First impressions matter.

Finally ready, he headed downstairs.

The master bedroom and the main bathroom of his Chelsea townhouse were on the building's second floor. A staircase led upwards to three spare bedrooms and Michael's home office, and down to a large first-floor bedroom suite. At its bottom was a ground-floor reception, a showroom-standard lounge that was hardly ever used, and a large extended kitchen that was the reason for its neglect.

The kitchen was a whirl of activity. Barely through the door, Michael was ambushed by the cloud of smoke that streamed in all directions from the range cooker at the far end of the room.

Michael stepped back out of the room with a smile and a shake of the head, unfastened the buttons on his suit jacket and slipped it from his shoulders. He hung it up in the hallway, where it would be safe from the cooking fumes.

'I know you're out there, Michael Devlin!'

Sarah Truman's American accent cut through the British voices that were emanating from the kitchen radio.

'Get your butt in here and get your breakfast.'

Michael strode back through the door, his grin growing wider as he surveyed the chaos of the kitchen. Smoke was still billowing from a thick-bottomed pan containing what had probably once been bacon. Less dramatic were the scrambled eggs that were already on a plate. And as for the sizzle he could hear from a pot of baked beans?

Best not to ask about that one, Michael thought.

'Effortless as always, sweetheart?' he asked playfully, stepping behind Sarah and wrapping an arm around her waist.

'I don't have time for silly games this morning, Michael.'

Sarah spoke without turning. She ignored Michael as he kissed the back of her neck. Instead she reached out for the plate with the eggs to add the rest of his breakfast.

'Now sit at the table.'

'How could I do that?' Michael took the plate from Sarah's grasp with one hand as he spoke. He held it high, out of her reach. With his other arm already around her waist, he pulled her into him.

'When I've got the most beautiful woman in London standing right in front of me?'

'I'm going to drop the pan!' Sarah laughed as Michael pulled her close, pinning her back against him. He buried his freshly shaved skin into her hair as he kissed her neck again. This time he got the reaction he wanted; Sarah turned her head and met his lips with her own.

'Happy now?' she asked as she pulled her face away, at least as far as she could manage.

'As happy as any man in a burning building could be,' Michael replied, laughing as he released his grip on Sarah's waist.

'Screw you, Devlin!' Sarah's mock outrage was well acted, but Michael did not buy it for an instant. 'It's not that bad.'

'Not that bad?!' Michael laughed as he reached over her shoulder and switched the cooker's extractor fan to maximum. 'I almost went looking for our fire blanket.'

'Do you want your breakfast or not?'

Honest answer? Michael thought. One look into Sarah's startling green eyes stopped him from saying the words aloud.

'Yes, yes please,' he said instead. 'Sorry.'

'There's nothing to be sorry for.' Sarah sounded disappointed at her own impatience. 'Cooking's just not my forte and it's frustrating.'

'I get that,' Michael replied, placing two glasses of fresh orange juice on the kitchen table and taking a seat. 'But no one's good at everything. Sometimes you've got to accept your own limitations.'

'Says the most competitive man on the planet,' Sarah laughed at her own response as she plated the food, set the plates down on the table and took her seat.

All the while Michael watched, marvelling that his life had turned out this way. That he had found his perfect woman. And that *she* had found *him*.

They had met less than two years ago, in the most extreme of circumstances. They had made a connection then that had only grown stronger. What could have been a crush had become something much more. And so here he was. Thirty-nine years of age, with the twenty-eight-year-old fiancée he adored.

It was more than Michael could have ever hoped for.

'So what's today?' Sarah asked. She dashed some Tabasco sauce onto her meal as she spoke.

'Wandsworth Prison,' Michael replied, taking the same hot sauce and adding it to his own petrified bacon. 'First meet with Simon Kash.'

'The boy in the murder trial?'

'Yep.' Michael drained half of his orange juice. 'Bad business. What about you? What time are you out?'

'Not until ten, back early evening. Will you deal with dinner tonight?'

'Could do. I'm out of the prison by midday, then chambers, but I shouldn't be late home. I'll have to check with Anne, though. I think she said she wanted to cook tonight.'

Neither spoke for a few moments while they finished their breakfast, with Michael surreptitiously discarding the worst of the charred edges and Sarah pretending not to notice.

'Will you make sure Anne's out of bed before you go?' Michael asked once both plates were empty, gesturing upwards with his eyes.

'I'll head up to her as soon as you're gone,' Sarah replied.

'Thanks. And look, I'm sorry to put that on you. I—'

'She's family,' Sarah interrupted. 'It's no trouble.'

Michael reached out and gently gripped Sarah's hand. She meant what she said. He knew that. It made the answer more welcome.

'But thanks anyway.'

The moment lasted for a few seconds, only ended by Michael's glance towards his watch. What it told him made him stand and kiss Sarah on her forehead.

'Time to go,' he said as he pushed his chair beneath the kitchen table. 'Can't be late for young Mister Kash, now, can I?'

THREE

Kathy Gray counted herself lucky for many things. Her husband of thirty years was one of them. They had enjoyed a long, happy and comfortable marriage. Never rich, they were also never less than comfortable. Together they had done much more than keep the wolf from the door.

Then there were her children. Four of them, all very different from each other. The eldest – John – was a carpenter, like his father. A strong, moral man with a growing family of his own. Next came Eric, another manual worker. No wife. No children. But happy, and with a thriving business. Katie was third. She had married young and had dedicated herself to her five children. Which left Chris. Last but by no means least: the baby who grew up to be the surgeon. His mother's pride and joy.

And of course there was Kathy's job. Her other life. For almost four decades she had been with the Longman family. She had watched with pride as Phillip Longman soared in his chosen career, basking in his reflected glory whenever his name appeared in the press. He was an important man – a great man – and yet he had always taken the time to make his housekeeper feel needed.

Kathy had the same affection for the rest of the Longman family. For Phillip's wife, Carol. A wonderful woman, kind-hearted and generous. She had passed at the age of eighty and yet it still seemed she was taken too soon. And for their children; Matthew, Russell and Peter. All of them had been near grown by the time Kathy's employment had begun, but each had still shown her enough respect and kindness that she cared for them almost like her own.

It had been with great sadness that she had watched the three boys drift from their father in the years since their mother's death. She had sometimes thought to speak to them on the subject. To give them a piece of her mind. It had never happened. No matter how close she felt to them all, Kathy was *not* family.

Sadder still had been Longman's decline over the past five years. Kathy had seen the strength of spirit that had once filled him evaporate as he mourned his late wife. It had been painful to witness yet not once did Kathy think to quit, despite her own advancing years. She had made a commitment to the Longman family that was as solemn to her as the commitment she had made before God on her wedding day. She would see her job to the end.

Her morning routine had changed little over the years. The house was quieter now, with just its single occupant, but that made little difference. As she had on most days for over three decades, Kathy closed the heavy front door behind her, walked to the kitchen, filled a kettle and placed it on the stove. Phillip's refusal to upgrade to an electric appliance might be amusing but, deep down, Kathy preferred the old ways too.

She turned the stove's gas knob and clicked for a flame.

Nothing.

Kathy tried again. And again. Still nothing.

She reached out to check for the sensation of expelled gas and immediately felt the problem; a current of air rushing past her outstretched hand. Kathy had not noticed it until now. It had been cold outside as she travelled to work, and she was not yet warmed enough to easily feel the chill breeze that had been sweeping past her.

Kathy turned and followed the stream of cold air back to its source. It brought her to the open pantry door. A door that should have been closed. Feeling her heart beginning to beat a little faster, she looked inside the small room. There was broken glass on the floor, from a small hole in the window. No larger than would be caused by a cricket ball, the hole could easily have been the result of an accident. At least it could have, if the window itself had not been left open.

Kathy span on her heel, her heart was racing. She knew Phillip was not responsible for the window. It had been years since he could reach the pantry without help.

Someone had broken in.

But who? And what for?

Only one man alive knew the answer to that question.

His pale eyes watched her, reading her expression for some hint as to what she would do next. Would she run? Or would she look for the man who had loyally employed her for who knows how long?

She would never know how important this choice would be to her continued existence. Or how lucky she was that loyalty won out.

A smile grew as he watched the housekeeper steel herself to do the right thing. But it grew alone. His pale eyes remained fixed as he watched her take a final deep breath to calm her nerves before starting up the stairs.

The first stair creaked as she took a faltering step into the unknown. The second time it had done so in six hours. Her observer avoided it as he climbed the steps behind her.

Whatever he decided to do in the next minutes, she would have no warning of his presence.

He hung back, watching silently. His mind was made up. Her reaction would be everything. The right scream. The right hysteria. That was what he wanted. That was what would satisfy him. If she gave him that then she would live. If she did not . . . well, then her fate was in her own hands.

Kathy Gray counted herself lucky for many things. But she would never know that her luckiest moment was walking into Phillip Longman's bedroom and screaming for all she was worth.

FOUR

The first two police officers had arrived in less than ten minutes and had gone straight to Phillip Longman's bedroom. One had thrown up on the spot. The other had called in the carnage that had awaited them.

The same horror would greet a stream of police personnel over the next thirty minutes. Each was a hardened professional, but still a surprising number were reacquainted with their breakfasts at the sight.

This was no ordinary murder scene.

'Who's been cleaning this place?' Detective Chief Inspector Joelle Levy could smell bleach as she climbed the stairs towards Longman's room. 'Someone's been disinfecting.'

'No, ma'am.' The answer came from Police Constable David Wright, who had been one of the first two officers on the scene. The one with the stronger stomach. 'That smell was strong when we got here.'

Levy gave Wright a quizzical look.

'You're sure?'

'Yes, ma'am. It was the first thing I noticed. You know, before we went in.'

Might make this interesting, Levy thought.

They continued to the top of the stairs and along the hallway, passing two open doors. Inside each was an immaculate, seemingly untouched bedroom. They suggested diligent housekeeping and a shortage of overnight guests.

The third room said no such thing. Inside it was a hive of activity, filling the air like an electric charge. Here the smell of bleach – now combined with a distinct hint of vomit – grew stronger.

This is what we're here for, Levy knew.

She stepped inside the room. Her gaze swept from one wall to another, taking in everything in between. An experienced detective, Levy had been prepared for the worst. And the worst was exactly what she got.

In his heyday Phillip Longman had been able to dominate a room. But he had never done so as completely as he did now in death. The sight of his frail body transfixed Levy. His nakedness was shocking. His mutilation was worse. Most appalling, though, was the way he had died. Longman had been crucified against his own bedroom wall. The nails that had been hammered through his wrists suspended him several feet above the floor.

'Jesus Christ.'

Levy spoke without irony. She had seen terrible things in her professional life. Sights far gorier than this. Yet there was something about the ritualistic nature of this man's death. It suggested deliberation. Levy had witnessed first-hand the damage a gunshot could do. The injuries caused by a bomb. Even a landmine. But what she was looking at now? Never had she seen such horrific injuries caused so very carefully.

Levy turned away from the still-hanging corpse and scanned the rest of the room. There was a pool of vomit at her feet. Not ideal forensic conditions, but far enough from the body to be no risk of contamination. The other weak stomachs had held out until their owners had reached the hallway and the room looked otherwise untouched.

That won't last, Levy thought. Already a team of white-suited crime-scene examiners were scouring every inch of Phillip Longman's last moments.

'What do you make of it, Steve?' Levy recognised Detective Inspector Steven Hale through his white suit and hood.

'Nasty business, ma'am.' Hale shook his head as he got to his feet. 'Whoever did this was a sick bastard. This poor old sod had his tongue cut out and replaced with his own balls. Whatever of his own teeth he had left were pulled out one by one. Then he was bled. Slow. They cut vein after vein, up and down his arms and legs.'

'Any idea which of the injuries killed him?'

'I think we can take our pick, ma'am. Maybe bleeding him out was what did it, even if it was slow. If that didn't then the crucifixion would have. No way he could have survived that in his shape.'

'I'm not sure you or I would have fared much better,' Levy replied, her eyes never leaving Longman's corpse. 'Let me know when we get a definitive answer on cause of death.'

'Ma'am.'

Hale moved back as Levy stepped closer to Longman. She circled around his body as much as the wall would allow, looking closely at his wounds. Finally she leaned close to one of the open cuts on Longman's right leg and inhaled deeply through her nose.

'Yeah, that's where the bleach seems to have been used,' offered Hale. 'No evidence of writhing on the back of his legs or on his back, though. Suggests he was already dead by the time it was thrown over his wounds. Small mercies, I suppose. Would've been agony if he'd still been breathing.'

Levy did not reply. Instead she walked to the far side of the room and picked up a chair that sat in the corner. Placing it beside the corpse's dangling legs, she stepped up. Levy was not a tall woman – little more than five foot five – but then Phillip Longman had not been a tall man. The seat of the chair was level with his crucified feet.

'Pass me a glove.'

Levy did not look down as she spoke, or as she took the glove from Hale's hand. Pulling the latex onto her fingers, she carefully opened Longman's mouth. His castrated testicles had already been removed from inside, leaving a cavity with no teeth and no tongue. A blackened mess.

Levy leaned forward, putting her nose as close as she could without risking contamination of the evidence, and took a deep breath.

'What is it?' Hale was intrigued. 'What can you smell?'

'Bleach.' Levy carefully closed the mouth and climbed down from the chair. 'They filled his mouth with it, too.'

'After he was dead? Why? What's the point?'

Levy did not answer immediately. Instead she looked around and caught the eye of PC David Wright, who stood a little more upright under the DCI's gaze.

'Has a bleach bottle been removed from this room?' she asked.

'No, ma'am. Everything's exactly as we found it. Other than any investigation of the body, obviously.'

'What about downstairs? Or in the bathrooms? Have any bleach bottles been taken from any of them?'

'I've no idea, ma'am.'

'The body was discovered by the housekeeper, right?'

'It was.'

'Then go ask her. Take her to the rooms. We need to know.'

PC Wright left the room without another word.

Hale looked bemused.

'What does a missing bleach bottle matter?'

'It matters because it kills DNA, Steve.' Levy had encountered the theory before. She had never seen it used. 'The bleach wasn't thrown over him to torture him. It was done to destroy evidence. That's why the whole body's drenched in the stuff. Whoever did this got down and dirty. Maybe that was the point. The thrill. But they also don't want to get caught. They know what they're doing, Steve. We won't find anything on the body. And judging by the smell, the only DNA we'll find in this whole bloody room is in that pile of sick by the door.'

Hale turned to look in the direction of the vomit. He then looked back at Levy.

'But I don't get why it matters if the bleach was taken? They won't have left an empty bottle with fingerprints on it. Not if they're that careful.'

'It matters,' Levy explained, 'because if it was taken from here then it was a brainwave. An impulse. But if the killer brought the bleach with him, well, then we're dealing with a professional. Someone who knew exactly what they were coming here to do. And how to cover their tracks. Important we know that, don't you think?'

Hale nodded.

'So what's the point in examining the room, then?' he asked. 'If you're sure we won't find any DNA or prints or anything?'

'Because right now this crime scene's our only lead. Who knows if the bastard missed a spot.' Levy took a final glance around the room. 'We've got to clear this one up.'

'What's so important about this one?' Hale asked. 'The fact he was crucified? Is it a religious angle?'

'Maybe,' Levy replied.

She turned to the room and raised her voice.

'I want that kept out of the press, by the way. Not one mention of how this man died. Not one.'

Levy turned back to Hale, taking him by the arm and leading him out of the room and back into the hallway. She felt a small rush of gratitude that he was beside her in this. Hale had been on her team for three years now. There was no one on the force she trusted more.

'But no, Steve. It's not the crucifixion,' Levy said in a low voice, barely more than a whisper. 'It's who this guy is. Who he was, I mean.'

'You know him? Who is he?'

'It's Phillip Longman. The former Lord Chief Justice.'

Levy saw the blood drain from Hale's face. The name was obviously as familiar to him as it was to her. As she knew it would be.

The role of Lord Chief Justice was as powerful as its holder wished to make it, and Phillip Longman had not held back. In eight years in the role he had been responsible for many of the most controversial legal decisions of modern times. Decisions that had brought down criminal and terrorist organisations alike. The mutilated corpse currently nailed to a bedroom wall had been one of the British establishment's most influential men.

'The political pressure on this is going to be a nightmare,' Levy continued. 'And so is the suspect list. Longman had a lot of enemies back in the day, and there are plenty of bastards with long memories.'

Hale nodded but said nothing as Levy looked back through the open door, staring at Longman's corpse.

Nothing about the pale, pathetic body suggested the status of the man it had once been. A man whose shocking death would grab all the headlines. A death that was Levy's to solve.

There was no time to lose.

FIVE

Wandsworth Prison had barely changed in the seventeen years since Michael Devlin's first visit. The building itself dated back to the 1850s, and every day of those near two centuries were etched across its imposing façade.

The inside was less grim and more modern, but not by much. The reception area – used by both lawyers and social visitors – was an unfortunate mix of stark and run-down. Metal benches with hard steel seats offered no comfort to anyone unlucky enough to sit upon them, while yellow walls painted perhaps a decade ago were still deemed 'good enough'.

The same complacency applied to the lockers for the valuables of visiting lawyers. Undersized, insecure and mostly broken, still they were neither replaced nor even repaired.

An original stone staircase led into the building from the quiet street outside. All visitors to any of the 1,900 prisoners had to climb those aged steps and pass through the security that separated the inmates from the freedom that lay beyond the walls.

Michael's recent promotion to the rank of Queen's Counsel – the mark of distinction separating the very best barristers from the rest – was no grounds for exception. His first visit to Wandsworth seemed a lifetime ago, when he was aged twenty-two and newly qualified. Back then Michael had been surprised to be searched as intimately as were the social visitors waiting alongside him. Any special treatment he had expected – any goodwill that allowed lawyers to pass through with a nod and a wink – had been missing then.

It was still missing now.

'Who are you here to see?'

The middle-aged prison officer behind the elevated reception desk was all business. No greeting. No small talk.

'Simon Kash.'

Andrew Ross was Simon Kash's solicitor and he answered for them both, passing up a formal letter addressed to the Governor of HMP Wandsworth. It introduced Ross and Michael as solicitor and barrister and confirmed their 9.30 a.m. legal appointment with their client.

'ID?'

Both Michael and Ross removed their photo identification from their wallets and passed them up for inspection without a word. They were returned within seconds and the two men were nodded through.

'Phones, coins, keys. The usual.' This request came from a second officer. A woman, younger than the desk jockey and standing instead of sitting. She was the next stop on the security conveyor belt.

A small black tray was slid across the desk as she spoke, which was quickly filled. Wallet, keys and coins from Michael's pockets. The same, plus cigarillos and lighter, from Ross. Each retained a lever-arch file that contained the bare bones of the prosecution evidence against Simon Kash, along with a notebook and a pen.

The black tray was placed into a single thin locker beside the reception desk. The locker key was handed to Ross, the only other item either man was permitted to bring inside.

The third security station sat at the other side of the reception area. Manned by two more prison officers, the large X-ray machine was beaten, battered and practically obsolete. No doubt it had once been state of the art and the envy of airports far and wide. But state funding had been falling for decades. Airport security had caught up, overtaken and since lapped what the Prison Service could afford. Antiquated X-ray machines and the occasional metal detector were as good as it now got.

A long metal bench barred their path to the X-ray machine. Designed to provide extra seating for when the reception area was busy, it seemed poorly placed when the room was as quiet as it was today. At six foot one, Michael was tall enough that he did not have to walk around the inadvertent obstacle. Instead he just stepped over. Ross was shorter and so had to take the longer route.

'Everything in the tray, then step over here.' A third prison officer reciting his mantra.

Soul destroying, Michael thought. *They've made these poor sods into automatons.*

This time the black tray was larger. One per person. Michael placed his few permitted items at the bottom, followed by his suit jacket, wristwatch and belt. Then he placed the tray into the machine and waited for the tatty conveyor belt to splutter into action.

With his back to Ross, the slowness of the X-ray machine gave Michael time to think. To consider – not for the first time – why he was here at all.

The official answer to that question was a simple one. There are certain cases in which only a Queen's Counsel was deemed qualified to act. Sometimes they do so alone. Sometimes with a junior barrister to assist. Simon Kash's was one of those cases: a complicated murder allegation that included elements of revenge, of low-level organised crime and which featured more than one defendant and so carried the risk of what was called a 'cut-throat defence'.

No, it was clear why the Kash trial required a QC. What bothered Michael was the fact that he held that rank at all.

It was not Michael's age that made him question his promotion. At thirty-nine, he was certainly one of the youngest barristers to be elevated to Queen's Counsel, but it was not unheard of. What *was* unique, however, was the fact that his promotion had come without application or interview.

Although unexpected, Michael had needed no explanation when he had received the news six months earlier. It was certainly not based on merit. He realised that immediately; he had not applied and so his merit could not have been assessed. Instead it was a thank you from a grateful government. A reward for his silence following the events in London and Belfast twenty months ago. Sarah had enjoyed something similar as a response to the news story she had put out in place of the truth. Her career had sky-rocketed, taking her from a CNN cub reporter to one of ITN's leading correspondents.

Neither of them had asked for the career boost, but in Sarah's case it was well deserved. For Michael, though, he would have preferred to have reached his new rank the right way. Through recognition of the hard work, dedication and skill that he had shown throughout his life at the Bar. Rather than because he had kept his mouth shut. Without that recognition, he doubted his right to call himself a QC, the one thing he had always wanted to be.

It means a lifetime of not knowing if I'm actually good enough, he had thought.

This had been Michael's mindset for six months. But now? Now his wavering confidence had been joined by guilt. The background to the Simon Kash case – how Michael had been brought in to it – had made things worse.

'Step over here please, sir.'

The voice of the fourth security officer broke into Michael's thoughts.

He looked up as the speaker gestured towards a lone step. Michael knew the drill. He stepped up, placed his feet shoulder-width apart and raised his arms to shoulder height. The speaker then spent twenty seconds patting Michael down. She checked beneath his collar, then his cuffs, his waistband and the hem of his trouser legs. She even checked inside Michael's mouth. Satisfied that he was smuggling nothing into the prison, she allowed him to retrieve his belongings from the X-ray machine.

Michael slipped his jacket back on and moved to the back of the visiting crowd. Ross joined him within a minute, having suffered the same indignity. They waited in silence while Michael let his mind drift back to that first visit.

Seventeen years ago.

Back then he had been surprised to endure the strict security he had faced. Almost two decades later and the only surprise was how little things really change.

SIX

Simon Kash made an uncomfortable chair look downright painful. He looked younger than his twenty-one years. Much younger. His grey prison-issue tracksuit did not help. It swamped Kash's small frame as he fidgeted in his seat.

Michael's eyes swept up and down as he surveyed the figure in front of him. What there was of it, anyway. Kash was accused of a crime of extreme violence – double murder. Already it seemed unlikely, and not just because of Kash's size.

True, the skinny boy did not look strong enough to overpower a teenage girl, let alone two brothers with violent reputations. But that impression alone meant nothing. Michael had encountered men half his own size who somehow possessed twice his strength. No. It was *everything else* about Kash that gave Michael pause. His nervous manner. His haunted expression. Michael just could not reconcile this frightened child with the animal who had massacred the Galloway twins.

'Tell me about Darren O'Driscoll, Simon.'

Kash seemed to shrink at the mention of the name. Michael had expected no less. Darren O'Driscoll was Kash's co-defendant and yet in the thirty minutes they had been in the small, dirty room in HMP Wandsworth's legal visits block, Kash had neither mentioned O'Driscoll's name nor alluded to the man's involvement in the case.

And Michael thought he knew why.

Together, Kash and O'Driscoll were accused of hunting down and killing two brothers in South East London. In their thirties and strong from a working life of manual labour, the Galloway twins were not among life's obvious victims. Yet they were now dead. Murdered – according to the prosecution – for the grave crime of disrespecting Darren O'Driscoll's uncle on a construction site in the City.

The motive behind their death was not surprising. Michael had seen many killed for much less. But how they had died? That was another story entirely.

London can be a violent city and Michael had been involved in his fair share of criminal trials arising from that violence. There was little he had not seen. Yet even he was shocked by the attack upon the Galloway twins.

The jury would never see the autopsy pictures.

They should be thankful for that small mercy, Michael thought.

The details would have haunted them. The sight of Martin Galloway alone – his body beaten so badly that every bone in his torso was either fractured or crushed entirely; his hands removed; his knees shattered; his skull caved in from one side – was horrifying. The injuries inflicted on his brother Mark Galloway were worse still.

According to the prosecution it was Mark Galloway who had 'disrespected' Darren O'Driscoll's uncle. If true, the man had more than paid for his 'crime'. Suffering the same treatment as his brother, the second Galloway had received much more attention *after* death. The machetes that had been used on both men had focused on Mark Galloway once the twins had breathed their last. His head, arms and legs were all removed, before his broken body was torn apart through sheer ferocity.

It brought to mind nothing less than a medieval execution. An execution that Michael's mind refused to connect with the nervous, unusual young man ahead of him.

'Tell me about him, Simon. Tell me about Darren.'

'What do you want to know?' Kash did not look up as he spoke. The words were mumbled into his chest.

'Everything,' Michael replied. 'But for now, do you think he was capable of what happened to the Galloways?'

'Nothing to do with Darren.'

Kash's answer was quiet. Inaudible, almost. And as short as he could make it. It was a pattern that had developed over the past thirty minutes.

'I didn't ask if he did it. I asked if he was *capable* of it. If he can be this violent.'

No answer. No eye contact. Kash's gaze did not leave the floor.

Michael pushed his seat back and exhaled heavily. He lifted his hands to his head and ran his fingers through his thick blonde hair.

The sound of Michael's chair scraping the floor as it moved backwards made Kash jump. It did not make him speak.

'Look around you, Simon.' Michael gestured around the room as he tried again.

A small, rickety table and three plastic chairs filled it to capacity. It was hot and dirty. The walls were covered in laminated rules that governed a prisoner's life.

'This is your future, son. If you're not careful you're going to be stuck in rooms like this for the next twenty-five years. At least. This isn't a game, Simon. You either help us on this – help *us* to help *you* – or you'll be in here until you're fifty.'

Kash looked up, his eyes following Michael's gesture. It took a few moments for the words to sink in.

'I didn't do it.' The words were soft when Kash finally spoke. Like a schoolboy disputing a punishment. 'I shouldn't be here.'

'We know that, Simon.' Andrew Ross cut in. His voice was more sympathetic than Michael's. 'That's why we're here. That's why Mr Devlin's here—'

'But we can't do it without you,' Michael interrupted. He needed Kash to understand. 'We can't just make this stuff up. We need *you* to be honest with *us*. If you give us the weapons then we'll go to war for you. But if you hide things from us – if you keep quiet to protect Darren O'Driscoll – then we're fighting a losing battle.'

'And if we lose, it's *you* that pays the price.' Ross took up the charge. He no longer sounded sympathetic as he followed Michael's lead. 'Us? We both go home. We'll be disappointed, but we'll move on. But you get a life sentence. Twenty-five years inside. Maybe longer. And certainly longer than you've been alive already.'

Kash did not respond. He just sank further into his seat, seeming to grow even smaller still as Ross's words settled.

If Kash had been too afraid of Darren O'Driscoll to help himself – and Michael was sure that he had been – then that fear should no longer be his number-one concern.

SEVEN

It was midday as Michael walked down the prison steps, Ross still at his side. The sun had come out in force while they had been inside. It was hot for noon. A few more hours and the tarmac beneath their feet would be melting.

Michael removed his suit jacket and loosened his tie as they passed the building's boundaries and stepped into the street.

'Where are you parked?'

Michael watched as Ross fingered a car key.

'In the garden centre,' Ross replied, indicating to the left.

Michael's route would take him right. Towards Earlsfield train station. Which meant that any further conversation needed to happen here.

'So what's your take on this?' Ross asked.

'The boy's a mess.'

Michael leaned back against an uneven brick wall as he spoke. The past two hours had been exhausting. Sometimes a client saying nothing is harder than a client who won't shut up.

'He knows what happened. And he knows who did it. He's just too scared to tell.'

'You think it's Darren O'Driscoll he's afraid of?' Ross asked.

'Without a doubt.'

Michael had formed a case theory after reading the evidence. His morning with Kash had done nothing to change it. What it *had* done was strengthen his determination to protect the boy from himself.

'Darren O'Driscoll killed the Galloways,' Michael offered. 'Him and whoever else; I don't believe he could have done it alone. But I don't buy that Simon was part of it. Not hands-on, anyway. Not in the role Colliver gives him.'

Terry Colliver was the prosecution's main witness, and certainly Simon Kash's biggest problem.

'So you believe him?' Ross sounded pleased. 'Simon, I mean. You think he might actually be innocent?'

Michael did not answer immediately. Instead he took a few seconds to compose his thoughts. It was important to get this right.

'Derek thought so,' Michael finally replied. 'He spent a lot of time with the boy and he's a better judge of character than I'll ever be. I'll go with his gut.'

Derek Reid had been Kash's barrister until two days earlier. That had changed when the trial judge ruled the case was suitable for a QC. Reid had never reached that status, and so the case had been taken from him and given to Michael. None of which would be unusual were it were not for the fact that Reid was Michael's close friend, his former pupil-master and the man Michael consistently rated as the most talented advocate he had ever seen.

It was another reason Michael felt uncomfortable – and a little guilty – about his premature promotion. The fact that he was now deemed – wrongly, Michael felt – a safer bet than Derek Reid.

He wondered if Ross perhaps shared the same view.

'About Derek,' Ross began. 'You know I didn't want to lose him, right? It wasn't my call.'

'I know.' Michael needed no explanation. 'But Simon would've been better off if it had been. Your call, I mean.'

'He has *you* now, Michael.'

'He would still have been better served. There's no one better than Derek.'

'Not even you?'

'Not even me. Especially when I have less than a week to get myself ready for trial.'

A clanking mechanical sound interrupted Ross as he opened his mouth to respond. Both he and Michael turned to face its source.

The prison's automated metal gate was slowly opening. It was the one route in and out of the complex that did not sit at the top of a staircase. As it slid aside, the sound of aggressive rap music filled the air.

For a moment Michael thought it was coming from inside the gate. He quickly realised his mistake as he spotted the source of the harsh lyrics.

A black BMW M760Li sat barely thirty feet away, parked against the kerb in a long line of cars. Until now its tinted windows had hidden its occupants and suppressed the beat of its stereo system. But now its doors had opened.

Three young black men in their early twenties – if not younger – stepped out.

'Seriously? They're in a hundred-thousand-pound car? Outside of a bloody prison?' Ross did not keep the disbelief from his voice. 'They turn up here of all places, in that thing, blaring out music about guns and gangs. And then they wonder how the police find them?'

'You know them?'

'Not those three. But plenty like them.' Ross indicated the car with a nod of his head. 'I remember when villains had to be smart to earn that kind of cash.'

'Maybe someone else is smart.' Michael gestured towards the prison gate as he spoke. Subtly, so only Ross could notice.

The gate was now fully open. Large enough for a prison van to pass through. The width and height were unnecessary. A lone figure stepped out as the gate began to close. He was older than the BMW's occupants by a generation. Tall with broad shoulders, he carried the few belongings he must have accumulated in prison in one hand, inside a transparent plastic sack.

One of the BMW men approached and was handed the sack without a word of greeting. A clear indication of rank. The man ignored the car's other occupants, too, as he climbed into the front passenger's seat and closed the door. The music that had filled the quiet street stopped an instant later.

The newly released prisoner had asserted his unquestioned authority.

'Christ,' muttered Ross.

They watched the original three men climb into the car. The air of menace that had surrounded them minutes before had been utterly dispelled. Replaced by complete subservience.

'Have you ever seen anything like that?' asked Ross.

'A few times.'

Michael's answer was half to himself. Ross had no idea how intimately Michael understood such criminal hierarchies. What they had just witnessed had been the reality of his childhood and it brought back unwelcome memories of his father. And of his brother.

'I'd best be getting back to chambers,' Michael announced abruptly as he tried to force the memories down. 'There's a lot to do to be ready for trial.'

'Understood. Anything you need from us, I'm on the end of the phone.'

The sound of the BMW's engine interrupted Ross's reply. It roared as the car sped south from its parking space. The 20 mph speed limit was broken in barely a second.

'I'll probably call tomorrow, I expect.' Michael spoke again once the sound of the engine had faded. 'First I need to read the rest of the evidence and see exactly where we are.'

'I'll be waiting, then.'

'Good to know.' Michael reached out his large hand, grasped Ross's own and shook it firmly. 'Speak soon.'

Their observer had never believed in fate. In any guiding force other than his own will. His own determination. That certainty had never been shaken, and it was not shaken now, as his pale eyes took in the unexpected sight of Michael Devlin.

It could be no one else. Devlin was as distinctive now as he had been then. Maybe more so. Older, certainly, with a few extra pounds on his frame. A few more lines on his face. The difference between a man and a boy. But he had kept both his thick blonde hair and his slim, strong build.

He had always wondered if he would see Michael Devlin again. Now he had. But would Michael Devlin ever see *him*? That was the question.

He had not yet decided. But whatever the answer, Devlin was not his concern today and no unexpected appearance outside of Wandsworth Prison would change that. There were other priorities. Other people much more deserving of his attention.

There was no fate. Only coincidence. He would follow his own path. And today that path led elsewhere.

EIGHT

Sarah Truman felt the first trickle of sweat as it passed the base of her neck.

June in London. It should not be this hot. The city traded in the mild. A little snow in winter. Rain when it was least wanted. Sunshine so weak that the English had invented warm beer instead of cold lager.

The lack of extremes had been a selling point for Sarah. Too many Boston winters made the predictability of the British weather attractive.

But for the past three weeks the climate had been off-message. Day after day of cold mornings leading to extreme dry heat. Today offered no reprieve. It was barely noon and so the heat would only increase as the hours passed.

Sarah looked back longingly at the outside broadcast van in which she had travelled. Remembered fondly the feel of its air conditioning.

It had been less than five minutes.

'How long do you think?'

Sarah turned to face the questioner. Nathan Benson. One of the network's new breed of cameramen. Technological whizz-kids without a lick of experience or a jot of common sense. Sarah missed the old guard. One in particular. She felt the familiar pang of sadness that hit her whenever she thought of Dan Maguire. He had been killed in an explosion less than two years ago. Just before Sarah had started running for her life. Just as she had met Michael.

'How long for what?' she asked, shaking off the distracting thought.

'How long will we be here? There's nothing happening.'

'It'll take as long as it takes,' Sarah replied. Advice she had been given years ago, by a cameraman Benson could never hope to be. 'We'll wait until they're ready to tell us something.'

Benson nodded. Sarah's tone was clear: no follow-up questions were welcome. Instead he concentrated on his state-of-the-art equipment. Digital adjustments that would mean nothing to anyone outside of his industry.

Sarah watched for a few seconds, bemused, but Benson's camera could only hold her attention for so long. Quickly bored by his tinkering, she walked back towards their van. It was parked on the nearest kerb. Five others – identical but for the network logos – were parked close by.

Sarah passed them all. Across the street. Far enough now, she turned and looked back at the scene she had left behind.

The house itself was impressive. Big, even for the location. Sarah would expect perhaps six bedrooms, none of them small. The driveway was visible from the road, behind automated iron gates. A large space, block-paved across. An intricate jigsaw that had no doubt taken patience and back-pain to complete. Everything about the property said 'Family Home'.

Sarah knew that it was no such thing. Not any more.

Wiping a sheen of sweat from her brow, Sarah looked around. The neighbouring houses seemed quiet. Not a single face at a single window. Not that Sarah expected anything else. When Scotland Yard's Major Investigation Team come to a community like this, no one's head comes above the parapet. Friends become acquaintances, acquaintances become strangers. With MIT around, the best neighbours would rather be left alone.

The heat was rising. Sarah could feel it. She crossed the street once again, this time heading straight for a small huddle of three reporters, one man and two women. From the visible effects of the heat, all three had been here a while.

'Miss Truman.' The male reporter greeted her. He was perhaps the same age as Sarah. Certainly not yet thirty. But like the others, he was on a much lower rung of the career ladder. 'We don't usually see you at this sort of thing.'

'What can I say? I thought I'd catch some sun.' Sarah smiled as she spoke. Hoped friendliness would disguise the fact that she knew none of their names. 'Has anyone heard anything from inside?'

'Only what Joanne overheard.' The CNN reporter. A tall, pretty American. Maybe twenty-two years old. Everything Sarah had been back when she was a CNN cub, only this one must have started even younger. 'Is that why they sent you?'

'What do you mean?'

'I mean if Joanne was right and the victim really *is* a judge. Your husband's some big-shot trial lawyer, right?'

'My *fiancé*'s a barrister, yeah. Not sure I'd call him a big shot,' Sarah answered. 'And that wouldn't give me any angle I can see. There are a lot of judges and a lot of lawyers. They don't all know each other. Besides, we're not sure if what Joanne overheard was right.'

Sarah was being disingenuous; the cub had called it. Michael's profession *was* the reason she had been sent. And far from being unsure about the victim, Sarah had known since just after 10 a.m. that the murder scene was the address of former Lord Chief Justice Phillip Longman. There were few upsides to the marathon legal dinners she had to endure for Michael. Having contacts at the Ministry of Justice was one of them.

'Joanne heard what she heard,' the man insisted. 'She doesn't miss much. Then she reports back to ITV and suddenly she's gone. Replaced by the big guns. That seems fairly cut and dried to me.'

'You may be right.' Sarah relented, still with no intention of sharing her information. 'But if they *do* know something back at the network, they haven't shared it with me. I wish they would. At least I'd know I'm not melting out here for offending someone.'

The murmur that passed between the three was hard for Sarah to read. It could be agreement. It could be disbelief. Frankly, it didn't matter. And before anyone could speak again, the automated iron gates began to open.

'Nathan.' Sarah was ready. Her cameraman was not. 'Nathan!' The second call was louder than the first, her exasperation clear. It worked. Benson's lens was quickly up and pointing in the right direction.

The gates had been closed since at least 9 a.m., when the press had started to arrive. Since then a mix of uniformed and white-suited police officers had been moving in and out of the house. Now they walked out en masse, twelve in all.

'Her,' Sarah whispered, gesturing towards the only person on the driveway who wore neither a police uniform nor a forensics suit. 'That's who we need to speak to.'

Benson adjusted his lens with the press of a button, zooming in on the woman Sarah had pointed out. A glance at his camera's screen confirmed Sarah's deduction: the woman in plain clothes was in charge.

NINE

Detective Chief Inspector Joelle Levy had no issue with the press. They were necessary. They could even be helpful. There were any number of murder investigations that would have failed without them, she knew. Despite this, some of her colleagues were far from media-friendly. Some actually saw reporters as the enemy.

Levy had noticed that those same colleagues often had the most to hide.

'Is there anything on me that shouldn't be there, Steve?'

Detective Inspector Steven Hale reacted immediately; it was a drill he and his DCI had perfected long ago. Levy was about to speak to the press after two hours in a messy crime scene. If so much as a spot of Phillip Longman's blood were to show up on screen it could be a PR disaster. And so Hale studied her carefully.

'You're clean,' he finally offered.

'Thanks.'

Levy reached up and removed the band that held her hair tight to her head. She felt her heavy black mane fall against her neck, settling just above her shoulders.

'Wicked Witch to Scarlett O'Hara,' Hale said with a smile.

'Very funny,' she shot back. Levy had no particular interest in her appearance but she was a realist. Like it or not, as a woman she would be judged. Hair pulled back equalled stern. Hair down equalled approachable. Any detail that brought the public onside was worth doing.

She turned towards the now fully opened gate. 'Bring them in.'

Hale gestured to the officer at the gate, who promptly led the reporters and cameramen onto the driveway. Towards where Levy and Hale stood by the property's front door. The questions started even before the small press pack had come to a halt.

'Officer, can you comment on reports that the victim was a senior judge?'

'Is it correct that a judge has been murdered inside the house?'

'Officer, is there any connection between the victim and any ongoing court case?'

'Ladies and gentlemen, we can't and won't answer any questions that can identify a victim of crime at this sensitive time.' Levy's answer left no room for discussion. The questions stopped.

'What I can do is share with you the bare bones of what we have, and as always if you play ball with us now, you'll have the benefit of our thanks later. Everyone on board?'

'Quid pro quo?' The question came from the only reporter who, until now, had stayed silent. Levy recognised her as Sarah Truman. 'Whatever comes out later, we hear it first?'

'That goes without saying, Miss Truman.'

'Not always.'

Levy smiled. She respected professionalism, in her own industry and in any other, and she was well aware of Sarah's reputation.

'Then take it from me personally. All four of you will get priority on any information we can release, as and when we can release it. Just as long as you're all onside for now.'

'Good enough for me.' Sarah moved sideways as she spoke, giving her cameraman the clearest view as Levy prepared to make her statement. 'Ready when you are.'

TEN

The Thames shimmered as Michael looked down from Waterloo Bridge. The cloudless sky reflected blue in the otherwise murky water. An illusion that added to the beauty of London's finest view.

Michael had always enjoyed this walk. Waterloo Station to Middle Temple. A bare mile, door to door, the route took him across Waterloo Bridge and its unmatched vista of London's most iconic landmarks. Each one a reminder of how far Michael had come from the grim streets of his childhood. It was why Michael had chosen this spot – dead centre between the Strand and South Bank – to propose to Sarah only twelve months after they had met.

That memory had only increased his fondness for the bridge.

In its own way Michael's destination was just as impressive. The Temple area of London – just a short walk from the end of Waterloo Bridge – was living history. Built around a nine-hundred-year-old church, the area had been the English home of the Knights Templar. Following the violent destruction of the Templar Order in 1312, the district had passed from owner to owner at the whim of a succession of medieval kings. A hundred years of uncertainty finally ended at the end of the fourteenth century, when the lawyers arrived to stake their claim. A near millennia of barristers had come and gone since that time, and still the majority called the Temple home.

Michael glanced to his left as he walked the first hundred yards of Fleet Street, towards Middle Temple Lane. After all these years, he still found the sight impressive. London's Royal Courts of Justice had been built at the peak of the British Empire. The power Britain had then possessed was evident in the building's sheer scale. The largest court building in Europe, its massive stone edifice had bewitched Michael from his first glimpse.

Middle Temple Lane itself was less impressive but no less unique. Its entrance was an inconspicuous white gate directly across from the court building. Michael had walked through that gate almost every working day of his career, and yet still he marvelled at the dichotomy of the threshold. On one side – the Fleet Street side – was the modern world: a typical bustling London road. On the other was a scene from the past. Cobbled streets. Gas lamps. Centuries-old buildings that leaned sideways with age. It was a Dickens novel brought to life, and it fascinated Michael now as much as it had on his first day.

Michael looked at his watch. 1.15 p.m. His decision to walk had made him late. It had also made him sweat. He had not factored in the heat. Pulling his mobile phone from his trouser pocket, he saw he already had a text message: *Tardy bastard*.

The message was expected. Michael knew its author without a glance at the name.

Two minutes. Sorry, he texted back.

Michael accelerated as he covered the last short distance to Middle Temple Hall. Once there he ran up the short stone staircase and through the black iron gates that led inside.

Middle Temple Hall – like the streets that surrounded it – was a glimpse back in time. Built in the sixteenth century by order of Queen Elizabeth I, the Tudor hall had stood almost unchanged since its construction, as had its purpose. Hall, as it was simply known, had always been a working building. A place for lawyers to meet, to eat and to discuss their cases. Difficult though it was to reconcile the five-hundred-year-old beams, the antiquated oak tables and the marble statues with an office canteen, for hundreds of London's barristers, Hall was exactly that.

Michael spotted Derek Reid in an instant. He was impossible to miss. At six foot three, Reid stood two inches taller than Michael, but it was not just his height that made him distinctive. When the two had met seventeen years before, when Michael had began his practical training as

Reid's pupil, Reid had been much heavier than was healthy. Now aged fifty-seven, he had become almost spherical.

'I'm sorry I'm late.' Michael noticed an empty used plate on the long oak table in front of Reid. The time had not been wasted. 'Wandsworth dragged.'

'Doesn't it always?' Reid pushed his first plate away as he slowly rose to his feet. 'I'm still bloody starving. Let's get some food in and then you can moan about prisons and trains.'

The two men made quick work of filling their plates. Regular lunch companions, they had the hot roast carvery down to a fine art. Within minutes they were back at the space Reid had secured, their plates piled high with roasted meat, potatoes and vegetables.

What Reid had already eaten did not seem to have dented his appetite. His plate was five potatoes and an extra portion of beef lighter before he spoke again.

'So how was he?' Reid asked between mouthfuls.

'Just like you said he would be. He's scared.'

Reid nodded thoughtfully before tackling another potato.

'Do you think you'll manage to break through?' he finally asked, sending two flecks of potato to the corner of his mouth. 'Enough that he'll help himself at least a little bit, anyway?'

'I doubt it,' Michael replied. 'Not on today's showing. That kid doesn't have what it takes to name names.'

'Yeah.' Reid wiped his mouth as he spoke. 'Yeah. That's what I thought.'

Reid pushed his now-empty plate away. As he always seemed to do, Michael found himself marvelling at his friend's ability to put food away; his own plate was still three-quarters full.

'If Simon could find the courage to stand up for himself,' Reid continued, 'you could nail O'Driscoll and show up Colliver for the lying – and probably murdering – little bastard that he is. All Simon has to do is untie your hands and let you do it. Twenty minutes with those shits in the witness box and you'd have them coughing to the lot, if you were allowed to. I know you will.'

'Thanks for the vote of confidence.'

Michael realised that his response sounded flippant the moment he said it, and he regretted it just as quickly. Whether Reid knew it or not, his trust in Michael's ability to pick apart a witness meant everything to the younger man. The fact that Michael, as a QC, was now the senior of the two was nothing but a twist of fate. Michael regarded it as a scandal that Reid had not attained the rank himself – and years ago at that – but to him it did not change a thing. With or without those letters, Derek Reid was the most talented barrister he had ever known.

'Don't worry,' Reid responded. 'I know you don't need the ego boost.'

Michael knew his friend hadn't taken offence at his words, but he still felt uncomfortable. And now Reid was looking at him searchingly, sensing his discomfort.

'Listen to me, Michael.' Reid's tone had changed, becoming more serious. It made Michael sit up and take notice, as though sixteen years had not passed since they were pupil and pupil-master. 'I know what's wrong with you, and you have to stop. You can't keep feeling bad about taking the case. It was leaving me as soon as the judge granted a silk's certificate. At least it's gone to you. With you, Simon's still got a chance.'

The compliment made Michael's heart beat a little faster and brought a smile to his face. A reaction which both embarrassed him and reminded him of the strange relationship that would always exist between a barrister and his former pupil-master. For six months, aged just twenty-one, Michael had been Reid's shadow. They had worked together, travelled together, eaten and – most of all – drank together. It was an experience unique to being a pupil barrister; no other profession involves such intense proximity in its training. Sometimes it doesn't work. Mostly it works well. And sometimes – most rarely – it forms the basis for a lifelong friendship and mutual respect. Michael and Reid were very much within that rare third category, and yet it did not take much for Michael to feel like that twenty-one-year-old kid again, basking in his pupil-master's praise.

He wondered if that would ever change.

'They still should have kept it with you.'

'Water under the bridge.' Reid's tone signalled an end to the matter. 'Now tell me: have you met your junior yet?'

'Not yet.'

It was common in the most serious cases for a defendant to have two barristers instead of one. A leader – often a QC – and a junior. With both usually chosen by the solicitor, it was not rare that the two would not know one another before taking the case. And so it was not unusual that Michael had never met Jenny Draper.

'What's she like?' Michael asked

'Very bright and very hardworking.' Reid was almost smirking as he spoke.

'The perfect combination.' Michael smiled. He could read his friend like a book. 'But that's not telling me what she's *like*, is it?'

'Blonde and attractive.' Reid laughed aloud. 'So be bloody careful.'

Both men broke into laughter at the conversation's sudden turn.

'As if you need to tell me that,' Michael finally managed to say. 'I'm not in my twenties any more!'

'Piss off,' Reid replied, making no attempt to keep his voice down. 'You were just as bad in your early thirties. And you'd still be now if you hadn't met Sarah.'

'But I *did* meet her, Derek, didn't I?'

'More's the pity for her, poor girl.' Reid lowered his voice again. 'But seriously, Michael. Jenny Draper's got a reputation. The girl likes a silk.'

Michael had heard the same thing. That his new junior had been involved in some messy relationships with more than a few QCs, or 'silks' as they were often called by other members of the Bar, a reference to their robes being made of silk instead of the coarser material worn by a junior barrister.

'You mean that's the only reason she'd be interested?' Michael asked, feigning both outrage and ignorance. 'Well now you're hurting my feelings.'

'Stop pissing about.' Reid had a point to make. For once he wanted it taken seriously. 'Just be careful of her. That's all I'm saying.'

'Derek, I'm not about to risk my relationship with Sarah. Especially for someone who's only interested in the letters I've got after my name.'

Michael pushed his plate away and placed his napkin on the table.

'Now forget about all of that. We've got more important things to occupy us: that dessert trolley over there's got your name on it.'

'I don't need telling twice,' Reid replied, getting to his feet with his eyes fixed on the dessert selection that sat thirty feet away. 'On either point.'

ELEVEN

Russell Longman sat and stared at the wall. His eyes did not focus on any of the laminated signs and paper posters that covered the room with medical information. Barely an inch of the room's white paint was visible.

For Russell Longman, the wall could have been blank. His mind was somewhere else entirely. Lost in an unbearable mix of grief, shame and dread. The grief was natural. The shame less so, brought on by the fact that months had passed since he had last visited his father. That it had been weeks since they had spoken. And dread at the thought of what was to come next: identifying his father's mutilated corpse.

I can't do this. The quiet voice in Longman's head seemed to come from somewhere else. Somewhere distant. At first he could hardly hear it, but its volume grew with each repetition.

I can't do this. I can't do this.

Slowly he began to realise what he was hearing. And he began to listen. To agree. He *couldn't* do this. It was asking too much.

I CAN'T DO THIS!

Russell Longman was not an impressive man. He had enough self-awareness to know that about himself, and to know that he was simply not capable of what he was about to be asked to do. It was devastating enough that he had lost his father. But to have to witness what had been done to him? To see with his own eyes what his father had suffered?

It's too much. It's too much.

Longman rose to his feet, his thoughts now stumbling from his mouth.

'It's too much,' he repeated. 'It's too much.'

He could feel his heart race wildly as he scanned the room, looking for the belongings he had dropped absentmindedly when first shown to his seat. With his mind spinning, it took Longman longer than it should have to spot his discarded jacket. A fact which only increased his growing anxiety.

Aware that nothing in the room – not even the walls – now felt as stable as they should, Longman steadied himself against the door frame and forced down a series of deep breaths.

Perhaps the breathing would have worked. Perhaps not. Either way, Longman was forced to stop and take a step back as the door to the room opened and Joelle Levy entered.

Levy's arrival broke through Longman's growing confusion. At first he was relieved to see her; a welcome distraction from his own frantic thoughts.

'Are you ready, Russell?' Levy remained at the door as she spoke.

Longman did not move. He just stared at her with tired, bloodshot eyes burning into hers. Her arrival had been a respite. But now he realised why she was here.

To take me to Dad.

The thought buckled his knees, forcing him to retake his seat. All without a word.

And somehow Levy seemed to understand. She walked across the room, hooked a chair and slid it close to Longman's. She did not speak. Instead, her hand began to gently run back and forth across his shoulders. A slow, calming rhythm. He was grateful for the effort and for the continued silence as he tried to gather himself. But still he could not face what lay ahead.

'I'm not going to be able to do this,' he finally said, his voice barely a whisper.

'You will, Russell,' Levy replied gently. 'You will for your father.'

'I . . . I can't. You don't understand. I can't see him like that. I can't face that. Not with what . . . not with what was done to him.' Longman felt his voice start to crack.

'I do understand, Russell.' Levy's voice was still gentle, but there was an added firmness that somehow cut through Longman's initial urge to interrupt. 'Believe me, I've seen some terrible things in my life. When I was eighteen years old I joined the Israel Defense Forces. I spent eight years there, as part of the IDF and then in another organisation called Shin Bet. In those eight years I saw sights I wouldn't wish on my worst enemy. Innocent people massacred with automatic weapons. Children blown to bits by suicide bombers. Once even the aftermath of a chemical-weapon attack. And then I came back to England and joined the Met Police and ended up in the Major Investigation Team, where I've seen nothing but death and violence every day for thirteen years.'

'I don't . . . I don't get it. Is this supposed to make me feel better?'

'No. I wouldn't insult you by trying to make you feel better. Not after what you've lost. But I do want you to understand this: with all that I've seen, with all of the violence and the murder and the gore, the hardest thing I ever did was stand above my grandmother as she passed away peacefully in her bed. The grandmother who had raised me.'

Longman could see the pain in Levy's eyes as she relived the memory. He was beginning to understand why she was telling him this.

'You see, no matter *what* you live through, there is nothing harder than losing our loved ones. And sometimes that loss comes with responsibility. Sometimes to watch them die. Sometimes you have to do what we're asking you to do now. And no matter who you are – whether you're a soldier or a spy or a cop who deals with death every day, or whether you're just a regular guy – you have to bear that responsibility. That's what you have to do now, Russell. It's a shitty thing, but you have to. Because your dad deserves at least that. Doesn't he?'

Longman sat silently for a moment as her words sank in. Her tone had been kind, empathetic, but the underlying message had been unmistakable.

Be a man, dammit.

'But you don't have to do it alone,' Levy offered. 'We can wait, if there's someone else to be here to support you?'

They were the words that made him realise he had no choice. The task was his, and his alone.

He took a final deep breath, forced down the anxiety that was rising in his gut and looked Levy in the eyes.

'What will he look like? Will he be bloody?'

'No, Russell.' Levy's tone had not changed. 'Your dad's been cleaned up. He'll look asleep. That's all.'

'But what about his injuries? His mouth? What the officers told me—'

'That's all been dealt with. We wouldn't have left him like that.'

Longman thought he saw a flash of anger cross Levy's face before she replied. He realised in that moment he had been told more about his father's manner of death than Levy would have liked. Not that it mattered to him. He had other concerns.

'And the cuts? Over his body?'

'They've been cleaned and covered up, Russell. You won't need to see them.'

'Have they not been stitched? Why have they been left open?' Longman's voice began to rise. His mind had found an outrage onto which he could cling.

'That can't happen, Russell. It's a murder investigation. That means we have to carry out an autopsy. Until that's over there's only so much we can do to your father's body, otherwise we risk compromising evidence. I know how it must feel. Really I do. But believe me, it'd be worse if we did something that let this evil bastard walk once we've caught him.'

Longman nodded again. This time with more focus in his eyes. The good sense of Levy's words once again cut through the confusion in his mind.

They brought clarity, but also more questions.

'Do you have any leads yet? Any at all?'

His voice was stronger now. Less emotional.

'It's much too early, Russell, but we will.' Levy spoke with utter confidence. 'Your dad probably made a hell of a lot of enemies over the years, what with his position and who he was. But what was done to him? That was a special kind of evil, and that narrows the field. So we'll find the bastard. He won't walk away from this.'

'Will you promise me that?' The emotion that had disappeared from

Longman's voice had returned. Tears began to fall. 'Will you promise you'll catch whoever did this to my dad?'

'I promise, Russell.' Levy's hand began to run back and forth across Longman's shoulder's once again. 'We'll catch him. I promise.'

Longman did not respond. He could not, not through the tears that were now flowing. Instead he placed his head in his hands, obscuring his face.

Levy stood up and stepped away, back towards the door, where she waited in silence until Longman rose to his feet and wiped the tears from his face.

'I'm ready,' he said. His breaking voice was no indicator of his new determination.

'Are you sure, Russell?' Levy asked again. 'We can wait for someone else to be here to support you? Your wife? Brothers?'

'No one else is coming,' Longman replied. His voice sounded stronger. 'Matthew and Peter still don't know; it's not something I want to break to them over the phone. And Alice? Well, she doesn't think of herself as my wife any more so she won't be coming any time soon.'

'What about a friend? Anyone?'

'I don't want to put anyone else through this, Inspector Levy.' Longman's resolve was increasing the longer he spoke. 'Someone has to do it, and the way it's worked out that's me. Like you said, it's the least my dad deserves.'

TWELVE

Derek Reid reached out for the large packet of salt and vinegar crisps from the small pile near the far corner of his desk. He opened it and devoured the contents absentmindedly, in just a few handfuls. All the while his attention stayed focused on the case papers upon which he had been working, and so it took him a few moments to realise that the bag had been emptied. Once noticed it was quickly remedied. A second pack was open within moments.

The case Reid was preparing was unusual. There had already been a trial and it had not gone Reid's way. His client had found himself convicted by a jury of a complicated banking fraud. It had been a majority verdict, which usually means that no more than two jurors disagreed with no less than ten others. This case was different. A single juror had been 'lost' in the course of the trial; ill-health had forced her discharge. Down to a jury of just eleven, the only majority could be ten against one. Anything less was unacceptable.

This had been explained to the jury. In careful detail and in the simplest of language. There could be no mistake, Reid had thought. Only it now seemed that there *could*. Following the conviction two jurors had written to the judge, reporting that the jury had been split eight to three. A majority, yes, but insufficient for a lawful majority verdict.

It was an extremely unusual situation. Not to mention a difficult one. There are very strict rules governing the absolute secrecy of a jury's deliberations. Their workings are regarded as sacrosanct. That cannot be broken. And yet it now seemed that those very workings had failed. If the verdict was unlawful then Reid's client's conviction could not stand. This made an appeal necessary. But how to prepare that appeal without breaching the sanctity of the jury room? The problems it posed were exceptional and Reid was finding it difficult to see the way through.

Reid took his eyes away from the papers and looked around his room. At nothing in particular. He just needed to see something that was not an A4 typed page or a computer screen. Whenever Reid felt this way the features of his room – some personal, most professional – provided a welcome distraction.

Reid had been a member of the same barristers' chambers for thirty-four years. An entire career. His pupillage – the same process Michael Devlin had gone through under Reid's own guidance – had been elsewhere. But he had joined Eight Essex Court immediately afterwards, and he had been here ever since.

In that time Reid had seen the chambers grow from just twenty-eight working barristers to the current number of eighty-three. A huge increase in number, if not necessarily in ability. Successive cuts in legal aid had seen the earnings of publicly funded criminal barristers devastated, driving the best potential applicants elsewhere. Into professions willing to pay market rates for their skills.

But while the ability of many applicants had fallen, their numbers had not. And so Eight Essex Court now had three times as many bodies, shoehorned into a centuries-old building barely big enough for the original number. Most rooms were overflowing, with both paper and with people. Even some of chambers' seven Queen's Counsel – which now included Michael Devlin – shared their office space with others.

Somehow Reid had secured a room of his own. Old it might be. Beaten up and with ageing bookshelves creaking under the weight of endless files. But it was Reid's and Reid's alone. His brilliant reputation may not have secured him the rank of 'silk', but at least it counted for something here.

Reid's office carried little concession to the modern world. He was proud of that. But for two or three items the room could have existed at any time in the past 150 years. Reid considered himself a throwback to a simpler time. A time when a barrister's skills in court were all that mattered for success. It was a conscious decision that his room should give the same impression, one only broken by the presence of his laptop, a small flat-screen television and an expensive coffee-machine. All of which were essential as far as Reid was concerned.

It was the television that attracted Reid's attention as he looked up from his desk and saw the face of Sarah Truman on the screen. This alone would have ordinarily brought Reid to a halt; he enjoyed watching his friend's work. But the sight he saw behind Sarah banished all thoughts of work from his mind. It was Phillip Longman's old family home.

Reid reached out for the screen's remote control. His heart was suddenly pumping fast. He could feel himself beginning to panic as he fumbled with the buttons, desperate to switch off the TV's mute setting. Finally he managed to make the damn thing work.

The sound of the television – of Sarah's voice – immediately filled the room.

'. . . discovered at approximately 8 a.m. this morning by the property's housekeeper. Police say that the housekeeper remains in a state of some shock at this time, and is currently in the care of her family. She will be spoken to at greater length once she has had time to recover from the sight she witnessed. I understand, however, that the police do not anticipate that she will be able to assist much further in their enquiries.'

Reid could feel the vein in his temple throb. His blood pressure was peaking. Every word spoken was confirmation of his worst fear. Sarah was now speaking directly to the news anchor, which meant it was a live broadcast.

'As I understand it, David, the exact cause of death has yet to be established. An autopsy will be performed but there is no doubt that the former Lord Chief Justice's death was violent. This *is* a murder enquiry, and it's already under way.'

Sarah's tone signalled that her report was over, but Reid was no longer listening anyway. He was staring at nothing, paralysed by disbelief as shock started to set in.

Reid had experienced panic attacks before. More often than he cared to remember, and certainly enough to recognise the symptoms. He felt the sensation of his chest tightening, almost like a heart attack. He knew he had to bring it under control; at their worst, panic attacks release enough cortisol that they can tip over into genuine cardiac arrest. Focusing on a single spot above the office door, he began to breathe as deeply as he could. Long, greedy breaths through his nose. Exhaling steadily through his mouth. Slowly. Rhythmically. It was a struggle to bring his heart rate – and with it the flow of cortisol and adrenaline – back down to where it should be; every time he came close the thought of Longman facing his 'violent death' returned, causing the attack to strengthen.

It was over thirty-five years since Reid had first met Longman. Back when Longman was in his forties and at the top of his game. He had been less than nine months away from his promotion to Queen's Counsel then, and still years away from his first appointment as a judge. Reid, on the other hand, was still in training. His Bar Exams passed, Longman had been appointed the younger man's pupil-master. As it had with Michael and Reid, that pupillage forged a friendship that had lasted ever since. A friendship now ended by tragedy.

As close as the two men had remained, their relationship had differed from the one enjoyed by Reid and Michael. Longman always remained much older in his outlook than Reid. Much more serious. And so it had created a father/son feeling between them, very different from the big brother/little brother vibe that existed between Reid and Michael. But all relationships differ, and those differences do not make one friendship count for less than another. Reid loved Longman as much as he loved Michael. To lose either one of them was unthinkable.

Reid sat back in his chair, suddenly aware that the threatened attack had passed. He immediately reached for his mobile phone and scrolled down through his contacts, thinking of the people who would be finding this even harder. For a moment his eyes rested on the name Phillip Longman. A number he would never call again.

Reid felt tears begin to threaten his eyes at the thought. He wiped them away as he looked at the other names on the screen. Matthew. Peter. Russell. Phillip's sons. Instinct and experience said that the police would have contacted Russell. He lived closest to his father, by some margin, and so was the logical choice to identify Phillip's body. Which meant he was the one most likely to know something.

Reid listened to the ringtone chime out six, seven, eight times. He had begun to mentally compose the inevitable voicemail he would have to leave when the call was suddenly answered.

'Derek, I was going to call.' The voice at the end of the line sounded both exhausted and bereft. 'I'm sorry you had to find out through the news.'

'You have absolutely nothing to apologise for, Russell.' Reid's tone was as kind as he could make it. He felt nothing but sympathy for Longman's youngest son. The closest in age to Reid himself, Russell had always been the friendliest of the brothers to their father's former pupil. 'I'm not calling to complain. I'm calling to tell you that I'm here. For anything you need. For anything I can do. You're not alone in this, Russell.'

Russell did not answer immediately, but the change in his breathing told its story. A story of relief. Russell Longman had needed a friend. Now he had one.

'Thank you, Derek.' Russell finally found his voice. 'I really appreciate it. You have no idea.'

'Not another word.' Reid shut off his laptop as he spoke, closed his files and rose to his feet. 'Now tell me exactly where you are, Russell. I'm coming to you.'

THIRTEEN

Leon Ferris sat back into his leather high-back chair. In front of him was a crystal glass, a large dash of oak-coloured whisky within. It sat on a coaster to protect Ferris's expensive mahogany desk. It was the only item on there. Ferris's desk was not for paperwork. He had people for that. Like the rest of Ferris's dark but expensively furnished office, the desk was there to create an impression.

Ferris reached out and picked up the glass. Savoured the smokey taste of its contents. It had been a long time – eight years – since Ferris had tasted top-end scotch. It was exactly as he had remembered.

As was his office, he noted with satisfaction as his eyes roamed around the room. More a statement of status than a practical working space, it took up an entire floor of the narrow building. And it seemed that nothing had been touched since Ferris was last in the room.

He knew that could not be true. Ferris had been in this room when the Serious and Organised Crime Agency had come through his door. When they had dragged him out in cuffs, accused of crimes both financial and violent. Every inch of the office had been combed as the country's most powerful police unit searched for evidence to convict him. That the decimated office had since been pieced together so completely showed the respect of Ferris's subordinates.

The charges Ferris had faced were many: conspiracy to murder, conspiracy to assault, drug trafficking, people trafficking, blackmail, demanding monies with menaces, money laundering. Every crime a gang boss could be accused of. A huge coup for the police. Ferris had known from the start that he could not beat the rap completely. He was a clever man. Clever enough to recognise a lost cause. But he was also clever enough to know when he *could* win, and he had expensive lawyers to fight those battles he carefully picked.

In the six months following his arrest Ferris had studied the evidence that faced him. Until he knew it better than anyone. Better than his solicitor and his barristers. He was guilty of every allegation, of course, but he also knew which charges the prosecution could prove and which they could not. Ferris used this knowledge to guide his lawyers and by the time the case came to court the most serious charges were gone. No more murder. No more trafficking. All that remained was the allegation of being a drug dealer. Still serious. Still a crime that carried a heavy sentence. But very far from the literal lifetime of imprisonment he would have faced on the original charges.

Ferris had pleaded guilty to what was left and was sentenced to sixteen years' imprisonment, of which he expected to spend a total of eight years in custody. He would be aged forty-four when he was released. Not exactly in his prime, but close enough. Ferris could live with that, and so he set about making the best of those years.

Ferris served his entire sentence in one prison. HMP Wandsworth. A London prison, less than five miles from his own neighbourhood. It had cost a small fortune in bribes to keep himself so close, but every penny had been worth it. It had allowed Ferris to run his empire from prison. A prison he ruled.

Leon Ferris had not stepped foot in his office for eight years. Yet he had never really left.

The one thing Ferris had been unable to do in that time was to issue his orders face to face. But now he could, and so for the past five hours he had been taking visitors. All here to pay tribute to the returned boss.

Ferris had dealt with each and every one. Demonstrating his intimate knowledge of his business interests, he had rewarded those who deserved it and dressed down those who didn't. It had been a full day, but it was necessary. Ferris wanted his return to be visible.

Only now, with the day at an end, did the stream of visitors stop. But it was no breathing space. Instead, it was time for Ferris to be debriefed by his lieutenants.

He looked around the room in silence. Looking back at him were three men.

Kevin Tennant, Ferris's right-hand man. His closest friend since adolescence. Completely loyal.

Harvey Ellis. Ten years younger than Ferris and Tennant. Bright, capable and ruthless.

And Ty Leach. Ten years younger again than Ellis. The driver who had collected Ferris from HMP Wandsworth that morning. A kid who wanted to be a gangster. Leach had found the right company.

Ferris was in no hurry to speak as he studied his men thoughtfully. He took another mouthful of whisky, savouring its welcome burn. For longer this time. Like all good whiskies, the second mouthful beat the first.

Leach, standing by the room's single door, shifted his weight. He was too young to have experienced Ferris's way of doing things. The other two men seemed more comfortable. They had been here before.

'So is that it?' Ferris finally spoke. He indicated towards the door with a tilt of his head. To give his question meaning.

'No one else expected,' replied Ellis. The organisation of the day had been his responsibility.

'And what about who we *should* have expected? Do we know who should have arranged to see me but didn't?'

'Not yet.' Ellis hesitated only slightly, but it told Ferris that he had expected the question. There were a few gaps in the appointment diary. Individuals who should have attended to pay tribute. Failing to do so was a statement; that they had parted ways with Ferris. And *that* was a statement that could not – that *would* not – go unpunished. 'I'll have a list by midday tomorrow.'

'Sooner. A message needs to be sent.' Ferris turned to Tennant. 'Any of the no-shows strike you as strange?'

'None.' Tennant was and had always been a blunt man. 'All of 'em predictable. All with Burrell.'

Ferris reacted with just a nod of the head. He understood Tennant's meaning. Ed Burrell – a man based less than a quarter of a mile from this office – was the latest pretender to Ferris's throne.

Just another in a long line, Ferris thought.

New gangs would always appear. And the bigger ones would get ambitious. They would try to compete. Sometimes Ferris would lose people to them; the grass often seems greener, especially when the boss is in prison. But so far Ferris had seen off every new face. Burrell would be no different.

Ferris turned back to Ellis.

'That right?'

'I think so, yeah. Didn't want to jump, though. Just in case.'

'Fuck "just in case".' Ferris spoke without any loss of temper. This was business. 'We're gonna jump. Get the list done and get every fucker on it dealt with. No excuses.'

'What about Burrell?' Tennant again.

'He can wait. Let him stew when he sees his new people lost. He'll be in touch soon enough.'

'And when he does that?'

'Do I need to answer that?'

As loyal as Tennant was, Ferris sometimes lost patience with his friend's need for instruction. He did not let it show. Tennant deserved at least that much respect. Instead he changed the subject.

'Moving on. Tell me about the Taylor boy I saw today. He seems switched on.'

'He is, Leon.' This time it was Leach who spoke. 'He's a friend of mine and—'

'Who asked him to talk?' Ferris did not address Leach. Not even a glance. He knew full well why Leach had spoken up; Leach had introduced Taylor to Ferris's outfit. It was his chance for some credit. Something Ferris was not in the habit of giving. 'Why is he talking to me?'

Leach fell silent. Not another word. He focused on a spot on the floor. Ferris let a silence hang, just long enough to increase Leach's discomfort.

'Does *someone else* want to tell me about Taylor, then?'

'He's a good kid,' Ellis replied.

No one so much as glanced at Leach. Not that he would have seen them if they had. His stare remained fixed on the floor.

Ellis continued.

'He runs about twenty boys already. He's a good earner.'

'Worth moving up, or is that too soon?'

'Depends what you want out of it?'

'I want to give our people options. Other than going elsewhere.' Ferris could see from Tennant's expression that he was not following the logic. His understanding of gangland politics had always left much to be desired. Ferris continued for Tennant's benefit. 'We'll deal with those that have gone over to Burrell. That sends the message. But at the same time we set Taylor up as an *alternative* to Burrell. Someone young who the boys can attach themselves to. Someone who's on the up, but who's loyal to us. Controlled by us.'

'So instead of the ambitious lads defecting, they can throw in with Taylor without us losing them?' Ellis replied. 'Makes good sense.'

'So is he ready for it?' Ferris wanted an answer. 'And right for it?'

Tennant and Ellis did not answer immediately. The question demanded due consideration. Leach, still smarting from his chastisement, kept his eyes down.

'It worries me,' Tennant finally said. 'He reminds me of you at that age, Leon. What would you have done if someone had backed you like that?'

'I'd have probably ironed them out and taken over the whole thing. In the end, anyway.' Ferris smiled. He could see what was concerning his old friend. Ambition and loyalty did not make good bedfellows. 'But we'll keep an eye, won't we. And I'd rather we had him in the tent than out.'

A smile spread across Ferris's face. He had made his decision and was happy with it. In fact he was happy with everything. Things had remained good while he was in prison. Not perfect, but better than he could have hoped for. And his move to back the kid Taylor was a first step to reasserting whatever little control – whatever respect – had slipped.

Soon, Ferris thought, *we'll be stronger than ever.*

The thought had barely crossed his mind when he sat up alert. A movement at the far end of the office – behind Leach – had caught his eye. His next reaction turned every head in the room.

Except one.

'I thought I told you to keep that fucking door closed!' Ferris bellowed at Leach.

The door had opened quietly and a small figure had entered the room. It had then been closed again, all without Leach seeming to notice.

He noticed now.

Ellis and Tennant were on their feet within an instant of Ferris's shout. Leach reacted just as quickly. Closer than the others, he moved towards the intruder without hesitation. No doubt keen to prove his value.

All three were stopped when Ferris spoke again. Anger had given way to confusion.

'That ain't you?'

It was not a question. Not really. Ferris would know that face anywhere. Especially the eyes. The cold, pale eyes.

'It is you, ain't it?' he asked again.

No answer.

'I asked you a question.'

Still no answer. Ferris was both irritated and amused. Conflicting reactions. He did not know which to follow.

Tennant, Ellis and Leach all remained rooted to the spot. None seemed sure of how to react, and Ferris knew why. An unremarkable man had walked into the office of their boss, unannounced and uninvited. A man who seemed unconcerned as he disrespected Ferris with his silence.

That just can't happen, Ferris thought.

He moved around the desk. Annoyance had won.

'You see this little bitch?' Ferris moved slowly. Directing his words towards Tennant and Ellis. But his eyes never left the newcomer. 'He was in Wandsworth with me. Until three years ago. Ain't that right?'

No answer. Not a flicker of the pale eyes.

Ferris moved closer.

'And do you know what we did with him in there?'

The room was silent until Ferris spoke again, emphasising every word and every pause between them.

'*Anything* we fucking wanted.' More slowly. More deliberately. '*Whenever* we wanted. Ain't that right?'

No answer. Ferris was almost within reaching distance. Still the pale eyes held his stare.

'And do you know why? Because this little bitch didn't fight back.' Ferris's tone was now mocking. Full of the menace it takes to terrorise a prison. 'And now he's here. Standing his ground. Is that what you're doing, is it?'

No answer. Ferris stepped in close. His spittle had barely inches to travel.

'Or is it something else? That's it, ain't it, little bitch? You're here for another go.'

Ferris smiled wide as he spoke. Disguising his intent. Then, without warning he lunged at the intruder.

Ferris was a big man. His hands large. Shovel-like. Their target was much smaller, inches below average height. His wiry build was no match for Ferris's slabs of gym-honed muscle. Ferris expected to need no more than a single punch.

But Ferris was very wrong. Their past encounters had made him over-confident. Careless. Ferris had no reason to expect this occasion to be different to the others. A big man physically dominating a small one. And so the punch was powerful but slow.

The speed of the intruder would have surprised Ferris, if only he had had time to consider it. The smaller man was built for quick, agile movement, but nothing in their past had hinted that he could fulfil that potential. This time, though, he did *not* hesitate.

Ferris's arm had barely moved before his opponent stepped inside the intended blow, his own arm thrusting upwards. Ferris had no time to think. No time to question. A long knife appeared in the intruder's hand. It found its way expertly to the underside of Ferris's chin.

Any resistance there was overcome by momentum. The blade entered Ferris's brain before he could blink.

*

Shock and disbelief combined as Kevin Tennant watched Ferris fall. His oldest friend and the most dangerous man he had ever known, killed in a heartbeat. No warning. No fanfare.

Tennant's mind could not quite accept what he had seen; it tried to reject the impossible. The others seemed to do the same; all three seemed to freeze. Just for a moment, but it was a moment they did not have.

Because the intruder was *not* in shock. And he moved fast. A second knife appeared in the same hand. Pulled from its hiding place in the same swirl of movement that brought the small man closer to Ellis and Tennant, via a rigid Leach.

It was Leach who fell first. His murderer hardly glanced at him as the knife slashed across Leach's throat. Blood hit the wall six feet away, making a second blow unnecessary. Only a severed carotid artery fired blood so far from its source.

Less than a second had passed.

Ellis was next in line. Tennant behind him. Less than a yard apart, but Ferris's killer was closer still. The distance gave Ellis no time to think, removing his only natural advantage.

If Ellis had been a natural fighter he would *not* have reached for his gun. There was no time to pull and aim; the intruder was too close for that. The best course was to attack with fists and feet, with Tennant at his side. Two against one. Ellis's instincts told him none of this. His mind resorted to a simple equation: gun versus knife.

Tennant could do nothing as Ellis reached for his holstered weapon just as his attacker reached him. Without a free arm to strike or to block, Ellis was defenceless as the second blade was thrust deep into his exposed chest.

Maybe two seconds had passed. Certainly less than three.

All resistance left Ellis' body as the knife pierced his heart. He slumped forwards. His murderer span aside as Ellis fell. It avoided an impact with Ellis' body but it also checked his momentum, bringing him to a standstill.

Face to face with Kevin Tennant.

Tennant stood at six foot three inches tall. Weighed north of two hundred and thirty pounds. He looked like a bear in comparison to his opponent. But Tennant had thrived in this world for reasons other than just size. It took more than mass to win a fight. It took skill. It took speed. Most importantly, it took a ruthless capacity for violence. Tennant had all of these and more.

The past seconds had shown that the intruder had them, too.

Neither man moved. There were now perhaps two metres between them. Whoever closed that gap would be putting themselves on offer. Leaving themselves open to a counter-attack. The element of surprise was long gone.

Tennant had seen what his opponent could do. Overconfidence would not end him as it had ended Ferris.

Tennant used his peripheral vision. Searching for an advantage. Within short reach was one of the bronze statues that Ferris had liked so much. Tennant remembered them being heavy. To most men, anyway. Perhaps Tennant's superior size and strength could matter after all.

The intruder's pale eyes had not left Tennant. They seemed to be staring into his soul. They made the bigger man uncomfortable. Frightened, even. It was a rare feeling.

Tennant felt his own gaze flicker away. Back to the bronze. His opponent would have noticed the glance. He had to act now.

Tennant was fast for a man so large. His right hand snatched out and grabbed the foot of the bronze before the intruder could take a step. He launched the statue in the direction of his opponent. Used all of his strength. The heavy bronze hurtled across the two-metre space. Tennant's body was close behind, his massive fists clenched.

The plan had been a simple one. The bronze would either hit its target or at least cause Pale Eyes to raise his arms in defence. Either way he would be on the back foot. Vulnerable for a second. Perhaps less. But long enough for Tennant to bring his size and strength to bear. A simple plan. Not an effective one.

The intruder had followed Tennant's eyes. Had seen them fall on the statue. In that instant he had known what Tennant would do, and so he had been prepared. Fast as Tennant was, his opponent was faster. Pale

Eyes span clear of the bronze as it hurtled past his head. Using the same momentum, he brought himself around to the exposed right-hand side of the rushing Tennant.

Tennant's right arm flayed out at his opponent as he registered the movement, but his forward motion worked against him. Pale Eyes dropped to a crouch, below Tennant's reach. Now low, the same knife that had killed both Leach and Ellis slashed deep into the sinew at the back of Tennant's right knee.

Tennant crashed to the floor. Hard. His arms broke his fall, protecting his head from the impact. Tennant tried to climb to his feet immediately, aware that he could not stay down. He pushed upwards with both hands and it was then that he realised two things. First, the fall had broken his right wrist. The pain that shot through his arm told him that. But it was a pain quickly forgotten. Overtaken by the panic of Tennant's second realisation.

His sliced right leg was now useless. A deadweight.

Blood was beginning to seep through the back of Tennant's jeans. It stuck the denim to his skin, confirming the worst. Whatever the cost, he could not climb to his feet.

The fight was over.

It was now just a question of how he would die.

FOURTEEN

Michael Devlin exhaled deeply as he climbed the steps to his front door, an involuntary sigh. It had been a longer day than he had anticipated. Much longer. Exhausted, he stepped inside and parked his wheeled bag against the hallway wall, slipped off his suit jacket and slung it across the bottom rail of the staircase. A far cry from the care he had shown it that morning.

He unfastened his cufflinks as he walked towards the kitchen, before rolling up his shirt and unbuttoning his waistcoat, freeing himself from the confines of his tailored working clothes. Michael loved his job, but he had never grown fond of the suits that came with it.

The kitchen was the most indulgent room in the house, as well as the largest. That was perhaps inevitable. Michael loved to cook, and both he and Sarah loved to eat. But even when doing neither, they still found themselves here rather than the lounge.

The ornate Clive Christian design had been installed by Sarah's father shortly before he gifted them the property as an engagement present; an extravagant gesture from an extremely wealthy man. The installation had cost more than Michael had earned in his first two years as a barrister, yet neither he nor Sarah had ever questioned its value. It was one of those things that reminded Michael of how much his life had changed.

For all this, Michael was surprised to find the kitchen empty. A glance towards the open door in its far corner offered the explanation. The door led outside, to a small stone staircase that snaked down to a patio that was carefully designed to resemble a courtyard. Beyond that was a long, well-kept lawn surrounded by flower beds.

Michael walked towards the door, taking a detour on the way to pick out a bottle of Corona from the pantry's refrigerator. He popped the lid as he walked. Took a long swig as he headed outside.

The sight that greeted Michael as he reached the top of the stairs was exactly as expected. Sarah and Anne Flaherty were seated around the long metal garden dining table with a wine glass each. Sarah's glass was half full. Anne's less so. An empty bottle of white wine sat in front of her, next to a cooler.

Both women noticed Michael at the same time.

'Do I need to ask?' he said, in reaction to two welcoming smiles, nodding towards the empty bottle as he spoke.

'If you insist, Mikey,' Anne replied. Her voice was full of affection. It always was when she spoke to Michael.

Michael returned the smile before doubling back into the kitchen for another bottle. He reappeared less than a minute later, walked down the steps and poured a fresh glass for Anne. He then topped up Sarah with barely a drop before putting the new bottle into the cooler and taking a seat between them.

'Quitting again tomorrow, are you?'

Michael had noticed the cigarette in Sarah's hand. He smiled as he spoke, making it clear that his question was light-hearted.

'Leave the girl alone, Mikey.' Anne seemed to have missed Michael's playful tone. He could see why. She had clearly put away more of the first bottle of wine than Sarah. 'She works hard. She's allowed to relax.'

'But she only relaxes this way when she's with you,' Michael replied. 'You're a bad influence, Anne Flaherty.'

This time Michael's tone was unmistakable. He was teasing both his wife and his oldest friend. It was a relief to finally be playful.

'So how was your day, Mikey?'

'Long and emotional,' Michael replied. He noticed his own Northern Irish accent becoming more pronounced, as it so often did when he was with Anne. 'Everything went a bit mad with Phillip Longman's murder.'

'Is that the judge Sarah was telling me about?'

'Yeah. He was a big name in the legal world. A huge name. The whole Temple pretty much shut down when the news came out.'

'How's Derek?' asked Sarah. 'Have you spoken to him?'

'Earlier, yeah. He's holding up. He's with Longman's son. Helping him through. To be honest, I think he's keeping himself busy so as not to fall apart.'

'Did Derek know him, then?' Anne asked.

'He did, yeah,' Michael replied. 'Longman was Derek's pupil-master. Like Derek was mine. Knowing Derek, I really don't think he could have lost anyone closer.'

'Jesus. The poor man.'

Anne lit another cigarette and took a sip of wine. Michael could see the sympathy in her eyes. If anyone could empathise with Derek's loss, it was Anne Flaherty.

'Are you going to see him?' Sarah asked.

'Tomorrow. I've got to meet the junior in my murder trial in the morning. Then I'm going to head to Derek's place and make sure he's OK.'

'You'll give him our best?' Sarah said, her voice concerned. 'And make sure he knows that we're here for him?'

'I already have, sweetheart.' Michael reached across and squeezed Sarah's hand, grateful to see her genuine care for his friend. 'But for now there's nothing we can really do for him. For now it's Derek who's being the moral support, to Longman's sons. But it'll come. He'll need a shoulder sooner or later.'

No one spoke for a few moments. All thoughts were on Derek Reid. Michael took another long swig of lager. Anne did the same with her wine. Sarah stubbed out her cigarette and took a sip from her glass.

Finally Sarah spoke.

'Don't share this with Derek, but from what I gather it seems Longman died badly. Real nasty stuff.'

'What did the police tell you?'

'Nothing, really. But you know how it works. If it was straightforward – if it was just the average murder, no matter the victim – they'd let us know that, off the record. But they won't tell us anything on this one yet. Nothing at all. Ninety-nine times out of a hundred, that's a bad death.

Add in the team in charge of the investigation and the story nearly writes itself.'

'Which team?' Michael asked. 'Who's in charge?'

'Joelle Levy. Major Investigation Team One from Scotland Yard.'

'They're taking this seriously, then.'

'You know that team?'

'I know Levy. I've cross-examined her.' Michael's career had included many major cases. In that time he had encountered most of London's top cops. 'She's good. Formidable.'

'She seemed fairly reasonable to me,' Sarah observed. 'None of the uncooperative crap we sometimes have to deal with.'

'Just stay on her good side,' Michael advised. 'You won't want to see the bad one.'

Sarah nodded. 'I'll make sure and stay friendly.' She squeezed Michael's hand as she spoke. Nothing more needed to be said on the subject.

A comfortable silence fell between them all. Michael took another long taste of his beer and sat back into his chair, enjoying a light, warm breeze that had grown out of nowhere. Sarah did the same, only to see the small sip she had taken from her wine glass replaced by far more from the bottle now in Anne's hand. What was left was then poured into Anne's now-empty glass, before she climbed to her feet and headed towards the kitchen.

'There's time for one more,' Anne said, speaking over her shoulder as she climbed the first step.

'How many has she had?' Michael asked, his voice now quiet.

'This'll be the third bottle.' Sarah answered. 'And she's had most of them.'

Michael shook his head.

Already one too many.

Anne's drinking had been a concern for months. Longer, maybe. But so far Michael had been unable to bring himself to confront her about it. He had tried to rationalise his reluctance, telling himself that it was not *that* bad. Then that it was *her* life. But deep down, he knew the cause.

Michael did not raise the subject of Anne's drinking because, ultimately, he believed it was his fault.

Anne had been Michael's sister-in-law in all but name. The partner of his brother Liam since they were teenagers, she had stayed in Liam's life when Michael had not. And she had still been there when Michael had returned after two decades, running for his life from a professional killer hunting both him and Sarah.

Michael had brought that threat into Anne and Liam's world. A threat which had ended in Liam's death and with Anne a shell of her former self.

Michael would have given anything to turn back the clock. To keep his brother alive. *That* was impossible. But he *could* take responsibility for his brother's broken 'widow', and that was exactly what he had done.

'How was she before I got here?' Michael asked.

'She had on a brave face like always,' Sarah replied. 'But I could tell she'd been crying before I got home.'

'And drinking?'

'Didn't seem like it,' said Sarah. 'But then she can hold her liquor a hell of a lot better than I can, so maybe.'

'Look, I'm really sorry.' It was not the first time Michael had apologised for imposing Anne on Sarah's life. Guilt built upon guilt. 'This won't be forever. I promise that. Anne will get better, and when she does we'll find her her own place. It's not like she can't afford it.'

'Michael, how many times do I have to tell you? Anne is not *your* imposition on me. It wasn't just *you* who went to Liam. It wasn't just *you* Liam was protecting. Christ, if it wasn't for me then *neither* of you would have been in that cabin. I owe Anne as much as you do. And besides, she's family now. She can stay with us as long as she likes, on one condition.'

'That we help her get better.' Michael had heard the condition before.

'That we help her get better, yeah. We're doing her no good by enabling her. But as long as we're helping, as long as she's getting better, then she's got a home here.'

Michael reached out and gripped Sarah's hand once again. Tightly this time.

'You really are perfect, Sarah Truman.'

'Nobody's perfect, Michael Devlin,' Sarah replied with a broad grin. 'But yeah, I run it close.'

'Just that humility that's missing, eh?' Michael laughed.

'Just that, yeah!'

'What's so funny?'

Michael and Sarah were still laughing as they looked up to see Anne walking down the steps, a fresh bottle of wine in her hand.

Michael rose from his chair and moved towards her.

'Change of plan.' He was careful to keep his tone playful as he reached out and took the wine bottle from her hand. 'Enough booze for tonight. I'm taking my girls out to eat.'

'I'm not hungry, Mikey,' Anne protested. 'Let's stay here and enjoy the garden.'

'Don't care,' Michael replied. 'After the day I've had I'm bloody famished, and I hate eating alone. Now go get yourself ready. We're leaving in ten.'

FIFTEEN

Adam Blunt did not try to suppress his smile as the news report ended.

It was the fourth time he had watched the same bulletin.

The first had come as a shock. But the repeats had been for entertainment. And he was not tiring of it yet.

I could watch this all day long, he chuckled to himself.

Blunt had hated Phillip Longman for almost twenty-five years, although their first encounter had been years before that. Early in Longman's judicial career. Back then Longman had been the legal world's rising star. Blunt had heard that long before meeting the man. What he had *not* heard was that Longman was also an uptight, preachy hypocrite. At least that was how Blunt remembered it. True or not, there was no doubt that the two men disliked one another intensely.

Every time Blunt appeared in Longman's court he seemed to be criticised. And that criticism hurt. Not personally – Blunt couldn't give two shits for what Phillip Longman thought – but professionally? Such repeated attacks by a well-respected judge could only be damaging. Still, Blunt had survived them. Bloody and bruised, but still standing. Until their final case, where Longman went further than ever before and ended Blunt's first career.

Blunt could never forget that. And he would never forgive.

In the years that followed, their paths had crossed only occasionally. Blunt was never more than an ambulance chaser as a solicitor, and so was rarely involved in cases serious enough to come before a judge as important as Longman. That had become only more true as Longman had risen through the judicial ranks. And yet, every now and again, Blunt had still found himself in Longman's court.

Each time had brought back memories. Each time had made him hate the man more. Which was why he smirked to himself now, as he watched the report of Longman's murder with grim satisfaction.

I hope the bastard suffered, he thought, for what could be the hundredth time that day.

The pleasure was short-lived, banished in a moment by the familiar stabbing pain in Blunt's gut. It distracted him from his enjoyment, just as it distracted him from everything else. It was not a constant pain. Sometimes it went away. Sometimes the drugs worked. But mostly it was there, crippling and mocking in equal measure.

He gritted his teeth and forced the pain from his mind as best he could. He would not allow it to destroy this moment for him. He had so very little left. He would at least enjoy today.

The diagnosis had come a year before. Bowel cancer. Six months at most. But here he still was, twelve months later. Alive and kicking. Well, alive at least. Something had kept Blunt going. Not family, of which he had none. Not friends, of which he had just as few. And certainly not hope for the future; Blunt had sold his law firm before his illness and had retired to the Suffolk coast alone. What future was there?

No. It had been none of these things that had kept Blunt alive. It had been God, he now realised. God – or whatever the higher power was – had kept Blunt here long enough to see Longman's violent death.

Blunt looked towards his wall. The clock hanging upon it read 3.10 a.m. He no longer kept normal hours. He just slept when the medication made him. And when he *did* sleep it did not matter where. Blunt had slept in his armchair much more than his bed in the last few months. If anything, that was a relief. The effort of moving from seated to standing was becoming more than he could take.

The medication did not control his bladder, however. Blunt's bowels had rebelled against him. They were slowly killing him. But right now his need to urinate was a more immediate problem.

He climbed to his feet. Slowly. Painfully. The closed door of the living room was perhaps ten feet away, give or take. Blunt could make that distance, but any further would have been a problem.

He took a few moments to regain his breath. Just getting out of his chair was getting much harder, he realised. The beginning of the end.

Still, I beat Longman.

The first steps had to be steady. A stumble could be fatal. Blunt knew that, and so he took a few seconds more before moving. Right foot first. Slowly, but not so slow that he would lack momentum. One step. Two steps. Three steps. The door came closer with each. Four. Five. Six. Closer still. Seven. Eight. Nine. The door was in reach. Blunt put out an open hand as he took the final two steps. He gripped the door handle and rested his shoulder onto the frame. To take the weight that now threatened to fall.

His breaths came thick and fast. Eleven steps had sapped his energy.

Eleven fucking steps.

The thought angered him. How had it come to this? How could he end this way, broken and alone? Only the thought of Longman's fate held off a bout of despair.

It took over a minute for Blunt to recover enough energy to continue. Hopefully enough to see him through the four more steps to the washroom on the other side of the closed door.

It would have to be. His bladder would not wait.

He gripped the handle tight and pulled hard to open the door.

The sight that greeted him put everything else out of his mind.

'Right.' Blunt spoke almost to himself as he faced the palest eyes he had ever seen. Eyes from his distant past. Their appearance was almost a relief.

He began to smile as he uttered his final words.

'Well, that makes sense.'

SIXTEEN

L evy glanced at her watch as she finished setting the table for breakfast.

Still on time, just about.

'Richard, it's on the table,' she called out, raising her voice just slightly. The house was not big. Just two bedrooms and a bathroom upstairs. It did not take a bellow to be heard.

The sound of fast footsteps on the staircase was immediate and moments later her ten-year-old son Richard burst into the kitchen. He took a seat at the small dining table and tackled his breakfast enthusiastically.

They ate in silence. Levy had raised Richard to be well-mannered, which included not speaking with a mouthful of food. She had also taught him the importance of eating when he had the chance; that he would never know for sure when the next meal would come. It was a lesson Levy had learned in the Israeli military. Breakfast – like every other meal – was, first and foremost, functional.

'You were late last night, Mum,' Richard said when he had finally finished his food. 'I woke up when you got home.'

'I know I was, Richard. I'm sorry.'

It was not unusual for Levy to keep unpredictable hours and to miss her son's bedtime. The frequency did not improve her feelings of guilt.

'Yesterday was a very long day.'

'What happened?'

'You really don't want to know, Richard.'

Levy was used to her son's questions. He was an intelligent boy, well educated and mature. She would sometimes tell him about her cases – just the broad strokes and heavily edited – but this would not be one of those times.

'It was a nasty business.'

Richard nodded his head. Young as he was, Richard knew when his mother did not want to answer, and he understood enough about her job not to press her.

'Will you be late again tonight, Mum?'

'I hope not.' Levy was not about to make a promise she could not keep. She had made that mistake before. 'I don't think so, I mean. But you never know after yesterday. Don't worry, I'll make sure Claire is around to look after you if I get stuck.'

Claire Gordon was a local girl well used to Levy's last-minute need for her services. Over the years she had been paid a large chunk of Levy's salary in childcare fees.

Which means more money out, Levy thought to herself. *Along with everything else.*

Levy had fallen pregnant aged twenty-eight, barely two years into her time with the police. It had not been planned and she had not known the father. Levy was far from promiscuous; she could count her sexual partners on one hand. Only once in her life had she slept with a man she could not call her boyfriend. Richard had been the result.

Levy had spent the next eleven years turning that accident into a blessing. And a blessing it had become in every way but one: her finances.

Driven to give Richard as full a life as she could, Levy had pushed hard for promotion. She had achieved it and had used the increased salary to find a home in a good area, close to the best schools. But a detective chief inspector's salary did not go far in a place like Highgate and so Levy had settled for a small house. It was barely big enough for them both, but was in the best location for her son's future.

'Are you driving me to school today, Mum?'

Richard's question broke the silence that had fallen.

Levy looked at her watch. 8 a.m.

'Yes, definitely.' Levy reached out and ruffled her son's hair as she spoke. Her mind had been drifting back to Phillip Longman. One look at Richard's face banished those thoughts. 'But we'll have to leave a little early, OK?'

'OK.'

Richard smiled wide. Levy knew how eagerly he looked forward to spending time with her and she was happy that they still had that closeness. She wished she didn't have to disappoint him so often.

'I'll get my satchel packed.'

He was already leaving the table as he spoke, his excitement palpable. Levy watched him go. She finished her coffee as he ran from the room and, knowing he would not be long, she began to pack his lunchbox.

She was almost done when she was interrupted by the sound of her mobile's ringtone, muffled from within her jacket pocket.

Pulling out the phone, she checked the caller ID: Steven Hale. At 8 a.m. it would not be a personal call.

'Steve. What's happened?'

'Gang murder, Jo. A bad one.' Out of the office, Hale dispensed with the formalities of title. When they were at work, he would never for a moment forget she was his superior, but after so many years working together, they'd become close. Their line of work did not lend itself to particularly sociable hours and this had left her with very few friends. Hale was one of them.

'Where?'

'In Brixton.'

'Why are they calling us in? Surely this one's for Trident?'

'Trident have been called,' Hale replied. 'But Scotland Yard want us to work with them on this one.'

The answer made Levy sigh.

Trident. Another bloody problem.

'OK,' Levy finally said. 'I'll be there in an hour or so. I just need to drop Richard off at school first. Text me the address.'

A crucifixion yesterday, a gangland massacre today, she thought as she disconnected the call. *Hell of a week so far.*

Levy glanced down at Richard's lunchbox. Looking back at her were a group of superheroes from the movies. The Avengers. A fantasy world. Where good always triumphed over evil.

She pulled on her jacket, picked up the lunchbox and walked to the foot of the staircase.

'Hurry up, Richard,' she called out. 'It's time to go.'

SEVENTEEN

Michael was due to meet Jenny Draper at 9 a.m. He had chosen the Starbucks coffeeshop on High Holborn. At the top of Chancery Lane. Draper's chambers was close by, inside Gray's Inn. Barely a stone's throw. It was one of the reasons Michael had chosen the location. When one barrister leads another in a case there is always a clear hierarchy. That can be off-putting on a first meeting; a one-sided match. Michael figured that home ground might tip the balance back towards her.

He had arrived fifteen minutes early; he liked to settle in before a meeting, to watch people arrive. He took a sip of his large black coffee – or Venti Roast, as he had had to call it when ordering – and glanced at his watch. 8.58 a.m.

The coffee shop was narrow but deep, stretching to the far end of the building. Dotted along its length were tables of differing sizes, as well as lone chairs and sofas. At the very back was a large square table that was big enough for four. Michael's choice.

Once settled he had kept an eye on the panoramic window that looked out from the shop. It ran the length of a pedestrian walkway that led to Gray's Inn.

8.59 a.m.

Michael's attention was caught by movement in the walkway. It was a busy route, but when he looked up this time one person stood out. A tall woman with long blonde hair pinned neatly against her scalp, late twenties maybe, early thirties at most, walking purposefully in the direction of the entrance.

Jenny Draper.

9.00 a.m. exactly.

Punctual to the minute. According to Michael's watch, anyway.

Draper walked through the door and strode towards Michael. Reid had been right. She was an attractive woman. Slim with pale skin and aquiline features, she wore a tailored grey suit that fit perfectly. It was very different to Michael's choice. For him, no court meant no suit. The jeans and casual T-shirt made him look more like a client than a colleague.

'Michael.'

Her accent was pure public school. It belonged to someone born to privilege and in no doubt of their place in the world. Her tone was just as confident. Draper was not asking; she was using Michael's name as a greeting.

She offered her right hand.

'Jenny.' Michael responded in kind, taking her hand and shaking it gently. 'It's nice to meet you at last.'

'And you. It's exciting to be working with you.'

Michael did not know what to say to that, so he just smiled in response and gestured for her to sit.

'What can I get you?' he asked, still standing.

'Espresso Macchiato, please.'

'Anything to eat?'

'Can I be bad and have a chocolate muffin? I need the sugar hit.'

'Whatever keeps you going,' Michael joked.

Michael headed back to the counter and placed the order. When it was ready he carried the tray back to the table.

Draper had settled in while Michael was at the counter. A single A4 lever-arch file was now on the table ahead of her. Next to it was a thin laptop. Next to that an iPad. And next to the iPad an iPhone. Michael wondered why anyone would need all three devices at once. A subject for another day.

'You've come prepared.'

'I wouldn't want to give a bad impression the first time we meet.' Draper smiled coyly. 'Plus I thought you'd want to hit the ground running.'

'We need to,' Michael replied. 'We don't have long.'

'We'll get you up to speed in no time.'

'Here's hoping.' Michael sat forward in his seat and clasped his hands between his spread legs. 'Now, tell me what *you* think of Simon Kash?'

For the next hour Michael and Draper discussed various aspects of the case. The allegations. Kash's character. What had happened up to now and Derek Reid being replaced.

Draper had agreed that Reid was more than up to the task. But in the next breath she was saying how happy she was that Michael was the replacement. How privileged she was to work alongside such a brilliant young QC.

Michael ignored the flattery. Perhaps she meant every word, but barristers are adept at massaging each others' ego face-to-face while saying something very different when out of earshot. And he also remembered Reid's warning.

'So you don't think Kash is innocent?' Michael asked.

The conversation had come full circle, returning to Draper's answer to Michael's original question.

'I didn't say he *wasn't* innocent,' Draper replied. 'I'm just not convinced that he *is*. Not like Derek was convinced. Not like Ross.'

'How old are you, Jenny?'

'Thirty-one. Why?'

'And how long have you been in your chambers?'

'Eight years. Nine if you count pupillage. Again, why?'

Draper was certainly confident. Perhaps overconfident. It did not concern Michael. Faith in oneself was a big part of what they both did for a living.

'It's just unusual to hear someone as young as you – as inexperienced, at least relatively – openly disagreeing with the likes of Derek Reid and Andrew Ross.'

Michael realised as he spoke that his meaning might not be clear. He continued.

'It's refreshing, I mean. A lot of people in your position would have just agreed with their leader's assessment. Especially if that leader is Derek.'

'Thanks very much.'

Michael could tell that she was pleased at the compliment.

'So you feel the same?' Draper asked. 'You think they've read Kash wrong too?'

'No, not at all.' Draper's reaction to the answer made Michael laugh. She seemed to visibly deflate. 'I had exactly the same feeling about Kash as Derek did. I don't think that kid did any of the things he's accused of. I just don't buy it. But it's good that *you're* cynical about him. One of us should be. You can keep your eyes open and your wits about you while I'm off on a crusade.'

Draper did not answer, which did not surprise Michael. It was very unlikely that she in her eight years at the Bar she had encountered a QC who seemed pleased that his junior disputed his assessment. Many barristers in Michael's position would take such disagreement as an insult. A challenge to their superiority.

Ego, Michael knew, was usually everything.

He watched as Draper thought it through. If she had the mind that her reputation suggested then she would see the good sense in having a team made up of half passion and half sceptical logic. It covered all of the bases, even if it was an unusual approach.

'So you *want* me to stay off-side?' Draper asked. 'You *want* me to keep doubting everything our client says?'

'I think I *need* you to keep doubting,' Michael replied. 'I've bought into this boy, Jenny. More and more so as I read the evidence. But belief can cause blind spots. You stay as you are and that will help us avoid them.'

Draper sat back into her chair as a smile spread across her face. The good sense in Michael's approach was not lost on her, he could see.

Maybe the reputation's deserved after all, Michael thought. *So let's see.*

'What do you think of Terry Colliver's evidence?' he asked out of nowhere. He had already identified Terry Colliver as their best line of attack. He wanted to know if Draper had done the same.

'I think he's the prosecution weak spot,' Draper replied. 'At least from a jury point of view.'

'Why?'

'Because he has motive to lie. He was arrested for the murder. The telephone evidence places him near the scene, if not *at* the scene. He was facing a trial as the killer and he suddenly gives up O'Driscoll and Kash's names. In return for a plea for a much less serious offence.'

'Correct.' Michael nodded, pleased with the answer. She had identified the witness's primary weakness, but she had missed another.

'And why would the police have taken his word as gospel?' he asked. 'Why did they basically swap him for O'Driscoll and Kash?'

'Because their intelligence told them O'Driscoll was involved,' Draper replied. 'They just didn't have enough admissible evidence to support what they already knew. Colliver's testimony gave them that admissible evidence.'

'But why name Kash too?' Michael was nudging Draper forward. 'Why not just give up O'Driscoll?'

'Because Colliver's telling the truth?'

Too obvious, Michael thought. *A swing and a miss.*

'Tell me why that is,' he said.

'Because it explains why the circumstantial evidence is so compelling against Kash. His name wasn't even on the radar before Colliver made his statement. There's no other reason to mention him except that it's true.'

'Are you sure about that?'

'I'm guessing from your tone that I shouldn't be.' Draper smiled. 'What's your take on it?'

'My take is that O'Driscoll didn't kill the Galloways alone. No one man can have killed them both. Not the way they died. It was a two-man job. Two-man minimum.'

'Then surely that points more closely to Kash? It's exactly what Colliver's saying.'

'It points more closely to *someone*, Jenny. *Anyone*. What it says is that there were numbers. Someone *with* O'Driscoll. Colliver knows that. Especially if Colliver *was* the second guy.'

Draper leaned forward. Her mind was swiftly processing Michael's theory.

'So you think that Colliver *had* to offer up another name? That he's telling the truth about O'Driscoll, but that Kash has been pulled in to fill a Colliver-shaped gap in the story?'

'Exactly.'

Michael was impressed at how succinctly Draper had distilled the point. A natural advocate. The way she put it, she almost sounded like she agreed with him.

'Food for thought,' Draper said, once again sitting back into her chair. It wasn't quite acceptance of Michael's new theory. Which in itself was a good sign. She continued. 'But of course it means that our best defence is that our co-defendant is guilty and lying. And that the primary prosecution witness is also guilty and lying.'

'I didn't say it was simple.' Michael could not miss Draper's amusement. Hell, he shared it. 'Could be fun though.'

'It'll be fun to *watch*, that's for sure,' Draper replied. 'Suddenly I'm glad that it's you and not me who'll be speaking in this trial.'

'Thanks for the vote of confidence. There is one small problem with all of this, though.'

'What?'

'Kash.'

'What do you mean?'

'I mean that at the moment he won't say a word against O'Driscoll. And *we* can't say or do anything that *he* tells us not to.'

'So we can't attack O'Driscoll? Which means we can't say that Colliver is telling the truth about him but lying about Kash. To cover his own involvement, or for any other reason. Doesn't that kind of undermine the approach you want us to take?'

'You *could* say it undermines it. Probably more accurate to say it destroys it, though.' Michael was still smiling. 'But of course, that's only if Kash sticks to his guns.'

'You think he might not?'

'I think there's every chance of that. Which is where *you* come in,

Jenny. I want you working on him. Every day of the trial. Until he gives us what we need to take out Colliver *and* O'Driscoll.'

'You want me to manipulate our client?' Draper sounded shocked. It was another first, Michael was sure. 'You want me to make him change his instructions?'

'What I want is for him to tell us the truth, Jenny. That boy is his own worst enemy. He's too young and too naive to protect himself from a life sentence, so it's our job to protect him from himself. And if you have to nudge him in the right direction to do that, well, that's fine with me.'

EIGHTEEN

Joelle Levy tapped the steering wheel impatiently. The cars moving south along Brixton Road were at walking pace. Perhaps slower. It had been that way for the past fifteen minutes of the journey.

These people must be wondering what's causing this, Levy thought as she looked at the cars crawling along ahead of her.

Maybe they were, but Levy was not.

The police cordon that was up ahead – not yet within her sight – was doing what they always did: causing people to slow. To take a look. It was a natural human reaction. The traffic was just a by-product.

Her destination – the very corner of Brixton Road and Electric Avenue – wasn't far. Maybe a quarter of a mile away. But it still took another ten minutes. Far longer than it should, even by the standards of Brixton's always-slow traffic.

Finally Levy turned left onto Electric Avenue, through the police cordon. She did not need to show her Metropolitan Police warrant card for the tape that blocked the road to be lifted; the closest officer had recognised her on sight. Once through she parked next to the kerb, exited the car and surveyed the scene.

Electric Avenue was both a retail and a market street, named for the fact that it was the first street in London to be lit by electricity. The narrow permanent shops sat on the ground floors of identical, connected three-storey buildings. They ran the length of the long, curved street, on both sides of the road. The lack of any gap between the buildings was unusual; it turned the buildings on each side of Electric Avenue into a single, continuous block.

On any other day these permanent shops would be complemented by market stalls running from the top of the street to the bottom. None were visible today. Electric Avenue had been closed, its makeshift businesses a further victim of the crime that had brought Levy here.

'They're in this building over here, ma'am.'

The voice of a police officer Levy did not recognise interrupted her thoughts. Like the flicking of a switch, it focused Levy's mind.

'What time did the cordon go up?' she asked, noting the door number of the building to which the uniformed officer had indicated. It was not necessary. It was the only one open on the street.

'About two hours ago, ma'am. Shortly after the bodies were found.'

'Which was what? 7 a.m.? 7.30?'

'Around then, ma'am, yes.'

'Then the market stalls must have been out already?' Levy indicated the now-empty road.

'Yes, ma'am. We had the stall holders put them away so we could secure the scene.'

'What about upstairs? What's the thoughts on time of death? This morning or last night?'

'Definitely last night, ma'am. No question.'

Levy considered the answer for a moment, gazing again at the long, empty road as she did so.

'Shorten the cordon,' she finally said. 'Bring it back so that it's twenty metres from the entrance to the building in both directions.'

'Ma'am?' Levy could hear the confusion in the officer's tone. 'But the forensics team haven't been up and down the road yet?'

'And nor will they.' Levy had no need to explain her decisions, but there was nothing to be lost in educating a potential future detective. 'This is one of the busiest roads in the area but it was only closed off this morning – once the market had already opened – to secure a crime scene that was already maybe ten hours old. Any forensics on the road itself will be long gone. Trampled away overnight *and* this morning. All we're doing by keeping this road closed is hurting the local trade. People *we* might need to rely on for what they've seen or heard.'

The officer nodded his understanding.

'Twenty metres, ma'am. I'll get it done.'

'Thank you.'

The officer moved off to follow his instructions. Levy called after him as he went.

'And make sure the shops and stalls outside of the new cordon know they can open for business, please.'

Levy turned towards the open doorway. The shopfront beside it was of a modern pawn shop. The kind that takes electrical and valuable goods, never really expecting to see the pawner again. Never really believing the goods were anything but stolen.

Cash business, Levy thought. *Helpful thing for a gang to control.*

There was nothing remarkable about the doorway itself, other than the number of police officers moving in and around it. The irregular stream stopped as Levy approached. A line of officers stood aside to let her pass.

Levy walked through the door and up the stairs. It was a short climb. One flight. At the top were two doors and the start of a further flight.

One of the doors led to a toilet. The other was open wide, exposing a room that was out of keeping with both the exterior of the building and the common areas Levy had seen so far. She stepped inside.

The dark decor of the room provided was a stark contrast to the cracked white paint of the stairwell. Even the inside of the door itself showed the difference: whitewashed and unremarkable from the outside, on the office side it was carefully varnished and maintained, and its brass handle shone. Someone had taken care to disguise this room from without, while a lot of money had been spent for the *inside* to give a very different impression.

Four victims.

Levy noted the four sheets laid carefully on the office floor. Each covered a body. If the crime scene had been a TV show the bodies and the sheets would be long gone. Replaced by a chalk or taped outline. This was a quirk of poorly researched cop shows. In the real world, it was only worth moving a victim and risking forensic evidence when a life could be saved. There was no such urgency when the victim was already dead.

In those circumstances the body stayed where it fell, with the integrity of the crime scene taking priority.

And nobody but God was going to be helping these guys, Levy thought.

The room was big, almost as large as the building's footprint. At its far end was a large mahogany desk and behind that a high-back leather chair. Both items were larger than the room's other furniture. A clear message of the importance of the table's owner.

The artwork on the walls looked expensive. Levy was no expert – she had no time to be – but she *had* seen valuable art before and it always had something about it. Levy saw that something here, in the hanging art and in the furniture and the bronze statues that were dotted around the room.

Levy saw and processed all of this in just moments, before her eyes finally settled on Steven Hale near the far end of the room.

'Dressing to impress today, Steve?' Levy asked.

Hale was wearing a suit and tie, rather than the forensic outfit he had sported in Phillip Longman's bedroom. It made him stand out as – other than Levy – everyone else in the room was dressed in their crime-scene whites.

Hale turned at the sound of his name and saw Levy.

'Heavy traffic, ma'am?' Hale asked as he walked towards her.

Back at work, back to formalities, Levy thought, and she noted – far from the first time – that a suited and booted Hale looked every inch a police officer. Tall, heavily built and just a little out of shape. But still formidable, with a face that carried the reminders of a violent life.

'Hellish,' Levy replied. 'What do we know?'

'A little bit more than when I called you an hour ago,' Hale replied. 'We had a little chat with the pawnbroker when he turned up to open the shop. It's amazing how forthcoming the likes of him can be when it avoids a property search.'

'How has what he told you avoided that?'

'It hasn't.' Hale smiled as he replied. 'But he doesn't know that, does he?'

Levy nodded. She was used to Hale enjoying the trickier side of the job. It was her least favourite aspect of what they did – Levy had used enough deception to last a lifetime during her six years in Shin Bet – but it was sometimes necessary. When it was, she was grateful for Hale's enthusiasm.

'So what did he tell you?' Levy asked.

Hale indicated to the large, body-shaped bulk beneath the sheet that was nearest the door.

'Well, to start with, this fella here is none other than Leon Ferris. You know that name, right?'

'Shit.' That response could have been answer enough. 'Yeah. I know the name.'

'Cause of death is already established,' Hale continued. 'A single knife wound to the underside of the skull. The knife is still in his brain.'

'The underside?'

'Yes, ma'am. Through the lower jaw. Only route other than the eyes that misses hard bone.'

'Someone did *that* to Leon Ferris?' It did not fit with what Levy knew of the crime boss. Ferris was a monster. As ruthless and as tough as they come.

How did anyone even get close enough to kill him that way?

'They had to have been face-to-face, right?' Levy asked, pushing aside her disbelief.

'According to David, yeah. Must have been.'

Hale could only be referring to David Christie, a pathologist who worked closely with Levy's Major Investigation Team. He had been and gone, Levy now assumed.

Hale continued.

'No other way the knife could have entered at that angle.'

'Shit,' Levy repeated. She turned away from the first sheet. It was already providing too many problems. Maybe the others would be simpler. 'Who else do we have?'

'This one we don't know,' Hale replied, turning to the sheet nearest Ferris. 'One of Ferris's lads, according to the pawnbroker. He doesn't know the name. The other two, though. We sure as hell know them.'

'Who are they?'

Hale pointed to the last sheet in what Levy now realised was an almost neat line of three.

'This one's Harvey Ellis,' he said, before turning to the fourth sheet, which was away from the others. Towards the other side of the room. 'And that's Kevin Tennant.'

Levy did not answer immediately. The killing of Leon Ferris – the way he had met his end – had bothered her. But she was familiar with the other two as well. Both violent, dangerous men. The idea that all three could be taken out at the same time and on their own turf was absurd.

And yet here they were.

'This doesn't make a jot of bloody sense.'

'What do you mean, ma'am?'

'I mean that it's one thing to kill Leon Ferris face on and at close range. Not that I can think of many who could do it. But Tennant and Ellis, too? These are three tough bastards with serious reputations. Who the hell could have done this?'

'Really? It's too early to—'

'I wasn't looking for an actual answer, Steve. Even the press don't expect results *that* fast.' Levy continued to circle the scene, taking in every detail. 'Ellis was basically running Ferris's operation while Ferris was inside, right?'

'Right.'

'Which I thought was still the status quo. So when did Ferris get out?'

'He was released yesterday.'

'You're joking?' Levy was genuinely shocked. 'This was done to them within twenty-four hours of Ferris getting out?'

'Closer to twelve hours, according to David. He puts time of death before 10 p.m.'

Levy exhaled heavily. She did not need this right now. With the Longman investigation less than a day old, the timing could not be worse.

'Any thought on how many it took to kill all four?'

'We think it was one or two guys.'

She looked up at him sharply. Even four against four sounded unlikely, considering the identities of the victims.

'Go on.' Levy made no attempt to hide her scepticism.

'Look, I know how that sounds,' Hale began. 'But everything points towards it. Look around the room. Almost nothing is disturbed. If we've got three or four or even five attackers in a room like this, things get messy quickly. Especially considering the bodies are all so close together; the killers would all be getting in each other's way. Also, to get a bigger number into the room takes away the element of surprise. You have them shuffling through the door, it gives the victims time to react. And yet three of the bodies have no defensive wounds, so they must have been taken by surprise pretty quickly.'

'I can see the thinking,' Levy conceded. 'Do we know how they all died?'

'John Doe there had his throat slashed. Ellis a single thrust to the heart. David didn't notice anything else. And from the positioning of the bodies, it's likely that Ellis was killed by the same man as Ferris and John Doe. He was barely a step away from Doe, and so – again – a second man would likely have gotten in the way.'

'So the theory is that one guy does this, basically in one fast, continuous movement?'

'That's what we've got so far.'

'And how does Tennant fit into it?' Levy gestured across the room. 'He's not in the same line-up of bodies, so we think there was a second man for him?'

'Impossible to say yet, ma'am. Could have been. Or the same guy.'

'Cause of death?'

'He was killed with that statue over there.' Hale indicated a large bronze figure on the floor by the body, obscured by what was left of the man it had killed. The one detail Levy had not noticed. 'It was used to cave in his head. At least three blows.'

Levy looked down at Tennant thoughtfully. The theory made sense if you discounted who the victims were.

'If you're right, this looks like a professional hit,' Levy finally observed. 'It's not street-gang violence. Not *this* clean.'

'That's why we were called in, ma'am. Because the Trident boys think the same. They think a rival group brought in a contractor. That sort of thing is outside of their wheelhouse, and so the higher-ups want us on board too.'

'You mean working alongside Trident? Or instead of them?'

Levy was dreading the answer. Operation Trident was a *very* different section of the Metropolitan Police, focused entirely on gang crime in London. And from what Levy had experienced of them, the way they worked was a million miles apart from the Major Investigation Team.

'Working *with* them,' Hale replied, his tone almost apologetic.

Levy exhaled deeply and shook her head at the answer. Phillip Longman's murder had already been a headache. Now this.

Two wholly exceptional murders less than twenty-four hours apart. And now with the added complication of Trident.

For the first time in her career, Levy was worried. This might be more than she could deal with alone.

NINETEEN

S arah leaned back in her seat. It was a comfortable, mesh design, built to mould around the sitter. Nineteen identical models joined it around the glass conference table. At £400 per chair, the cost was £8,000 just for a room full of reporters to park their backsides in comfort.

And they wonder why network TV can't turn a profit, Sarah thought.

Only half of the remaining seats were taken. Eight by reporters from the network's Home Affairs section – Sarah's section – and the tenth chair by James Elton, Independent Television News' UK Editor.

Elton's status placed him at the top of the table. Sarah's – as ITN's senior Home Affairs Correspondent – placed her first among the others in the room, in the chair to Elton's right.

It also made Elton her immediate boss.

'Where are we on Longman's murder?' Elton asked. The question was directed at Sarah. 'Is there anything new we can run in the next bulletin?'

'There's not,' Sarah replied. 'MIT are keeping their cards close to their chest. They're releasing no details. At the moment we'd just be reporting the same facts as yesterday.'

'Can't we get anything from the guys on the scene? Maybe tap up one of the officers?'

'Not this team, James,' Sarah replied. She wished she had better news. 'It's not the local bobbies this time. It's the Major Investigation Team from Scotland Yard. If they've been told not to talk, they don't talk.'

Elton nodded his head. Sarah could guess what he was thinking. People in his position rarely took 'no' for an answer. But sometimes – just sometimes – 'no' really was the answer. The question was: did he trust Sarah's instinct that *this* time was 'sometime'?

'What about a family angle?' Elton finally asked. The question told Sarah that her boss had decided to go with his reporter's gut. 'Can we get anything from his kids? Has anyone contacted them?'

'No one from us, no.'

'From who then?'

'Pretty much everyone else. BBC. CNN. Sky. They've all doorstepped Longman's sons, looking for information.'

Elton's demeanour changed in a heartbeat. The answer was clearly unwelcome.

'And why haven't we, exactly?' Elton asked, his annoyance unmissable.

'Because I've spoken to someone very close to the family this morning,' Sarah explained, being careful not to mention Derek Reid by name. 'And I know exactly what reaction Longman's sons would have had if we'd doorstepped them as well.'

Elton almost smiled. Sarah's answer had salved his irritation, at least for a moment. But he still wanted more.

'Which I assume is the reaction the others have all suffered?' he asked.

'Exactly the same,' Sarah replied. 'A lot of anger and a few broken cameras. Nothing newsworthy, certainly not for the competition; they don't look so good intruding and shoving mics in Longman's sons' faces. Especially when you consider what those men have just suffered.'

'So your plan is what, then? In terms of securing the story now the other networks have queered their pitch?'

'As far as the family is concerned, we wait. In a few days, when it's all a little less raw, my contact will arrange for us to sit down with them. Just us.'

'Why would they do that?'

'Because the family trust my contact implicitly. And my contact trusts me. He knows that they will have to speak at some point. It's inevitable, with a figure as public as Phillip Longman. And he knows that if it's me they speak to, I'll keep it dignified.'

Elton smiled again. And again Sarah knew why.

Doorstepping was the one aspect of Sarah's job she disliked. The idea of forcing her presence on those who had just lost those closest to them had always seemed distasteful. But since her own losses almost two years ago – back when she had first met Michael, ironically on his doorstep – it had become unthinkable. She now understood the suffering of those left behind by tragedy, and it made her avoid the act all the more.

It was a dislike which had forced her to find alternatives. Other routes to a story. In other words, it had made her a better reporter.

That, Sarah thought, *is why he's smiling*.

'Good work. Really good work,' Elton finally said. 'Although it doesn't help us a jot with filling this afternoon's bulletin. So when do you think the police will start opening up?'

'I really don't know. It's unusual for them to release literally nothing after this long. But then this case is unusual, considering who the victim is. In any case, we should be the first to know when they finally are ready to open up.'

'OK.' Elton didn't look happy, but again he seemed to accept Sarah's answer. 'Just keep your ear to the ground on this, right? Stay in with Longman's family, and stay on top of these MIT people.'

'Absolutely,' Sarah replied. 'I'll make sure we're at the front of the queue when the time comes.'

Elton turned to address the rest of the room.

'Right. That's Longman's story into the long grass for now. So how do we fill the gap for today's main news?'

Seven of the other eight Home Affairs correspondents opened their files simultaneously, to pull out the stories they had each brought to the meeting. The eighth person – Alex Redwood – left his unopened. He had no need to trawl through papers for *his* story.

'I can fill it.' Redwood's voice was deep but clear. Each syllable pronounced in a cut-glass English accent. Every head in the room turned towards him.

'What have you got?' Elton asked.

'Another murder.'

'Where?'

'Southwold, in Suffolk.'

'The coastal town?'

'The very same.' Redwood was unusually sure of himself. Sarah had always thought that about him. His answers now did nothing to change her view. 'And we *do* have details on this one.'

Sarah knew that the final comment was aimed at her.

Redwood did not share her distaste for the darker side of their job, she knew. He had no problem with doorstepping or revealing information that made a story more salacious. It was often information he could not have come by through legitimate channels, and it was this that worried Sarah the most.

'It's another old guy,' Redwood continued. He looked at Sarah as he spoke, his mouth breaking into a conceited smile.

What an asshole, Sarah thought. *He actually thinks it's a competition. Who's got the best dead geriatric.*

Redwood looked back towards Elton and when he spoke again he did so with exaggerated dramatic effect: 'And he died badly.'

'Oh get on with it, Alex.' It was obvious that Elton was unimpressed with the strained delivery. 'What do we know? Simple and quick.'

'The murder scene was a bloodbath.' The acting had stopped. Redwood stuck to the facts. 'The victim was crucified, James. Literally crucified.'

A murmur shot around the room.

Sarah had not been expecting *that*. And from what she could tell, neither had anyone else. Including Elton.

'Crucified?' he asked, disbelief in his voice. 'Are you sure?'

'Oh, I'm sure. And it didn't stop there. He also had his balls cut off and stuffed into his mouth. And he was cut up all over. Deep cuts that bled him out, like a slaughtered animal.'

Sarah could hardly believe what she was hearing. She had seen enough in her career that she was hardened to most horrors. To rapes. To murders.

But not this. This is a new one on me.

The details left her with questions.

'Do the police think it's a religious thing? Because of the crucifixion, I mean?'

'That's their lead theory, yes. Probably Islamic extremists if you ask me.'

'Where was the body found?' Sarah asked.

'In his own home. In Southwold. Seems he was murdered in his living room.'

'Was there anyone else in the house?'

'You mean apart from whoever crucified him?'

'Don't be clever, Alex.' Elton interrupted the exchange between his reporters. 'Just answer the question.'

Redwood did as instructed.

'No, Sarah, there wasn't anyone else,' he answered, the sarcasm gone. 'The victim lived alone. Retired.'

'Was there anything else on the scene to suggest the same thing? Messages? Videos?'

Sarah's instincts were kicking in. Something did not feel right.

'Not according to my source,' Redwood replied, his tone beginning to betray impatience. 'But the crucifixion alone seems to speak for itself, doesn't it?'

'Maybe,' Sarah said, grasping the issue that had been floating in her mind from Redwood's answers. 'But it's a big change of approach. Extremism is usually a spectacle. Either a shocking amount of deaths, or shocking deaths done very publicly. This is one man, killed in private.'

'So what are you saying?'

'Just that we shouldn't be jumping to conclusions,' Sarah replied. 'And that we should be reporting this carefully. We should be keeping any suggestion of religious extremism out of the story, at least until the police are more certain.'

Redwood opened his mouth to speak, but was silenced by Elton raising his hand and shaking his head.

'Agreed,' said Elton. He looked directly at Redwood. 'This needs to be reported responsibly. We don't want to be accused of stirring up some sort of anti-Islam campaign, especially if this turns out to be something else entirely.'

Elton turned to Sarah.

'Do you want to take this one?'

Sarah looked at Redwood. She was tempted by Elton's offer. Not because she particularly wanted the story; no, it would just be for the pleasure of seeing Redwood lose it.

It'd be no more or less than the unscrupulous bastard deserves, Sarah thought. *After all, there's no way he came by these details ethically.*

'No,' Sarah finally answered. Her *own* ethics had won out. 'It's Alex's story. Besides, I don't have the close contacts Alex has in Suffolk Police. They probably wouldn't be so keen to cooperate with me.'

Redwood showed no gratitude for Sarah's generosity. Just anger that she had been offered the story at all. He did not need to speak for Sarah to read him.

'Then I guess the story stays with you, Alex,' Elton said. 'Does the crucified man have a name?'

'Adam Blunt.'

The name hit Sarah's ear like a hammer. She had heard it before. Not recently and not often. But there was something about it. Her mind went into overdrive, shifting through long-forgotten memories, searching for why that name might be relevant.

'Do you know anything else about him?' Sarah asked.

'No. Nothing.' For the first time Redwood seemed hesitant. 'Why?'

'I'm not . . . I think . . .'

Got it!

It was all Sarah could do to keep the thought inside.

'Why?' Redwood asked again.

'Because I've heard of an Adam Blunt,' Sarah could finally explain. 'He was a lawyer Michael used to speak about. A solicitor. They'd worked on a few cases together back when Michael was much younger. Nothing since I've known him; the only reason I know the name is that Michael was invited to Blunt's retirement party a while back. He didn't go and I remember him telling me why; he absolutely hated the guy. And he said a lot of people in the law felt the same. It's why the name stayed with me. Michael doesn't dislike a lot of people. So for him to hate someone, that's pretty unique.'

'Look, this insight into your personal life is all very nice,' Redwood interrupted, his impatient tone undisguised, 'but I'm sure there are a lot of Adam Blunts in the world, Sarah. The odds on it being the same guy are fairly infinitesimal.'

'I know the odds, Alex,' Sarah replied. 'But I also know how odds get shortened. And if you'd allowed me to finish, you'd be able to follow the point. Because that retirement party Michael didn't go to. Guess where the guy was retiring *to*?'

Redwood didn't answer. He didn't need to. The look on his face said it all.

And so Elton spoke for him.

'Southwold in Suffolk?'

'Southwold in Suffolk,' Sarah confirmed. 'And if it *was* that Adam Blunt who died last night, that gives us two controversial lawyers, both murdered with unusual levels of violence within twenty-four hours of one another.'

She turned to Redwood.

'Now tell me the odds on those murders being unconnected?'

TWENTY

Michael waited in Derek Reid's living room, listening to the sound of plates and cutlery that was coming from the kitchen, where Reid was preparing a lunch he had insisted on making.

Michael still felt a little uncomfortable whenever he visited Reid here, which had once been Michael's own home. The Islington townhouse from his bachelor days. Those days were now gone, and the memory of the events that had ended them had made it impossible for Michael to ever again think of this place as 'home'.

The ground floor of the house had changed dramatically since Michael had lived here. The bomb damage the building had suffered almost two years ago had made extensive repairs necessary.

Michael had paid for the rebuilding work, but he had never returned.

And so Reid, freshly divorced and in need of a place to stay, had moved in. At the time Michael had been splitting himself between London and Belfast, keeping his career alive in the capital while doing his best to identify and sell off or close down the complicated business interests of his murdered brother, Liam Casey. It had been a hard few months – stressful and emotional – so Michael had been grateful for the house-sitter; one less worry off his mind.

The arrangement continued after Michael returned to London full-time, proposed to Sarah and moved into the engagement present of a Chelsea home they had been given by Sarah's father. That gift had allowed Reid to remain in Michael's Islington house and he had been here ever since, enjoying the benefits of the low rent charged by a friend who no longer needed the money.

Reid walked into the room, a large tray in his hands that held an open bottle of red wine, two large glasses, two plates that were empty and a full-sized chopping board that was not. Reid had carefully arranged a host of foods onto the wooden board. Expensive, acorn-fed Iberico ham. A selection of blue and hard cheeses. Various raw vegetables – peppers, cucumber, celery and tomatoes – sliced for easy consumption. A mix of roasted and sun-blushed vegetables to complement. And artisan bread, to round off the meal.

Michael was impressed by the spread, but then he would have expected nothing less from Reid, mourning or not.

'Help yourself.'

Reid indicated to the board as he spoke. Not waiting for his own invitation, he was already placing forkfuls of cured Spanish ham onto his plate.

'So how are you?'

It was Michael's first chance to ask the inevitable question. Reid had guided him to the living room upon arrival before disappearing into the kitchen.

'You won't believe what they did to him, Mike.'

Reid spoke without looking up from the board. Continued to pile food onto his plate.

When he finally sat back and looked Michael in the eye, tears were filling his own.

'It's no way to go. No way at all.'

'How did he die?' Michael would not have asked if Reid had not given him the cue.

'He was crucified, Mike. He was beaten, cut to pieces and *fucking crucified*.'

Michael did not know what to say. Reid's emotions were raging, barely concealed beneath the surface.

'That's . . . that's just . . . just unbelievable.' Michael could think of no other words.

'You're telling me. I've never heard anything like it.'

'Look, no offence but are you sure? I mean, there was nothing in the press about it. And Sarah has no details like that and *she's* spoken with the lead investigator. Where did it come from?'

'It was *from* the lead investigator,' Reid replied. 'A detective called Levy. She told Russell. Well, confirmed it, anyway. After one of her team told him. He probably shouldn't have told me if it's not being released to the public, but it's what happened. Phillip was crucified, Mike. He was bled out by cuts all over, and his testicles were removed and left in his mouth.'

'Jesus Christ.' Michael immediately saw the inappropriateness of the expression. He moved on. 'Did you tell Sarah any of this when you spoke to her?'

'I didn't know any of this when I spoke to her,' Reid replied.

That makes sense, Michael thought. *Explains why she didn't say anything.*

Michael moved the conversation forward.

'Do the police have any suspects? Anything at all?'

'Doesn't look like it. Russell said that Levy seemed capable. That she seemed driven. But I get the impression that they've got nothing.'

'I know Levy.' Michael jumped at the chance to say something positive. Anything that could give Reid hope. 'Joelle Levy. She's been involved in a couple of my cases in the last few years.'

'I've heard of her,' Reid said. 'But I've never come across her. I hear she's good. Is she?'

'She's excellent, Derek. Exactly who you want on a case like this.'

'Maybe a little young?'

'She's probably about the same age as me, give or take a couple of years,' Michael replied. 'But she's got an old head and she's got fire in her gut.'

'That description sounds like a Michael Devlin girl.' Reid smiled for the first time since Michael's arrival. It was a welcome sight. 'Anything you want to tell me about her?'

'There's *nothing* I want to tell you! *Ever*!!'

Michael and Reid were laughing before Michael's answer was finished. For Michael it was mostly a laugh of relief, relief that – for all of the tragedy of the last twenty-four hours – his friend was still capable of the act.

The two men continued to chuckle, until a comfortable silence fell between them. A silence that can only exist in a true and confident friendship.

They worked their way through the food that remained on the board, with Reid eating at least twice as much as Michael. Only when the food was done did they speak again.

'You didn't answer my question.' Michael picked up his wine glass, sat back into the comfortable armchair and looked Reid in the eye. 'How are *you*?'

'I've been better.' Reid's answer was as matter-of-fact as Michael would expect. Close friends do not need to dress up the truth. 'Hearing that Phillip had been murdered was bad enough. But finding out what had been done to him? I almost didn't get through that, Mike.'

Michael nodded his understanding but said nothing.

'If I hadn't been with Russell . . . if I hadn't needed to hold *him* together. It was the only thing that got me through.'

Once again, Reid's eyes filled with tears as he spoke. Michael instinctively reached out and placed a hand on his friend's right knee. He squeezed it reassuringly.

'I know exactly how you feel, mate,' Michael said, knowing that Reid was one of the few people aware of his own past. 'I know how empty you are. How you feel you won't make it with this hole right in the centre of yourself. But you will. It'll be hard as hell, but you will.'

Tears were now flowing down Reid's cheeks as Michael continued.

'I've been there, Derek. You know that better than anyone. I lost a friend as close to me as Phillip was to you. And I lost my brother. I watched Liam die. And believe me, I wanted to die with him. With *both* of them.

'I didn't see how I could carry on with them gone. How I could live with what had happened to them. Now not a day goes by that I don't think of them both, Derek. They're in my mind when I wake up and they're there when I go to sleep. But we carry on. Whatever it is – human nature, evolution, whatever – we are *made* to move on. Something allows us to keep going. Even to laugh again. You might not believe it now but you'll get over this. You'll never forget him, Derek. But you *will* get over it.'

Reid said nothing in response. His tears were now flowing freely. Michael had shed a few himself, brought on by the memory of his own losses.

No words were needed. Instead, Reid reached out, placed a hand on top of Michael's and squeezed. It was all the acknowledgement Michael would need.

The two men sat in silence for a few minutes more. Both drained their glass. Reid first, Michael not far behind.

Michael refilled both and took a mouthful before speaking again. It was time to move the conversation on.

'I met Jenny Draper today,' he finally said.

'What did you think?'

Reid wiped away the last of his tears as he spoke. He was grateful for the change in subject.

'She's pretty impressive,' Michael offered. 'Confident, too.'

'And?'

'And nothing.' Michael saw the mischief returning to Reid's eyes. 'Sarah has absolutely nothing to worry about.'

'Jenny might think differently,' Reid laughed. The humour diluted the lingering sadness in the room 'Watch your back on that one, old boy.'

'I'll keep my eyes open.' Michael welcomed Reid's teasing. It proved his own earlier words. Reid had not lost his ability to laugh. 'Anyway, since you keep mentioning it, is there something you want to tell me about *you* and Jenny?'

Reid snorted out the wine he had just sipped. From both his mouth and his nose.

'Me?' Reid bellowed the question as he caught his breath. 'Christ, Mike. Did she *look* like she'd been crushed under an elephant?'

Both men roared with laughter at the comment, with Michael still chuckling when he felt his mobile phone vibrate in his jeans pocket.

He took it out and the sound of 'Boom Boom Pow' by The Black Eyed Peas – the personalised ringtone he had set for Sarah – filled the room.

With a silent apology he got to his feet and walked towards the hallway door before putting the phone to his ear.

'Hello gorgeous. What's up?'

'Hi, sorry, I've got to be quick. I was just wondering about that solicitor you mentioned a while back. The one who retired. It was Adam Blunt, wasn't it?'

Michael's smile disappeared. Replaced by confusion. Adam Blunt was a name he was never happy to hear.

'Yeah, that's right,' he replied, careful to keep his voice low. The name would be even more unwelcome to Reid, and Michael did not want to dampen the relatively good mood he had worked hard to achieve. 'Why?'

'And is it right that he retired to a place called Southwold?'

'Yeah, so I was told. Look, what's this about?'

'Any chance you know his address there?'

'Not off-hand. I'm sure chambers would have it. In case anything came up with one of his cases. Give the clerks a call, if they have it they'll give it to you.'

'What about Derek? Would he have it?'

'No chance.' Michael's tone was now firm. 'I'm not asking Derek. Blunt's a bit of a sore point with us, I'm not scratching it while he's in this state. Anyway, why do you need it?'

Michael could feel the colour draining from his own face as he listened to what Sarah had to say. And one word in particular made his blood run cold.

Crucified.

It took him a moment to accept what Sarah had told him. When he did, the connection was undeniable.

'Sarah,' Michael finally said, 'I think you need to know how Phillip Longman died.'

TWENTY-ONE

New Scotland Yard's four Major Investigation Teams occupied about a third of the building's fifth floor.

A large communal work-space occupied by the bulk of the teams accounted for most of that. Open plan and cavernous. It was joined by a separate Exhibits Room. Smaller, but not by much. Designed as storage for the evidence accumulated in ongoing investigations and for upcoming trials.

Then there were the senior staff's offices.

Chief Superintendent David Rogers ran the Special Crimes and Operations Directorate's Homicide Command (Central), and so technically oversaw the four Major Investigation Teams under the Command's umbrella. A political and public role, it came with the largest office and was where the buck ultimately stopped. The chief superintendent's day-to-day involvement in any of the teams below him was, however, minimal.

Next was Superintendent Carol Walker. An admin rank, there to do what most would consider Rogers' job.

Joelle Levy and three other detective chief inspectors came next. Each responsible for their own MIT and the fifty officers supposedly assigned to each of those four units. It was here that the everyday command of the four central Major Investigation Teams rested, with DCIs high-ranking enough to deserve a substantial office but still low enough that their hands stayed dirty.

Steven Hale was one of four detective inspectors who worked under Levy as part of MIT One, and he was also her most trusted. None of which made a difference to his office rights. Like his three MIT One colleagues of the same rank, Hale had to join two hundred other members of the Command's four teams, hot-desking in a newly furbished office space that looked more like a Seattle coffee house than a working police station.

The incredible panoramic views of the River Thames, the South Bank and the London Eye did not make up for the impractical modern design of this 'new' New Scotland Yard, a relatively recent replacement for the far more workable, much larger New Scotland Yard that had now been sold and demolished to make way for more luxury residential homes.

It did not come close.

It was in this working area that Levy and Hale now sat, behind an empty desk in the team's main workspace. Ahead of them were three tables, pulled together to sit end to end. All were piled high with case files. Four stacks per table. Twelve in all. How many cases per stack depended on file thickness. They varied wildly.

Six detectives sat between Levy, Hale and the files. Four men. Two women. All of them looked equally tired. It was not yet lunch, but for all of them it had already been a long day.

'What was the filter?' Levy asked, indicating the files. 'How did you settle on these cases?'

'We concentrated on crimes of extreme violence only.' The reply came from one of the women. Detective Inspector Natasha Pickett. Ten years older than Levy. A talented but overstretched investigator, Pickett was no leader. Nonetheless she had earned Levy's trust. 'We just don't have the manpower or the resources to review all of Longman's cases. So we narrowed it down to those with defendants who have somehow shown themselves capable of the sort of violence that was done to him.'

Levy nodded. She was well used to working with limited resources; of the fifty officers who should have made up her MIT One, she had never had more than thirty at any one time. And that was just the easiest example of the underfunding that blighted every investigation.

It was for this reason that Levy had approved the plan to at first limit the investigation's focus to Longman's cases that featured ultra-violence. Such a focus would allow her to best deploy her limited manpower.

It had not worked as well as she had hoped; the large number of files still left was a disappointment.

'There still seems a lot,' Levy said. 'How can we focus it further?'

'We already have.'

This time one of the men answered. Detective Sergeant Pat Tucker. Another older officer, he was even more the stereotypical copper than Hale: tall, broad and carrying more than a little weight, he was an imposing figure on the streets. He continued.

'We've removed completely every case where the defendant is dead or still in custody. That accounted for over half. These three tables are what's left.'

Levy nodded again. She had hoped that the process would have narrowed the field more. Investigating the remaining files would still take thousands of man hours. Thousands of man hours she simply did not have.

'Then we divided what was left into three categories,' Tucker was still speaking. 'One per table. The first table is for one-off offenders. Where violence is an anomaly on their record. The second table is for any offender released more than three years ago. On the basis that if they were looking for revenge they would be unlikely to wait so long, particularly with such an old victim who could easily have passed away in the meantime. And the third table is for cases of extreme violence, repeated offending *and* relatively recent release.'

'So table three cases would be the priority, then,' Levy said in frustrated agreement.

She considered the piles of paperwork in front of her. Sifting cases for prioritisation in this way was far from a perfect system. Ideally she wanted to go through all of them. But with an underfunded thirty-officer squad and a second serious murder to investigate alongside Longman's, she really didn't have the resources. Still, she knew where the blame would fall if the murderer did turn out to be on tables one or two. And so at the very least she wanted to review their filtering system; to check that the cases in those piles definitely deserved to be there.

'OK, I agree with the approach,' she announced. 'It's the best we can do with what we have. Before we start, though, I want to give the filter a test run. Make sure files are in the right categories. Everyone grab a file at random, three from table one and three from table two.'

She waited while all six officers did as instructed.

'Tucker, who do you have?'

Pat Tucker opened the file he had taken from table one. At the front was a short set of notes. Not his handwriting. One of the others had reviewed the file. Tucker read the notes aloud.

'Arthur Hart. Single count of murder. Domestic. Killed his wife when she threatened to leave him. Disposed of her body by dismemberment. The offence happened at the end of a long period of stress, both professional and personal. He was released two years ago after eighteen years in prison. Fifty-one years old when convicted. No history of violence prior. Positive progress in prison. Assessed as probably too old to have killed the victim the way Longman died. More importantly, he has shown no propensity for violence of any sort outside of his one offence.'

'What was Longman's involvement in the case?' asked Hale.

'Longman chaired the hearing that refused Hart's appeal against his sentence.'

'So he wasn't the trial judge?'

'No.'

Levy considered the facts. Everything she had heard supported the initial file assessment. Hart was not their man.

'Agreed,' Levy finally said. Turned to Pickett. 'Natasha? What do you have?'

'This one's from table one,' Pickett's file was one she had assessed herself. 'But it could also have been on table two.'

'Tell me.'

'Karl Hirst. One count of manslaughter. One count of GBH. Two counts of kidnap. One count of blackmail.'

'Table one?' Hale was already questioning the process. 'It hardly sounds like violence was an anomaly with this guy.'

'Except this violence was all on the same single occasion,' Pickett explained. 'Eighteen years ago. Hirst was twenty-eight and had no criminal history at all before his arrest. He kidnapped the two children of a local bank manager and threatened their lives to get access to the vault. The bank manager went to the police. Hirst got wind and carried out the threat. Killed the son, seriously injured the daughter. The prosecution couldn't prove that the death of the son wasn't accidental suffocation, so he was convicted of manslaughter rather than murder. Longman was the trial judge. Sentenced him to life with a minimum of fourteen to serve. Hirst was released after fourteen, almost to the day. That was just over three years ago.'

Levy thought through the facts. It still did not feel right.

'Are you sure he really qualifies for table one?' she asked. 'The offence might be a one-off but it was no crime of passion. It suggests a capacity for cold violence, surely?'

'Maybe, ma'am,' Pickett replied. 'But it's still manslaughter, not murder. There's nothing to say he meant to kill the boy, which means we can't actually guarantee a one-off capacity for murder. Plus there's his prison record, which is what convinced me he belongs on table one. In a nutshell, he was an exemplary prisoner. No violence. No insubordination. Nothing. He made parole on the first attempt with the full support of prison staff and psychologists. Everything points to one-off violence.'

Levy nodded again, lost in her own thoughts. Whatever Pickett said, the crimes still worried her. They involved planned and calculated violence. But the other factors *did* meet the sift criteria. A one-off episode of violence against forty-six years of peace.

Plus three years of freedom, Levy thought. *Pickett didn't concentrate on that, but waiting three years for revenge? Against an old man who wasn't exactly hard to reach? If anything, that's the better argument against Hirst.*

It was the final point that called it. Levy had her misgivings, but no system was perfect.

'OK,' Levy finally said. 'Put him back where you found him.'

She turned to the second female officer. Detective Constable Sally Ryan. Twenty-nine years of age, Ryan was Levy's rising star.

'What do you have, Sally?'

'Nicola Allan, ma'am. Two counts of murder. Her husband and his mistress. A nasty one, too. She followed them to the second victim's home. Waited for the lights to go out. Then she broke in and stabbed them both to death in their bed. By all accounts it was a bloodbath.'

Hale interrupted.

'Which table is this one?'

'Table two, sir. There was a history of violence here. Nothing so extreme. But she had attacked another woman in the street six years before, using her high-heeled shoe as a weapon. Cut the victim's face wide open, leaving a deep nine-inch scar. She was sentenced to eighteen months imprisonment for that. Plus there were incidents of attacks while in custody. So she doesn't meet the criteria for table one.'

'But she meets it for table two?'

'And then some, sir. Longman was the trial judge. He gave Allan a life sentence with a minimum of eighteen years' custody. Because of her behaviour inside – the violence against guards and prisoners – she ended up serving twenty-three. She was released aged fifty-two, and that was eleven years ago.'

'So she could have taken whatever revenge it is she thinks she's owed aged fifty-two, but waits until she's sixty-three,' Levy observed. 'I think that makes table two a safe bet. And I doubt a woman in her sixties would be capable of physically lifting a body several feet off the floor and then crucifying him to a wall, no matter how old or frail he might have been.'

'She could have had an accomplice?' Hale offered.

'But then why wait eleven years. If she has back-up then she doesn't need to wait until Longman is weak. She'd have killed him much sooner.'

Hale hesitated for just a moment.

'OK, I see the logic. But I don't like this. We're finding reasons not to investigate viable suspects. I'm worried we should be looking at some of these other people.'

'I agree, and if it comes to it then we will. But for the moment we just need to find a way of prioritising the more likely suspects. The likes of Hirst and Allan aren't off the hook. If the files on table three end up giving us nothing, we'll go back to the others. But we don't have anything like the resources to do them all at once, so for now we haven't got a choice.'

Hale took a deep breath. Levy could tell that he had no argument left. He knew that she was correct.

'OK,' he finally said, passing the file back to Sally Ryan. 'Then let's put her back on two.'

Levy turned to her fourth team member to ask for his file, but was interrupted by a young officer who had approached from across the room.

'Ma'am, I'm sorry but there's a call for you.'

Levy looked up. She was irritated that the process had been stalled just as it was starting to roll.

'Take a message and tell them I'll call back,' she said, returning her attention to her team.

The officer seemed uncertain. Levy's voice carried a natural authority when she wanted it.

'The caller says that's it's very urgent, ma'am.' The voice lacked confidence, but he continued nonetheless. 'I *really* think you need to take the call.'

Levy looked up again. And this time she paid attention. It took her a few moments to place the young officer, until the name Ollie Cleary came to her. A new recruit to MIT One.

Levy turned back to her six-man team and to Hale.

'Excuse me,' she said as she rose to her feet and followed Cleary to the other side of the room, where the telephone was waiting.

'This is Levy.'

'Hi Joelle. This is Sarah Truman from ITN. We met at Phillip Longman's home yesterday.'

'Yes. I remember. What can I do for you, Miss Truman?'

'I have some information for you, on the Longman case. I think whoever murdered him has killed again.'

TWENTY-TWO

Sarah looked at her watch: 3 p.m. The distance from Grays Inn Road in London to Mill Lane in Southwold was around 120 miles. A little over three hours, door to door. Sarah had arrived fifteen minutes earlier.

Levy and her team can't be far behind, Sarah reasoned.

Alex Redwood had contacts in the Suffolk police. That much was clear. But Redwood was no longer a part of the story. Twenty minutes of enquiries had proved that the deceased Adam Blunt was the man Sarah had suspected. A well-known lawyer who had retired to Southwold over a year ago. His identity alone raised a likely connection to Longman; two retired lawyers, murdered in their homes within a forty-eight-hour time frame.

Any lingering doubt on that connection had then been erased by Sarah's call to Michael.

Once the Blunt story merged with the Longman story, Redwood's involvement was at an end. Sarah was the senior correspondent. That alone gave her precedence. She was also the more talented of the two reporters. The more well known. And by far James Elton's preference.

There was only going to be one winner.

Nathan Benson had remained in the outside broadcast van. Sarah had not.

She lacked Redwood's local resources. His informants within the local police. Sarah did not know how he had built those relationships. Bribes, perhaps. Or charm; he was a very good-looking man, Sarah had to acknowledge. And he was charismatic. At least until his true self broke through the veneer. It didn't matter either way.

If Sarah was going to get more information, she would need to make some friends.

The local press were already on the scene. Television news and print media. Ten reporters, maybe more. Sarah did not count. They were huddled together outside of the police cordon. All were obviously well known to one another. And all were no doubt wondering why the national press – Sarah Truman, no less – had taken an interest in a local death.

Sarah approached the group, smiling broadly. Once again felt the 'us and them' divide. Once again she ignored it.

'Perfect day for the beach, huh?'

The weather, Sarah thought. *Guaranteed to get the Brits talking.*

'Too hot to be standing around here all day.'

The answer came from the closest reporter. A middle-aged man, slim and dressed for the cameras.

The main man around here, Sarah's instincts told her.

'Totally.' Sarah slipped in an Americanism. One she never used. Designed to lower the local defences. 'How long have you guys been here?'

'Since 10 a.m., some of us.'

The answer came from a much younger man. Barely in his twenties, his unironed shirt and stained jeans indicated a newspaper reporter. Certainly not the clothes he would wear on-screen.

'And I guess you're one of the early risers, huh?' Sarah turned her full attention onto the youngster and smiled wide. 'Any news from inside since then?'

'Not much,' the print cub replied. 'We know it's a murder, obviously. And a few police have let it slip that it's a bad one. But not a lot else.'

Sarah listened. She kept her smile throughout, then scanned the rest of the press when the youngster had finished speaking. The faces that looked back at her were now a little more open. More welcoming. None showed any disagreement with the young reporter's assessment. It confirmed Sarah's suspicions.

Redwood's police source was not shared by others.

'So no details released about the way this guy died?'

Sarah knew the details already, but it was the natural question. The others would wonder had she not asked it.

'As Tony said, just that it's real nasty.' The answer came from the group leader. The middle-aged guy from local TV. Sarah turned back to him. 'Not suitable for early evening news, anyway.'

That settled it. With the exception of Redwood, the press had been told next to nothing.

'Then I guess we're in for a wait,' Sarah said, once again smiling as she spoke.

The charm offensive had had the desired effect. Sarah was a famous face – certainly in reporting circles – and celebrity came with expectations. People presumed aloofness and arrogance. When they instead found something more positive – more likeable – they were easily converted.

Sarah held out her right hand in the direction of the group's leader.

'By the way, I didn't catch your name. Mine's Sarah.'

Ten minutes passed, full of small talk and big tales. Typical of when reporters get together with nothing to do but wait. A pleasant way to pass the time, it got them through one of the downsides of the job.

Sarah was laughing hard at a joke that did not deserve it when something caught her eye. It was activity, close to the four outside broadcast vans parked on Mill Lane.

Her gaze slowly focused on her own ITN vehicle, which sat furthest back of the four vans. She watched as it began to reverse, creating a gap that widened as a second van – marked up as Anglian Regional News – reversed in the opposite direction.

The space created was large enough for a vehicle to access the police cordon. Which Sarah now realised was exactly as intended. A convoy of three – two cars and a van – drove towards the police tape. One word from the driver of the first car and the tape was lifted. The three vehicles drove under. Once through they parked in the spaces available.

Sarah watched as Joelle Levy stepped out of the first car. She was its only occupant. Levy looked around. She seemed to note the Detective Inspector from Suffolk's own MIT. A man in his early fifties, balding and hiding it badly. Levy acknowledged him with a wave then glanced away before he could return the gesture. She seemed to be looking for something. For someone.

Finally her gaze fell on the press pack.

Sarah's eyes met with Levy's. The DCI gestured with her head, which Sarah took as an indication to move away from the other reporters. Further along the cordon. Sarah did as indicated. Levy did the same.

'Thanks again for the tip,' Levy said, once they were close enough to speak quietly.

Levy's voice was low. The two women were yards from anyone else but still Levy was being careful. She indicated the local press.

'You know any of them?'

'For the past five minutes I do.'

'Long enough to tell me how compromised my case is?'

'They don't know any details. Aside from working out that it's a bad one.'

'What about you? Are you going to report what you told me over the phone?'

'Like you said yesterday. If I play ball you'll thank me later, right?'

Levy smiled and nodded her head. It was all Sarah needed.

There was something about Levy that she trusted. Just an instinct. And one she might not usually follow. But today she was willing to go with her gut. Levy had given Sarah her word, and for Sarah that was enough.

'I'm going to have to get inside,' Levy finally explained. 'This is going to be a jurisdictional bun-fight.'

'Any chance you'll lose?'

'What do you think?' Levy smiled as she spoke. Sarah returned it. 'Can you stay for a few hours? Until I'm done here? We should talk.'

'My thoughts exactly.' Sarah smiled again. 'I'll be here.'

'Good.'

Levy turned her back without another word and strode towards the house at the centre of the cordon; towards the Suffolk Detective Inspector who waited for her at its entrance.

Even from a distance Sarah could see the friction as the two officers met. The hostility. The jurisdictional battle was brewing.

Rather you than me, pal, was her only thought.

TWENTY-THREE

'**V**odka tonic. Lots of ice.'

Sarah placed two glasses on the wooden table, stepped over the bench and settled opposite Levy.

'Wine drinker,' Levy observed.

'No imagination, I guess.' Sarah picked up her wine glass by the delicate stem and held it out ahead of her, halfway across the table. 'Cheers.'

'Cheers,' Levy said in return. 'And thanks. I need this after the last few days.'

The clink of the glasses was a starter's pistol. Both women took a mouthful of their drink. For Levy the relaxation was instant. Not from the alcohol; that would take a little longer to work its way into her bloodstream. No, it was the dopamine rush that did it. The brain's reward for that first sip.

Sarah had waited for less than an hour in Mill Lane. She had been ready to stay longer. Levy, it turned out, had not.

Levy had known exactly what she was looking for in Adam Blunt's home. And she had found it all. The more detailed forensic analysis was left to her crime-scene investigators.

Once outside Blunt's house she had approached Sarah and told her to follow. A short drive out of town and they were here: the empty garden of a quiet country pub.

Levy had found a table in the shade while Sarah bought their drinks.

'So I guess I was right?' Sarah broke the silence. 'It's the same guy.'

'It looks like it, yeah.' Levy could not hide the resignation from her tone. Having to confirm Sarah's instincts was an unwelcome task.

'So that's two within forty-eight hours,' Sarah observed. 'That's a solid strike rate.'

'I've seen better,' Levy replied, 'but not the way this guy does it.'

'What do you mean?'

'I mean I'd expect those numbers from a spree killer. Or more, if it was a lunatic shooting at random, or someone killing a partner or family member, then driving a hundred miles and killing another. But those guys are crude. Blunt. They kill, they get caught. Or they commit suicide.'

'This guy's different, then?' Sarah seemed fascinated. 'What is it? The crucifixion? The castration? What does that tell you?'

'That tells me he's a sick son of a bitch. Same thing it tells you. But no, that's not what worries me.'

'What does?'

'Off the record?'

'Goes without saying.'

'No it doesn't, Sarah.' Levy always believed in being direct. At least where possible. Right now, it was essential. 'I'm taking a big risk talking to you. Which I'm only doing because you've shown yourself as trustworthy. But if I'm wrong about that – if you screw me over – you won't want to deal with the consequences.'

'So I've heard.' Sarah smiled. She took another sip of wine. 'My fiancé said the exact same thing.'

'Your fiancé? Do I know him?'

'Not really, no. At least not personally. He's a barrister. Michael Devlin. I think he's defended in a couple of your cases.'

Levy did not answer immediately. Instead she trawled her memory. It did not take long. Her time in Shin Bet had included training in absolute recall. By its very nature, a talent she could not forget. The picture of a tall man with blonde hair focused in Levy's mind.

'Michael Devlin,' Levy said, almost to herself at first. 'I remember him. He's good, Sarah.'

'Thanks.'

'Handsome too. Lucky girl.'

'Thanks again.' This time Sarah laughed. 'But seriously, anything you say to me is off the record. Hell, I could report what I already know – none of which comes from you – but I'm not even going to do *that*. There's nothing you can tell me that's more headline-grabbing than crucifixion.'

'OK,' Levy replied. 'Then here's what worries me. These killings, they're identical. Ritualistic. Except it's no kind of a ritual I've ever heard of. More a personal perversion of some sort.'

'You mean sexual?'

'I don't think so, no. More a perversion of the killer's humanity, if that makes any sense?'

'I'm not sure I know what you mean,' Sarah said.

'Maybe that's not the perfect description,' Levy continued. 'But whatever it is, this guy is *not* a blunt instrument. He's not killing just to kill. Just to cause death. He's enjoying every inch of it. The torture. The dismemberment. The terror, no doubt. And the aftermath. Some of the sick stuff he does is post-mortem. And that's for us. For whoever finds the bodies.'

'And you don't get that with a spree killer?'

'Not in my experience. They just kill; the killing is *all* it's about. But it's not only the sickness that sets him apart. It's his intent.'

'His intent?'

'That he fully intends to keep going. Spree killers, they kill until they're caught or cornered. And they don't do much to stop that happening. But this guy? This guy is covering his tracks and he is doing it very, very well.'

'How? What is he doing?'

'He's using bleach, to cover his tracks. He soaks the body in it. He pours it down their throats. And then when he's done he uses it to cover any part of the house he's been in.'

'To kill any DNA he's left behind,' Sarah observed.

'Exactly,' Levy replied, impressed that Sarah knew how effective simple bleach was as a crime-scene sanitiser. Most did not. 'And a spree killer doesn't do that. But someone who wants to kill again? They *do*. And that's terrifying when he's killing at this rate.'

'Shit.' Sarah sat backwards on the bench. The thought made her exhale deeply.

'Exactly right,' Levy replied, her own ramrod straight bearing unchanged.

The two women fell silent. Levy gave Sarah a moment to digest the details. It was the first time Sarah had heard it, Levy knew, because it was the first time Levy had said it out loud. She was taking a risk sharing so much with a reporter, she knew that. But she considered herself a good judge of character and she felt Sarah was worth trusting. And in any event, without Sarah's earlier tip off, it might have taken days for her and her team to be told about this latest murder.

Finally Sarah broke the silence.

'Whoever this bastard is, he's a different breed.'

Sarah reached into her handbag as she spoke. Peeling the wrapper from an unopened pack of cigarettes she had bought inside, she took one for herself before offering the open pack to Levy.

'Do you smoke?'

'Once,' Levy replied. 'I gave up years ago.'

'So did I.' Sarah lit the cigarette. 'But sometimes, you know?'

'Yeah, I know.'

Sarah inhaled deeply, taking a moment to ride the nicotine hit. Levy looked on. She could remember the same feeling; could understand an ex-smoker lapsing in moments of stress. It was not something she could allow of herself. Not when stress was such a constant in her life.

'What about suspects?' Sarah asked. 'Have you got any leads at all?'

'We've got lines of enquiry. I'd be lying if I called them leads.'

'Longman's past cases, right? I mean, Longman must have been the target of a lot of grudges from his time on the bench. So I guess you must have started trawling through his case files, looking for someone who might be capable of this sort of violence.'

'Sounds like you should be working for me.' Levy smiled. Took a sip of her drink. 'But yes, that's exactly what we're doing. Or at least it's what we *were* doing. Problem is the man's caseload was huge. Even after we'd used a bunch of filters to whittle them down.'

'Surely that will have changed now, though? With Blunt's death?'

'That depends,' said Levy. 'If they were targeted because of a connection then that narrows down the case files we have to shift through.'

'Because it must relate to a case where Blunt was the lawyer,' Sarah suggested. 'Which massively cuts down which files are potentials, right?'

'Right,' Levy confirmed. 'But the problem is, Blunt's death also raises the possibility that this is just a maniac targeting lawyers. Or retired lawyers. However unlikely that is – and trust me, I know it's bordering on the absurd – if it somehow turns out to be true then this just got a whole lot harder. Because if this is all random, then studying Longman's cases won't help at all.'

'Then surely you need to focus your best bet?' Sarah suggested. 'If it's a maniac who's just offing random lawyers and covering his tracks this well, catching him is just going to be a case of getting lucky, isn't it? And like you say, it's just not that likely a scenario. But if you assume that there is a connection – that Longman and Blunt were targeted for some old case they were both involved in – then at least you have *something* to pursue. And if it *is* that, well, Blunt's death must have just massively reduced your list of subjects.'

Levy did not answer.

The files on tables one, two and three had been on her mind since that morning. And the imperfect filtering system her team had needed to apply had been right there with them. But Sarah was right. That filtering system was irrelevant. A solicitor like Adam Blunt could not have appeared in as much as one per cent of Longman's cases. It would bring the number to a manageable level. Certainly single figures.

But not zero, Levy thought. *Because zero means no connection and no connection makes the killings random. A lunatic just hunting lawyers.*

Levy got to her feet. Her drink less than half done.

'I'm sorry, Sarah, but I've got to go. We've got to act on this now.'

'Understood.'

'And Sarah?'

'Yeah?'

'Thanks for the pep talk. And the drink. I needed them both.'

Pale Eyes kept the volume of his speaker audible as he watched Joelle Levy walk away from the table, leaving Sarah Truman to finish her drink and her cigarette alone.

The information coming from the speaker was worth hearing, but he would have much preferred to hear what the cop and the reporter had just discussed. There had been no way to get close enough, not with the pub garden empty.

He would find out soon enough. Certainly sooner than *they* would find *him*. The latter would happen, of course. But only when he was ready. When he was done.

He watched as Truman stubbed out her cigarette, left the table and walked towards the car park. She would not pass him. He had positioned his vehicle to ensure that neither woman had any reason to pay it any attention. And so he could continue to observe, as Truman reached her own car and drove away.

Sarah Truman. The big guns.

It gave him an unexpected feeling of satisfaction. Just two killings so far, and already he had a famous reporter on his tail. And by the time he was done, she would have one hell of a story.

TWENTY-FOUR

Michael Devlin recognised every guard at the entrance of London's Central Criminal Court. He greeted each of them warmly as he queued. Each guard greeted him back, most by his first name.

More commonly known as the Old Bailey, the Central Criminal Court housed many of the country's major criminal trials. This in turn attracted the country's leading barristers. Michael was counted in that number.

And today he was here to begin the murder trial of Simon Kash.

The entrance to the court building was unusually secure. Heavy, metal-framed doors led from the street to a security foyer. Lawyers, police officers, defendants and witnesses could pass through. For everyone else, that foyer was as far as they would get.

After all these years the security process was familiar. Knowing what was ahead, Michael could pass through the isolation tubes at the end of the foyer and then the magnetic gate that followed in a matter of seconds, delayed only by the speed of the conveyor belt on the X-ray machine through which he had to pass any bags and belongings.

This morning was no exception. Michael was through the process in under a minute and making his way down the three steps that led to the building's basement-level elevator bank.

The basement elevator bank was almost identical to the banks on every other floor. Six elevators. Three a side. Ornate but ageing. The only difference was the large wooden door that sat at the far right-hand corner of the bank.

It led to the court's cell area.

The cells where Michael would today meet Simon Kash for only the second time.

Michael boarded the elevator nearest to the cell-area door and pressed 'four'. The outdated lift mechanism kicked in and his stomach lurched with the sudden upward movement.

When the doors opened at 'four' Michael stepped out and turned left. At the end of the bank – left again – were the antique oak and glass doors that led to the Old Bailey's robing areas, where barristers changed from their twenty-first-century clothing into the eighteenth-century outfits unique to Britain's courts.

The doors led to three rooms. The largest by far was the male robing room, directly behind the doors. The others were much smaller. One was the female robing area. It sat on the right, immediately after the main entrance. A recent addition. Or, more accurately, an after-thought. The size of the room practically an insult.

The remaining room was the QC's robing space, which sat behind an antique oak door at the far end of the male area. It was as small as the female robing room, but in this case the size was justified. QCs were massively outnumbered by junior barristers.

Michael still felt strange going into that last room. He had been coming to the Old Bailey for seventeen years. In all of that time he had used the main robing room. It seemed unnatural to do otherwise, but rules were rules. Especially here.

He took less than five minutes to change clothes, transforming him from modern lawyer to traditionally dressed Queen's Counsel. The wig was the same as always. The same horsehair he had bought in Ede and Ravenscroft when he was just twenty-one. His wing collar and court bands were also unchanged. But the rest of the outfit was new. In place of his suit jacket was a QC's court coat; a cross between a waistcoat and a jacket, the three buttons at the end of each upturned sleeve was one of the clearest ways for a QC to be identified on sight. Finishing the costume was a thick, silk QC's robe instead of the more flowing cotton robe Michael had worn for almost two decades.

At the entrance to the men's robing room was a hundred-year-old wooden staircase. It led only upwards, to the Old Bailey Bar Mess. A huge, high-ceilinged dining hall where only advocates were permitted.

Michael took the stairs two at a time. It was 9.15 a.m. Already the Bar Mess was busy. Scores of barristers, seated on row after row of tables. All preparing themselves for the day with every kind of breakfast.

Trials. Politics. Gossip. All were being discussed as Michael made his way across the room. He stopped at the coffee dispenser and filled a mug.

'Michael.' He looked around at the sound of his name. Jenny Draper had spotted him. 'Over here. I've saved you a seat.'

He headed towards her. Like him, she had already changed into her court outfit.

It suits her, Michael thought. *Like she was born to wear it.*

He took the empty seat, placed his coffee cup on the table and dropped his battered wig next to it.

'Have you tried the cells yet?'

'I did,' Draper replied. 'I went down at 9 a.m. No vans had arrived and they had no ETA. The custody officer said she'd tannoy when the vans turn up.'

'Right.'

Michael was not surprised by either Draper's efficiency or the lateness of the prison vans.

'Did you hear about Adam Blunt?' Draper almost whispered the question. As if Blunt's death was gossip. 'Did you know him?'

'Didn't everyone?' Michael replied, surprised to hear the name so quickly. As always it made him uncomfortable, but he would not let himself show it.

Draper seemed to take the hint from the tone of Michael's reply. When she spoke again her voice was louder and more professional.

'He instructed chambers before he retired. I did a couple of trials for him years ago.'

'But did you ever meet him, Jenny?'

'No. Never face to face.'

'Then you've got sensible clerks. Adam Blunt would have been all over you like a rash.'

'No he wouldn't!' Draper's feigned outrage at the suggestion, but the act was betrayed by laughter. She tapped Michael's wrist. A playful telling off. 'So *did* you know him then?'

'Since I was younger than you,' Michael replied. 'I knew him before he became a lawyer.'

'My God, Michael.' Draper's face fell. Her reaction genuine. 'I'm so sorry. I didn't realise he was a friend of yours. What must you think of me, gossiping about him?'

'Knowing him didn't make us friends,' Michael said. 'To be honest I couldn't stand him. Nasty old bastard, he was. And bitter.'

'Well, OK, Mr Devlin. Tell us what you *really* think!'

Michael forced a smile at the sarcasm, but he didn't reply. Instead he drained the second half of his coffee cup.

The less said about that man the better, he thought.

'So did you hear anything about what actually happened to him?' Draper's whisper was back. 'The news reports hinted that he died badly.'

'Why would *I* have heard anything?' Michael asked.

'You knew him. I thought maybe . . .'

'Really, Jenny? You don't mean, "Has your reporter fiancée told you anything off the record?" now, do you?'

'No, Michael.' Once again the whisper was gone. Draper appeared horrified at the suggestion. Except she wasn't. Michael could tell. 'Honestly, I didn't even register the connection.'

'Well then that's for the best, isn't it. Because we wouldn't want something like that to be an issue between us as we move forward, would we?'

There was a clear message in Michael's tone. A message he ensured that Draper could not miss.

In almost two years Michael had kept Sarah's every confidence. To do otherwise was a slippery slope. Especially in Michael's world. Barristers were great when it came to client privilege. Watertight with information relating to their own cases. But gossip? It was air to them. Taken in with one breath. Spilled out with the next.

It was not a risk Michael would ever take with Sarah's reputation.

Draper did not respond, but her surprise and embarrassment at Michael's reaction were clear.

Michael had made his point, but he did not want it to cause friction between them. And so he leaned forward across the table and spoke again.

'But whatever was done to the old bastard, I'd be surprised if he didn't deserve every bit of it.'

Draper looked up. Her eyes met Michael's, whose broad smile cut through the tension in an instant. Satisfied that no lasting damage had been done, Michael got to his feet.

'I'll get us another couple of coffees before the van arrives.' He pointed at Draper's empty plate. 'Now have you eaten enough or are you wanting another muffin?'

TWENTY-FIVE

Michael and Draper exited the elevator on the basement level. There was already a queue for the cells. It passed the antique wooden door that led from the elevator bank to the custody suite's security gate.

At least thirty barristers were there, waiting for one of the eight secure client conference rooms. All needed to speak to their clients before their hearing began. Less than half would do so. It was another perfect example of an imperfect system.

Michael looked at his watch. 9.35 a.m. Less than five minutes since the tannoy announcing that the prison vans had arrived and already the line was unmanageable.

Draper joined the back of the queue. Michael did not. Instead put his mobile phone to his ear.

'Don't bother doing that,' he said before turning his attention to the call. 'Andrew, it's Michael. We've just seen the queue. Please tell me you're already in it?'

The response was the one he wanted.

'Perfect. See you in a second.' He disconnected and turned back to Draper. 'Andrew's at the front. Come on.'

Draper did as instructed and followed as Michael walked alongside the waiting barristers.

As they reached the closed wooden door Michael offered an explanation to the barrister closest to it.

'My solicitor's through there, Matt,' he said.

Michael knew the man. Draper only recognised him. Matthew Cole QC. Older than Michael by perhaps ten years and as high-flying as they came. Cole was Darren O'Driscoll's lead barrister, which for now made him an ally. That would last until Simon Kash gave Michael permission to attack Cole's client. If he ever did.

'You always were a jammy bastard, Devlin.' Cole's accent was broad Liverpudlian. Unusual for a London-based barrister and all the more effective for its rarity. He pushed the door ajar for Michael and Draper to pass. 'Go on then.'

'Cheers.' Michael stepped through the wooden door, into a small, crowded waiting area outside of the main cell gate. He turned back to ensure Draper was still behind him, and then remembered his manners. 'By the way, Matt. Have you met my junior?'

'I've not had the pleasure.' Cole stepped back to let Draper pass, putting his hand out in greeting as she did so. 'But I've heard all about you. Nice to meet you, Miss Draper.'

'Jenny, please,' Draper replied as she took Cole's hand and shook it. She deployed the same coy smile she had used when first meeting Michael. 'It's a privilege to be working with you, Mr Cole.'

Honed to perfection, Michael thought.

'It's Matt,' Cole replied. He smiled and looked back towards Michael. He did not release Draper's hand. 'And as for working *with* me? Is that what's happening, Mike?'

'You'll have to wait and see on that one.'

Michael's smile was genuine. As was Cole's. The two barristers knew that their cases might conflict, but they nonetheless liked and respected one another. Professional adversaries could remain civil. In fact they could sometimes be good friends. It was something that many defendants would never understand.

'I'm sure I will,' Cole replied. His smile did not waver. A genuine smile, suggesting he was pleased to have Michael on the case. It made Michael wonder why.

Is he happy because he'll now get a decent fight? Michael thought. *Or because he isn't up against a proper QC?*

There was no way for Michael to know the answer. Like he had said to Cole, he would just have to wait and see.

Pushing the thought from his mind, Michael glanced around the waiting area. The queue of lawyers snaked through it. From the wooden door all the way to the secure entrance to the cells. An entrance that sat open, with Andrew Ross standing beside it.

'Hurry up, you two,' Ross called out.

Michael realised that the opening was waiting for him and Draper. Both sped up and manoeuvred around the queue, bringing them through the heavy oak door just in time. A moment later it was closed and locked behind them.

Beyond the main entrance was a narrow white corridor. Five legal teams – each one some three lawyers strong – were crammed in. Waiting for the second security gate to be opened. This required a second set of keys held by a second security officer. It was a simple, perhaps obvious precaution; no single set of keys could open every door between the custody suite and the outside world.

They waited for three minutes. At least according to Michael's watch. To his body it felt much longer, the effect of being pressed up against a wall on one side and a person on the other. The sound of metal on metal announced the welcome arrival of the second key-holder moments before the metal bars of the second entrance swung aside.

Once inside the cell area Michael was searched, his laptop and phone stowed and finally he was allowed to pass the barred metal gate into a passageway that led to the interview rooms.

He did not wait for Draper or Ross while they endured the same security process. Instead he strode along the corridor towards their assigned interview room.

Draper entered moments later and took the seat next to him, facing the door. Ross was seconds behind and he sat opposite them, leaving just one seat next to him at the already cramped table.

'How do we all feel?' Ross asked. It was not an enquiry after health. Ross's only interest was Simon Kash.

'We've got a lot to work with,' Draper replied. 'Michael has some excellent theories.'

'They're only excellent if Simon lets us pursue them.' Michael was as realistic as ever. 'If he doesn't take our gloves off then those theories are worthless.'

'Understood.' Ross nodded as he spoke. 'Then I guess we'll just have to convince him.'

Michael opened his mouth to respond, then stopped himself at the sound of approaching footsteps in the passageway outside.

The sight of Kash gave Michael the same gut reaction he had experienced days before.

There's just no way this kid could have done what they're saying.

Kash was wearing what Michael was sure was his first suit. Cheap and at least a chest size too large. Perhaps two.

Next to Kash was a member of the cell staff, to whom he was handcuffed. The guard lifted both his arm and Kash's as he removed the cuffs. The man's gym-built bicep was visible as he did so. The size contrasted with Kash's small head and torso, highlighting the physical insignificance of Michael's client.

'Take a seat, please, Simon.' Michael spoke once the guard had left the room. 'But close the door first, would you?'

Kash did as he was asked, then climbed over the secured chairs and settled opposite Michael.

All three lawyers watched as he did so. Observing the awkward movements. He had the lack of body awareness that Michael would more expect in an adolescent.

'How are you, Simon?' Michael asked.

'I'm OK.'

Kash did not look up as he spoke. His voice was quiet. Almost inaudible.

'It's a big day today,' Michael continued. 'You know what's going to happen, right?'

'My trial.'

'Well not your *whole* trial, Simon.' Draper cut in. 'It's the start of your trial. Today we'll select a jury and then the prosecution will make an opening speech. Which means they'll explain to the jury what they say happened. But there won't be any evidence. Not today.'

Kash had already had this explanation from Ross. Michael knew that. But he allowed Draper to continue, giving him the opportunity to observe Kash's reaction to her.

How he responds to Draper's going to be the key, he thought to himself. *The route to making Kash do what we need.*

The reaction Michael saw told him everything. Kash had practically folded in upon himself as Draper spoke. The boy was painfully shy. No doubt sexually inexperienced. And so Draper's daily attention might just have the effect that Michael hoped for.

'Have you given any more thought to Darren O'Driscoll?' Michael asked.

Kash shook his head. Repeatedly. Almost violently. His left hand touched a darkened area of skin on his temple. A subconscious tell.

'Did O'Driscoll do that, Simon?' Michael had spotted what Draper and Ross had not. 'The bruise you've hidden under your hair. Was it him?'

Draper and Ross looked more closely. Kash's lank brown hair was a little more than medium in length. Its style was out of date, parted in the centre like a cool kid from the early 1990s. The left-hand side of the 'curtained' style had hidden the bruise, but it was less effective now that Michael had pointed it out.

'Why did O'Driscoll hit you, Simon?'

Michael's earlier question had been unanswered and he was taking Kash's silence as a 'yes'.

Once again there was no answer.

'Did you tell him what we discussed when we first met, Simon? That you had to protect yourself, not him? Is that why he hit you?'

There were no answers to any of the questions, and Kash looked weaker with each one. Looked more terrified.

Michael knew that he could only push his questions so far. He had to be careful not to break the boy.

'Simon, you need to listen to me now.' He tempered his voice, speaking as softly as he could. 'You can't let fear of Darren O'Driscoll get you convicted of something you haven't done. You can't be so afraid that you don't let me defend you. We can make arrangements that protect you from him. You just have to tell me that you *need* protecting.'

Kash looked up and met Michael's eye. The first time he had ever done so.

'No one can protect me from them.'

'From *them*?' Michael grasped the first lifeline Kash had thrown. 'Who's "them", Simon? It's not just O'Driscoll?'

'I'm not saying any more, sir.' Kash's voice was quiet again. It was steeped in fear. 'I just want to get through this.'

'You need to want more than that, Simon. You need to want to be *acquitted*. To be found *not guilty*. You can't serve a life sentence just because you're afraid.'

'I can, sir.' A tear threatened to escape Kash's eye as he spoke. 'Because at least a life sentence means I'm alive.'

Michael began to answer, only to stop.

What the hell do I say to that?

For the first time in as long as he could remember, Michael had no response. Not a real one. Not a truthful one. Michael had grown up in a world alien to Ross and Draper. But a world that Kash might understand. And so Michael knew that there was truth in Kash's words. There *were* consequences to what Michael wanted Kash to do. A price to pay for putting the blame where it truly belonged.

Those consequences could be exactly what Kash feared. For Michael to tell him otherwise would have been a lie.

'We can make sure that they can't get to you, Simon. I swear.'

Draper told the lie that Michael would not.

Maybe she thinks that's true, Michael thought. *Or maybe she doesn't give a shit about Kash's safety.*

Draper continued.

'If you let us take on O'Driscoll we can make sure he's kept away from you. But you need to let us do what's best for you. You have to let Michael prove that O'Driscoll is guilty of this murder, but that he didn't do it with *you*.'

Kash shook his head again. The movement released the tear that had been building in his eye. That tear and some more. Kash looked down once again.

'Darren had nothing to do with it.' His voice was weak. Unconvincing.

Michael recognised the answer for what it was. A mantra. Drilled into Kash by bigger, stronger men.

'I'd like to go back to my cell now, please.'

'Simon, you really need to listen—'

This time is was Ross who spoke. The beginning of a plea to Kash's good sense. Michael reached out, gripped Ross's forearm and stopped him from saying more with a shake of the head.

'Maybe that's best, Simon,' Michael said. His instinct was that further pressure at this stage could backfire. 'Maybe you should go back to your cell, and we'll head back upstairs. We can all speak later.'

'Thank you, sir.'

Once again Kash spoke without looking up. As soon as the words were out he got to his feet, manoeuvred himself awkwardly from his seat and walked to the doorway. Where he stopped.

Kash stood almost a foot below the six-foot-six doorframe, with almost as much space between his sloping narrow shoulders and the frame's sides. The contrast made look as small as Michael had ever seen him, but nothing could have prepared him for what Kash did next.

Simon Kash turned and looked back directly at Michael and spoke just two more words before leaving.

'I'm sorry.'

TWENTY-SIX

J oelle Levy was back behind the same desk in the MIT New Scotland Yard communal working space. Levy's office was on the same floor, and it was both quieter and more comfortable. But it was also away from her team people, and so away from the case.

Ridiculous as she found the idea of police officers hot-desking, Levy preferred to be here. In the beating heart of the Major Investigation Team.

Two of the three tables from yesterday were gone. The files that had sat upon them were back in the archives; the evidence of Phillip Longman's life in the law once again gathering dust.

Only one table remained. A table that now carried just five files.

'The sift was a hell of a lot more productive this time,' Levy observed as Detective Constable Sally Ryan placed a sixth file onto the small stack. 'How many more to come, Sally?'

'This is it, ma'am,' Ryan replied.

Levy allowed herself a relieved smile. Adam Blunt's death had made all the difference. Cross-referencing cases where Longman had been the judge and Adam Blunt the solicitor had narrowed the field enormously. It also erased the search terms that had bothered both Levy and Hale so much.

'Is there overlap with any of the cases identified yesterday?' she asked. 'On any of the three tables?'

'There are two.' The more focused search had required far fewer man-hours, which had allowed Sally Ryan to take on the case analysis alone. 'One from table one. And one that met all of the criteria and made it to table three.'

'OK, then let's begin with a quick look at the four that don't overlap,' Levy instructed. 'We'll make sure they don't deserve further scrutiny before we move onto the prime suspects. Tell me about them.'

'None of them are criminal cases, ma'am. And none of them involve anyone with any criminal convictions, or even any suggestion of violence.'

'Then what are they?'

'Three High Court disputes, all property related. Blunt's firm had a fairly busy property department. The fourth was an application for a press injunction on a minor sex story.'

'OK, so no violence. What about bad blood? Did Blunt or Longman do anything controversial in any of those cases?'

'No, ma'am. In fact, all four of them ended in favour of Blunt's clients, so none of them had anything to complain about at all. Turns out he was a fairly able civil lawyer.'

Levy smiled. Ryan really was efficient.

'Then I think we can safely rule them out,' Levy concluded. 'At least for now. We still need the i's dotted and the t's crossed, though, so have all four spoken to.'

'It's already happening, ma'am.'

Levy smiled again.

A whole team of Sally Ryans and our clean-up rate would be a hundred per cent.

'OK. Move on to the possibles, then. Remind me of the first one.'

'The Arthur Hart case, ma'am,' Ryan replied. 'The domestic murder where the husband just seemed to snap.'

'I remember.' Levy replayed the briefing in her mind. She recalled every detail. 'The facts of that one still don't ring true to me, but we can have someone pay him a visit today.'

Levy's eyes shifted to the second of the two files. She could already tell that it was Ryan's pick.

'And our friend from table three?'

'That's the interesting one, ma'am.' There was a hint of excitement now in Ryan's voice. 'He's a real nasty piece of work.'

'What's his name?'

'He's called Wisdom Penfold, ma'am.'

Ryan waited for the name to sink in. She did not wait long.

'Are you serious?'

'Yes, ma'am.'

'Is that a name change? Deed poll?'

'No, ma'am. It's his given name.'

'Seriously? No wonder he turned out nasty.'

'He certainly did, ma'am.'

'OK. Tell me about him. What's the case?'

'As you'd expect from table one, it was another murder. A commercial deal that went bad. Seems Mr Penfold saw himself as a bit of an entrepreneur. Buying and selling cars, land, industrial goods vehicles. Anything, really. Provided it was expensive.

'He must have been good at it as he made a lot of money. But it seems that on one deal he was duped. He sold a property – a piece of land – to a buyer, not realising that the buyer had secured building planning consent on the property without Penfold's knowledge. With that consent the property was actually worth seven times what Penfold was paid. When Penfold found out, he arranged to meet the buyer in a local pub under false pretences. When the guy showed up, Penfold confronted him, they had a brief discussion and it ended with Penfold smashing a beer bottle and sticking the jagged end into the guy's neck. In full view of everyone in the place.'

'Did he fight the case?'

'The murder allegation, yeah. He ran a defence of provocation, claimed the victim had laughed at him during the discussion and that was sufficient provocation that he should only be guilty of manslaughter.'

'Sorry? He fought a trial on the basis that being laughed at in an argument was a defence to murder?' Levy did not hide her disbelief. 'Well if that's the kind of legal advice Blunt was giving out I'm surprised someone didn't kill him sooner.'

'You're not the first to say that,' Ryan replied, glancing across the room in Steven Hale's direction. 'And in fact Longman blew the defence out of the water anyway when he addressed the jury before verdicts, virtually guaranteeing Penfold's conviction for murder.'

At first Levy did not speak as she carefully assessed the facts.

It sounded promising.

'It certainly sounds like Penfold has the capacity for pre-planned extreme violence. And a willingness to kill if he thinks he's been wronged. But what about the manner of the killing? In his local pub? There was no way he wasn't getting named for that, while our new hero has been exceptional at covering his tracks so far. That doesn't fit, does it?'

'It is the one discrepancy, ma'am, yes,' Ryan replied. 'Although it isn't fatal. For once thing, Penfold may have been a victim of overconfidence last time. From what the file indicates, he was feared by everyone in his local area. Basically the local gangster. There's a good chance that he thought no one would dare to identify him. And if that's wrong, remember he was in prison for fifteen years. That's a long time to plan and prepare if he's after revenge, and to find out better ways to avoid detection.'

Levy listened carefully. She agreed. Career offenders learn from their mistakes; they will rarely make the same one twice. Penfold had been easily caught the first time. If he was clever – and if he was their guy then he was certainly *that* – he would have learned to be better in the intervening years.

'So just to be clear on this, Longman was the trial judge and Blunt was Penfold's lawyer, right?'

'Yes, ma'am,' Ryan replied. 'Penfold was convicted of murder and Longman sentenced him to life with a minimum of fourteen years. He ultimately served fourteen and a half. Released six months ago.'

'How old is he now?'

'He was thirty-two when he was convicted, so he's now forty-seven.'

'Which makes him young enough. What about his history? Apart from the offence itself? Is there anything to suggest he's capable of any of this?'

'There is, ma'am. Convictions for violence going back to his mid-teens. A reputation as a fighter. Bare knuckle stuff, for money.

And he was a suspect in two murders where nothing seemed to stick. Witnesses refusing to cooperate. That sort of thing. Based on what he *has* done and on what he's *suspected* to have done, Penfold is one violent bastard.'

'What about Blunt?' Levy asked. 'Did he badly represent the guy?'

'Apart from the whole provocation bullshit? No, not at all other than that. But it seems they fell out anyway. Penfold wanted the sentence appealed, argued that the minimum term should have been lower. Blunt refused. Rightly, too; Penfold's minimum tariff was pretty bloody reasonable. Still, it pissed Penfold off and there were a lot of threats made to Blunt, although over time they stopped. But Penfold definitely held it against him, and I think we can safely assume that Longman got some of the blame for the conviction as well, since he was the one who actually passed the sentence. For my money, the belief that he'd been denied a defence to murder and that he had lost more years of his freedom than he should have – however ridiculous those beliefs might be – would definitely be sufficient motive for a man like Penfold.'

Levy sat back into her chair and considered everything she had just been told. Wisdom Penfold ticked the boxes. He was violent, capable and ruthless. And he clearly had a taste for revenge.

'And what about prison,' she finally asked. The last factor that pointed elsewhere. 'If he was released after fourteen and a half years of a minimum fourteen then he must have behaved himself. That suggests his violent streak might have disappeared.'

'I did think of that, ma'am,' Ryan replied, not surprising Levy for a moment. 'So I made some enquiries. There's a lot to suggest that he didn't behave himself at all, actually. When I looked at the prison files I saw an increase in 'faultless' injuries to other prisoners at every prison Penfold was sent to. Looks to me like he stayed violent. He was just clever enough – scary enough – that no one spoke. Like I said, fourteen years is plenty of time to get better at covering his tracks.'

'But isn't that something the Parole Board would look at?'

'Only if it's brought to their attention, ma'am. But if no one's reporting the violence then what is there to tell them?'

Levy nodded, impressed. Ryan had thought of everything. She had done her job with the diligence Levy knew she would. And she had finally given them a suspect.

Wisdom Penfold.

TWENTY-SEVEN

Steven Hale glanced across the room. Towards Joelle Levy and Sally Ryan. They were working through a number of files. Far fewer than had confronted them yesterday.

Progress, Hale thought. *Pity we can't say the same over here.*

The murder of Phillip Longman and the massacre of Leon Ferris and his men had posed a problem. Just like every Major Investigation Team, MIT One often took on two or more cases at a time. It was the nature of the beast. But they were not usually cases like these.

Longman's murder carried its own political pressures. The murder of a Lord Chief Justice – retired or not – needed fast resolution. Add in the manner of his death and it became a once-in-a-career investigation.

The Ferris case might not have had the same profile, but it did have similar difficulties. Community pressures, in a part of London where the police were far from popular. It also required cooperation with another specialist unit: the anti-gang team known as Operation Trident. Like Longman's, the case was unusual enough that in any other circumstances it would be the team's 'case of the year'.

And so both had earned Levy's focused attention. Until the death of Adam Blunt changed everything.

Blunt and Longman had the same murderer. That much was undeniable. A killer who, at his present rate, would secure infamy. A murderer is classified as a serial killer after three individual deaths. Longman's killer had dispatched his first two within thirty-six hours. It suggested that he would earn the title before the week was out.

This meant that Levy's full attention was now needed on the Longman/ Blunt case. Most of MIT One's resources and manpower – insufficient as they already were – were similarly directed. But this did not mean that the Ferris case could be ignored. Far from it. Levy had appointed Hale to lead the investigation. To choose his own small team of seasoned investigators and discover just what had happened in Electric Avenue.

Hale turned his attention away from Levy and Ryan. Back to his own debriefing, which was about to begin. The only positive to the new MIT communal space was that it was large enough for several meetings at once, far enough apart that none would interfere with the others. And Hale's debrief needed that space, as his own six officers had been joined by another ten from Trident. With them was their own Detective Inspector, John Wild, Hale's co-lead on the Ferris investigation.

Hale leaned his backside against the empty table that faced the mixed teams. Wild had taken a seat behind it, indicating that Hale was holding the floor on this one.

'As you all know, the autopsies on each of the bodies are complete. As is the scene of crime investigation by my forensic team. The results of both support the working theory of a single killer, starting with Ferris at the door, through to Leach, then Ellis and finally Tennant.'

Hale had already detailed that theory to both his own team and to the officers from Trident. At first there had been protests and disbelief. Familiar with the formidable reputation Ferris had built, the Trident team in particular had shared Levy's initial scepticism. But with all the evidence from the scene laid out, eventually they had accepted it as the most likely theory.

'This was no ordinary gang warfare,' Hale continued. 'It was too precise, too efficient. Whoever did this was clearly a professional. So, who hired him?'

A murmur went through the group as some of the team shuffled in their seats.

'Ferris had a lot of competitors.' Finally an answer. It came from a member of Trident. A young black officer who clearly came from the same streets his team policed. 'There's a lot of gangs in and around that part of South London.'

'You are?'

'Anton Campbell, sir. Detective Constable.'

'OK, Anton,' Hale replied. 'But can any of them *really* be called competitors? Ferris's organisation may have started out as a gang and it may still have gang members working for it or associated with it. But it really became a full-on criminal organisation, didn't it?'

The Trident team looked between themselves, searching for some consensus. Finally Campbell replied.

'That's a fair assessment, I guess.'

'And if we use that as a filter? Who's left who could really be called a competitor? An organisation, rather than a gang? Who would actually benefit from the vacuum Ferris would leave?'

'There are a few, sir,' Campbell explained. 'But I think everyone would agree that the obvious candidate is Ed Burrell.'

'Tell me about Burrell.'

'Burrell's an up-and-comer.' This answer came from an older Trident officer, who Hale recognised as George Dixon. 'He started like everyone else. Like Ferris. Small-time gang violence. Petty crime. A few years ago he stepped up. We have him fingered for armed robberies, drug supply, gun trafficking, extortion. Moving up fast.'

'Compared to Ferris's set-up?'

'Nothing like it, sir. A fifth of the size.'

'So a full-on war doesn't go well for Burrell?'

'No. If he takes on Ferris man-for-man, he loses. Badly.'

'But if he has Ferris and his top men killed? Cuts the head off the snake. What about then?'

'Then he becomes the biggest name in the area by a margin. Burrell doesn't come close to Ferris, but everyone else is just as far behind *him*.'

Hale nodded his head. The assessment of Ed Burrell made the man a candidate. A good one. But Hale was well trained. He had learned from Levy.

Burrell could not be the only option.

'What about what's left? Are there any others who've made the jump from gang to proper gangster? We can't assume that one of the smaller fry hasn't let his ambition get away from him.'

'I can think of three.' Campbell again. Building on his earlier answer. 'None in Burrell's league, but still a step above the usual. Maybe ambitious enough to think they could gain out of this.'

'OK.' Hale pushed his backside away from the table and drew himself to his full height. 'Then I need you on the smaller fry, Campbell. The three you've identified and any others that get suggested as possibles. Choose two of your team and two from MIT One to assist.'

Hale surveyed the room and picked out another Trident officer, Dean King. King was probably more familiar with Ferris and his organisation than anyone else. It had made him the most reluctant to accept the one-man theory. But it also made him the perfect man to investigate Ferris's main rival.

'And I want *you* taking the lead on Burrell. Get your ear to the ground. Chase down contacts. Grasses. Ferris's men moving across. Anyone and anything that could indicate Burrell being behind this. Choose four from Trident to help you.'

Hale then turned to Detective Sergeant Pat Tucker. One of his own.

'Pat, you're heading up the Burrell enquiries alongside King. Select two from MIT One. For now Burrell's our most likely suspect. Go and find me a reason to kick down his door.'

Hale next turned to the final MIT One officer. Natasha Pickett, who was, by common consensus, the unit's best data analyst.

'Natasha, I want you on records. I want you to look at every suspected professional hit in the last ten years. Solved and unsolved. There must be some similarities with what we've seen here. This guy can't be a first-timer. DI Wild will assign two of his team to assist.'

Finally, Hale faced the group as a whole.

'We're not going to let this slide. We've got plenty to go on. We know who stands to gain from this. We know Ferris's competition. And we know that whoever did this was a serious professional, and that leaves footprints of its own. We'll find whoever did this. And if that means taking out another pit of murdering bastards when we do, well, I won't lose any sleep. Now, let's get going.'

TWENTY-EIGHT

'And that, members of the jury, is almost all I have to say to you in opening this case. All that's left are two very important things to remember. One applies to everything you have heard from me today. The other is without question the most important principle in this process; the principle upon which the entire criminal justice system is built. So it is vital that you listen to and understand these final two points, and that you keep them in mind for as long as you sit as a jury in this trial.'

Peter Epstein QC had been speaking for two hours. It was his opening submission, which was how every trial began: with a speech from the prosecuting barrister. Epstein's had been fair. It had also been captivating.

Michael had expected no less from Senior Treasury Counsel, the Old Bailey's number-one prosecutor and the closest thing the UK had to a US District Attorney.

Epstein continued to address the jury, covering the general principles they were bound to follow regarding the evidence they would hear, and the fundamentally important principle that the burden of proof rested on the prosecution, with the defence needing to prove nothing. But by now Michael had stopped listening. He had heard every possible version of the recital more times than he could count. His focus was firmly on what was still to come.

The sound of movement as Epstein finished speaking and took his seat brought Michael's eyes up from his papers and his mind back to the moment.

He looked down the long wooden bench on which all six of the seven barristers sat. At the far end, closest to the judge, was Epstein. Next to him was his junior, Claire Wells. Behind them was the prosecution's second junior, Martin Maguire. Maguire's was a lower rank, unique to prosecutors, that was usually reserved for promising but very newly qualified barristers.

'Did I miss anything?' Epstein asked Claire Wells in a whisper.

'Not a thing,' Wells replied. 'Brilliant opening.'

'Thank you.'

Their voices were low, but Michael's hearing was acute and he could not close out the sound of the exchange. It made him smile; it was reassuring that even barristers as successful as Epstein still second-guess themselves.

'Well, members of the jury, that's that as far as guidance goes. Mr Epstein has set out the Crown's case very clearly and very well, so if I . . .'

The voice of His Honour Judge John Levitt QC filled the courtroom as he now addressed the jury, to remind them of their duties and obligations as trial jurors.

Michael tuned him out, too. Another speech he had heard a thousand times. They never changed. And if the unthinkable happened and they *did*, Draper was busy taking full notes of every word.

Michael had other things on his mind. Or, more accurately, one thing: the safety of Simon Kash.

The bruise on Kash's head had concerned Michael. But it was Kash's demeanour that worried him most. The boy was absolutely terrified. Of O'Driscoll. Of others. Of going back to Wandsworth Prison that night. So scared that he would not risk sitting in the same room as his lawyers in case it was perceived as in some way 'grassing', Michael had realised.

Kash was helpless, and it was Michael's natural instinct to protect anyone in that position. But how? What could he do when intervening was against his client's instructions? How could he help Kash to help himself without violating the strict rules of his profession?

Distracted though Michael was, his ear remained attuned enough to know that His Honour Judge Levitt QC was bringing his brief address to an end.

'And on that happy note, members of the jury, I am going to let you go. Please be in the building and ready to start by 10.30 a.m. tomorrow morning, when the Crown will call its first witness.'

Levitt sat back against his high-back wooden chair. An antique from the earliest days of the court. Maybe a century old. From here Levitt could see into the dock, which was raised to the same level as his seat. Considerably higher than the jury box that sat against the north wall and the barristers' benches that sat against the south.

The jurors were escorted from the court without a word by the court usher. The courtroom itself remained equally silent as they left. The sound of the door to the jury area clicking closed behind them was the signal that the jurors could no longer hear the courtroom, which was the cue for the lawyers to resume their work.

'Is there anything else we need to deal with this afternoon?' Levitt's question was to all three QCs.

Michael's mind raced. The thoughts that had concerned him were still bubbling to the surface. He knew the step he needed to take to protect Kash. The step he wanted to take. He also knew he should not. Kash could not have been clearer.

He mulled over the decision as both Epstein and Cole answered Levitt's question.

'Not from me, My Lord.'

'Nor me.'

Then it was Michael's turn, and in that moment he made the decision. He would do what he should not. What his conscience told him was right.

Michael rose to his feet.

'Actually there is something, My Lord.'

All eyes in the room were on him. Even his own team – Draper and Ross – did not know what he was about to say.

'I have reason to believe that my client is suffering the undue influence of his co-defendant in this case. To Mr Kash's significant detriment. I therefore respectfully request that My Lord orders that the defendants be kept apart while in the court cells, and that further guards are present in the dock throughout the trial to further protect Mr Kash. *And* I request that My Lord orders that Mr Kash be taken to a different prison to his co-defendant this evening, on separate prison transportation, and that this arrangement stays in place throughout the trial.'

Michael took his seat without another word, while the courtroom erupted around him.

TWENTY-NINE

'I take it what you did in there wasn't in the script?'

Michael had not seen Sarah in the public gallery, watching her fiancé work. The gallery was thirty feet up from the courtroom, out of the barristers' sight, with its entrance on a different street.

Sarah had left the gallery once the arguments started. She had seen from Michael's body language that he would not be engaging in them; he had said his piece and that was that. It was a dogged stubbornness she recognised, and one she both loved and dreaded.

Instead she had made her way outside and walked the short distance to Old Bailey – the street from which the Central Criminal Court took its far more famous nickname – and down it to the court building's entrance. That had been thirty minutes ago, which was a longer wait than Sarah had expected. Not that it was a problem: another scorching day had given way to another balmy evening, and so it was just a pleasure to be outside.

'No, it wasn't in the script!' Michael laughed, reaching out and kissing her hello. 'And neither was this. Thanks for the lovely surprise.'

'Too many late nights recently,' Sarah explained. 'I thought I deserved an early one tonight, and some one-on-one time with my man.'

'And what a lucky man he is.'

Michael kissed Sarah again. Longer this time. Even when their lips separated their foreheads still touched. An intimate moment that neither wanted to end. They would not be so lucky. The sound of the court building's heavy metal door broke through, and a woman Sarah did not recognise walked towards them.

'Jenny. I didn't realise you were behind me.' Michael stepped back. It gave Sarah both room to move and a clear view of Draper. 'Let me introduce you. Jenny, this is my fiancée, Sarah. Sarah, this is my junior. Jenny Draper.'

'Pleasure to meet you, Jenny.'

Sarah held out her hand. Draper took it with a friendly smile.

'You too, Sarah. I'm a big fan of your work.'

Draper's eyes were already leaving Sarah's as she spoke, and within an instant she had turned back to face Michael. Sarah rolled her eyes in a mixture of amusement and annoyance. She was sure that Draper had intentionally positioned herself partly in front of Sarah, physically excluding her from the conversation.

'Simon is refusing to speak at all, Michael. He's absolutely terrified.'

'I told you he would be,' Michael replied. 'It's all in the moment for him. But trust me. A few days outside of O'Driscoll's influence and he'll come out of himself. We needed them separated.'

'But he didn't tell us to do that, Michael,' Draper said.

'He didn't tell us not to, either,' Michael replied.

'Kash's wishes were still clear. Whether he said it expressly or not.'

'Which we disagree on,' Michael replied, his voice staying lighthearted. 'If I've misread him then it's on me, isn't it?'

Sarah knew that tone and watched the exchange with some satisfaction. Draper was wasting her breath. Michael had made a decision and he was not going to be swayed.

'OK, but what about Cole?' Draper asked. 'How is he going to take what you did? The message it sends about his guy?'

'Matt won't give a monkey's,' Michael replied. 'The jury won't notice the extra security. And they won't know which prison they're both held at. It makes no difference to O'Driscoll at all, so Cole won't care.'

'He certainly seemed like he did,' Draper argued. 'His objection was pretty angry.'

'That was for his client's benefit, Jenny. Don't be fooled by it. Matt's pleased with what I did.'

'Pleased?'

'Because it tells him where we're going. I've separated the boys. Matt knows I've done that so we can influence Kash. So we can convince him into letting us attack O'Driscoll. So now Matt knows what he's up against. He'll be happy we've drawn the battle lines.'

Sarah watched with a smile as Draper was lost for words. It was not the first time she had seen Michael have that effect, but she enjoyed it more on someone who had been so instantly arrogant.

Michael's approach was unorthodox. Sarah knew that. He was motivated far more by doing the right thing than he was by abiding by rules when they made that impossible. It was a risky way of working – one which had brought him close to the edge a number of times – but ultimately Michael could not live with himself if someone else paid the price for protecting his professional skin. That was why he was willing to stand up and protect the likes of Simon Kash from their own bad decisions. And it was why, Sarah knew, most lawyers struggled to work with him.

Draper will be no exception, Sarah thought. *She's a classic barrister. By the book. Which means the Michael Devlin way will* not *be a natural fit.*

'OK, that's enough law for one day,' Sarah said, stepping forward.

She reached out and took Michael by the hand. It turned him towards her and he smiled. If her words could be called a hint, that hint had been taken.

They both turned back to face Draper.

'Sarah's right, Jenny,' Michael said. 'Time to call it a day. It's not often we get to travel home together. I'm not going to miss the chance now.'

'Oh. Yes. Sorry. OK.' Draper seemed caught off guard by the abrupt end of their discussion, Sarah noted with pleasure. 'Well, then, I guess I'll see you tomorrow, Michael.'

'I guess you will. 9 a.m. in the Bar Mess?'

'Yes, perfect. I'll see you then. Have a lovely night.'

'And you.'

'Goodnight, Jenny,' Sarah called as Draper began to turn, not quite believing that she had done so without a goodbye. 'It was nice to meet you.'

'Oh, yeah.' Draper turned. She seemed surprised by Sarah's farewell. 'You too, Sarah. You too.'

Draper turned away again and began to walk away, towards Holborn and Gray's Inn.

Michael and Sarah watched her go. Just for a few moments.

'Well *she's* interesting.'

Sarah's observation was pointed. She made no attempt to hide it.

'You think?' Michael laughed as he placed his arm affectionately around Sarah's shoulder. Sarah wrapped her right arm around Michael's lower back in response as they began to stroll in the evening sun towards Ludgate Hill, in the opposite direction to Draper.

'I'm pretty sure I don't like her,' Sarah admitted. 'The way she looked right through me.'

'I get the impression she's not a girl's girl.'

'And then some. How long before she makes a move on you?'

'Does it matter, sweetheart? It's not like she'll be getting anywhere, is it?' Sarah looked up at him, raising an eyebrow in response. Michael would have to do better than that

'OK, OK. Look, I'll find a way to palm her off on Matt before she tries. He'll be happy to step in.'

'So you've thought this through then.' Sarah laughed at Michael's nonchalance, tightening her grip around him. 'Don't be so sure she'll go for Matt. You're much more handsome.'

'Thanks, gorgeous. But he's much more successful. They don't come bigger than Matt Cole. That means more to girls like Jenny Draper than a face.'

'Just watch her, Mikey.' Sarah was no longer laughing, and she had called Michael by the name only Anne Flaherty used. Sarah did it rarely. When she did, she knew Michael listened. 'She's got an agenda.'

'Now you sound like Derek.' Michael stopped and turned her to face him. 'But believe me, sweetheart, you've nothing to worry about. There's only one girl for me.'

Satisfied, Sarah allowed Michael to pull her close again, as they continued their walk in comfortable silence.

'DEVLIN!'

Sarah felt Michael loosen his grip immediately in response to his name. The voice that had shouted it had not sounded friendly.

Both Michael and Sarah turned and saw a young man walking towards them.

'Can I help you?' Michael took his arm from Sarah's shoulders and stepped in front of her as he spoke. She was both amused and grateful at his instinctive reaction to protect her.

'I think you can, yeah.' The man had lowered his voice, but his tone was no less threatening. 'I wanna know what went on in there today.'

'And who might you be?'

'I'm Patrick O'Driscoll. Darren's brother. And I wanna know what you were doin', slagging off my brother like that.'

'Then speak to your brother's lawyer,' Michael replied. 'I've got nothing to say to you.'

O'Driscoll did not move. His stance said that he had no intention of it.

'You said my brother's bullying Simon Kash. Where'd you hear that? Did Simon say it?'

'I just told you, Mr O'Driscoll. Speak to your brother's lawyer. Because you're not speaking to me. Now get out of the way.'

'You don't wanna ignore me, Devlin.' O'Driscoll stepped closer as he spoke. Within inches of Michael. 'Bad things can happen. Even to the likes of you.'

Sarah looked down as O'Driscoll spoke and saw that Michael had clenched his right fist. Tight. She knew he would be running through his options. Preparing for the worst of them.

'Don't make a stupid mistake here, son.' Michael's voice had lowered. It was unwavering. 'Don't think that what I do for a living makes me a victim. I've been dealing with shit like you since I was a kid. It won't worry me to flush another one.'

O'Driscoll took a step back in confusion, clearly unprepared for this response. Sarah had seen it before. No one else ever expected Michael to react in the way he just had. But then no one else knew the real Michael Devlin. The boy from the streets of Belfast who would do anything to win.

O'Driscoll seemed unsure how to react. Unsure what to do next.

Michael was not. O'Driscoll's backwards step was a sign of weakness, and Michael's peculiar upbringing had taught him how to exploit that moment. He stepped forward, closing the distance that O'Driscoll had put between them.

'What's it going to be, Patrick? Are you going to do yourself a favour and fuck off? Or do I need to leave you in that gutter there?'

Sarah could see the realisation dawn on O'Driscoll's face. This was no soft lawyer in front of him. This was a bigger man. A stronger man. A man whose eyes said that *he* could deliver on his threat.

'Take this as fair warning, Devlin,' O'Driscoll growled, trying to save face. As he spoke he stepped hastily backwards, putting a few metres between himself and Michael. It made a mockery of his own parting threats. 'Any more of this shit against my brother and I'll be paying you a visit. You *and* your missus there. And it won't just be me.'

'YOU'D BETTER MAKE SURE IT'S NOT JUST YOU!' Michael shouted as the younger man retreated, his two fists now gripped vice-like. Sarah had feared that O'Driscoll's mention of her would strike a nerve, and she had been right. Michael was suddenly close to losing control.

'BECAUSE YOU COME ALONE AND YOU WON'T LEAVE BREATHING!' He continued to shout, pulling his arm free of Sarah's as he did so. 'YOU HEAR ME? YOU WON'T LEAVE BREATHING!'

Sarah could tell that he was itching to run. To chase O'Driscoll down. And so she made the decision for him. She grasped his hand tight, pulling him back towards her.

'Calm, Mikey.' Sarah's voice was soothing. 'Calm.'

Michael turned towards Sarah's voice. His eyes met hers but they did not focus. Sarah could tell that he was struggling. That his control was on a knife edge.

Desperate, she took his face into her hands and stared hard into his eyes.

'Calm down, Mikey,' Sarah repeated. 'It's just a stupid boy making stupid threats. It's not worth the trouble. All we have to do is call the police. We know who he is. We know what this was about. We just need to call the police. So calm. Just calm.'

Michael's eyes began to focus. Sarah's words were getting through the fog.

'I'm sorry.' The shame in Michael's eyes said that he meant it. Sarah did not need that proof. She knew him better than he knew himself. 'I'm sorry.'

'You don't have to say sorry.' Sarah reached into her handbag as she spoke and took out her mobile phone. 'I'd have lost it too, if that little shit had said that to me.'

She tapped a number into the phone. Eleven digits. Michael had been expecting three nines.

'Who are you calling?'

'A new friend,' Sarah replied. 'One who'll make Patrick O'Driscoll regret every word he just said.'

THIRTY

'What time was he brought in?'

Joelle Levy was at her desk with her telephone at her ear. She glanced at the clock and noted the time. 9 p.m. Richard's bedtime. Levy had missed it again. The familiar guilt ate at her gut.

'OK. Has anyone spoken to Sarah Truman and Michael Devlin?'

'Yes, ma'am,' came the answer. 'They thanked us for picking O'Driscoll up, but neither one wanted to make a witness statement.'

'I didn't think they would. In that case, interview him, hold him until his twenty-four hours are up and then release him without charge.'

'Ma'am?' The caller sounded confused. 'That's not appropriate if we know we won't be getting any evidence. Why would—'

'Because I said so, Sergeant. If anything comes of it, I'll make it clear you were acting on my instruction. Just hold him.'

Levy placed the receiver into the phone dock and shook her head. Having her judgement questioned by a police sergeant was irritating, but that was especially true when the sergeant was right. Levy had known that neither Sarah nor her fiancé would make a witness statement against Patrick O'Driscoll. Sarah had been clear about that in her call; that it would make it too difficult for Michael to continue as Simon Kash's lawyer.

Without those statements there was no real evidence to justify the arrest. Less still to keep O'Driscoll in custody for twenty-four hours. The sergeant had reminded Levy of this, but a debt was a debt, and Levy still felt that she owed Sarah.

Levy did not have time to dwell on her irritation. A knock at her office door forced it from her mind.

'Come in.'

Steve Hale looked tired. The darkness beneath his eyes was the first thing Levy noticed. The pressure of a high-profile murder had already taken a toll. It could hit that quickly. Levy knew from experience.

Levy gestured to the two chairs ahead of her desk. Hale took the right-hand seat, his usual choice. As he sat, Levy opened her desk drawer, took out two glass tumblers and poured a large measure of Jack Daniels into each.

Hale reached out, took his glass and touched it to Levy's own.

'L'chaim.' Hale used the Hebrew version of cheers. He always did when drinking with Levy.

'Cheers,' Levy used the English. Repaying the gesture. An unconscious ritual.

Both Levy and Hale savoured the sweet bourbon, with Hale taking a second sip before speaking.

'How's it looking? Any luck locating this Penfold guy?'

'Not yet,' Levy replied. 'We've spoken to his probation officer. Turns out he missed his last two appointments. For some reason it wasn't reported, despite Penfold being on licence. Which is something the probation officer will have to answer for in the long run, but for now we've got to concentrate on finding the bastard.'

'Then for the PO's sake I hope Penfold isn't your man. The shit-storm of not reporting a guy on a life-licence while he's on a bloody killing spree? That's just not worth thinking about.'

'Well for my sake I hope he *is* our guy, Steve.' Levy had no sympathy for a probation officer who had not done his job. 'Because if it's *not* him, well, then we're all out of leads.'

'But what about the other files? There were six potential suspects, weren't there?'

'There were, yeah. But only Wisdom Penfold held up. The rest were a mix of too old or too sick. And for the most part motive-free.'

'You've traced them all already?'

'Not all of them yet. The only other one with any suggestion of violence on his record was simple enough as he's on a life-licence.

Required to keep the authorities informed of his whereabouts at all times. We've seen him already and he's no good for this. And we've seen two of the other four; no violence on their record, no motive in respect of either victim. And the last two we're still tracking down but from what's in their files we can pretty much discount them already; again, no obvious motives and both are older than Longman was, assuming either is still alive.'

'Lucky break.' Hale's tone suggested that he could use some of the same luck himself. 'So you really think Penfold's your man?'

'He ticks the boxes.' Levy's answer was as close to commitment as Hale would get. 'He's capable of that level of violence. Plus he had motive – revenge – against both Longman and Blunt. And now it looks like he's gone off-radar just in time for the murders. Long enough to do his homework and get started, not so long that anyone would have looked for him before the fact. He meets the criteria perfectly.'

'Hard to argue against it,' Hale observed. 'So what's the next step? A warrant to search his home?'

'Done. We executed it four hours ago.'

'Anything?'

'Nothing. The home address he'd given to probation obviously wasn't. It was just a bare one-bedroom flat. Unfurnished and dusty. There's no way he ever lived there.'

'Shit.' Hale's tone had changed. Perhaps he had re-evaluated his assessment of Levy's luck. 'So what else is there to do, then? Go public?'

'Shit no.' Levy's answer was emphatic. 'We can't say for sure that Penfold's good for this. I mean, it *looks* like he is but what if he *isn't*? What happens if I start a nationwide manhunt and we then find out that he's just buggered off on holiday without telling probation?'

'I see that but come on, Joelle.' Hale used Levy's first name, meaning they were off the clock. 'The timing? And the apartment that was never lived in? Take that into account and it's not likely he's doing anything innocent with his life, is it?'

'Maybe not, but that doesn't mean he's massacring lawyers for pissing him off decades ago.' Levy sighed deeply. She was exhausted. 'It's a mess,

Steve. I realise it looks like Penfold. Shit, I'm praying that it *is* Penfold. But at the moment it's just not enough. Not for a step as big as going public. If it goes wrong we'll be annihilated by the press. Especially on *this* case.'

Hale nodded. He took a sip of his drink, then looked his DCI in the eyes.

'How do you do it, Joelle?' The question seemed to come from nowhere. 'How do you deal with all of this shit? The press. The politicians. The pressure. I've had it for a day and I'm whacked. You get this twenty-four seven.'

Levy met his gaze and realised then that they had been concentrating on her problems. It reminded her that she was not just speaking to a friend, but also to a subordinate. A subordinate who needed her guidance.

'You get used to it, Steve. And anyway, we are where we are.' Levy shrugged off her previous despair. 'It'll all look different in the morning. It always does. So where are we with Ferris?'

It was Hale's turn to sigh. He did so forcefully. Then he answered.

'We're moving forward.' He paused. 'No, that's a lie. We're pursuing every lead but at the moment we're moving bloody nowhere.'

'How are the teams getting on?'

'I've mixed them up, like you suggested. Got them to play to their strengths. We've got one team chasing down Ferris's main rival. Another following up on the other less likely competitors. Then a final team researching all professional hits in recent years. To see if we can spot any similarities.'

'You've got Pickett leading that last one, right?'

'Right.' Hale grinned. 'Who else?'

'Exactly. It feels like I've lost my right arm not having you *or* Pickett on the Longman case. So you'd better make the fact you've stolen her from me worthwhile.'

'I will,' Hale replied with a smile.

'Good. Although even with Pickett on the job that research will take a while. There's nothing about the MO on this that rings a bell for me.'

'Nor me. I've never heard of a hit like this before.'

'Are we still confident that's what this was?'

'More than ever. The Trident boys couldn't have been clearer. No simple street gang could have done this to Leon Ferris and his men. Christ, if you heard the reaction of *some* of that team, we must be looking for Batman. That's over the top, obviously, but I can't see how this was anything but a professional job.'

Levy listened carefully. As Hale spoke she reached out and took his now-empty glass and refilled it with a bigger slug than before. Then she did the same to her own.

They both enjoyed a sip before continuing.

'What's your gut saying?'

It was the only question Levy could ask. There was no evidence. Not yet. But that did not mean that Hale had nothing. Something only another investigator would understand.

'It says we need to be looking at Ed Burrell.' Hale's answer was instant. 'No one else gains out of this. Not like Burrell does.'

'Burrell's the main rival, I take it?'

'That's right. Nowhere near Ferris's league. But a very clear second. Burrell's the only other player in that part of London.'

'Then it makes sense that it's him.' Levy followed Hale's reasoning. 'But you said there were others? Less likely but still competitors?'

'Yeah, but not really. It's more just a case of being thorough. There *are* other gangs in the area with ambition, but I don't buy them for this. They'd stand to gain from offing Burrell, not Ferris. Ferris leaves a gap that they can't hope to fill.'

'But maybe you're crediting them with too much intelligence, Steve. Maybe they don't *know* they couldn't fill it?'

'I did think that, and maybe it's right. But then I looked at the murder again. And I'm convinced that whoever did *that* – whoever stepped into that room and offed all four of them – *that* guy isn't even on our radar. Or Trident's. So much so that I had Pickett contact the NCA for help this afternoon, in case *they* recognise the MO. Whatever the outcome of that, I just don't see one of the street gangs engaging a professional of that level to take out Ferris. Or knowing where to find such a person. No.

The only player that gains from Ferris's death *and* has a chance of finding that kind of a hitman is Burrell. I just know it.'

'Then you know where you're going, Steve. That's half the battle won already.' Levy tipped her glass at Hale as she spoke. An unspoken congratulation. Then she a took a mouthful before continuing. 'So how long before Burrell gets a knock at his door?'

'As soon as I can find a bloody excuse.' Hale laughed. Levy was happy to see it. It was what made their job bearable. 'And what about you? Do you think sitting in this office into the night is going to catch Wisdom Penfold any quicker? Go home, Joelle. Go home and spend some time with your son.'

Levy smiled and got to her feet.

'You're right,' she said, taking Hale's once-again empty glass from his hand. 'We should *both* be getting home. This day's been too long already.'

THIRTY-ONE

Michael sat at his desk with one hand on his unopened Simon Kash working file. His eyes, though, were on something else entirely.

Michael's office sat at the very top of the house in what would no doubt have been the maid's quarters years before. Converted long before Sarah's father had bought the property, the space had been an obvious choice for a working room. Big enough for two large bookcases, three half-height floor cupboards and a comfortable L-shaped desk, it was exactly what Michael needed.

But tonight Michael had achieved little. The encounter with Patrick O'Driscoll was still playing on his mind. But that paled into insignificance next to Michael's real concern: the danger that faced Simon Kash.

Michael's eyes had been drawn to the photograph from the moment he had taken his seat. At first he had not understood why. It had sat there since the office had been furnished. And he had seen it countless times before that. But gradually he realised its significance, and with it he began to understand why saving Kash from himself had become so important to him.

Two faces stared back at Michael from the photo. Two young men, one with blonde hair, one with brown, but unarguably brothers. Both younger when the photo was taken than Simon Kash now, but, Michael knew, much more streetwise. Not that it changed what was about to happen to the elder boy who, unknown to him, was just weeks away from facing allegations almost as serious as those that now hung over Kash.

Michael's gaze bored into the face of his dead brother, Liam. The face in the picture was the Liam that Michael preferred to remember; the young, carefree force of nature that his brother had been, rather than the violent, angry man he became in prison. A prison term that should have been Michael's.

You were taking bullets for me even then. A threatened tear was now staining Michael's cheek.

He stood up and placed the photo back onto the windowsill ahead of his desk. Hard as the memories were to take, he was grateful for the clarity it had given him. Seeing Liam so young and remembering what he had gone through for a crime he did not commit – for *Michael's* crime – Michael understood his own urge to 'save' Simon Kash.

Protecting Simon is the closest I'll ever come to protecting my brother. The closest I'll ever come to repaying him.

The sound of chinking glass drifted through the open window, interrupting Michael's thoughts.

It had come from the garden patio, three floors below the office. Michael knew what it meant. Sarah and Anne were in the garden. And the wine was now flowing. He was surprised it had taken this long; Sarah might be determined to cut back Anne's drinking, but Anne rarely took 'no' for an answer.

Michael tapped the photo unconsciously, closed the office door and headed downstairs.

In just minutes he was taking a seat in the garden, an open bottle of beer in his hand.

'So, Sarah's told me what happened after court.' Anne did not skirt around a subject. 'Well done for holding that temper of yours.'

'I had a little help with that one.' Michael reached out, took Sarah's hand and gave it a gentle squeeze. 'Besides, there are better ways of dealing with that sort of thing.'

'You think he'll try it again? Once you've *really* gone after his brother?'

'Who knows?' Michael was not concerned. 'Maybe. Maybe not. Whichever it is, it won't stop me defending Simon Kash properly.'

Sarah squeezed back, telling Michael that she agreed with the sentiment.

'Do you really think your boy's innocent, Mikey?' Again, Anne's question was blunt.

'I absolutely believe he is, yeah. And every moment I spend with him convinces me more. He's a child and he's scared. He's no murderer.'

'How can you be so sure?'

'Because he only has to do one thing to help get himself out of this. He only has to point the finger at his co-defendant and let me off the leash. But he won't. Guilty clients tell me lie after lie, Anne. Whereas Simon hasn't done that at all. He's telling me *nothing*. They've terrified him into staying silent. Into protecting Darren O'Driscoll, at the cost of his own future. And I'm not going to let that happen.'

Anne smiled. Michael knew why. He had heard the passion in his own voice. It sounded like he was taking the Kash case personally. Which, of course, he was. From the smile on her face, he knew that Anne had heard the same thing.

She said nothing at first, as she took two cigarettes from her packet, passed one to Sarah and lit them both before refilling her own wine glass.

'This passion of yours, Mikey. It wouldn't have anything to do with who this kid reminds you of, would it?'

Michael smiled wryly, always surprised by how well his friend could read him.

'I guess that could be true, yeah.' Michael placed his now-empty beer bottle on the table ahead of him. 'It's not everything, but yeah, when I look at him, when I see him making decisions that will hurt him, like Liam did for me, I want to protect him from himself. But it's not just that. It's also the evidence. It just doesn't stack up.

'I really believe that Simon's been dragged into this and now he's lost. Too terrified to fight for himself. Like I said, *I'm* not going to watch that convict him. If he can't fight for himself then I'll do it for him.'

With a sad smile, Anne looked into Michael's eyes as he spoke, before raising her glass in a toast.

'Then here's to Simon Kash. The luckiest kid in the world to have found you.'

THIRTY-TWO

Wisdom Penfold clicked the Wi-Fi icon at the top right-hand corner of his laptop's screen, selected the sole available network and entered in the password he had been given at the hotel's reception. Then he waited for a connection.

It took a little longer than he expected. He was still getting used to how the world had moved on during his years in prison. Wi-Fi was one of those changes.

A few moments more and the connection was made. Penfold brought up the Stena Line booking page and selected the Harwich to Hook ferry, 7 a.m. on 20 June. The first of the day that still had space.

He looked at his watch. 3 a.m. Just four more hours and he would be gone. Out of England. The first time in twenty-two years.

And I won't be back, he thought. *I'm done here.*

The booking page asked for details. Passenger name and a bank card for payment.

The latter was no problem. Penfold had been careful since his release. He had purchased a dormant bank account registered to someone else. Credit and debit card use was unavoidable these days. Before his imprisonment cash had been king, but it had been dethroned during his sentence. This had forced Penfold to use both types of card many times in the past few months.

If those cards had been in his own name then a trail would have been created, and by now the police might be looking for him. With what he was doing, Penfold could not risk his real name being flagged up on any police system.

The other requirement – travel and identity documents – was

similarly dealt with. Penfold had done his homework in the past six months. Passports were getting harder and harder to fake, but without one he could not board the ferry. He could not even book the ticket.

As difficult as fake documents might be to come by, no one was better placed to 'know the right people' than someone who had just spent the best part of two decades living with every type of criminal. It had not been cheap, but as Wisdom Penfold looked at the pristine burgundy passport in his hand – naming him as the same non-existent person who owned his bank account and credit cards – he knew that the investment had been worth it.

Penfold entered the information and waited for payment to be confirmed. It took less than a minute. He then accessed his email inbox and opened his e-ticket. The ferry was confirmed.

It was his only connection to the transaction under his own name. He had not anticipated the need for email and so he had not set up a new address under the fake name.

He closed the laptop and packed it away. Next he undressed, carefully folding the clothes he had been wearing. To wear again tomorrow.

Everything was in place. Tomorrow, Wisdom Penfold would leave England behind.

Either that, or I spend the rest of my life in prison.

THIRTY-THREE

Steven Hale glanced at his watch as he strode into the MIT working area. 7.30 a.m.

The place was already busy. But then Scotland Yard never sleeps. Hale scanned the floor. Looking for the members of his team, both MIT One and Trident.

The Trident officers were the easiest to spot. They were unfamiliar with the space and had crowded in the far corner of the room. Some of the MIT One operatives were with them.

All seemed part of the same discussion. A discussion Hale needed to hear. He made his way towards them.

'What have we got?' Hale asked as he got closer. Near enough to see that DS King had the floor. 'Dean? What's the news?'

'News on Burrell, sir,' King replied. 'Might be something we can use.'

'What is it?'

'He's been muscling in.'

'On who?'

'On everyone, pretty much. He hasn't wasted any time. Almost like he knew the opportunity was coming.'

Hale smiled. He had hoped that Burrell would show his hand. But to do so this quickly? That was unexpected.

'What's the source, Dean? Anything we can use in court? Or is it just street talk?'

'Mainly street. But I think we have a few business owners who'll come forward. People Burrell's men have visited, looking to take over Ferris's protection rackets. They wouldn't have said a word against Ferris but Burrell's not as frightening as he'd like to think.'

Hale took a moment to think through King's information.

It's something. But is it enough?

'It's too tenuous.' Hale was a realist. 'Word's out about Ferris. To everyone, not just his killers. Burrell must have known which businesses Ferris was extorting. He might be stepping in fast, but it's not enough. It doesn't justify pulling him in.'

'What about for extortion, guv?' The question came from DS Dixon. 'The evidence seems pretty clear on that.'

'Maybe, but that's not what we want him for. *Trident* can bring him in on *those* charges when we're done. But if we do it now and then we ask him *anything* about the murder when we've nothing to support it? We'll end up with a bloody mistrial.'

Dixon seemed to understand Hale's logic; he did not debate it further.

King had other ideas.

'What about one of Ferris's men?' he asked.

'What do you mean?'

'I mean what if one of Ferris's men told me that Burrell had approached him? *Before* the killing. Like, two days before.'

'And said what?'

Hale felt a flutter in his stomach.

Say the right thing. This might be just what we need.

'He was told that a change was coming,' King said. 'A big change. And that he would be safest if he was on the right side before it happened.'

'Anything else?'

'Is that not enough?'

'It might be. But more is always better.'

'It's all we have, guv.'

Hale paused. His mind was racing. The attempt to poach Ferris's man was not enough. But the talk of a big change was close and the veiled reference to the safety of Ferris's men took it further.

I think it's just far enough, he decided.

'OK. I think we can work with that. But it's got to be bang on, Dean. Are you absolutely clear on what your man was told? Because anything less than what you just said – even an inch less – and we're sunk.'

'It's *exactly* what I just said.'

King sounded as certain as Hale needed.

'And you're sure he'll stand by it?'

'With the shit I've got on *him*, guv?' King smiled as he spoke. 'Yeah, he'll stand up and be counted. I guarantee it.'

'Then bring him in. Right away. I need a section-nine witness statement before midday.'

'Consider it done.'

Hale turned to the rest of his team and spotted DC Campbell.

'Anton.'

'Guv?'

'I want you to draw up an application for a warrant. Liaise with Dean. Get the statement from his source, then have us ready for court by 2 p.m.'

'A warrant for where, guv?'

'For Burrell's place. I want this all done properly.'

Hale turned to address the full team.

'I want every angle covered,' he announced. 'This has to be watertight, people. Because we're taking this bastard tonight.'

THIRTY-FOUR

It was 8.45 a.m. as Michael left Eight Essex Court. It was unusual for him to visit chambers in the morning. At least once a trial had begun. His case papers were already at the Old Bailey, as was his court outfit, so there was nothing chambers had that he would need.

Nothing but its proximity to Temple Church.

Michael walked straight ahead as chambers' main door closed behind him. Towards the archway and alley that led to Pump Court, then onwards to Cloisters at its end. A scattering of Tudor-era pillars sat beside Cloisters. They marked the boundary between Middle Temple and Inner Temple.

It had taken him just a minute to walk from the door of Eight Essex Court to Temple Church. Usually he would have strolled. He liked to take his time and admire the living history that had fascinated him since his first visit. But not today. Michael was here for a reason.

For a friend.

He spotted Derek Reid the moment he passed the final Cloisters pillar and entered Temple Church's courtyard. Reid was standing alone, thirty yards – maybe more – from the door to the church.

A door at which he was staring intently.

'Derek.'

Reid had not noticed him, nor did he react to Michael's use of his name.

'Derek.'

This time Michael voice was louder. It worked.

Reid turned and saw his friend.

'Michael. What are you doing here?'

'I wanted to make sure you were OK,' Michael explained. 'How're you doing?'

'It's not my best day, mate.'

Michael did not need to be told. He could see it in Reid's face. In the way Reid stood. He was just about holding it together. Michael knew why.

The strength was for Longman's sons, Michael realised. The last good turn Reid could do for his friend. He was achieving that through sheer determination, and Michael could see the toll it was taking.

'Is there anything I can do?' he asked.

'Nothing, Mike. Really, nothing.'

Michael did not reply. What was there to say? He put a hand on Reid's shoulder and turned to face the same direction as his friend. Towards the church door.

The two men stood in silence for minutes, just watching as mourners arrived. Lawyers mainly. All come to pay their respects to a giant of their profession. They were entering the church in twos and threes.

'You need to go inside, Derek.' Michael's voice was soft when he finally spoke. 'It won't be long now.'

Reid turned and looked into Michael's eyes. Tears were forming in his own.

'You can't come in?'

'I can't. We start at ten today. I've got to be there from the beginning.'

'I know. Sorry. I shouldn't have asked.'

'Always ask, Derek. Always.'

Reid nodded his head. A tear began to trace a path down his cheek. Michael moved his arm to the back of Reid's neck and pulled him close, hugging his friend's head to his shoulder.

'Just get through this,' Michael whispered into Reid's ear. 'Because you'll regret it if you don't. Get through it.'

Michael could feel Reid nod against his shoulder. He released his grip and Reid stepped back, wiping the tears from his eyes. A smile faltered on his lips.

'Thanks, Mike.' Reid's voice broke a little as he spoke. He indicated to the church door with his head. 'I best be going, eh?'

'I think so.'

Michael's hand was still on Reid's shoulder as the two men faced each other.

'Look, when I'm done in court I can come to your place. Maybe take you out for a bite?'

'No. No thanks. When this is all over I just want to go home. I'm going to open a bottle, get pissed and then get my head down. I'll be no use to anyone after this.'

'You're sure?'

'I'm sure. Give me a few days, Mike. You just concentrate on Simon. I'll get in touch when my head's back together. I just need to be alone for a little while, that's all.'

Michael could understand. Grief was nothing new to him, and he knew it was something that everyone dealt with differently. Michael's way had been similar to Reid's. Do what needs to be done, then go into isolation. To mourn alone.

Reid knew his own mind.

'OK. Then take care, Derek. And call me when you're ready for some company.'

'I will.' Reid reached out and hugged Michael again. He whispered in his ear before letting go. 'Thank you, Mike.'

Michael stepped back as Reid turned and watched his friend walk away, into Temple Church. He waited until Reid was inside before turning himself, towards a second archway and alley. This one led out of the courtyard and towards Fleet Street. And it was occupied.

It had been two years since Michael had last seen Joelle Levy in the flesh. Not usually long enough for a person to change too much. In Levy's case, she had not changed at all.

Michael did not doubt that Levy recognised him, too. One thing he remembered about her was her absolute recall. An unusual skill in anyone. It made her a difficult witness to challenge.

'Nice to see you, Chief Inspector.' Michael spoke as he walked towards the archway. Levy stayed still. 'No need to ask what you're here for.'

'It's always sensible to have eyes on the funeral, Mr Devlin. Freaks often turn up to see a victim buried.'

'But you don't think this one will, do you?'

'What makes you say that?'

'You're standing too far away for a good view. And no one's covering the Middle Temple side of the courtyard; I just walked through. So you've no chance of catching him, even if you did somehow manage to spot him.'

'Maybe you're underestimating me, Mr Devlin. I can move fast enough when I have to.'

'I don't doubt it.' Michael smiled broadly. He meant every word. It was obvious that Levy kept herself fit. The unflattering suit she chose to wear could not hide her athleticism. Michael changed the subject. 'I think I should be saying "thank you" for last night, shouldn't I?'

'You have your wife to thank,' Levy replied. 'I owed her a solid.'

'Still, thank you. It should save me some trouble moving forward.'

'I wouldn't count on it. We can't keep him longer than tonight. And he seems the stubborn sort.'

'Also good to know. I guess I'll have to stay alert.'

'That shouldn't be a problem for a man like you, Mr Devlin. You've dealt with worse, I'm sure.'

Something in Levy's tone said that she *was* sure. That she knew more about Michael Devlin than he would like.

Michael chose to ignore it. He changed the subject again.

'So what are you really doing here, Ms Levy?'

'Joelle,' Levy replied. 'I'm on first-name terms with Sarah. No reason you and I should stay formal.'

'In that case it's Michael, not "Mr Devlin".' The only polite response. A momentary tangent. 'And since we're now friends, Joelle, what *are* you really doing here?'

Levy smiled.

'To be honest, Michael, I was hoping to speak with Derek Reid.'

'Why?'

'Because he defended a man called Wisdom Penfold about sixteen years ago. Between us, Michael – and I really *do* mean between us – we think Penfold is good for the murders. We hoped Mr Reid might be able to fill in a few blanks for us.'

Michael recognised the name, and so he closed his eyes and thought back. He did not possess the total recall enjoyed by Levy, but he was a good second.

He had what he was looking for in moments.

'Yeah, I remember that case.'

'Were you involved?'

'No. But it wasn't long after I was Derek's pupil. So I still had an unhealthy interest in his career. All ex-pupils do. They use it as sort of a guide to where they want to go themselves. Plus Wisdom Penfold's an unusual name. Hard to forget.'

'Is there anything you can tell me about the case?'

'Not a whole lot. Derek didn't go into specifics. But I remember that Penfold was a nasty piece of work. So yes, maybe he's a good call on the murders. He certainly seemed capable of that level of violence.'

'Do you think Mr Reid could tell me more?'

'Definitely. Derek's got a mind like a safe. A bit like your own, Joelle.'

Levy smiled. It made Michael smile in return.

'You should do *that* more often,' he said. 'It makes you look a lot less intimidating.'

'Maybe I *want* to be intimidating,' Levy laughed.

'Just take the friendly advice!' Michael was still laughing as he reached into his suit pocket and took out a white business card. He handed it to Levy. 'My number's on there, Joelle. If I can help with anything that comes up, then just call. For now, though, I have to go. I've a trial starting at ten and I'm almost late.'

'Understood.' Levy took the card. She swapped it for one of her own and handed hers to Michael. 'Sarah already has my number, but in case you need it.'

'Thanks.'

'No, Michael. Thank *you*. It's been helpful.'

Michael smiled a final time. Levy did the same. She then stepped aside, giving Michael room to pass. He took it and Levy watched him go. She was still watching when Michael stopped at the end of the alley and turned to face her.

'Something just occurred to me,' Michael said. 'If Wisdom Penfold *is* your man, and he's come after both the judge and the defence solicitor, doesn't that make Derek a target? As his defence barrister?'

'Potentially,' Levy replied. 'But don't worry, he has protection. I've already authorised a team outside his house from tonight.'

'You might need to send them a little earlier,' Michael suggested. 'Because once this is over and Phillip Longman is buried, Derek's heading home to drink himself into a stupor.'

'Understood. Then they'll be there from this afternoon.'

Michael nodded. Satisfied.

'Thanks, then, Joelle. Again.'

Michael turned as soon as he finished speaking. In a heartbeat he was on his way. Left from the archway. Towards Fleet Street and the Old Bailey.

Levy reached into her jacket pocket and pulled out her mobile phone. If Michael was right – if Reid was going to be home earlier than the evening – then she needed to rearrange his protection detail.

She tapped 'work'. The call was answered before the phone had reached her ear.

'Dylan, it's Levy. I need you to revisit the arrangements for a protect—'

'Ma'am, we were just about to call you. We've found him. We know where Penfold is.'

'Where?'

'In the middle of the North Sea, ma'am. He's booked on the 7 a.m. Harwich to Hook ferry.'

'Hook?'

'A port in the Netherlands, ma'am.'

'How did we find him?' Levy felt a mixture of satisfaction and concern. 'Is he travelling under his own name?'

'No, ma'am. He's travelling under the name Clive Fountain. That's why his passport wasn't flagged up on boarding. But the e-ticket was sent to his personal email address. We found his email address on a separate data sweep, which led us to the ticket.'

Levy hesitated. It seemed a sloppy mistake for so meticulous a killer. But then Penfold had missed the explosion of email use that had occurred while he was in prison. Perhaps the mistake was explicable.

'What's the journey time for that ferry?'

'Approximately six and a half hours.'

'And London to Harwich by chopper. How long will that take?'

Levy could hear Dylan typing before he answered. He was no doubt Googling the answer.

'About forty-five minutes, ma'am,' Dylan answered.

'Perfect. Get a chopper scrambled. I'll be at the helipad in twenty minutes.'

'Ma'am, to get a helicopter at this notice I'll need—'

'I don't care what you need to do, Dylan. Just make sure the bloody chopper's there when I arrive. Then contact the ferry. Tell them to keep going for another thirty minutes. Then turn around and head back to Harwich Port.'

'You don't want them to turn back now? Why?'

'I haven't got time to explain myself, Dylan. Just do exactly what I say. Now.'

Levy pressed the red disconnect icon. Her heart was racing. Her adrenaline spiking.

There was no time to be irritated by her assistant's questions, because only one thought now occupied Levy's mind.

We've got him.

THIRTY-FIVE

It was the wet sea air that surprised Wisdom Penfold the most. That the sensation was so welcome.

Penfold had missed many things during his years in prison. And like most long-term inmates, what he was denied had become an obsession. The touch of a woman. The taste of a cold beer. The feel of a good suit. These had been what Penfold had pined for. But now, with the sea air whipping into his face as he left England behind, he could think of nothing he had missed more.

Penfold looked around the upper deck. At the other passengers. At the crew. All were making the most of the weather. Basking in the heat that had settled during their two and a half hours at sea. The morning had been cold, just like every other in the past month. But then the sun rose higher in the sky, replacing the cold with its burning rays.

The risk of being caught while travelling on a passport that read Clive Fountain had always been a small one, but it was still a relief to be clear of the port. He had felt a small thrill as he passed every British checkpoint without inquiry. The fear of being stopped was natural for a man who had committed such crimes, but he was going to have to learn to stop looking over his shoulder. Even now, he could feel the paranoia setting in.

It had started when they were still in the port. A man and a woman, apparently a couple. Something about them had bothered him, though he could not say what. But when the woman had met his eye twice while queuing for the ferry and the man had visibly avoided doing the same, Penfold's hackles had risen. He had forced them back down after watching them furtively for a few minutes. The couple had done nothing suspicious.

Penfold stared out to sea. He was not admiring the view. Instead he was thinking. Of the past. Of the future. Of how to make the transition from one to the other.

The past weeks had taken years of planning. Countless hours in his cell, plotting and perfecting every aspect of the crime to come. Now it was over. He had done what he needed to do. All debts were paid and he could look forward to a life free from his past. Free from the things that had weighed him down. And now free from England. The country that had imprisoned him. The country he hated.

He turned, leaned his back against the rail of the ship and raised his face to the sun. Within minutes he could feel his skin burning. Penfold did not care. He had been pale for far too long.

It can sometimes be difficult to gauge time. To have any sense of whether minutes or hours have passed. Different factors can influence it. Including the sun, which can be almost hypnotic.

This happened to Wisdom Penfold on the upper deck of the Harwich to Hook ferry. He lost all track of time as he enjoyed the feel of the sun on his skin.

Right up until the moment the ship began to turn.

Penfold had grown used to the movement of the ferry. The rhythm with which it rode the waves. Nothing about it bothered him. At least not until now.

The feeling as the boat now moved to its left was different. Not at first. At first it could be ignored. But a full minute later and it was still turning. At this speed, that meant a full ninety degrees. Enough to change the shadows on the deck and to cast them onto Penfold himself.

Confirmation of his worst fear.

We're turning around.

Penfold's heart began to race. His grip on his rucksack doubled as he moved along the deck. As fast as he could risk without drawing attention to himself.

A short distance away was a crewman. Not a steward, instead

someone who looked like he might actually know something. Penfold headed straight for him.

'Excuse me.' Penfold tried to seem unconcerned. 'We seem to be turning around. Are we?'

'I'm afraid so, sir. The captain has ordered us back to port.'

Stay calm. Stay composed.

'Why?'

'Problem with the boat, sir. We have to get her looked at.'

'What sort of problem?'

'A technical one. Nothing to worry about but it needs to be dealt with. That can't happen at sea, I'm afraid.'

Don't panic. Don't draw attention.

'Can't it wait until we get to Holland? I have friends waiting for me there.'

'Captain's orders, sir. If we don't get the problem dealt with we could cause permanent damage to the boat. Harwich is only two hours away. Hook is four.'

Might be bullshit. Might not. Roll with it.

'Sounds like a no-brainer, then.' Penfold forced a smile. 'I assume there'll be compensation for the delay?'

'I'm sure there will be, sir. Cheaper than ruining the ship.'

'Thanks.' Penfold maintained the smile.

Stay natural.

'Well, good luck with whatever it is.'

'Thank you.'

The crewman walked away.

Penfold stood still for a moment. Looking into the distance. Focusing, in the hope that he might catch a glimpse of Holland.

Nothing, he thought as he let his eyes wander.

By now other passengers had noticed the turn. Had noticed the moving shadows. Soon everyone would know they were headed back. It would inconvenience many, he thought, but he was sure that none was taking as big a risk as he was by returning to British soil.

THIRTY-SIX

The return journey took two hours.

Including an hour of hell, Wisdom Penfold thought.

The first hour had been OK. A concern, but a manageable one. Penfold had heard the explanation perhaps twenty times during that first sixty minutes. From crew members and from other passengers. It had not changed. A technical difficulty with the ferry. A need to return to the closest port.

Inconvenient but believable.

The second hour had been much worse, from the moment England came back into view. Penfold had experienced an incredible feeling of relief when it had disappeared earlier in the day. His paranoia was just as great now that the coastline was back.

For sixty minutes Penfold's fears had grown. Not helped by the couple from the port. He had seen them again on deck and had noticed the man glancing in his direction. Not once but twice. If Penfold had been calm he would have dismissed it. Of course they'd be on the upper deck, he would have thought. Almost everyone was. And the glances in his direction? That was not surprising, either.

But after a whole hour of his heart racing. Of jumping at every shadow? Penfold's behaviour was now erratic. And it was drawing attention.

Who *wasn't* looking at him?

It could not be helped. The fate that might await him in the UK was too much for Penfold to bear. A return to the walls that had held him for so long, a sentence well-earned by his recent crime.

Penfold could not stay calm. Not with that hanging over him.

He made his way to the lower deck. The dock was fast approaching. He had maybe ten minutes before the moment of truth. Before he would know the real reason for the ferry's return.

Please God this isn't a set-up.

Penfold found a quiet corner. Most passengers remained on the upper deck, still enjoying the sun. It offered him space and Penfold took it. He settled into a cushioned bench next to a wall and began to breathe deeply. For a moment he managed to clear his head. To calm his nerves. To overcome his fear.

Stop thinking about it. It might be nothing. It's probably *nothing. And if it's not, well, then you'll deal with it.*

You've done it before.

Penfold listened to his own advice. It was working; he could feel his racing heart begin to slow, the pain in his temple begin to lessen.

It's nothing to worry about. We'll be moving again in no time.

Hindsight is a wonderful thing. And a frustrating one. If they had stayed on the upper deck then Penfold might have waited. He might have stayed calm.

If they had just stayed with the other passengers. If they had just stayed in the sun.

Penfold's decision was made the moment he saw them. The couple from the port. From the upper deck. The same man and woman Penfold had noticed before. They had seemed a little too interested, which had set off his survival instinct. Penfold had tried to ignore it; he had put it down to paranoia.

But what are they doing here? he questioned himself. *When everyone else is upstairs? Too much of a coincidence.*

Penfold got to his feet and for the first time he did not grip his rucksack. Instead he left it where it was, giving him two free hands.

Penfold directed his eyes at the floor as he began to walk towards the couple, keeping a single bench between himself and them so as not to be heading straight at them. Relying on his peripheral vision, Penfold could tell that the couple had remained standing: looking out of the window towards the approaching port and resolutely *not* looking at him.

It was this that finally convinced him. There were almost no passengers or crew members below deck. Of the few that *were* there, one was now walking towards them. They *must* have noticed him. Yet they kept their eyes averted. It wasn't natural.

And told Penfold all he needed to know.

Three metres. Far enough for the couple to have time to defend themselves.

Two metres. Closer. Making defence more difficult. But not impossible.

One metre. Too close. It would take a miracle.

Penfold cleared the bench with a fast, powerful stride. His hands were outstretched as he moved. Aimed at the man's head. A head that was now turning, but turning too slow.

The man stood no chance. Before he could react Penfold had both hands on his skull. The momentum that had taken Penfold over the bench was still with him. He used it well. With a combination of his own weight, his strength and the speed of his movement, Penfold brought the man's head crashing into the thick metal rail that circled the whole lower deck.

The sound said everything. A deep, dull boom.

No bone could make that noise and stay intact. But Penfold already knew that. He had felt the give in the man's skull and did not need the confirmation of sound before he turned on the woman.

It had taken Penfold a second to deal with the man. Long enough for the woman to turn; to know what was coming. She could have run. Perhaps she would have made it. She chose to do the opposite: to attack. Brave and foolish, all at once.

The weather had made a coat or a jacket impracticable, and so she had nowhere to carry a concealed weapon. Without one she could only attack with her hands. A lost cause, maybe, but she would go down fighting.

Penfold did not see the blow coming. He had underestimated the woman. Concentrated too much on the man. Her thumb dug deep into his left eye, cutting the eyeball. And it stayed there. The woman had been trained well. Not to go fist to fist with a man like Penfold. Instead she was trying to incapacitate him. To blind him. Her other arm swung up, targeting his last good eye.

Penfold, though, was a hard man to fight. He had an unusual tolerance for pain and a gift for giving it back. He caught her arm before her thumb reached his good eye. Gripped her wrist tight and pushed it backwards and down, against the joint. An instant later he felt it snap beneath the skin.

The woman screamed. The pressure in Penfold's eye disappeared. Her right hand had pulled back, towards her left. Human nature had taken over.

Penfold stepped back and watched her fall to the floor, cradling her arm. A red stain was growing fast across her white T-shirt. The broken wrist bone had pierced her skin.

He looked around. The few passengers and crewmen on the lower deck had heard the scream. Most were stunned. But two had reacted. They were hurtling in his direction. Penfold was not stupid. He did not know either man. There was a good chance he could win, but just as good a chance he could not.

He did not intend to find out.

Penfold turned back towards the fallen woman. Helpless on the floor, all her attention was focused on her devastated wrist. Penfold accelerated towards her, timing his steps with the precision of a footballer. His right leg cocked back as the woman came within range. An instant later and it was swinging forward, powered by muscle and momentum. Penfold's foot struck the woman's jaw, cleanly and with full force. The impact sent her head reeling backwards and she was unconscious before her head hit the metal floor with a sickening thud.

Penfold did not stop to inspect the damage. Instead he hurdled her and headed back the way he had come. Towards the stairs to the upper deck. He grabbed his rucksack as he passed, hardly breaking stride.

Two short flights of stairs and Penfold was back in the sun. The metallic sound from below told him that his pursuers were close behind. Already on the staircase. Penfold took no chances. He ran to the bow of the ferry. Estimated the distance to the port.

Five hundred metres. Maybe a little more.

'GRAB THAT MAN!'

The shout came from behind. Further than Penfold had expected. His pursuers had stopped at the top of the stairs and it had taken them a few seconds to spot him.

It gave him time.

Penfold turned away from the shout, while every other passenger on deck turned towards it. They all saw the same thing: a crewman, his arm thrust out, a finger pointing directly at Penfold.

The odds were against him. Massively. If only ten per cent of the passengers played hero, it was still one hundred per cent more than Penfold could handle.

He had to move before they could consider it.

Penfold sprinted away from the crowd closest to him before he could be stopped. A few reacted quickly, giving chase. Others stayed rooted to the spot.

A few of the chasers were slower than Penfold. Others were not. The quicker ones were gaining on him fast. Penfold could feel them closing.

He looked ahead and saw a wall of bodies forming. A wall he could not pass.

His decision was made in an instant. No time for second thoughts. No time for hesitation. Penfold had perhaps two seconds left. He would need them both.

Penfold swung his rucksack behind him as he ran. As far back as he could stretch. Once he reached his limit he launched the bag forwards. Over the main deck rail. Down to the deep tidal river that led to the port.

He reached the rail just as the bag went over. Grabbing the thick metal, he used it to launch himself over.

The man closest to him reached out. Almost managed to grip Penfold's trouser hem. Almost. But close is not close enough. The chaser's arms were still outstretched as he watched Penfold fall. Ninety feet. From the top deck to the deep water below.

Joelle Levy stood on the dock. On the spot where the ferry's passengers would disembark.

Four men from MIT One stood behind her. Behind them were ten more police officers. Members of the Essex Police Firearms Unit.

No chances were being taken.

Levy had been at the port for thirty minutes. As long as the ferry had been in sight. She had timed the trip from London perfectly.

Since her arrival the boat had come ever closer. Its size more obvious and so the scale of any search more apparent. *If* a search was needed.

'How long before they dock?'

Levy was speaking to the man beside her. Stephen John. The Stena Line's operating manager for Harwich International Port.

'I'd say seven minutes or so,' John replied.

'OK.' Levy turned to her team. 'Keep your wits about you, people. Penfold is on that ship but he is *not* getting past this port under any circumstances. Understood?'

'Ma'am.'

The team spoke as one. Regimented. Every officer knew his or her duty; knew exactly why they were here.

Levy turned back towards the ferry. It was close enough now that she could make out the crowds on the upper deck.

She reached inside her jacket for her shoulder holster and removed her pistol. A Glock 19. Smaller than the standard issue Glock 17, it was still plenty big enough for the job.

Levy checked the weapon. Fully loaded. Fifteen 9×19mm Parabellum rounds. Levy took good care of her weapons. She had undergone extensive firearms training with the Metropolitan Police, training which had not come close to the expertise already instilled in her by the Israel Defense Forces or Shin Bet.

Levy rarely expected to use the pistol she carried.

She felt differently today.

She returned the Glock to its holster and her eyes moved back to the ferry. It was closer. Clearer. The movement on the top deck was now plain to see. Movement that seemed unusual.

Levy squinted her eyes and tried to block out the sun with her hand as she focused on the bow of the ferry. She could see what looked like a surge of the passengers. Similar to a tide or a Mexican wave.

The crowd on the deck seemed to be moving as one. First forward. Then left.

'What the hell's going on?' Levy's question was as much to herself as to anyone else.

'I've no idea.' Stephen John's answer was not helpful. Nor was it needed.

Levy's eyes followed the movement, trying to get ahead of it. To discover what was causing the deck's strange motion.

Whatever they're moving towards is what matters, she observed. *Not the crowd itself.*

The answer came almost immediately. Preceded by an object thrown over the upper deck's safety rail. A bag, it looked like. From this distance Levy could not be sure.

An instant later and she did not care. The object was followed by something much more compelling. The unmistakable sight of a man, leaping from the ferry to the river below.

'It's Penfold!' Levy shouted the name as the realisation hit her. She was already running as she shouted again

'GET TO THE RIB!'

The four MIT One officers followed, in the direction of the rigid-inflatable boat that was moored close by. The RIB was there for exactly this situation: an attempted escape at sea.

The firearms officers did not move. This was no accident. Levy had briefed her team on every scenario. Every officer knew what she expected.

The RIB was moving within moments. Piloted by a specialist. Levy pointed him in the right direction, to where Penfold had hit the water.

A seven-minute ferry journey, Stephen John had estimated. It took less than two in the high-performance speedboat.

The RIB reached Penfold quickly. He was still where he had fallen. Levy raised her pistol and aimed it at Penfold's head.

She quickly realised that the weapon was unnecessary.

Penfold was in no condition to resist arrest. He was barely able to tread water; his head repeatedly went under as he struggled to stay afloat.

The impact with the water had taken a toll. Penfold's right arm was useless. Broken, it seemed. Or dislocated. Levy could not tell which. Nor did she care. All that mattered was that she had him.

Levy holstered her pistol and turned to the nearest two MIT One officers.

'Fish him out of there and read the bastard his rights.'

THIRTY-SEVEN

Michael had watched the jury carefully as Keith White presented his evidence. White was the UK's leading expert in cell-site and mobile-phone data, a field of evidence that had, since the late 1990s, hugely increased in importance.

Mobile phones were everywhere. It was difficult to find a person – old or young – who did not own one. They were the ultimate modern convenience.

They also happened to be the most effective individual tracking system ever devised.

It was the people-tracking aspect that had brought White to Court Number Two of the Old Bailey. The prosecution expert, he was there to demonstrate to the jury what that data proved.

The morning had been taken up with White's presentation of his findings. Peter Epstein QC had questioned him in a way designed to guide him in his explanations to the jury. Cell-site data can be complicated and so it was essential that it was explained clearly. But Michael could see that Epstein's guiding hand was unnecessary; White could do this in his sleep.

He had begun by explaining how the mobile-network operated, and how its data could be used to locate the position of a mobile phone at the time of that phone's use. To do this he handed out a detailed map of a random location in West London with a single mobile-phone mast in the centre. The jury then watched as White used a marker pen to draw a line upwards from the cell mast to the edge of the map, another diagonally down to the left, and a third diagonally to the right, dividing the map into three sections, with the mast at the centre.

These sections, White explained, were the mast's cell zones: A, B and C.

Michael listened intently, making sure all the information was presented clearly. White went on to explain that any mobile phone used at a location inside the map's right-hand section – cell zone A – would usually register in that same zone, because the telephone was designed to seek out the nearest *available* transmitter. But sometimes cell zone A would already be busy with as many users as it could take at one time, and so the telephone would seek out the *next* nearest transmitter. This might be in the lower or the left-hand triangles – cell zones B or C – of the same mast, or it could be a different mast altogether.

'But the vast majority of the time,' White had explained, 'the cell zone that registers the call will be the cell zone in which the phone is physically located. So we can say that during the call, the phone itself was – most likely – within the geographic area covered by cell zone A.'

Michael had watched the jury throughout the explanation. All of them seemed to have followed so far. But Michael knew that things were about to get a bit more complicated.

With the general explanation done, White produced another map – less detailed this time and covering a much larger area of five miles – and once copies had been handed to the jury he began to mark up all of the cell masts within that five-mile area. Not for the first time, Michael was amused by the jury's surprise as mast after mast was identified; few realise quite how many of the things are hiding in plain sight.

With all masts highlighted, White then circled one mast in particular. He explained that this was the same mast they had looked at on the previous map and then drew the same three lines emanating from it: a line upwards, a line down to the left, and a line down to the right. As the map was of a far larger area, however, none of these lines extended beyond an inch in length. Done, he went on to highlight a main road that ran through the mast's cell zone A. He then traced the route of that road through the full five miles covered by the map, which, by the end, was very far away from the initial identified cell mast.

'Now imagine that the call was made from *this* street,' he had continued, indicating the highlighted road, 'and that the caller was in a car travelling south. If that call continues during the journey, at some point it will no longer physically be within cell zone A – the right hand of our first mast, which we'll call Mast One. Once Mast One is no longer close enough, the telephone will look for the *new* nearest mast. And when it finds it, it will jump to that mast. So, if the caller is driving along the road highlighted and reaches *this* point . . .'

White indicated a spot that was a mile or so further along the road.

'. . . then in all likelihood the signal will be picked up by *this* mast . . .'

He indicated a different mast, the one now closest to his hypothetical car, and he identified the bottom cell zone section it would now be travelling through by deftly adding the three one-inch zone lines as with Mast One.

'. . . which, using our same 120-degree triangulation, is cell zone B of what we will call Mast Two.'

Michael watched the jury nod in understanding. It was not just courtesy.

Still with him so far, he thought. *Let's hope they can keep up.*

White continued, demonstrating the likely cell masts and cell zones for every half mile of movement along the highlighted road. When he was done the jury had a list of mast hits on a southern route which, White explained, would be strong evidence of that imaginary journey.

'But what if one or some of those masts or cell zones were working at capacity, Mr White? What if one or some of them had taken all of the simultaneous users they are able to carry?'

Epstein knew the potential lines of attack. His questions were designed to close them.

'In those circumstances, where would the phone uses be registered?'

'In those circumstances, Mr Epstein, the telephone would look for the *next* nearest transmitter. Which could be on the same mast but in one of the other two cell zones. Or it could be a different mast entirely. Still relatively nearby, but not quite as close.'

'And how likely is it, for example, that the nearest available mast would be, say, over a mile away from where the phone is being used?'

'Not very likely at all, Mr Epstein.' White had held up the larger map to assist. He continued. 'As you can see, there are many, many masts in this five-mile area. Each has three cell zones, as we've seen. Each cell zone has a significant capacity, and the phone use on each mast is prioritised. The top priority are the calls that come from telephones on the mast's own network. You see, each mast is owned by a particular network. For example, our Mast One could be owned by EE, while our Mast Two could be owned by Virgin. Each mast will give preference to calls or texts that come from its own network. But assuming it has capacity left, then it's first come, first served; it will take calls from phones of *other* networks. So most of the time *any* mast will take a call from *any* network. It is therefore very, very unlikely that all masts within a small area would *all* be at capacity. The idea that a phone wouldn't be able to use one of the masts close by, that instead it would need to connect to one that is, say, a mile away from the phone's physical location, is extremely unlikely indeed.'

With the jury up to speed on the theory, White moved on to the evidence in the case.

Using cell-site data relating to O'Driscoll and Kash's telephones, he explained how their movements could be tracked, placing both phones at the scene of the Galloway murders. He then used the same data to show the jury the route he believed at least Darren O'Driscoll's telephone had taken. A route, he said, which mirrored the Galloways' own journey and so suggested that the brothers had been followed. And then, he said, the same data showed both telephones leaving the area shortly after the brothers' time of death.

By the end of White's evidence to Epstein, the jury had a clear picture of all the cell-site evidence, a picture that wholeheartedly supported the prosecution's case. And a picture that Michael was sure was wrong.

Once Epstein had finished and taken his seat, Cole had cross-examined White for his own client, O'Driscoll. He had attempted to undermine White's conclusion that O'Driscoll's telephone had been at the scene of the Galloways' murders. Although Cole's questions had been asked skilfully, Michael knew he was coming at it from the wrong angle; White's evidence had not been hurt.

But Michael was not concerned. As he rose to his feet, he knew he could do better.

'Mr White, I'm going to ask you some questions on behalf of the defendant Simon Kash.'

'I understand, Mr Devlin.'

White had encountered Michael before.

'Then you'll also understand, Mr White, that I have nothing to ask you about Mr O'Driscoll's telephone.'

'I think I've been asked all there is on that one.'

White smiled as he delivered his answer. The jury did the same. They seemed to agree.

'And it *is* possible for me to leave Mr O'Driscoll's telephone alone, isn't it?' Michael continued. 'Because you don't actually suggest that Mr O'Driscoll's telephone and Mr Kash's telephone travelled together, do you? Or that they even took the same route?'

'I don't suggest either of those things, no. I couldn't. But I think I've made that very clear, haven't I?'

'Indeed you have, Mr White. You've made it *very* clear. So let's look at your evidence as it relates to Simon Kash's phone.'

'Yes, please.'

Michael picked up a bundle of bound papers forty pages long, which contained all the various data that White had used in his evidence. The jury had copies of the same documents.

Michael opened his own copy at page six. He asked for White, the jury and the judge to do the same.

Page six was a map, similar to the one White had used in his example, and with the same five-mile scale, but this time the area it covered was the Borough of Bromley in South East London. Where the Galloway brothers had been butchered. White had concentrated on this map when giving the jury his conclusions on the evidence.

'Can we do this backwards, Mr White? And start at the scene of the murder?'

'We can start wherever you like, Mr Devlin.' White's voice was dismissive. Unconcerned.

'That's very kind of you.' White's arrogant tone did not bother Michael in the slightest. He was going to enjoy this.

Michael picked up the map, pointed to the red spot that indicated the murder site and continued.

'We're agreed that the scene of the murder was here, are we not?'

'Yes.'

'And we note that the last recorded use of Simon Kash's telephone on the night of the murders registers to cell zone C – the left-hand section – of Mast Twenty-two. Which you've told us is a mast owned by the O2 network.'

Michael pointed to the mast, more for effect than anything. By this point everyone knew Mast Twenty-two.

'That's the same mast that registered Mr O'Driscoll's telephone use at around the same time. Correct?'

'I thought you had no questions about Mr O'Driscoll's telephone, Mr Devlin?' Judge Levitt interrupted.

'Apologies, My Lord,' Michael replied. 'I meant *specific* questions. I won't be able to avoid *any* reference to Mr O'Driscoll. Much as I'd like to.'

'Perhaps no more promises you immediately break, then, Mr Devlin?'

'I'll do my best, My Lord.'

Michael turned back to White.

'So, again, that's the same mast as Mr O'Driscoll's telephone. Correct?'

'Correct.'

'And you suggest that this puts them at the same location at the time of the uses.'

'Correct.'

'Which was 8.45 p.m.'

'That's right.'

'And of course you say that the remaining telephone evidence shows the defendants moving out of the Bromley area almost immediately after 8.45 p.m.'

'Correct.'

'OK. I just wanted to make sure we were clear on that. Now, let's go back in time, Mr White. Not long. Just, let's say, ten minutes. Can you tell me the mast that picked up Simon Kash's telephone use at 8.35 p.m.? Just ten minutes earlier?'

White checked his report.

'Mast Twenty.'

'And the network that owns Mast Twenty?'

'EE.'

'So a different mast?'

'Yes.'

'And Mast Twenty, owned by EE – that's *this* mast right here, correct?'

Michael pointed to the map. To a second mast, perhaps an inch further away from the murder site. White checked his own papers.

'Yes, Mr Devlin. That's correct.'

'How far is *that* mast from the site of the murder?'

'Judging by the key, it looks to be just over half a mile.'

'Can you tell me, is Mast Twenty closer to the site of the murders than Mast Twenty-two?'

'No. It is not.'

'What's the difference in distance?'

'Around half a mile again. Mast Twenty-two is less than two hundred yards from the scene of the murders.'

'OK. In that case is Mast Twenty at least the *second* closest mast to the site of the murders?'

White took a few moments to look at his map. Michael could see White counting under his breath. He had anticipated the question that would follow his answer.

'No, Mr Devlin. It is not the second closest mast.'

'That's interesting. I wonder, do you have any idea how many masts are in fact closer?'

'Five, Mr Devlin. Mast Twenty is the sixth closest cell mast to the murder scene.'

Michael nodded his head as he glanced towards the jury. Most had started to look confused by the exchange. He needed to make sure that they were grasping the point.

All still a bit technical so far, he thought. *So let's make it crystal clear.*

'How can it be correct, Mr White, that Simon Kash's phone use places him at the scene of the murder, when his telephone was ignored by the five cell masts closest to that location?'

'As I explained very clearly to Mr Epstein, it is perfectly possible that Mast Twenty-two was at capacity. In those circumstances Mr Kash's telephone would seek out the closest available cell site. The important word there is *available*. It is perfectly possible that Mast Twenty was the only one of the next five masts that was *not* at capacity.'

'But you said earlier, Mr White, that each mast had three cell zones, and that it was very, very unlikely that a telephone signal would travel up to a mile before finding an available cell. Isn't that right?'

'It is, Mr Devlin, yes. But this wasn't a mile, was it? It was half a mile. Plus you have to consider the number of masts. Look at the map in your hand. For some reason the Bromley area has far fewer masts than the average and so the phone's signal has far fewer options. Plus each mast has to take on far more signals. All of this suggests that masts in this area are much more likely to reach capacity. Now I accept, of course, that Mast Twenty is not the *ideal* mast. But its use in no way suggests that Mr Kash's phone was somewhere *other* than the murder site.'

Michael took a few moments, keeping his eyes on White, before responding. The expert witness clearly thought he had batted back the best point. Which was exactly what Michael *wanted* him to think.

'OK. Now, at the risk of breaking my promises again, can you confirm that a call was made by Mr O'Driscoll at the same time as Mr Kash's phone use? At 8.35pm?'

'It was.'

'And can you confirm that the cell site that picked up *that* call – Mr O'Driscoll's call – was Mast Twenty-two?'

'It was.'

'So the same mast that picked up the phone use of both Mr O'Driscoll and Simon Kash ten minutes later?'

'That's correct.'

'Thank you. Now, back in time a little more. In the hour before the

8.35 p.m. call, Simon Kash's telephone was used a further seven times. Is that right?'

White checked his report.

'It was.'

'Thank you. Now, can you please tell me how many masts picked up one or more of those seven telephone uses?'

White checked his report. Then rechecked it more carefully. Michael watched him, amused. The expert was beginning to see the flaw in his analysis.

'Two masts, Mr Devlin.'

'Were either of those Mast Twenty-two, Mr White?'

'No. They were not.' White suddenly sounded much less sure of himself.

'What about Mast Twenty?'

'Yes. A number of the uses went to Mast Twenty.'

'How many, Mr White?'

'Five.'

'Five of the seven. That's very helpful. And the other two uses, Mr White?'

'They were picked up by a different mast, Mr Devlin.'

White held up the map and pointed to another circled mast. One which seemed even further from the murder site.

'Mast Thirteen.'

'And Mast Thirteen is owned by?'

'The EE network.'

'And is that mast closer to or further from the site of the murders than Mast Twenty?'

'It's further away, Mr Devlin.'

There was a resignation in White's voice. He knew what was coming. Michael could tell. White had seen his own mistake and there was nothing he could now do to rectify it.

'How much further, Mr White?'

'Perhaps half a mile.'

'And how many other cell masts are there between Mast Twenty and Mast Thirteen?'

White counted. Twice. The expert was rechecking. Hoping his first count had been wrong. His face told Michael that it had not. Finally White answered.

'Four, Mr Devlin.'

'Four, Mr White? Four?'

'Yes.'

Michael looked at the jury, feigning puzzlement. Some jurors seemed genuinely perplexed in return. But others were quicker; they had already reached the conclusion Michael had intended.

Michael pressed on for the remaining few jurors. Playing to the crowd.

'So, Mr White. You told this jury today that Simon Kash's phone signal being picked up by Mast Twenty-two proved that the telephone was at the site of the Galloways' murders, very soon after their deaths.'

'Yes.'

'You also used the same data to conclude that Simon Kash's phone was in that same location for a lengthy period *before* their deaths.'

'I did.'

'*And* you told this jury that this second conclusion was *not* undermined by the same phone being picked up by Mast Twenty just ten minutes before.'

'That's correct.'

'You said that although Mast Twenty was half a mile from the scene of the murder and that there were *five* closer masts, it did *not* rule out the phone being at the scene.'

'That's correct.'

'But we *now* know that the same phone was used a further *seven* times in the hour before the 8.45 p.m. use.'

'Yes.'

'*And* we know that *none* of those uses were picked up by Mast Twenty, either.'

'That seems to be the case, yes.'

'Which *must* suggest that Simon Kash's phone was *not* at the murder scene during the hour period in which the Galloway brothers were tortured and killed, mustn't it?'

'Not, erm, not necessarily.' White was on the ropes. 'As I've explained, it's about the nearest *available* cell—'

'Yes, we've all heard and understood that,' Michael interrupted. 'But are you really suggesting that for an *entire hour*, every mast closer than Mast Twenty – all *five* of them – was so full to capacity that they couldn't cover the phone use?'

'That is . . . that is possible, yes.'

All certainty had left White's voice.

'But what about the two uses picked up by Mast Thirteen, Mr White?'

'I don't understand.'

'Of course you do. The two uses of Simon Kash's phone that were *not* picked up by Mast Twenty. Because that mast was probably at capacity too, according to your logic. Those two uses could *not* have come from the murder site, could they?'

'I think it's a stretch to say that, Mr Devlin.' White was standing his ground. He was not doing it well. 'It is perfectly possible that cell usage and capacity was such that this was the nearest available cell mast at that time.'

'But doesn't that completely contradict what you have already told this jury, Mr White?'

'I don't think that it does.'

'Then I think we're doomed to disagree.'

Michael had White beat. Both men knew it, and all Michael had left him was a choice: admit the error. Or refuse and look unreasonable.

White had chosen the latter.

Michael pressed on.

'Because earlier you were asked about the possibility that a mast one mile from a given location would pick up a signal from that location. And your answer – in your own words – was that "a call using a cell a mile away from the caller is extremely unlikely indeed". But now we have identified *two* calls. Calls which, if the phone is at the site of the murder, have registered on a mast over a mile away. And suddenly you're saying that this is perfectly possible? *Come on*. The answer you've given flies in the face of your earlier evidence, doesn't it?'

White did not answer immediately. He seemed to be struggling for a compelling answer. Or maybe just a passable one.

Michael knew that none existed. Only stubbornness remained.

'I don't agree, Mr Devlin. There are differences.'

'Well let's just leave that one for the jury, then, shall we, Mr White?'

Michael glanced at the jury as he spoke. He could see their distaste for White's response. His point was made.

Michael continued.

'But just so I'm clear, you're maintaining that the use of Simon Kash's phone in the hour before 8.45 p.m. – registering as it does on EE's Mast Twenty-two and EE's Mast Thirteen, and never in that hour on any of the five closer masts – is consistent with that telephone being at the site of the murder.'

'Yes.'

'And therefore consistent with that telephone being in the same place as the telephone of Mr O'Driscoll? Despite the two phones registering on different masts?'

'Yes.'

'On the basis of a mast's limited signal capacity.'

'Yes.'

'OK. In that case, just one more thing, Mr White. You explained earlier how a mast will prioritise its own use.'

'I did.'

'So the O2 masts we have looked at would prioritise O2 users, and the EE masts would prioritise EE users.'

'Yes.'

'There is another aspect to this though, isn't there? The aspect that comes into play *after* capacity has been reached. Because the prioritisation continues even then, doesn't it?'

'Yes, that's correct.'

'Which means that if a mast is at capacity and then a user from its *own* network comes calling, the mast will eject a user from a different network to make room. That's right, isn't it?'

'It is, yes.' White was relieved to be back on firm ground. 'That's why mobile calls are sometimes mysteriously cut off. Because, let's say, an EE phone is using up the last space on an O2 mast, then an O2 user tries to "log on". In those circumstances the O2 mast will eject the EE signal to accommodate the O2 signal.'

'That's what I thought. And I'm glad you used that particular example, Mr White. Because, as you've told us, Mast Twenty-two belongs to the O2 network, doesn't it?'

'That's right.'

'And it also happens to be the mast closest to the murder site and therefore the mast most likely to be used by a phone user at that location.'

'If it has available capacity—' White began.

'Yes, we appreciate all of that.' Michael denied White the chance to digress. 'And it's right, isn't it, that Mr O'Driscoll's telephone was picked up by that same O2 mast on each of its uses in the hour prior to the last use at 8.45 p.m., correct?'

'Yes.'

'Which is why you conclude that Mr O'Driscoll's phone was at the murder scene during that time.'

'Yes.'

'Exactly.' Michael picked up the telephone bundle once again. 'Mr White, can we turn to page four of the bundle?'

White did as requested. The judge, jury and all other barristers did the same.

'If we look halfway down the log of phone uses, we see that two of Simon Kash's eight uses are almost simultaneous to two of Darren O'Driscoll's uses. Can you see that?'

White studied the data.

'Yes.'

'Mr O'Driscoll made a call at 8.11 p.m. For three minutes. Registered at Mast Twenty-two.'

'Correct.'

'And at 8.12 p.m. Simon Kash made a one-minute call, registered at Mast Twenty.'

'I see that, yes.'

'Then we look further down. To 8.31 p.m. Mr O'Driscoll made another three-minute call. Mast Twenty-two again. A minute later Simon Kash made what seems to be an aborted call. Registered at Mast Thirteen. A mast that is a full mile away, as we know.'

'Yes.'

'And which is an EE mast.'

'Yes.'

'Are you aware of the phone networks that provide service to Mr O'Driscoll and to Simon Kash, Mr White?'

White stared straight ahead. He finally understood.

'No, Mr Devlin. But I now think I can hazard a guess.'

'Let's not hazard anything, Mr White. It's a matter of agreement between all parties. Mr O'Driscoll is registered to the TalkTalk network. Simon Kash's phone is registered with the O2 network.'

'I see.'

'So please answer me this, Mr White. If Mr O'Driscoll was in the same place as Simon Kash and made a call from his TalkTalk phone, it *could* be picked up by the nearest O2 mast *if* that mast had capacity, could it not?'

'Yes.'

'But if Simon Kash then made a call from the same location and the nearest O2 mast was now *at* capacity, then one of the users from a non-O2 network – maybe Mr O'Driscoll, maybe someone else – would be ejected. Correct?'

'That is correct. Yes.'

'Which means what, Mr White? What is the *only* conclusion we can reach from the fact that Mr O'Driscoll's call was taken by the O2-owned Mast Twenty-two but that the *same mast at the same time* did not pick up Simon Kash's call from an O2 phone?'

White did not answer immediately. The only response he could give undermined him completely.

Hard words to utter, Michael thought. *But he's brought this on himself.*

'Well, Mr White?'

'It means . . . it means that Mast Twenty-two was *not* the closest mast to Simon Kash's phone at the time of those two calls.'

Michael looked towards the jury. He could see that they understood. Still, it never hurt to hammer a good point.

'Which means, Mr White, that at those times – during the hours that the Crown say the Galloway brothers were tortured and murdered – Simon Kash's phone was being used in an entirely different location to Darren O'Driscoll's phone. Isn't that right?'

'That's what the evidence now seems to suggest.' White could give no other answer. 'It seems that the phones were not together after all.'

'Thank you, Mr White.'

Michael took his seat and looked to his left. Simon Kash was facing him. Michael smiled. And, for the first time, Kash smiled back.

THIRTY-EIGHT

'How many passengers were on board?'

'It was a capacity ferry, Sarah.' James Elton's voice was quiet. Slow. 'Almost all on the upper deck, so hardly anyone saw the violence. But they caught the chase and then the guy's dive. And the arrest.'

'Mobile phones?'

'What do you think? I've seen six different videos already. One on YouTube. The rest on Facebook. Makes you wonder why we still pay for cameramen.'

'They've got their uses.' Nathan might not be the best cameraman in the world, but Sarah was warming to him. And he was definitely better than some bystander with a smartphone and a shaky hand. 'So why is this one coming to me? There must be a local team up there?'

'Personal relations,' Elton replied. 'Watch this.'

Elton turned the flat-screen computer that sat on his desk. Halfway, so both he and Sarah could see. Sarah leaned forward as Elton pressed play.

The footage was typical of a smartphone camera. Unsteady in the extreme. People forget that professional recording equipment is shaped as it is for a reason; to provide the cameraman with stability. Reduce that to fit in a palm and the result is what Sarah was now looking at. A recording shaky enough to induce seasickness. That the phone was already on a ferry only worsened the effect.

'What am I looking for?'

'Just wait. You'll see it in a second.'

Less than a second, in fact.

Sarah had spotted him before Elton had finished speaking. A large, powerfully built man sprinting to the front of the boat. The camera was on his right to begin with, its view blocked by the ferry's central structure. But once clear of the obstruction the man was unmissable.

'Do we know who he is yet?'

Sarah did not take her eyes from the screen as she spoke.

'Not yet,' Elton replied. 'Or what he was wanted for. That's where you come in.'

Sarah was about to ask why, but before she could speak the man moved again. This time sprinting towards and then past the camera. For a moment he was lost in the phone's movement as its owner turned, trying to follow his path. But then he was visible again. Moving fast towards the ship's rail.

'What's he doing?'

Sarah was speaking almost to herself. As she asked the question the man was throwing his bag over the rail, before taking a leap of his own. He quickly dropped out of shot as gravity kicked in. The man fell fast and had hit the water long before the camera could catch up.

'That's pretty damned dramatic.' Sarah looked away from the screen. Back towards Elton. 'But I still don't understand what it's got to do with me.'

'It's not over, Sarah.' Elton pointed to the screen. 'Keep watching.'

Sarah did as instructed. She looked back at the screen. The footage was now shakier; the phone's owner was struggling to keep focus. Mainly caused by the movement of the boat but not helped by imperfect equipment.

Sarah could just about see what she assumed was the same man, now in the water. He was not swimming. In fact, he was barely staying afloat.

'What is it I'm supposed to see?' Sarah could feel morbid anticipation growing in her stomach. 'Does he drown?'

'Just keep watching.'

Sarah did not ask again and just watched in silence, her eye on the footage timer.

One minute passed. The man was still above water. Two. Still there, but weakening fast. As the third minute approached the camera switched focus. It moved upwards, away from the near drowning man and towards a boat that was moving in fast.

The camera zoomed in, losing some definition as it did so. But the important part of the image became clear as the boat came to a stop: Joelle Levy, her gun raised and pointed towards the water.

'Levy?' Sarah looked back to Elton, genuinely surprised. 'Levy was making the arrest?'

'Looks that way,' Elton replied. 'Which tells us what?'

'That this guy's got something to do with Longman's murder. Why else would Levy be there?'

'My thoughts exactly. Which begs the question, Sarah: why the hell did *you* not know about this?'

Sarah was startled by Elton's tone. Her boss did not sound happy.

'What does that mean?'

'I thought the two of you had an arrangement. That we'd sit on what we knew for now. In exchange for which she'd keep you updated on all developments. So we'd be ready for an exclusive.'

'That's pretty much what we agreed, yeah.'

'Then what the hell is she doing in Essex? Making an arrest that's all over the bloody internet without giving you any kind of a heads-up?'

'It's not *that* strict an arrangement, James.' Sarah had not been entirely truthful when reporting her interactions with Levy. She had made no mention of what was amounting to a fledgling friendship. 'She can't involve me in everything.'

'Then what use is she to us, Sarah?' Elton was not hiding his irritation. 'We've sat on a big bit of news for her. The crucifixions. The connection between Longman and Blunt. For Christ's sake, we've got evidence of a bloody serial killer and we haven't reported it. And for what? Because I don't see anything coming back our way.'

'It's a long game, James. It's—'

'It's *too* long a game, Sarah. I'm through waiting for Levy to throw us a bone. The next information we get, *we* chase it and when *we're* ready *we* report it. No more keeping quiet to help the police. It's not like they'll ever acknowledge the assistance anyway.'

'But what about what Levy's already told us, James?' Sarah could feel her ethical code being dismantled. 'That was strictly off the record. If we go back on that then we'll never have any trust with the police again. We can't do that.'

Sarah knew that her point had been a good one; there were implications to what he had to decide. Both short term *and* long term.

A compromise was needed.

'OK,' Elton finally said. 'We settle it this way. Anything you've been told up to now – anything you've discussed with Levy on a promise you'll stay quiet – we can honour that; there's no point burning bridges when we don't have to. But anything *new*, Sarah. Anything new is *ours*. Levy is *not* your partner. You don't owe her anything. So the next lead – every bloody lead from now on – is ours. And they're *not* for sharing. You got that?'

'There are legs in the relationship I've built with Levy, James. I really don't think we should throw it away.'

'Then don't throw it away. Stay friendly, Sarah. And by all means be Levy's sounding board. Something good might come of it, so discuss the things you already know to your heart's content. But from now on it's a one-way street. Understand? *Our* leads are *our* leads. Simple as that.'

Sarah opened her mouth to respond. To argue her case one last time. The look on Elton's face told her it would be a waste of breath.

The conversation was over. And so was her deal with Levy.

THIRTY-NINE

Wisdom Penfold sat behind a small wooden table in the cramped interview room. His arms were stretched out ahead of him, joined at the wrist by solid, leather-covered handcuffs.

On Penfold's left was a lawyer. Peter Hughes, a local solicitor, called in to advise the prisoner and to protect his interests. On his right was a three-deck audio tape-recording machine. An antiquated relic of the 1980s. The last time a government had properly invested in its police force.

Penfold looked at the two empty chairs ahead of him and wondered when his interview would begin. His injuries had been treated – his dislocated arm re-set, his bleeding eye bandaged – but still Penfold was in pain. He felt like he had been hit by a truck and the discomfort was making him impatient.

Let's just get this over and done with, Penfold thought. *I know where I'm going*.

Penfold had no faith in God. So he was unsurprised when his 'prayer' went unanswered. The door did not open. His interrogators did not appear. The torment of anticipation continued.

Twenty more agonising minutes passed.

The room offered no distractions. Just pale blue walls, painted who knew how long ago. And Peter Hughes, to whom Penfold had no intention of speaking. He had not asked for a lawyer. He had not refused one, either. But that did not mean he intended to engage with the man.

Finally the room's only door opened and two people walked in. One he recognised: Joelle Levy, the woman in charge. Behind her was another officer. A tall man in his early thirties. Trim and wearing an expensive suit.

The two officers took their seats. At first neither spoke. The man sat closest to the tape machine and so it was for him to press its record button. A high-pitched tone indicated that the tape had begun.

The male officer turned to Penfold.

'Mr Penfold, we are now commencing your recorded interview under caution, following your arrest this morning. The interview will be taped and that tape will be made available to you or to your legal representatives if you are charged with an offence at the conclusion of the interview, or are charged with the same at a later date. Do you understand this as I have explained it to you?'

Penfold did not respond. Cooperation now would not help him. It would not result in a shorter sentence. Penfold knew that. He had nothing to gain from answering questions, and so he would not.

The male officer waited a moment before he continued.

'Can I assume from your silence that you do not intend to answer?'

Penfold continued to stare forward, unblinking. He held the officer's gaze, but he had no intention of responding to these people. The officer seemed unfazed and simply turned to Peter Hughes.

'In which case I will ask Mr Hughes to confirm that Mr Penfold has failed to respond to the question just asked of him.'

'Mr Penfold has refused to respond, yes.'

The officer returned his attention to Penfold.

'Next, Mr Penfold, we need to confirm who is present in the room today. I am Detective Inspector Thomas Chadwick, Major Investigation Team One. With me today is Detective Chief Inspector Joelle Levy, also from MIT One. With you is your legal representative, Mr Peter Hughes. And finally yourself, Mr Wisdom Penfold. Can you confirm that what I have just said is accurate?'

Penfold was determined to say nothing. Not a word. He kept up his stony gaze while the inspector continued to read the required script, informing him of his rights. For all the good they would do him. There wasn't a right in the world that could keep him from rotting in jail.

'Mr Hughes?'

'Yes, Inspector. That is correct.'

Levy leaned forward. An indication to the inspector that she was taking over. The man seemed to understand and sat back into his chair.

Penfold's eyes shifted to Levy.

Now for the real thing, he thought.

'Right, now we've got that out of the way, let's talk about Phillip Longman.'

Penfold's eyes narrowed. His first hint of a response, brought on by the familiar but unexpected name.

'Where were you in the early hours of June 16th?'

Suddenly unsure of where this was going, Penfold still did not answer.

'Let's put it another way then, Mr Penfold. Were you present at the house of Mr Phillip Longman – 14 Magdalen Road in Wandsworth – in the early morning of the 16th of June?'

Still no verbal response. But increasing confusion. *Where the hell is this going?*

'OK. What about on the 18th of June, Mr Penfold? Where were you in the early hours of that date?'

Penfold was shaking his head. He still gave no answer, but now because he simply did not have one.

'Were you present at the home of Mr Adam Blunt – 11 Mill Lane in Southwold, Suffolk – in the early morning of the 18th of June?'

Blunt? That piece of shit? What the fuck is *this?*

'Mr Penfold, these are very serious allegations. Right now you are very much the prime suspect for both crimes. Do you have anything whatsoever to say for yourself?'

Penfold glared at Levy with unadulterated malice, but still he did not speak. He did not know why, or even if it was still the best course. But until he knew more he would not risk giving an answer that could mean more trouble than even he deserved.

'For the benefit of the tape then, Mr Penfold, you are unwilling to tell us your whereabouts when former Lord Chief Justice Phillip Longman and Mr Adam Blunt were murdered in their own homes, on the 16th and the 18th of June respectively.'

Startled, Penfold's jaw literally dropped. He had been chased down by Scotland Yard, forced back to British soil, nearly drowned, and they had not even come after him for the right crime.

Of all the dumb fucking luck.

His shocked reaction was not lost on the woman, he could see that. When she spoke again her words tumbled out fast, concern evident in her voice.

'Mr Penfold, again for the benefit of the tape, you seem to be expressing considerable surprise at the few questions I've asked so far. Am I misinterpreting your body language, Mr Penfold? Or is there something you wish to tell us?'

Penfold looked from Levy to Chadwick. Then to Hughes. He was searching for something. Reassurance? An explanation? He didn't know himself, but nothing was coming.

Enough was enough.

'What the fuck are you goin' on about?'

Penfold's voice was deep. That was unsurprising; he was a big man, as tall as Chadwick and wider than Steven Hale. Levy had already noticed his arms, which seemed to have no wrists. Just thick forearms that connected directly to huge hammer fists.

'What I'm going on about, Mr Penfold, are the murders of Phillip Longman and Adam Blunt. The murders for which you were arrested.'

'The what?' Penfold's shock was convincing. 'Are you fuckin' serious?'

'You're here, aren't you?' The answer came from Chadwick.

'Yeah, I'm 'ere. But not for *that*, surely?'

Levy's unease was worsening. His reaction seemed much too real to be an act. She pressed on, desperately hoping that she was wrong.

'What else, Mr Penfold? What else did you think you were arrested for?'

'Not the fuckin' murder of a judge. And definitely not Adam fuckin' Blunt. I 'ad nothin' to do with any of that. I couldn't 'ave. I didn't even know Blunt was alive, let alone that someone killed 'im.'

Levy glanced towards Chadwick. He shook his head. Almost imperceptibly. It seemed that he had read Penfold's reaction in the same way. It seemed genuine.

But they could not just accept their instincts. Penfold had to be tested.

Levy turned back to the suspect.

'Mr Penfold, the judge who sentenced you to life imprisonment was murdered four days ago. Your lawyer, who refused to appeal that sentence, was murdered *two* days ago. Both in an identical and highly unusual way. In the weeks leading up to these crimes you abandoned your reporting responsibilities as a paroled offender on a life licence, which allowed you to go off the radar. And then today you attempted to flee the country. In the course of your capture you assaulted two individuals. Both of whom are currently critical in hospital, one of whom is unlikely to survive the night. Do you expect us to believe that this is all coincidence?'

'I don't give a shit *what* you believe.' Penfold seemed outraged. 'I've done what I've done, but I ain't bein' put on offer for two murders I knew nothin' about. Am I upset the old bastards are dead? No. No I ain't. Not one bit. But I didn't kill either of 'em.'

'Then what were you running from today?' Chadwick asked the obvious question. 'Because you *were* running, weren't you?'

'Wad' you fink? Did I look like I fancied a fuckin' swim?'

'Then what was it, Mr Penfold?' Levy asked. She could not believe the direction this had taken, but she was determined to follow it to the end. 'You were so desperate to get off of that boat that you nearly killed two people. One of them probably *will* die. *And* you jumped from the top deck. Nearly one hundred feet. What was all that for? What were you running from?'

'Oh, tha's clever.' Penfold's voice had dropped. It was deeper. Almost conspiratorial. 'Is that what this is? You accuse me of somefin' massive so I'll start talkin'? So I use somefin' else as an alibi? What kind of a mug d'you take me for, eh? Eh?'

Levy glanced at Chadwick, who again shook his head. Penfold's last question had clinched it. The man was telling the truth and it felt like a punch to the gut.

'I've no interest in anything else you might or might not have done, Mr Penfold. We're here to find whoever killed Longman and Blunt. If we're to count you out as a suspect then we need to know. What were you running for if it wasn't Phillip Longman and Adam Blunt?'

'YOU KNOW FULL WELL WHAT IT WAS ABOUT!'

Penfold bellowed the words, slamming his cuffed hands on the table as he shouted. It must have sent an agonising jolt through his injured shoulder, Levy observed.

'THEY WERE *YOUR* PEOPLE THAT TRIED TO STOP ME. YOU *KNOW* WHY THOSE COPPERS WERE THERE. SO DON'T TAKE ME FOR A FOOL!'

Levy looked towards Chadwick. It was her turn to be confused, and Chadwick had no explanation to offer; he seemed even more bewildered.

She turned back to Penfold. Her heart had started to race with the implications of his last words.

'What "coppers", Wisdom? The two people you hurt on the boat? Or someone else?'

Levy could not hide her concern or her confusion. She heard it in her voice, and from the ugly smile that now tugged at Penfold's lips she knew that he could read it on her face.

And she could tell that he was suddenly enjoying every moment.

'Are you saying that the man and woman were police officers? Or have you hurt someone else?' The desperation was still there, impossible to hide. And Levy did not even try. The entire agenda had shifted. Longman and Blunt were no longer Levy's first concern. The safety of other police officers had taken their place.

'Have you hurt someone else?'

Penfold's smile only widened in response to Levy's raised voice. He shook his head in amusement and fixed his eyes on Levy's. But he made no attempt to answer.

And nor will he, Levy thought. *Not when he thinks he has the upper hand.*

'This interview is suspended.'

Levy reached across Chadwick and pressed 'stop' on the tape machine. She stood up and opened the door to the interview room where two Essex Police officers stood guard. They were big men. Neither as large as Penfold, but enough for an injured, handcuffed man.

'Take him to his cell.'

The two officers did as instructed, taking Penfold by his arms and pulling him towards the door. Levy turned away as he passed, determined not to see his gloating face for a moment more.

She waited until he was gone before turning to Chadwick.

'Get to the hospital. Find out what you can about the couple from the boat.'

'What about Longman and Blunt?'

'Forget about them for now. This is our priority for the moment.'

'Do you really think the couple he attacked were on the job?'

'I have no idea. All I know is Penfold's not our man, but he was running from something. Maybe another squad was on to him for something, which means that we might have two coppers in hospital fighting for their lives. Right now, *that's* what matters.'

FORTY

'So is that it, Mr Devlin? Does that mean I can go home?'

Simon Kash sat in his regular seat in Interview Room Six. For the first time it did not seem to swallow him. Kash was still small, but he finally seemed energised.

'We're not even close to that, Simon.' Michael was sorry to disappoint him. To see the hope in Kash's eyes begin to fade. 'It's just one witness. There's a lot still to come.'

'But he agreed my phone wasn't there at the murder. That it wasn't with Darren's phone?'

'That's right, Simon, but what does that actually prove? It proves your *phone* wasn't there. It doesn't prove that *you* weren't there. It isn't like you and your phone can never be apart, is it?'

'But we weren't apart, Mr Devlin. I had my phone with me the whole time. I always do.'

Michael was pleased to see some passion. It was about time.

The separation from O'Driscoll is starting to work.

'I know that, Simon. But we've no evidence of that beyond your word. And the Crown still has evidence that they say puts you at the scene.'

'You mean Terry Colliver? But he's a liar, Mr Devlin. I was never there.'

'I know that too. And I'll try to prove that, Simon. But that's for later. That's still to come.'

Kash seemed to deflate. It made him look more childlike. As if Michael had taken away a new toy. Michael could not help but feel for him. He did not want him to lose hope.

'Look, Simon. I'm not saying that we didn't make great progress today. We did. It just wasn't quite as much as you'd like to think. It was very important that we undermined the phone evidence, because it was important evidence. And now it's gone.'

'It's better than gone,' Jenny Draper interrupted. The first time she had spoken since Kash had been brought into the room. 'Now it's evidence *for* us, Simon. To support that you were somewhere else.'

'But only to an extent.' Michael did not appreciate Draper's contribution. He did not believe in false hope. A sharp glance was enough to tell her exactly that. 'Like I said, it proves that your *phone* wasn't there.'

'But I don't understand.' Kash was as engaged as Michael had ever seen him. 'Why is it evidence for the prosecution but not evidence for us?'

'It *is* evidence for us, Simon.' Michael was surprised by the question. Kash was much more incisive – and much more confident – than he had ever been. 'But in the same way that your *phone* being there isn't absolute proof that *you're* there, the phone *not* being there doesn't automatically mean that *you're* not.'

Kash did not reply immediately and Michael did not rush him. He'd been startled but pleased by the uncustomary flash of spirit, and he wished that he had not been forced to dampen it with his answer. But still, even that single moment was progress.

It's got to be the separation from O'Driscoll. It's doing exactly what I'd hoped.

'What about the final call?' It was Draper who broke the silence. 'Simon's phone is still located close to the scene on the last call. Close to Darren's.'

Kash looked at Michael for an answer.

'That depends on what Simon tells us.' Their case still depended on Kash's instructions; neither Michael nor Draper – nor any barrister – could just invent the facts of a defence. They needed Kash to understand that. 'Because there are possibilities, aren't there? It could be that the signal was picked up by the nearest available mast while Simon was half a mile away, and that the same mast just happened to be the one nearest to

O'Driscoll's phone while he was finishing up with the Galloways. That's possible. But it's also very weak, especially after everything we achieved with the phone expert this afternoon.'

Michael paused and waited for Kash to look up. He needed Kash to understand this – to engage – because if he did not then they had lost, phones or no phones. He did not speak again until Kash had met his eye.

'Another possibility, of course, is that Simon *was* there after the murder,' he continued, satisfied that Kash was giving him his full attention. 'It's possible that Simon was ordered by Darren O'Driscoll – via a third party – to come and collect him, because Darren needed to get away from the scene of the crime. If Simon did as he was told by Darren then *that* would explain why his phone was present just before O'Driscoll left the scene.

'Those are the two possibilities I can see from the evidence, Simon. Either catastrophic bad luck with a phone mast, or you were doing what you always do, and by that I mean you were doing what Darren *ordered* you to do. I don't know which is true – I have a strong suspicion but I don't know – but you do. And I need you to tell me so I can win this fight for you. Because if I'm right and the answer is scenario two and you gave me permission to prove it, well, then you just might have a chance of going home.'

Michael stopped speaking. He had taken it far enough.

Kash had looked down again at the suggestion of O'Driscoll summoning him to the scene. In the same moment his visible discomfort returned. Michael read the body language for what it was. Confirmation that the 'second possibility' was not a possibility at all. It was the truth.

Michael tapped Draper's hand and indicated towards Kash with a movement of his head. A signal for her to step in.

'Is that what happened, Simon?' Draper's voice was light as she performed the delicate balancing act between charm and authority. She did so expertly. 'Were you forced to collect O'Driscoll? To drive him away? Is that what happened?'

Kash looked up, deep into Draper's eyes. Michael could see that he wanted to answer, to give Draper the thing she sought

Between us we're breaking through.

'You can tell us, Simon,' Draper continued. 'You're safe now. O'Driscoll can't touch you. Just tell us and we'll make sure it stays that way.'

Michael watched as Draper worked. The effect on Kash could not be clearer. Or more understandable. Draper's charms had worked on far more confident men, Michael knew. Directed against a bullied, inexperienced boy when the rest of world was against him? Kash did not stand a chance.

Thank God she's on his *side*, Michael thought.

'I . . . I can't.' Finally Kash spoke. 'I want to. I swear I do. But I can't. If I tell you the truth about what happened then I'll end up dead. I know I will.'

'How, Simon?' Michael stepped in. 'If you tell us the truth then Darren O'Driscoll will be in prison for the rest of his life. He can't hurt you from where he'll be.'

'He's not the only O'Driscoll, Mr Devlin.'

Kash's answer was simple. Darren's brother, Patrick. A man willing to threaten Michael in the street.

Michael had not found Patrick intimidating. But Kash would. Michael now regretted that he had not given in to his instinct and hospitalised Patrick O'Driscoll when he had the chance. Not for himself, or even for Sarah, but for the scared boy sitting across from him now.

'I don't want you to worry about Patrick O'Driscoll.' Kash raised his head. He seemed surprised that Michael knew the name. 'He's not worth your time, Simon. And he's definitely not worth a life sentence.'

Kash shook his head. His eyes began to fill with tears.

'I can't talk about any of this,' he said. 'I really can't. I just want to go back to my cell.'

'Simon, I . . .'

'I want to go back to my cell, Mr Devlin. Please.'

Michael studied Kash, wondering if now was the time to push the issue. He quickly concluded that it was not.

'OK, Simon. You go. We'll see you in the morning.'

'Thank you, Mr Devlin.'

Kash rose to his feet and reached out his right hand. It was the first time he had instigated a shake. Michael returned the gesture and felt Kash's small hand disappear into his own.

'And Mr Devlin,' Kash spoke in a voice now close to a whisper, 'thank you for today.'

FORTY-ONE

Derek Reid glanced to his right, towards the red wine glass that sat on the small table next to his leather chair. The glass was empty. Just a drop of Burgundy and a little sediment to show for the three bottles it had held so far today.

Reid had been home for three hours, give or take.

Phillip Longman's funeral service in Temple Church had taken an hour. It had been sombre and respectful, a fine tribute to a man who deserved it. Most mourners had left at its end, their respects paid. Those that remained had followed the hearse from Temple to Mortlake Cemetery in South West London – Surrey, practically – where Longman was finally buried.

The wake that followed was a final obligation. Reid did not want to be there; he wanted to grieve alone, in his own way. But he could not leave Russell Longman to deal with the wake alone, and Russell's brothers were sure to be no help. One of them – Matthew – was an unassuming man lost in his own grief. The other – Peter – was an abrasive, combative sod at the best of times; a problem, not a solution. So Reid had put off his own need to mourn and had accompanied Russell Longman to his home, where the wake was held.

An entire afternoon of manners and small talk. The last thing Reid wanted as he held back his own tears.

It was gone 3 p.m. by the time Reid reached his front door, exhausted and emotional. An entire morning and half an afternoon before Reid had the opportunity to properly grieve, in the only way he knew how.

Reid had always been a man with passions. In his younger days it had been women that drove him; the reason for his three failed marriages and why his personal worth had plummeted with each divorce. He had finally learned his lesson and had since grown to concentrate on his other passions: food and wine.

The first kept him overweight. The second kept him short of cash.

Within forty minutes Reid had made himself a gourmet meal. Fillet steak topped with creamy wild mushroom, onions and truffle shavings. Accompanied by fat, triple-cooked chips, first prepared the evening before. Next he selected a 2005 Maison Joseph Drouhin Chambertin. An expensive Burgundy red. £100 per bottle at retail. Far too expensive for Reid to drink alone. At least on any other day.

Neither the food nor the first bottle had lasted long. Reid worked through both in the reclining leather chair in his living room. His fifty-inch wall-mounted television had kept him company, playing a stream of recorded comedy from his TiVo.

Good food. Fine wine. The distraction of humour. Exactly what he needed.

Two more bottles had followed. Four more recorded shows. The comedies were increasingly just background noise, breaking the silence of the house. With each glass Reid thought more about Longman. About his loss. Until finally he could properly mourn his oldest friend.

The glass was empty. So was the bottle. Good reason for Reid to push himself to his feet. He did not notice the groan that accompanied his movement. It happened every time, caused by a combination of age and weight.

Reid picked up both the wine bottle and glass and headed to the kitchen. His stride was steady, even after three bottles. One of the few benefits of Reid's size was his alcohol tolerance. The three bottles *had* hit him. But not as they would have affected most. It would take a few more before Reid was as drunk as he wanted to be.

One last bottle of the same Chambertin sat on the kitchen worktop. Another £100. Reid was long past caring. He opened the bottle, filled a fresh glass and made his way back to the living room.

The sound of a mobile ringtone stopped Reid before he could take his seat. He looked around the room, trying to locate the sound.

At first he could not place it. The alcohol had taken at least *that* much of a toll.

Finally he spotted the illuminated handset. It was on a side table next to the living-room door.

Reid picked up the vibrating phone, checked the name of the caller and only then flicked the answer icon from left to right.

'Sarah.' Reid spoke once the phone was at his ear. 'Everything OK?'

'Yes, all fine. I just wanted to check up on you, make sure you're holding up after today.'

'I'm OK, Sarah. Really I am.'

'And how was the funeral?' Sarah asked.

'It was a lovely service. As lovely as they *can* be, anyway. He had a good send-off at least.'

Reid felt tears threaten his eyes as he spoke.

'That's good,' Sarah replied. 'Now listen. You don't need to be by yourself tonight if you don't want to be. Michael's just up the road from you. He can come and stay tonight if you like?'

'That's really nice of you, Sarah. But please, tell Michael I'm good on my own. I honestly couldn't face company right now.'

'What are you going to do?'

'Just have a few more bottles of wine and watch some TV. Then probably an early night, once the wine kicks in.'

'That's no good at a time like this, Derek. You need to be with friends. Please, let me send Michael over to you.'

Reid was unsure how much longer he could hold himself together. The call was not helping.

'Honestly, Sarah. I mean what I said. I don't need Michael to check on me. This is my first chance to be on my own since Phillip died and I need that time. Please, just tell him to give me a few days.'

'Well ... OK,' Sarah said, after a brief hesitation. 'But remember we're here the moment you need us, Derek. And remember we love you.'

'OK. I love you guys too. Thanks.'

Reid took the phone from his ear, disconnected the call and switched it off entirely. He frisbee'd the dead handset onto his couch.

No more calls tonight.

The fresh bottle and glass still sat on the table beside Reid's chair. He filled the glass without sitting, put it to his lips and drained the contents. Then he wiped a tear from his eye. It was replaced by another.

Reid no longer had control of his emotions. The drink had finally hit. *It's about bloody time.*

Derek Reid was not an intrusive neighbour. He took little interest in the comings and goings of the quiet Islington square in which he lived. Paid little attention to either his neighbours or their visitors. Reid respected the privacy of those around him, and he hoped those neighbours would return the courtesy.

It was an ethos shared by all in Lonsdale Square. A community of wealthy professionals, all seemed determined to keep themselves to themselves. These were people who relied on regular police patrols for their safety and whose trust in that protection made them complacent.

And so these were not people who would have noticed the pale-eyed stranger who had passed their doors three times in less than an hour.

FORTY-TWO

'But remember we're here the moment you need us, Derek. And remember we love you.'

Sarah listened to Derek Reid's response. Then to the sound of the line going dead. She took the phone away from her ear. Placed it back into her pocket.

I hope he really is OK.

Of Michael's two closest friends, it was Reid that Sarah knew best. That was inevitable. The other was Joe Dempsey, now based in New York but a man Sarah doubted she would really know even if he lived next door. She would never forget how much she and Michael both owed to Dempsey. How could she? But it was Reid with whom she had built her own friendship.

It was Reid she had grown to love.

Sarah knew that Michael was concerned for his old pupil-master. That he feared the impact of Longman's death. So did Sarah.

Like Michael, Reid was a man of few friendships. But also like Michael, when he had them they were intense. Michael was like a brother to Reid. Sarah knew that. And she also knew that Longman had been as close as a father.

It made her worry for Reid.

He'll be fine, Sarah told herself. *Let him get on with it. You've got a job to do.*

Sarah forced the thought of Reid from her mind and took a drink from the water bottle she held in her hand. It was much needed in the heat. Somehow it was still stifling at 6 p.m.

She dabbed a delicate sheen of sweat from her brow, careful not to take her on-screen make-up with it. She looked across the street as she did so. Towards New Scotland Yard and the mass of reporters and TV cameras that had formed outside of its main doors.

Two outside-broadcast trucks had parked end to end while Sarah had been using her phone. They blocked her direct route from the river side to the huddled press, but Sarah slipped between them and headed towards Nathan Benson. Her young cameraman had managed to position himself in the centre of the group, securing his lens the best line of sight.

He's learning fast, Sarah thought.

'Any update?' she asked as she reached Benson.

'Nothing we don't already know,' Benson replied. 'You really think what happened on the ferry was connected to Longman?'

'Has to be. Why else were Joelle Levy and MIT One there? The guy's got to be a suspect.'

'You'd think they'd at least give us a hint. We've all been here long enough.'

The comment came from a cameraman Sarah had never met. She would have remembered the birthmark above his right eye.

'Perhaps they're too busy trying to catch a killer.' Sarah felt the need to defend Levy. Not that Levy needed the help. 'Probably a bit more urgent than press relations, huh?'

'I guess we'll find that out soon enough.' Birthmark's tone was either naturally sour or Sarah had touched a nerve. 'You know, once they're finished with the important stuff.'

'Whatever, pal.' Sarah's tone was as dismissive as her words. She turned as she spoke, stepped closer to Benson and lowered her voice. 'When the statement starts, make sure all that guy's camera can see is your back.'

'With pleasure.' Benson smiled at the instruction. 'Where will you be?'

'Nothing to be gained from shouting out pointless questions,' Sarah explained. 'I'll head back across the street and give you a clear view.'

'Got it, boss.'

Sarah gripped Benson's shoulder. Just for a moment. It was both a 'thank you' and a 'good luck' in one gesture, and without another word she manoeuvred her way back through the crowd. Back towards the riverside of Victoria Embankment, where she had been standing when she had called Reid.

Sarah only felt her phone vibrating once she had come to a halt. She answered as soon as she saw the caller ID.

'Hi. Everything OK?'

'Have you got time to meet?' Levy asked.

'When?'

'Forty-five minutes. An hour at most.'

'Storeys Wine Bar. Across from the back of Westminster Abbey.'

'I'll be there.'

The phone line disconnected but Sarah did not put her handset away. Instead she tapped the messaging icon, found 'Nathan Benson' and began to type: *You're on your own, Nathan. I'll explain later.*

It was 6.30 p.m. by the time Joelle Levy walked through the pub door. Sarah had been waiting for half an hour. Less time than Levy had estimated.

Sarah began to get to her feet to catch Levy's attention. There was no need. Levy had already seen her, so Sarah retook her seat.

'That was quick for a press conference.'

'They don't drag out when you're not saying much,' Levy replied. 'It's my round, Sarah. Same order as last time?'

'Perfect.'

Sarah watched as Levy headed to the bar, noticing her unusual presence as she went. The DCI was not a tall woman and was in no way physically imposing, yet she had something about her which got her noticed. And which got her served immediately.

Sarah had experienced it herself the first time they had met. Back at Longman's house. Yet she still could not place what it was. An innate authority, perhaps? Or maybe just natural charisma? Whatever the answer, Levy had it by the truckload.

Sarah said nothing as Levy returned to the table, took her seat and passed across a large white wine. Only when Levy raised her own glass of vodka and tonic did Sarah speak.

'Cheers.'

'Cheers,' Levy replied, touching glasses. 'You've no idea how welcome this is after today.'

Both women took a mouthful of their drinks. Once again neither spoke as they enjoyed their brains' chemical reward. It made Levy exhale long and hard. Sarah waited for her to finish.

'Long one, was it?' Sarah finally asked.

'You could say that.'

'Successful?'

'Not for us, no.' Levy took another sip of her drink. Continued. 'We made a significant arrest, I guess. Just not in the right bloody case.'

'Any of this for public consumption?'

'Only the really general parts, Sarah. The rest is off the record.'

Sarah hesitated. What Levy had said was a problem in light of her earlier conversation with Elton. She considered telling Levy that but decided against it.

At least for now.

'Can I ask why you're telling me then, Joelle?'

'Same as before Sarah. So you can have your story ready for when it comes *on* the record.' Levy looked down for a moment. Then back up. Continued. 'And to be honest, I need to get a shitty day off my chest. Is that OK?'

'I'm happy to be a friend, Joelle. Once I know where the line is there's no way I'll cross it.'

Sarah welcomed Levy's request. It made the conversation personal, not professional.

Which means Elton can go to hell, she thought.

'Thanks, Sarah. I really appreciate it.'

'So. What happened?'

'Wisdom bloody Penfold happened.' Levy's face twisted as she said the name, like it had left a bad taste in her mouth.

'Is that the guy from the boat?' Sarah asked.

'One and the same.'

'I take it from what you just said that he *wasn't* involved in Longman's murder? Or Blunt's?'

'Correct. I thought he was good for it. He ticked every sodding box, Sarah. Every bloody one. He was represented by Blunt until the relationship fell apart. He was sentenced by Longman and he was recently released. Add to that a capacity for serious violence and it was like he was screaming "I did it!". That's why we went after him.'

'Well, you sure as hell got the capacity-for-violence part right. I heard the guy he attacked on the ferry didn't make it?'

'You mean the *cop* he attacked on the ferry.'

'The what?' This was news to Sarah. 'Are you serious?'

'As serious as it gets. The guy he killed was an undercover police officer. So was the woman he hospitalised.'

'Jesus Christ. Were they from your team?'

'No. We knew nothing about them.' Levy's voice was as weak as Sarah had ever heard it. 'We didn't know they were cops. Not until Penfold basically told us.'

'You mean after they'd been hospitalised? How is that possible?'

'Undercover officers don't carry ID. Too risky. So we had no way to know. Plus surveillance officers aren't routinely armed, so the poor bastards had no chance when he jumped them.'

Sarah took a moment to think. The news was a shock. It also led to an inevitable question.

'But if the victims weren't part of your team, why were they following him?'

'Because they thought he might lead them to some very serious players on the Continent. Turns out that while Penfold was inside he got very chummy with a guy called Barry Ireland.'

'The gangster?' Sarah had heard the name. Few in her profession had not. 'That's a dangerous connection.'

'But also a profitable one. Ireland has six years left to serve, but he's still under investigation for some serious stuff. Things that could turn that six years into the rest of his life. First among *them* is the Bond Street Jewellery Massacre.'

'Shit.'

There was no more appropriate a response. The Bond Street Jewellery Massacre was legendary. A robbery of three million pounds worth of cut diamonds in which every employee of the jeweller lost their life. Six men and women, all executed in brutal style. No one had ever been charged with the crime and no diamonds had ever been recovered.

'You think Ireland was behind it?' Sarah asked.

'It's not that *I* think it,' Levy replied. 'It's that the National Crime Agency thinks it. Or that they *know* it, to be more accurate.'

'Well if they know Ireland was involved why don't they arrest him?'

'Because it's not that simple. It's one thing for the NCA to know what's happened. It's something else entirely for them to prove it. They need admissible evidence, which is why they were following Penfold.'

'But how could Penfold have been involved? He was in prison when Bond Street happened.'

'He wasn't involved. But the NCA knew how tight he'd become with Ireland inside. They've got informants everywhere and bugs all over the place, including in prison. So they knew Ireland had made a deal with Penfold. That Penfold would collect half the diamonds from one of Ireland's old team, and that he would take them across to Holland. To where Ireland still has an operation. The NCA knew that was happening, so they were following Penfold. To catch him at Ireland's place in Amsterdam, diamonds in hand. Which would connect Ireland to the robbery.'

'And what was Penfold getting out of it?'

'The deal was five hundred thousand pounds. According to the prison bug, anyway.'

'The prison bug? So all this was recorded?'

'It was. For all the use that turned out to be.'

Levy shook her head at her own comment. Sarah understood why. It was a peculiarity of English law that recordings from covertly placed bugs are generally inadmissible as evidence. Instead the police use them for intelligence gathering, allowing them to catch criminals in the act. Often it worked. But sometimes it could go wrong.

Today, it seemed, was sometimes.

Levy took another mouthful of her drink. Her glass was almost done.

'Anyway, that *was* the agreement. Now it looks like Penfold went off script. The NCA raided Ireland's associate today. The guy who had been holding the diamonds. They found him beaten to death in his flat – his boyfriend, too – and all the diamonds gone. The theory right now is that five hundred thousand wasn't enough for Penfold. The NCA didn't realise it but he wasn't leading them to Ireland's men. He was planning to sell the entire diamond stash for himself.'

'So that's why he attacked those poor people? Because he'd murdered Ireland's guy?'

'That's what the NCA believe, yeah. Which scuppers their operation against Ireland. But at least they get Penfold on two murder counts. Well, three now. And in the meantime my case is back at square one.'

It was Sarah's turn to exhale. It was a lot of information to take in. Diamonds. Executions. Double-cross. Nothing Sarah had been expecting when she had taken Levy's call thirty minutes earlier. Nor when Levy had classed the conversation as 'personal'.

Sarah took a long sip of her wine as she processed the new material. Finally she had a question.

'If this guy is capable of murder – and clearly he is – why does that rule him out for Longman and Blunt? What's to stop him doing that *and* killing Ireland's guy for the diamonds?'

'NCA surveillance.'

Levy finished her own drink – hardly a mouthful – before continuing.

'They've had him under surveillance for two weeks. Not twenty-four seven; he managed to lose them when he collected the diamonds and killed Ireland's man – he was a bit more careful with his movements that day, for obvious reasons – but they were on him at the relevant times. So we know he wasn't anywhere near Longman or Blunt on the nights they died.'

'Shit.'

'My thoughts exactly,' Levy fidgeted with her empty glass as she continued. 'Which takes us right back to the beginning. Penfold was the only real suspect we found by cross-referencing Blunt and Longman's cases. Which means we're back where we started, searching for a needle in Longman's haystack of case files.'

Sarah sat back, slowly shaking her head from side to side. It was not a rejection of what Levy had said. It was despair.

They really are nowhere.

'So it's back to the three-file system?' she finally asked.

'Has to be,' Levy replied. 'What else is there?'

Sarah had no answer.

'I guess there is one upside for you, though,' Levy continued.

'What's that?' Sarah asked, confused.

'Well if it's not Penfold, that means Michael's friend Derek Reid's no longer under threat.'

Sarah smiled.

Finally some good news in all of the bad.

FORTY-THREE

'Have you ever been so bored in your life?'

The question was asked by Police Constable Richard Haye. He was twenty-two years of age, six foot seven and, as his colleague Police Constable Colin Moxon had noticed, seemed to lack anything resembling an imagination.

Making him the worst possible person with whom to be cooped up in a car for an eight-hour close-protection shift, Moxon thought.

Unlike Haye, Moxon had done this sort of thing before. Usually it involved staying close to a key witness before a trial. Only once before had it been to protect a potential imminent victim. In none of those cases had the protection ultimately proved necessary. Moxon did not doubt that the same would be true tonight.

'Why don't you step out of the car and stretch your legs?' Moxon asked. As much for his own relief as for Haye's.

'I can't do that,' Haye replied. He seemed shocked at the suggestion. 'What if someone sees me?'

'Are you serious?' Moxon could hardly believe what he was hearing. 'We're sitting in full uniform right outside this guy's house, in a fully marked bloody police car. Short of a neon sign, there's no way on Earth we could be any more conspicuous. Which is the whole bloody point.'

Haye still seemed confused.

'Jesus Christ, Richard. Is the oxygen not reaching you up there? We're not here to lure whatever crazy bastard is after this bloke into his home and jump him. If we were there'd be a whole lot more of us. We're here to be *seen*. So the crazy bastard stays away. It's not bloody rocket science.'

Haye nodded his head. At last he seemed to understand. Moxon could only wonder how long he'd remember; how soon he would need it explained again.

Christ knows where they find them these days, he thought to himself.

Haye was already halfway out of the car when its radio crackled into life.

'Sierra Granada to Sierra Four, over.'

Sierra Four was the call sign for the car. Sierra Granada was its home station, Islington.

'Sierra Four, over,' Moxon answered.

'Sierra Four, operation is suspended. Perceived threat was incorrect. Head back to the station, over.'

'Understood, over,' Moxon replied.

He turned to Haye, who was now fully back inside the car.

'Looks like you'll have to stretch your legs back at the station.'

'Why do you think that is?'

'You heard them. They got their information wrong. All we need to know.'

Moxon had already started the engine as he spoke. Within moments they were moving. Moments more and they had left Lonsdale Square behind.

The figure in the shadows watched as the police car drove away.

It had been parked outside Derek Reid's house since at least 5 p.m., but no earlier than 4 p.m., because it had appeared some time between Pale Eye's second and third passes of the address.

And it had posed a problem.

Maybe not a problem. But it was still not ideal.

Nothing could be allowed to get in his way. Nothing could be allowed to derail his plan. What was going to happen here was going to happen tonight. And if that meant that the men in the car died, well, then they died.

So no, not a problem. Just an inconvenience.

That inconvenience disappeared as the car drove away.

He had no idea why it was leaving. Nor did he know if it would return. The first of those facts did not matter. The second did. And so he would wait and he would observe. If they came back, then he would do what he had to do.

And when that was complete, he would do what he *wanted* to do.

FORTY-THREE

Steven Hale tightened his grip on his pistol. A Glock 17. Standard issue. Seventeen 9×19mm Parabellum rounds. It was seventeen more than he intended to use. But it paid to be prepared for the worst.

Hale looked around. Ahead of him were two officers. Huge men. Each at least six foot four. Each with fifty pounds or more on Hale himself.

The man on the right carried what they called 'the Big Key'. A sixteen kilogram battering ram designed to send over three tonnes of impact force through any door lock. His partner carried a Heckler and Koch MP5. The semi-automatic assault weapon preferred by the Metropolitan Police Unit SO19.

Beside Hale was DS Dean King. Though smaller than the two SO19 officers at the top of the stair, King was still a big man. Similar in natural stature to Hale but lacking Hale's expanding waistline. King was armed with the same standard-issue firearm: a Glock 17 pistol. Both men would have preferred the MP5 but neither had the training.

Hale looked behind. The short staircase that led up from the street to the first floor was full with officers from SO19. Twelve more firearms specialists, all standing two to a step.

The decision to bring SO19 support had been inevitable. Every item of intelligence the Trident unit held on Ed Burrell said the same thing. That the man was obsessed with weaponry. Everything from samurai swords to grenades, from ceremonial daggers to combat rifles. No one knew how many firearms Burrell possessed. Or what types they might be. All that was certain was that he and his men were armed and that they enjoyed the confidence that gave them.

A confidence that could only be dented by a show of overwhelming force.

The SO19 assault team had been assembled quickly. Fourteen men, all highly trained specialists. Hale had issued their orders: that an armed engagement was to be avoided at all costs. They were there for a clean arrest. Burrell was to be detained, questioned and his role in Ferris's death established. Nothing else would do.

With the mission statement clear, the team had travelled to Brixton: SO19, Hale and King. Sixteen armed police officers. A force to be reckoned with.

Hale had been surprised to note how similar Burrell's set-up was to Ferris's own. The same 'no questions asked' style of pawn shop below. The same first-floor office space. The same cramped staircase leading up from the street.

The only real difference seemed to be the location. Popes Road instead of Electric Avenue. Barely half a mile apart.

The team had made its way along Popes Road. Quickly and quietly and in tight single file. Moving as close to the shopfronts as space would allow. No one looking down from Burrell's office could have seen them approach. Within seconds they were through the stairway door and lining up as directed.

Ready to breach. Ready to make their arrest.

Hale looked back towards the office door and saw the left-hand giant raise his hand. His five fingers were extended.

Hale felt his stomach tense. The first telltale sign of the adrenaline rush that was sure to follow.

Here we go.

Four fingers.

First round chambered.

Three fingers.

Christ, we could use Levy right about now.

Two fingers.

Deep breaths

One finger.

Calm. Calm.

None.

'GO GO GO GO!'

The shout came as the left-hand giant lowered his last finger. At the same moment the right-hand giant swung the Big Key. It impacted the door at the top of the stairs and ripped through it like paper.

The signal to move.

Hale was second through the door with his pistol raised, sweeping the room. Ahead of him was the left-hand giant. Just behind was King.

Within moments the room was filled. Eight armed police officers. Highly trained and ready for anything. Eight more had continued moving up, climbing the second staircase. A safety sweep of the floors above.

Ed Burrell sat at the far end of the room, behind a desk near identical to the one Hale had seen in Ferris's office. A crude attempt to match his rival.

It'll take more than a table, Hale thought. *You'd need to grow eight inches for one thing.*

The raid had not been expected. That much was clear. Burrell and the room's four other occupants had frozen at the sight of the first weapons. Just three sets – Hale and King's pistols, plus the first giant's MP5 – had been enough. No one had moved. That was not going to change as five more MP5s entered the room.

Hale moved forward, towards Burrell and ignoring the other four. His pistol remained up, aimed squarely at Burrell's chest. Hale had heard stories about the man in the last twenty-four hours. Stories of irrational violence. He would not be taking any risks.

'Edward Burrell.' Hale spoke with authority. 'I am arresting you for the murders of Leon Ferris, Kevin Tennant, Harvey Ellis and Tyrone Leach. You do not have to say anything but it may harm your defence if you fail to mention when questioned something that you later rely on in court. Anything you do say may be used in evidence against you. Do you understand this caution as I have explained it to you?'

Burrell did not answer. Nor did he take his eyes from the pistol that was aimed at his chest. The man was suffering from shock. Hale could see that and it made him wary of getting too close. Shock can have many different effects; most common is inaction, but it depends upon the man. Burrell had a reputation. A tendency to erupt. There was no telling how he might react when taken by surprise.

Hale's pistol remained steady as he moved around the desk. Burrell's men were being dealt with by others. They were already on the floor. Already being cuffed. Burrell, though, was still in his seat.

'Get to your feet.'

Hale's voice was steady. Firm. And backed up by the weapon still aimed at Burrell's heart.

Burrell did as instructed, slowly and deliberately. The shock seemed to be fading, replaced with an expression of fury. Hale tightened his grip on his pistol and took a step back, well out of Burrell's range.

The difference in their size was significant – Hale large, Burrell surprisingly small – and right now only Hale was armed. But the look on Burrell's face said that he would act if he could.

Hale would not give him the chance.

'Get on the floor. Face first with your arms outstretched ahead.'

Burrell stayed exactly where he was. His eyes had now left the pistol. They were instead fixed on Hale's own, their message one of intense anger. Hale could see the murderous intent within them; he could somehow almost feel it on his own skin. Burrell's threat was now electric in the air. And surprisingly effective. Hale was not easily intimidated. But somehow Ed Burrell – a small man with eight guns now aimed directly at him – was managing exactly that.

'On the floor, Burrell,' Hale forced more confidence back into his voice. Raised it to a shout. 'NOW!'

Burrell did not move. Hale could see why. The man was weighing his options. Would he comply? Or would they have to force him? There was no doubt how this would end. With Burrell face down and cuffed. But the journey to that conclusion was in Burrell's hands.

'I won't ask again.' Enough was enough. A message that was clear in Hale's voice. 'Get on the damn floor or I'm gonna put you there.'

Burrell's intensity did not lessen, but his resistance did. He seemed to have realised the futility of his position. Slowly he put his hands behind his head and dropped to his knees. One at a time, his eyes never leaving Hale's as he descended. The anger was still there. The hate. But they had been overruled by reality.

Burrell could not win this. Not now. And there was no point in being injured for a lost cause.

He lowered his upper body to the floor and stretched his arms out ahead of him, awaiting the inevitable cuffs. Hale kept his pistol steady throughout; still aimed, but now at Burrell's head. He did not lower the weapon until two SO19 officers had secured Burrell's wrists behind his back and lifted him from the floor.

Hale stepped back as Burrell was pulled from the room. He returned Burrell's stare as the smaller man passed him. The animosity was obvious. Hale did not doubt that, if given the slightest chance, Burrell would have killed him where he stood.

'Nice guy.' Hale approached King as Burrell was bundled through the door. His heart was racing. 'He definitely chose the right career.'

'I don't think the priesthood was ever an option,' King replied. 'Nasty little bastard.'

'Let's hope we can keep him off the streets, then,' Hale said, before taking a few moments to survey the room. 'Does this remind you of anywhere?'

'You mean Ferris's office?'

'Exactly. It's like Burrell's paying tribute. Only with a cheaper version.'

'Makes sense,' King replied. 'By all accounts Burrell was obsessed with Ferris. But judging by this place it might be more than that. This makes it look like he wanted to actually *be* Ferris.'

'Doesn't that concern you?' A doubt was beginning to eat at the back of Hale's mind. The sort of thing that would bother Levy, he thought. 'That sort of an obsession?'

'Should it?' King asked.

'I don't know. It's just . . . it's just, you know, an obsessive killing their obsession? That's not unusual. In fact it's common enough that we know how they tend to do it: they almost always do it themselves. Close up and personal. But if Burrell was behind Ferris's death, he has to have hired *someone else* to do the job. It's . . . it's just not typical.'

Hale shook his head. Perhaps he was trying too hard to ape Levy. He forced himself to dismiss the thought.

'It's probably nothing,' he said. 'I mean, this was a business thing, first and foremost. So let's just get that little shit into an interview room and get some answers.'

Hale took one final look around the room and – as much as he resisted it – the same doubt resurfaced. He forced it back down once again and turned towards the door. Just as an SO19 officer walked through it.

'Sir.' The officer made a direct line for Hale. 'I think you'd better see this.'

'What is it?'

'Drugs, sir. More drugs than I've ever seen.'

Hale moved quickly. King too. They followed the SO19 officer out of the room. He turned left and moved up to the second tier of the staircase, followed by the more senior officers.

It took them up one more floor. To a room just as big as the office below.

'Jesus Christ.'

Hale could think of no other words. What greeted him as he stepped through the door did not need them. The sight spoke for itself.

'Holy fuck.' King was just a step behind.

The room was directly above Burrell's office but it had not enjoyed the same attention. It was nothing but floorboards, whitewashed walls and windows covered in masking tape. Like a room awaiting the attentions of a decorator.

That must be the intention, Hale thought as he gazed at the room's contents. *To fool the people in the buildings across the street.*

It would have been an effective deception from out there. But not from inside, where it was spoiled by four wooden pallets that sat in the centre of the room.

Each pallet carried a full load of conspicuous white powder, tightly wrapped into kilo-sized bricks.

'Is that what I think it is?'

King spoke without looking at Hale. His eyes stayed fixed on the pallets.

'It has to be.'

'Have you ever seen that much in one load?'

'I haven't seen that much *ever*. Not if you add up every arrest in my whole career.'

'Shit.'

King estimated the value of what was in front of them. He let out a whistle as he passed twenty-five million.

'That's one shitload of—'

King never finished his sentence. It was interrupted by the sound of gunfire.

In an instant King was out of the room, Hale just a step behind him. Both pulled their firearms as they rushed down the stairs. Towards the sounds coming from the street outside.

FORTY-FOUR

King reached the door first. He did not hesitate, running straight through and into the street. Hale did the same. It was the wrong move, one that none of SO19's firearm specialists would have made. It was contrary to their training.

And it cost King his life.

Hale would later count himself lucky to have been slower than King. It placed him second, the less obvious target.

The SO19 officers had taken effective cover as soon as the bullets began to fly, leaving the gunmen they faced with little to aim at. A fact which made King's wide, muscular frame an irresistible temptation.

King went down within three steps of the door. At least five shots had been fired. Two had hit. One had shattered his hip. The other his head. The force of the impact had sent him backwards into Hale, who was close behind.

It was King's falling body rather than Hale's tired reflexes that sent the older man to the ground and saved his life.

Hale landed heavily on the pavement. King fell next to him, a bullet hole unmissable in the centre of his skull. Hale scrambled for his own dropped pistol, picked it up and then grabbed King's too.

With a pistol in either hand he crawled the final few feet to the cars that were already providing his cover.

'GET BEHIND A WHEEL!'

The shouted instruction came from the nearest SO19 officer. Hale looked along the line of parked cars and saw that each firearm specialist was carefully positioned in the same way.

The sight brought his own firearms training came back to him. Lessons until now lost in the adrenaline of the moment.

The tyres give the best protection, Hale remembered.

He was moving in an instant, launching his body behind the nearest wheel. He tried to make sure his body was as covered as possible, although his bulk was working against him.

Hale signalled the attention of the same SO19 officer.

'WHAT THE HELL HAPPENED?'

He had to shout over the sound of gunfire.

'AMBUSH,' the officer shouted back. 'THEY HAD A TEAM IN THE BUILDING OPPOSITE. THEY OPENED FIRE AS BURRELL WAS BROUGHT OUT.'

'WHERE'S BURRELL NOW?'

'DON'T KNOW. WE LOST OUR TWO GUYS BRINGING HIM OUT STRAIGHT OFF. THEN BURRELL MADE A RUN FOR IT. ACROSS TO HIS TEAM.'

Hale nodded. His heart was racing but the initial shock was passing. He was beginning to calm. And to understand. With that much cocaine in the office upstairs, he should have expected this additional security. A team covering the entrance was just good sense.

'HOW MANY OF OUR TEAM DOWN?' Hale shouted.

'JUST THOSE TWO. THE REST TOOK COVER.'

'WHAT ABOUT THEIRS?'

'ONE DOWN IN THE FIRST EXCHANGE. I COUNT THAT LEAVES THREE MORE. PLUS BURRELL.'

'WHAT ABOUT THE GUYS FROM THE OFFICE?'

'IN THE VAN. LOCKED UP BEFORE THE SHOOTING STARTED.'

Hale took a moment to weigh the odds. Right now they were pinned down, but they heavily outmanned Burrell's men. Probably outgunned them, too. Plus it had taken five shots at a target as big as King? With only two hitting?

Means they can't shoot for shit, Hale thought, his calm returning. *Unlike my boys.*

The decision was made.

'OK. WHAT WE . . . SHIT!!'

Hale felt a ricochet pass him, less than an inch from his cheek. He could feel the heat of its movement.

'YOU OK?'

'I'M FINE. BUT WE NEED TO END THIS. NOW!'

'AGREED!'

The officer signalled down the line. Hale watched the same signal pass from man to man. If he had not given the order he would have no idea what the hand movements meant. To the SO19 officers, they were as meaningful as a spoken sentence.

The first officer held his hand level with his head. Three fingers this time. He turned first to Hale. Then to his right. He lowered a finger.

Two.

Here we go again.

One.

Oh shit.

'GO GO GO GO!'

The team stood up as one. Twelve firearms specialists and Hale.

It seemed longer, but it had been maybe half a minute since Hale had left the building. In that time Burrell's men had kept up a consistent rate of fire. It had kept the SO19 team pinned down, which was the aim. But it had also prevented Burrell's people from moving away. Movement meant pausing fire, and pausing fire against trained gunmen was a fatal mistake. This left Burrell's team where they had started; on the pavement just outside of the building directly across the street. A spot that did not enjoy the same coverage of a line of parked cars.

It was there that they stood as Hale and the SO19 team rose to their feet and opened fire as one. And so it was there that they fell.

Two went down immediately. A single bullet each. Precisely placed in the centre of their foreheads. One came from the officer next to Hale. The other from the left-hand giant.

Burrell's third man was taken just seconds later. Two bullets to the back as he ran, his bravado destroyed by the instant death of his friends.

Which left just Burrell himself.

In the moment he had had to think, Hale had wondered if Burrell had stayed for the fight, or if he had done what any sensible boss would and ran. Hale's gut preferred option one. Burrell was aggressive and arrogant. And Hale had offended him.

He won't let that go, Hale knew.

And he was right.

When the first two men went down, Burrell broke cover. Perhaps it was knowledge of what was upstairs: enough cocaine to imprison Burrell until his pension, inevitable now as his back-up team dropped like flies. Or perhaps he was just insane. Whatever it was, Burrell did not try to flee. Instead he came forward at a sprint, heading straight for Hale.

It was a journey he could not hope to finish alive.

It was a moment or two before Hale saw him, leaving Hale little time to think. Burrell was moving fast and Hale acted on instinct. With his own weapon already in hand, he aimed it at Burrell's chest with every intention of pulling the trigger.

Had Burrell been a yard or two closer, Hale would have done exactly that. But he was not, and so Hale had the extra instant to realise that his attacker was not only unarmed, he was in fact still restrained with his arms cuffed behind him. It made Hale hesitate, and it almost allowed the now near-berserk Burrell to reach him.

Almost.

Burrell was just feet away when a bullet tore into the very centre of his chest. Hale did not see the shooter, but it was enough to take Burrell down on its own. Four more bullets – which, from their directions of fire, came from at least two other MP5s – joined it in the next instant. Just to make sure. That was the difference between police officers with guns and a highly trained, specialist firearms unit. The latter did not hesitate when bullets were flying. For them, the questions could always wait.

With the shooting over, Hale stepped forward, towards Burrell's body.

He looked down and noticed again how small Burrell seemed; if anything the man somehow looked more insignificant in death. Then he looked around. At a road now devastated by gunfire.

He looked back to Burrell.

All of this to be the big boss, he thought. *And you didn't even make it to day five.*

FORTY-FIVE

Derek Reid had not slept a full night since Phillip Longman's death. If he was honest this was nothing new; his sleep had long been fitful, regularly interrupted by toilet breaks that were a symptom of his age. But since Longman's murder it had been much worse.

He was managing four hours a night. Maybe less. The rest of the time was spent tossing and turning.

Reid had hoped that four bottles of wine would change that. That they would at least see him through the night. But they had not. The thought of his friend's murder still ravaged him.

The bedside clock had read 2 a.m. when Reid first awoke.

He had chosen to ignore it. To try to sleep. But it proved a hopeless ambition. Forty-five minutes later he was still awake, his mind a bustling hive of images and thoughts.

It was time to accept defeat.

Reid threw off the light sheets that had covered him, exposing his naked body. It was not a sight that filled him with pride as he looked down, but as always he forced himself to ignore it as he slid his legs out of the bed.

He felt the cold of the wooden floor under his feet as he sat up. He stayed there for a few moments, on the edge of the mattress, as a new sensation kicked in. Reid's head had been filled with his thoughts while he was on his back, but now it actually hurt.

Fine time for a hangover to kick in, he thought.

What he needed now was water, and maybe some paracetamol. The bedside table held neither. A drunken Derek Reid was not a prepared Derek Reid, no matter how much practice he may have had.

Reid rose to his feet and walked towards the built-in wardrobe beyond the end of the bed. He took out a white robe, one he had 'borrowed' from a five-star hotel years before. It was just about the only thing his third wife had not taken in their divorce.

Old and beat up, he thought. *Like its owner.*

The robe was not a perfect fit. 'One Size Fits All' is a claim not made with Reid's body shape and height in mind. But it covered enough, protecting Reid's modesty from the grand total of no one with whom he shared his home. Still, there were mirrors in the house and Reid did not like what they told him about his naked body.

He slowly made his way out of the room and down the stairs, his legs unsteady from the evening's excess. It had become a regular night-time journey. Reid could trace the route in his sleep; in fact he probably had. Not that he needed to tonight. He was certainly groggy, but he was awake.

The medicine was kept in the downstairs bathroom, behind the sliding door of the mirrored cabinet. Reid went there first, found a packet of paracetamol and then noticed a single American-strength Alka-Seltzer sachet beside it. Two tablets, brought back from his last trip to New York and designed for exactly what was troubling him.

Reid ignored the paracetamol and took the sachet.

Next he moved to the kitchen. It smelled of spilled red wine and unwashed plates and pans. None of which helped the hangover. Reid tried to ignore it while he filled a tumbler glass with water and dropped in the two Alka-Seltzer tablets.

The fizzing sound would stop once the carbon dioxide was released. Indicating that the medication was ready. It would take at least a minute, so Reid used the time. He took another clean glass from his cupboard, filled it with water from his refrigerated filter jug and headed to his living room.

The lounge was pitch-black. The window shutters Michael had fitted when he had rebuilt the front of the house did their job perfectly, blocking out the street light.

Reid moved by memory alone. He was used to the darkness and knew where every obstacle would be. He found his leather chair as easily as if the midday sun were filling the room, sat and lifted the smaller glass to his ear.

The fizzing had stopped, so Reid moved the glass to his lips and drained the contents. Followed by a mouthful of filtered water to wash away the taste.

The TV remote was on the table next to the chair. Reid needed no light to tell him that. The presser, as Reid called it, was always on the table or in his hand. Never anywhere else. He reached out and flicked the flat-screen into life.

Sudden light in complete darkness can have a strange effect upon both the eyes and the brain. Especially a flickering light, like that generated by a television screen. Reid had grown used to it. To the strange images that would appear in his peripheral vision, only to disappear an instant later. It happened all the time and was no cause for concern.

Except for when it was. Except for now.

At first Reid had ignored the figure in the corner of the room, dismissing it as just another figment brought on by the change from dark to light. Reid had no need to convince himself that the image would go. That it would disappear. He just knew that it would.

But it did not. Not in an instant. Not even in a second.

Reid's heart rate doubled as he jumped to his feet, suddenly realising that what he was seeing was no figment. That it was no trick of his mind. His headache disappeared as the reality hit, his hangover washed away by shock.

'You've let yourself go, Mr Reid.' The voice was soulless. Empty. 'Too much luxury in your life.'

Reid could feel the vein in his temple thump. Blood pressure in action. His world was spinning, his breathing laboured from the shock of the last seconds.

Reid had to regain control. Had to calm.

'You feeling a bit sick?'

That voice again. Something Reid recognised. His brain tried to place it.

'The shock a bit too much for you, is it?'

There was no joy in the tone. The words were mocking but the voice remained flat.

'That'll be the heavy living, Mr Reid. All those expensive dinners.'

The voice was ever more familiar. Whatever memory was being jogged in Reid's mind was getting closer, and the effort to reach it was somehow calming him.

The figure stepped forward. Out of the corner and towards Reid.

The only light in the room was the TV. It was not enough. Reid could not make out the man's face in the darkness.

'Who are you?'

Reid's voice was strong. Not a trace of fear. It surprised even Reid himself.

'Me? I'm someone who hasn't had all those expensive dinners that made you so fat, Mr Reid. I'm someone who hasn't had all of that fine wine you're killing yourself with.'

'I don't understand.' Reid almost had it. The memory. So close he could almost touch it. A fact he did not intend to share. 'I don't know you.'

'*Oh*, you know me.' Finally some life in the voice. Some genuine bitterness. 'You'll have thought about me many times, Mr Reid. But not as often as I've thought about you.'

The figure stepped closer. Just as the flickering light brightened. It illuminated the room for just a moment. It was long enough.

'Hirst.' Everything about the man came to Reid at once. None of it was welcome. 'Karl Hirst.'

'See, Mr Reid. I told you you'd remember.' The words were gloating but the tone was empty once again. It gave nothing away. 'And do you remember everything else, Mr Reid?'

Reid took a step back as Hirst moved forward. The man's face became clearer with every slow, deliberate movement. The threat more imminent.

'Do you remember what you did to me? What you did to the man *you* were supposed to defend?'

Reid gave no answer. He had none. But he knew *exactly* what Hirst was referring to. All of it. And finally he knew why Longman had died.

FORTY-SIX

Sarah was still half asleep as she reached out for Michael. She expected her hand to find his chest. It was an unconscious routine; Michael usually slept on his back, and Sarah usually woke first. Today was different. Sarah's hand found nothing. Michael's side of their king-sized bed was empty.

She focused on the space beside her as she felt the last ties of sleep slip away. Michael's side had been slept in. That was clear from the ruffled pillows and sheet. Not that Sarah needed the evidence; she had seen it herself last night. Michael was in bed and asleep by the time Sarah had returned home.

The sounds of movement gradually seeped into Sarah's brain. The noise at first meant nothing. Now it told a story. Pots and pans crashing against one another. Fast running water. The sound of people talking. Sarah was used to it all. The soundtrack to a Michael Devlin breakfast.

Sarah glanced at the bedside clock. 7.30 a.m. Later than she had planned.

Shit.

She threw back the sheets, leapt out of bed and headed for the room's walk-in wardrobe. There she took the smaller of the two robes from the hook on the back of the door, slipped it on and made her way downstairs.

The sound and the smell of Michael's cooking strengthened as Sarah came nearer. So did the sound of Anne Flaherty's voice. It seemed odd to Sarah to hear her so early in the morning, up and awake instead of sleeping off the previous night's wine intake.

Michael must have kept her sober last night, Sarah thought. *A step in the right direction.*

Sarah walked into the kitchen and gave a wry smile at the scene that greeted her. It was one she had come to expect when Michael cooked. The range was an example of regimented organisation, with multiple pans on the hob at once. Eggs, bacon, sausages, beans, mushrooms, black and white puddings. All planned to perfection, to be ready at the same time.

The rest of the room, however, was a disaster. Unused pots and pans. Soiled plates and cutlery. Broken egg shells and food packaging. All discarded haphazardly across the counters. Another hallmark of a Michael Devlin meal.

'Sarah!' Anne turned the instant he heard Sarah's voice. 'Your man's making us all breakfast.'

'I can see that.' Sarah nodded. 'And is he going to be cleaning up *after* breakfast?'

'What? And leave you with nothing to do all day?' Michael grabbed her by her waist and pulled her towards him. Careful to keep her away from the stove, he planted a kiss on her lips before speaking again. 'What sort of man would that make me, eh?'

'I've got plenty to do.' Sarah pulled away. She knew he was joking. She just was not in the mood to join in. 'Plus a job.'

'Yeah, yeah. Big TV star,' he said with a smile.

Sarah did not respond and Michael seemed to finally take the hint. Falling silent, he began to move the cooked food onto the three plates as he spoke, replacing his Irish accent with a posh English version.

'Now if Mesdames would kindly take a seat, I will be serving presently.' He gestured to the table, already set for three. He placed down three plates before speaking again, this time in his broadest Belfast. 'Who's ready for an Ulster Fry?'

'So what brought on the big breakfast?' Sarah asked as she took her seat, trying to distract herself from rehashing the Wisdom Penfold incident in her mind yet again.

'I thought you might need it,' Michael replied. 'You had a late night.'

'I'm certainly not complaining. Just a nice surprise. So how did it go yesterday?'

'You mean in court?'

'Yeah. You had the phone guy, right? How did that pan out?'

'As well as we could have hoped. Took some doing because he didn't like being proved wrong, but by the end he'd accepted that Simon's phone was not with O'Driscoll's phone at the time of the murder.'

'Doesn't mean Simon wasn't.' Sarah was a reporter. Cynicism was her stock in trade, and today she was feeling especially negative. 'It's not like he's attached to his phone.'

'Try explaining that to Simon,' Michael replied. 'And Jenny. She's as bad as him. Only she doesn't have the excuse of being a kid. They both seem to think we've won the case already.'

'I thought Jenny was supposed to be the cynic?'

'So did I.' Michael sounded disappointed.

Sarah reached out and gripped his forearm.

'But it went well. That's what matters, right?'

'Yeah. You're right. Of course you're right.'

'So what's today? Is it the big one?'

'Terry Colliver? No. He's tomorrow. Today we get Colliver's pal.'

'Anything to worry about?'

'Nah. He's just a warm-up.' Michael smiled at the thought. 'Getting me ready for the main event.'

Sarah squeezed Michael's forearm again. She was happy to see the sparkle return to his eyes; the anticipation of another day of drama. It lightened her mood. She picked up her fork and took a mouthful of food.

'So what about you?' Michael asked. 'The ferry story kept you out late. There didn't seem much to report.'

'But there was plenty we *couldn't* report,' Sarah replied, disappointed that Michael had brought the subject back to here. 'That's what took the time.'

'Like what?'

'Mainly that the whole thing was connected to Longman's murder.'

'What?' Michael stopped eating. 'What do you mean? How?'

'The guy who was arrested. He was the prime suspect.'

'That was Wisdom Penfold?'

'Yeah.' It was Sarah's turn to be surprised. 'How did you know that name? Has someone broken the story?'

'No. I spoke to Levy yesterday. She was asking me about Penfold. Said he was good for Longman and Blunt.'

'Why would she be asking you?'

'She'd come to ask Derek about him, really, because Derek was the barrister in Penfold's case. But I saw her first and mentioned knowing a little about the guy. Just stuff Derek had told me back in the day. Anyway, what's the news? They've got him?'

'They've got Penfold, yeah. But he's not a suspect any more.'

'Really?'

'Turns out he had the perfect alibi. He was under police surveillance when both Longman and Blunt were killed.'

For just a moment Michael seemed deflated. Sarah thought she knew why. The arrest of Longman's killer would be the surest way to lift Reid's spirits. It made Penfold's innocence a disappointment.

'Where does that leave Levy's case?' Michael asked.

'Square one.' Sarah felt dejected. As if the failure was somehow hers. 'They're no further forward than they were on day one. Penfold was the only viable suspect with a link to Longman and Blunt. With him gone, it's back to finding someone with a motive from Longman's past.'

'That's a lifetime of suspects,' Michael said. 'It could take them weeks to track every case.'

'Maybe not weeks,' Sarah replied. 'Levy said they have a filter system. Criteria to let them concentrate on the most likely first. But there are no other links between the two. Longman didn't act as judge for any of Blunt's other clients. Not in cases that turned out badly, anyway. So it's still a big job and her team is already stretched to breaking point.'

Michael nodded his understanding, but Sarah could see that his sharp mind was already moving on. It got there quickly.

'Hang on,' he said, looking at her quizzically. 'What you just said about Blunt's clients. What about the other defendants where Longman was the judge? The ones Blunt arrested?

'What?' Sarah was growing confused. 'What do you mean arrested? Who did he arrest?'

'Plenty of people, I'd have thought. Blunt wasn't always a lawyer. Certainly not when I first knew him. Blunt used to be a cop.'

Sarah sat bolt upright. Michael's revelation changed everything.

'Which means it could be a case Blunt investigated. Rather than one he defended?'

'Exactly,' Michael replied. 'I would have thought the police knew that, but if Levy wasn't aware he was a cop then the parameters of her search could be excluding the wrong people. Her team might have found this guy already, only to dismiss him because Blunt wasn't the lawyer.'

'Jesus.'

Sarah thought for a moment. What Michael had told her could be the key to the case. A key that Levy would expect to be given. That was the arrangement. Sarah would help where she could, in exchange for an exclusive when the time came.

It was an arrangement that Elton had instructed her to end, but to hell with him. There were more important things than exclusives. More important things than her career.

Michael got to his feet while Sarah was still thinking and pulled on his jacket.

'I've got to get going.'

He walked back to the table and kissed Sarah as she rose from her own chair.

'Good luck today,' Sarah said. 'Give them hell.'

'I'll do my best,' Michael replied. He changed the subject. 'Will you be back before bed tonight?'

'Can't say. It depends how the whole "Blunt was a cop" thing plays out.'

'Then maybe I should have kept my trap shut,' Michael said, 'because there's a whole lot of bad bastards on Blunt's police résumé.'

'Like who? Anyone you know?'

'Personally? Just the one. A nasty piece of work from back when I was Derek's pupil. But it can't be him.'

'Why not?'

'Because he's still in prison.'

'You're sure?'

'I am. And if I weren't I'd be beating Levy's door down. Honestly, of all the people I've met in my career, this guy was the worst by a length and then some. Bad enough that I've kept tabs on him over the years.'

'How?'

'You're not the only person with contacts on the Parole Board. If this bastard ever sees fresh air I want to know about it. So I made arrangements.'

Sarah detected the grim note in Michael's voice. It spoke volumes and it intrigued her. Impossible suspect or not, she wanted to know more.

'I think you need to call Levy,' Michael said, moving the conversation on as he headed for the door. 'Let her know about Blunt's cop angle, if she doesn't already.'

'I will,' Sarah replied. She fully intended to ignore Elton's order, but right now her curiosity had been piqued. 'This guy you mentioned, though. She'll need to eliminate him as a suspect. What was his name?'

Michael looked back from the doorway, his face ashen. Sarah could tell that the subject – the memory – was unwelcome.

'His name was Hirst,' Michael finally said, as if the words were an effort. 'Karl Hirst.'

FORTY-SEVEN

'Will you be home early again tonight, Mum?'

Levy kept her hands on the wheel as she looked towards her son, who sat belted in the passenger seat of her Volvo for the morning school run.

When did 8 p.m. become 'early'? she thought. It said everything she needed to know about her work–life balance.

'I hope so.' Hope won out over expectation. It always did where Richard was concerned. 'And if I am then we'll go up to Highgate village for dinner. What do you think?'

'That'll be awesome.' Richard's face beamed excitement. 'We can have pasta.'

'We can have whatever you want.' Levy smiled. Sometimes the simplest things can bring so much joy. 'Except beer. You can't have any beer.'

'Mum!' Richard laughed aloud. 'I don't drink beer!'

'Well just as long as you don't.'

Levy was still smiling as she pulled out of the parking space, shifted into second and accelerated along the centre of the road. Richard was pushed back into his seat by the sudden speed. The sensation made him squeal with delight.

Richard's school was on the next road. Just around a corner. It took them another ten minutes to get there. They could have walked it in less than five, if there had been anywhere to park. Levy marvelled at how busy London's streets had become.

'Are you picking me up after school?' Richard's voice sounded hopeful as Levy brought the car to a halt.

'Now you're pushing it, Richard.' Levy's voice remained light. This was one subject about which she felt no guilt. She was hardly the only working mother forced to miss the afternoon school run. 'Claire will be there to collect you.'

'OK. But I'll see you after?'

'I'll do my best.' Levy leaned across, unlocked Richard's door and pushed it open. 'Now you be good today.'

'Yes, Mum.' Richard kissed Levy on her cheek. He pressed his lips in hard. His childish way of showing affection. 'See you later.'

'See you later too.'

Levy's last words were yelled after her son. Richard was already running towards the school gates.

Levy reached for the door. Pulled it shut. Put the Volvo into first and pulled away. In her passenger wing mirror she watched Richard pass the school gates. Into the safety of the playground. When he was gone she shifted to second and accelerated.

Levy's mobile phone sat in the centre console, connected to the car's hands-free system by Bluetooth. Levy pressed the green call icon on the car's central display and the system came to life.

'Call Steven Hale.'

She spoke clearly. Slowly. The system was impressive but it still made mistakes if Levy spoke in any other way.

Hale's name and number appeared an instant before the first ring tone. He answered almost as quickly.

'Morning, boss. You on your way in?' He sounded stressed.

'What's wrong?'

'Word from above. Rogers wants to see us both as soon as you're in the building.'

Levy's mood dropped. An impromptu summons from the chief superintendent was never good news.

'Any idea why?'

'I hear he's not happy about yesterday. Too much press attention on what he sees as failed operations.'

'Failed operations? Is he serious? Penfold wasn't our man but he's still good for three other murders. And Burrell was a good collar, even with what happened. What's his problem?'

'I think it's Burrell.' Hale sounded dejected. 'I think Rogers got wind that he's not good for Ferris after all?'

'Not good for Ferris? Where did that come from?'

'From me. I've got my doubts, boss. And I was stupid enough to mention them.'

'Shit.' Levy knew how the politics of their unit worked. She had thought that Hale did, too. It looked like she had been wrong.

'OK. I'm heading to you now. And Steve?'

'Yes, boss?'

'Keep your bloody mouth shut 'til I get there.'

FORTY-EIGHT

Michael reached the top step to the Old Bailey Bar Mess and looked around. It was less busy at 9 a.m. that it would be in thirty minutes. It made Jenny Draper easy to spot. That and the fact that she always sat in the same place.

Draper saw Michael at the same moment. She waved and held up what Michael assumed was a full mug of hot coffee.

'Prepared as always.' Michael smiled as he took the seat across from Draper. The coffee was steaming. No milk. Exactly as Michael liked it. 'And the perfect order.'

'Just making sure my leader is firing on all cylinders.' Draper broke out her practised smile. She reached out and lightly touched Michael's left forearm. 'I just want to say, you were amazing yesterday.'

'You said that yesterday, Jenny.' Michael pulled back his arm. 'And thanks. But you don't need to repeat it.'

'But I do, Michael. I kept replaying it in my head last night. What you did to White, especially with your hands tied by Simon's instructions. It was amazing.'

'The material was there.' Michael was not being modest. Just honest. 'If you gave it enough thought you could have done the same.'

'Matthew Cole didn't.' Draper's enthusiasm was not being dampened by Michael's calm. 'And *he's* supposed to be, well, *he's* Matthew Cole.

'Matt had nothing to work with, Jenny.' Michael was concerned. He had hoped that the presence of Cole – a much more prominent QC – would direct Draper's attentions elsewhere. It did not seem to be working. 'I'd have done no better than him if I was representing O'Driscoll. Matt's client's phone was on the scene the whole time. No way around that.'

'You're being modest, Michael.' Draper would not be dissuaded. 'What I saw yesterday? It was, well, it was powerful . . .'

Draper's voice dropped as she spoke, her message clear.

She's certainly confident, Michael thought. *That's a bad sign.*

'Look, Jenny,' he began, choosing to ignore her open flirtation, 'I like an ego boost as much as anyone, but trust me, this is still uphill. Cole knows what he's doing, and Epstein wrote the book on prosecuting cases like this. We're up against two giants. So let's leave the congratulations until the end, eh?'

Draper looked into Michael's eyes as he spoke, holding his gaze for a few moments once he had finished speaking.

'OK,' she finally said. 'I get it. There's a lot still at stake.'

'There is. Remember, we still need Simon to take our gloves off with O'Driscoll. I can only go so far without him doing that.'

'And that's *my* job. I know.'

Draper was about to say more, but before she could speak again she was interrupted by the court's speaker system.

'The custodies from Her Majesty's Prison Belmarsh have arrived. Any barristers needing to see their clients from Belmarsh are asked to attend the cell area now.'

'And as if by magic,' Michael said, nodding towards the Bar Mess loudspeaker.

'Earlier than usual,' Draper observed.

'Then let's take our luck where we find it. If you head down to the cells now you might get as much as an hour with him.'

'You want me to go alone?'

'I think it might be more productive, yeah. Just you and Simon. Lay it on thick, Jenny. Charm the life out of the kid. And make it clear how much *you* want us to win. Not me. How much *you* want us to be able to attack O'Driscoll.'

'You really think it'll work?'

'I honestly have no idea. But we need it to. And we need it to work *today*. Time's not Simon's friend on this one.'

'Why so urgent?'

'Because Terry Colliver's due to give evidence tomorrow. And if we're not allowed to attack O'Driscoll by the time Colliver gets in that box, well, I don't fancy our chances long term.'

'No pressure then.' Draper got to her feet and gently placed her hand on Michael's shoulder. 'I'll get him on board, Michael. Whatever it takes.'

Draper removed her hand with a final smile, turned and headed for the Bar Mess doors and the elevators that would take her to the Old Bailey's basement level.

You'd better, Michael thought as he watched Draper walk away. *Because if you don't, this is over.*

FORTY-NINE

The office of Chief Superintendent David Rogers was on the same corridor as Levy's, but that was as far as the similarities went. It was at least four times the size. Similar, Levy thought, to the room in which Leon Ferris had died.

In an era of police budgetary cutbacks and at a time when a unit as vital as MIT One was undermanned by almost half, no expense had been spared on Rogers' accommodation.

The desk was larger than any one man could need. It always reminded Levy of her time in Israel and of the tables wide enough to hold a detailed map ahead of military operations. *Their* size was necessary; they served a purpose. All Rogers' desk served was the man's ego.

'Take a seat, Joelle. Steven.'

Rogers spoke without looking up. Levy and Hale had stood to attention in front of the desk. Rogers had let them stay that way for almost thirty seconds. An indication of his mood.

As if it was needed.

Levy took the right-hand seat. Hale the left. Both looked towards Rogers. He was pointedly completing paperwork; he did not glance up from the page. A demonstration of relative importance.

It was lost on both Levy and Hale. Both were long past caring.

To Rogers' right was Superintendent Carol Walker. Rogers' immediate subordinate and Levy's immediate boss. Walker sat bolt upright in her chair. Two feet back from the desk. Her eyes fixed on Levy and Hale. If Rogers had not been present then Walker would have chaired the meeting. Today she had to defer to his greater rank. Levy could tell that it bothered her. Walker was itching to speak.

Rogers concluded his paperwork and took his time to carefully sign his name, doing so with a flourish. Next he held up the page and blew lightly on the wet ink, to dry it without causing the lines to streak. Rogers took his time. A message to everyone in the room. Confirmation of where the power sat.

Finally he placed the paper down, put his hands together and looked directly at Levy.

'So, Joelle. How do you propose we deal with yesterday's debacles?'

Straight to the point. Rogers was a politician to the public and to the press. But in here he was a police officer, getting to the heart of a problem.

'I don't see either incident as a debacle, sir.' Levy met Rogers' straight talking with some of her own. 'Yesterday's operations may not have resulted in arrests that benefited *our* investigations, but they were both successful in other respects.'

'That's a fascinating point of view.' Rogers' tone did not agree with his words. 'Why don't you enlighten me on that? What was the big success with the very public arrest of Wisdom Penfold? Because I was struggling to see that as it was plastered all over the evening news.'

'Wisdom Penfold was a murderer fleeing the jurisdiction. As we now know it, he had killed an associate of Barry Ireland and stole three million pounds' worth of diamonds. He is now in custody for that murder, the killing of the victim's boyfriend and the murder of one undercover officer and the serious assault of another. I fail to see how that's a disappointment.'

'It's a disappointment, Joelle, because he is *not* in custody for Phillip Longman's murder. Because you have wasted time and resources chasing a bloody red herring. We have two crucifixions thirty-six hours apart, including one of a very important man, and yet you then spend a day and a half chasing a lead that has nothing whatsoever to do with this case and a police officer ends up dead. Do you think the press will miss that?'

'With all due respect, sir, we can't be obsessed with what the press say. If they find out that Penfold's initial arrest was for Longman then yes, they'll crow about it. But only until we find the real killer. It'll be temporary.'

'Temporary? You think that matters? We're judged today on yesterday's results. And that judgement comes fast. Are you so sure you'll have time to put this right? That you won't just be replaced?'

'Well that's your call, sir.' Levy was shocked at the suggestion but she refused to show it. 'If you want to replace me then replace me. But it won't make me agree that Penfold's arrest was a bad result. We've put a murderer away for the rest of his life.'

'At the cost of a surveillance officer. How do you think that will play out? Have you watched the news? They're already suggesting that our intervention cost the officer his life. That if we hadn't turned the ferry around the team could have followed him and effected the arrest in Holland with the cooperation of the Dutch authorities.'

'Sir, the press—'

'It's not just the press, Levy. It's the bloody NCA as well. They've lost two valuable agents; one dead, the other likely invalided. And they say they've lost a whole operation, too. That because of us their investigation into Barry Ireland and that Bond Street business is dead in the water.'

'Now that's just a bloody lie, sir.'

Levy could not help but raise her voice. She could handle the truth. Even when it was spun and distorted. That was the job. But outright dishonesty was another thing altogether.

Levy continued.

'The NCA operation was dead the moment Penfold killed Ireland's man. Penfold wasn't leading them to anyone that could connect the diamonds to Ireland. The NCA know that. Penfold had *stolen* the diamonds. He was going to sell the whole lot and run. They *know* that. If they say otherwise they're lying.'

For the first time Rogers did not fire back. Instead he turned to Walker.

'You got anything to say on that, Carol?'

'It accords with my own information, sir,' Walker confirmed. 'The NCA operation was a bust. And they should have known that earlier. If they'd left surveillance on Ireland's associate – or if they hadn't lost

Penfold – then they'd have realised much sooner what had happened. It would have allowed them to call it and to arrest Penfold much earlier. Without the public fanfare or the loss of life. In my opinion, they're now using yesterday to cover their own embarrassment.'

Rogers stayed silent, considering her words. Levy met Walker's eyes as he did so and nodded her thanks. Walker inclined her head in return. A slow, formal tilt that said was just doing her job. Her conclusion had nothing to do with loyalty to her unit.

'On that information, that's rather how I read it, too.' Rogers turned back to Levy. 'It's still a shit-storm, though, Joelle. But I won't have those over-funded bastards casting mud on *my* unit. We'll protect you as far as the ferry's concerned. But that means I want some progress on the Longman case. Before any more bloody lawyers end up crucified.'

'Sir.'

Levy felt a mix of relief and pressure. The unexpected attack after Penfold's arrest was going to be defended. But the price was high: greater pressure for progress on Longman's murder.

Which is firmly back at square one.

'Which brings us to Edward Burrell.' Rogers' attention turned to Hale. 'You, Steven, took an SO19 team to a heavily populated street in South West London. Once there you proceeded to engage in a pitched gun battle ending in the death of three officers and four civilians – albeit known gang members – and the suspect himself. Do you see a problem with that?'

Hale was not used to direct interrogation. Such questions were usually reserved for Levy as the operational commander. But Rogers knew who *really* had charge of the Ferris case.

'Sir, we, erm, we carried out a clean raid. We apprehended Burrell. We apprehended him and his men inside of the building. We had no way of knowing what was waiting for us outside.'

'A clean raid, Inspector? Do I need to remind you of the cost?'

'I understand that, sir. I really do. But we had no intelligence at all about the back-up in the building across the street. We didn't know what we would find in Burrell's place; we had no knowledge that a drug consignment of any size was going to be there, let alone enough to flood London. So we had no reason to expect that Burrell had taken extra precautions with back-up outside.'

'Why was there no intelligence? How could you have gone in there so blind? You had Trident officers with you, Inspector. Surely *they* had some idea?'

'No one did, sir. Burrell holding that much cocaine? It was unheard of. He just doesn't operate anywhere near that level. At least he didn't.'

'And he doesn't any more. So silver linings.' Rogers' voice was flippant. Only for a moment. 'But a gun battle in the middle of Brixton does not read well in the morning papers, Inspector. Especially with officers down.'

'I realise that, sir. But it wasn't planned. We reacted to an ambush. And we won. I don't know how these things are done but surely that can be spun in our favour? Can't it?'

Rogers pushed his chair back from his desk. He reached up, put both hands on his head and locked his fingers across his hairless scalp.

'I was thinking that myself, Steven. I was thinking that this could be played to our advantage. Officers ambushed on a raid, the ambushers taken out. Maybe we can turn you into the hero of the hour.'

'That's really not necessary sir,'

'I'll decide what's necessary, Steven. And then I'll inform you what that is. Now, onto another issue. Quite an important one, given what occurred yesterday. I have heard a rumour, Steven, that you might be questioning yourself. That you now have your doubts that Burrell was involved in Ferris's death.'

'That's right, sir,' Hale answered. 'I have significant reservations.'

'Why?'

Levy glanced at Hale, interested in what would follow. They had not yet had a chance to discuss Hale's theory.

'First it was just instinct, sir. When we raided the address I took a look at Burrell's office. It was a carbon copy of Ferris's. Near on identical. It suggested to me that Burrell wasn't just in competition with Ferris. It suggested that he was obsessed with Ferris. Like, psychological obsession or whatever you'd call it. I've seen that before in murders, sir.' Hale indicated Levy. 'We both have. And whenever I've seen that, the obsessed person does the killing themselves. They wouldn't hire someone. It's part of the illness. It's personal.'

Levy nodded at the assessment. It made sense.

Rogers and Walker could not have missed her agreement. Rogers turned back to Hale.

'Is that all? Just your gut instinct?'

'No sir.' Hale seemed to be warming to his subject. 'It was also the drugs, sir. Our suspicion that Burrell was responsible for Ferris's murder was based upon his approach to one of Ferris's men. Burrell suggested that the guy might want to switch allegiances, because things were about to change. We thought he meant that Ferris was about to die. But a drugs shipment that size, sir? That would have changed the status quo as surely as Ferris's death. It would have made Burrell ten times as rich as Ferris. And money talks in that world. So I now suspect *that's* what Burrell was referring to.'

'That makes some sense,' Walker offered. 'And then you add the police attention that Ferris's murder would inevitably bring onto his rivals. Why would Burrell risk that with so much cocaine in his possession? It's just asking for trouble.'

'Exactly, ma'am.' Hale's assessment was finding favour. 'All of which tells me that Burrell was not our man.'

'And yet his building was raided, which led to a shoot-out in the middle of Brixton.' If Hale's response had also persuaded Rogers, it had not made him happy. Rogers continued. 'Which is another incident – within twenty-four hours – of public violence brought about by a misconceived arrest by MIT officers. Does no one else see the problem with this?'

'But it led to a major drugs bust, sir.' Levy interceded on Hale's behalf. 'The biggest on British soil in a decade. Surely that justifies it?'

'Guns, Joelle. Fired on the street of London.' Rogers' voice was rising close to a shout. 'We cannot have that happening for the wrong reasons, regardless of who fires first. This isn't about right and wrong. It's about perception. About how it will be reported. We cannot have our officers in pitched shoot-outs for arrests that turn out to be groundless.

'The drugs were lucky. Justification after the fact. But if the press gets wind that the reason for the raid in the first place was bad intelligence? A false conclusion? Dare I say it, *bad police work*? What the hell happens then? I'll tell you what happens. We get the same treatment as Longman. We get bloody crucified. *That's* what happens.'

No one responded. Not Levy. Not Hale. Not Walker. All stayed silent. Rooted to their chairs as Rogers rose from his own. They watched as he walked around the room. As he used its square footage to the full. The Chief Superintendent thought carefully as he paced to the door and back. Once. Twice. Three times before retaking his seat.

'Burrell was behind Ferris's death.' Rogers' voice was firm when he finally spoke. 'That's the official line, for now at least. I want you giving a press conference on that within the hour.'

'But sir, he wasn't. Surely you can—'

Hale was interrupted by Rogers' raised hand.

'The truth is irrelevant on this one, Inspector. It's not like there's going to be a trial anyway. Not since you killed the bastard.'

'Can I ask why, sir?' Levy spoke on Hale's behalf. 'I mean, if Steve has to lie. Doesn't he deserve a reason?'

'I don't think he deserves anything, Joelle. But perhaps it will assist him in the future if he understands.'

Rogers turned to Hale.

'The public need to have faith in us, Inspector. They need to know that when we raid a gangster's lair and risk a gun battle in which civilians could have been killed, that we do so for the *right reasons*. That we do so because we *know* what the bastards have done. You secured your search warrant on the basis of Ferris's murder. That can't be changed. But if suddenly we were *wrong* about the murder? Well, that's public confidence all gone to hell, isn't it. And you can bet your bottom dollar that the press would happily expose it. So Burrell had Ferris killed. Now he's gone too and everyone is happy. Understood?'

Levy saw Hale glance at her uncertainly. She sympathised; what he was being asked to do was outside of his experience. Hale was a cop. Not a politician.

She gave him a subtle affirmative nod. The only way to tell him what she wanted to say.

Just go with it, Steve. There's no other way.

Hale turned back to Rogers.

'Sir, if we proceed on the basis that Burrell ordered Ferris's murder, that still leaves the actual killer.'

'It does.'

'Then am I allowed to continue my investigation into him? Into whoever actually carried out the job?'

'As long as it isn't suggested that he worked for someone other than Burrell, you mean?'

'Of course, sir.'

'In that case yes. It would look a little rum if you did otherwise, in fact.'

'OK. Then I'm on board, sir.' Hale had little choice. 'How long until the press conference?'

FIFTY

'So what do we know about him?'

James Elton sat at the head of the conference room table. To his right was Sarah Truman. To his left Nathan Benson. The room's seventeen other chairs were empty.

Both Sarah and Elton wanted this conversation private.

Sarah and Benson had been working together for three hours, building on the little Michael had told Sarah. They had been productive, digging up information on Adam Blunt's career with the Metropolitan Police. At the same time Sarah had found everything she could on Karl Hirst. At first it had been to satisfy her own curiosity, piqued by the effect the name had on Michael. But only at first.

They had already brought Elton up to speed on Blunt. The subject now turned to Hirst.

'He was convicted of manslaughter, assault, blackmail and kidnap,' Sarah answered. 'Seventeen years ago. Longman was his judge and sentenced him to life with a minimum of fourteen years. Hirst served fourteen. As close as possible to the day. And despite what Michael told me this morning, it seems he was paroled on his first application.'

The revelation that Michael had been wrong had come as a shock. A shock that quickly turned to excitement. Hirst was a viable suspect.

But that's all he is for now, Sarah thought, forcing herself to contain her own enthusiasm. *Until I have more. He's not going to be another Wisdom Penfold.*

'OK. Violent and sentenced by Longman. That ticks the boxes. But what's the connection to Blunt? Was he the lawyer?'

'Better than that,' Benson offered. 'Blunt was the cop.'

'No shit.' Elton smiled at Sarah. The story wrote itself. 'And he headed the investigation, I take it?'

'He did,' Sarah replied. 'His last case, in fact. Blunt quit the police literally the day after the conviction. No warning. Still a few years away from his pension.'

'Anything that suggests why he'd do that?'

'Not that we've found. At least not yet. But it's damned strange. We're looking into it.'

'OK. So are there any problems you see with Hirst?' Elton was testing Sarah's judgement. He seemed concerned that yesterday's conversation could make her careless. 'Is there anything that says he might be a weak choice of suspect?'

'The two things I'm sure you've already spotted from what I've told you, James.' Sarah knew Elton well. She could anticipate what he would consider a problem. She continued. 'The fact that he was released on his first application suggests he wasn't violent in prison, and fourteen years is a long time to pretend at that kind of character change. So it suggests his violent streak was a one-off. Plus three years is a long time to wait between his release and the murder when the target is someone as old as Longman. Whoever killed Longman wanted him to suffer hugely, so why wait three years when he could have just died naturally any day and deny the killer that chance?'

Elton nodded.

'Both big black marks against him being our man,' he said.

'I thought the same,' Sarah replied, 'so I checked Hirst's prison record with my contact in Wandsworth. Hirst's last prison.'

'And?'

'It was impeccable. In Wandsworth and everywhere before. No violence. No insubordination. Hirst was the perfect prisoner. He did his courses. He got himself qualified in a whole host of different subjects. Criminology. Biology. Philosophy. Forensics. The guy's got degrees and diplomas coming out of his ears. But nothing on there to suggest any violent streak.'

'Still, the fact is it's unusual to be paroled from a life sentence on a first application, however good the track record,' Elton observed. 'Does your guy in Wandsworth have any idea what might have swung it?'

'He did, yeah. Hirst was targeted while he was in Wandsworth. He caught the eye of one of the main players there and ended up being used as a plaything. Beaten. Abused. You get the picture.'

'Did he give you a name?'

'No,' Sarah replied. 'He'd just said it was pretty much the big fish.'

'Was nothing done to stop it?'

'Not a thing.'

'Why not?'

'A combination of factors. For one thing, Hirst never complained, never once. And he also never fought back, so there was never an actual incident for any guards to deal with. Seems he just let it happen.'

'But the prison knew about it? Enough for the guy to tell you?'

'They knew, yeah. Unofficially. But the other factor mattered, too. The guy behind it was a special case. He had most of the guards paid off; hell, he probably had my guy, too, hence he wouldn't spill on who this man was. So there was no way anyone was stepping up. Especially when Hirst hadn't asked for any help.'

Elton shook his head.

'But it found its way onto Hirst's record?'

'Unofficially. But enough that the Parole Board would be given the gist. My theory is that this swung it. That the board will have taken the view that Hirst had been punished above and beyond, due to what he'd suffered. *And* they figured that his lack of a violent response was absolute proof that he was no longer a danger. That he was no longer violent. It would also explain why Michael's contact at the Parole Board didn't inform him that Hirst had been released. This was one they'd want to see just slip under the radar.'

'Seems a fair conclusion to reach,' Elton observed. 'And pretty bloody compelling. So what makes you think they were wrong? That he *is* still a psycho?'

'I *don't* think they were wrong, necessarily,' Sarah replied. 'But I do think he's worth tracking down. He's the only name we have right now, without access to Longman's case files. It may come to nothing – it'll *probably* come to nothing – but until Levy is ready to share I think Hirst's worth a look.'

Elton said nothing.

Sarah had made her case. Hirst ticked a lot of boxes, but she knew that there were compelling arguments against him. Her best point, though? What the hell *else* did they have?

Finally Elton spoke.

'OK, go after this Hirst guy. Find out everything you can about him and about his crime. And track down anyone else involved in that case. Any other lawyers, prosecutors, witnesses, the lot. Never hurts to speculate in this game, and if he turns out to be our guy then that's a hell of a story.'

Sarah nodded in agreement.

'But I want you working with Kendal and Cross on this,' Elton continued, referring to two of the younger reporters on his roster. 'Have them chase down Longman's other cases, concentrating on all live ex-cons who appeared before him and who have any record of serious violence.'

'So basically the police search criteria?' Sarah asked.

'Exactly. If they're doing that while you investigate Hirst they might just come across a suspect who better fits the bill.'

'OK. But where will they get Longman's case files?'

'Not my job to bring the horse to the water, Sarah. Tell them to use their initiative.'

'Right.'

'And one more thing. Remember what I told you yesterday. No more sharing with the police. At least not until I say so. I don't want any mention of Hirst or the "Blunt as a cop" angle to MIT. Understood?'

Sarah hesitated for just a moment. She knew what she wanted to say: that Elton's order disgusted her, and that in respect of the 'Blunt as a cop' angle it was already too late. She had left that message for Levy moments before this very meeting.

Sarah also wanted to say that she would share whatever she had to

– including the name Karl Hirst – if it would save lives. It was a fight she was willing to have. But for now it was unnecessary. For now Hirst was nothing more than a hunch, with a host of factors pointing away from him, and she would not risk sending MIT One on another wild goose chase. Until he was more – if he ever *was* more – she would keep Hirst's name to herself.

It allowed her to give the answer Elton wanted:

'Understood.'

FIFTY-ONE

Michael listened intently as Matthew Cole QC continued his cross-examination.

So far Cole had been effective. No more than that. But Michael knew what it was that Cole needed to prove for O'Driscoll to stand a chance with the jury. He also knew how exceptional a barrister Cole could be.

And so he knew that the best was yet to come.

The witness was Jay Price. An old friend of the defendants. At least according to him. Darren O'Driscoll said otherwise, Michael knew. So did Simon Kash. It was one of the few things Kash had been willing to tell them.

Michael had not known what to expect of Price. Nothing in the man's witness statement said anything significant about its maker. It made Price a blank slate. Someone to be analysed, his strengths and his weaknesses identified.

Michael had spotted them quickly. He did not doubt that Cole would have seen them, too.

Peter Epstein QC had questioned Price carefully, taking a very different approach to the one he had applied to Keith White the day before. The phone expert's delivery had been effortless. Today was different. Today Epstein had to control a witness just as eager to speak, but far less skilled at the task.

Most of Price's evidence matched his witness statement. He explained to the jury how he was a long-term friend of both O'Driscoll and Kash. How the three had been close since school. He also admitted knowing Terry Colliver. Not a close friend, he explained. More a casual acquaintance. A friend of a friend.

Price had gone on to tell the jury of his disgust at his friends' crime. How their murder of the Galloway twins had been the breaking point in his relationship with them. How they had tortured the brothers, how they had dismembered them and how they had boasted about their crimes.

The pleasure they had taken in what they had done, he explained, was the final straw.

Epstein had taken his questions slowly. He had concentrated on details Price could give of the killings; things that only the murderers could have told him, that he could not have known from anyone or anywhere else.

Epstein had made a point of turning to the jury whenever such a detail came out. Meeting their eyes whenever Price referred to something the jurors had already heard; a detail they would recognise as accurate. The message behind Epstein's theatrics was clear: how else would the witness know this? Other than from O'Driscoll and Kash?

It was a good performance. But not a perfect one. Price had not been controlled completely. That was not Epstein's fault. The rules of questioning his own witness prevented Epstein from suggesting the answers, which gave Price more latitude than Epstein would have liked. It was an opportunity to go off-script and Price had seized it time and again by adding evidence that had not appeared in his witness statement.

It was the classic mistake of a witness with an agenda: trying to make things worse for the defendants.

Michael and Cole had shared a glance every time Price had tried to twist the knife in this way. Both had seen this many times before and so they knew what Price was doing. And both knew how counterproductive it really was; how weakened the evidence became by each of these additional lies.

Once Epstein was done, it was Cole's turn to question Price.

Cole started gently. He made no effort to attack Price and instead seemed to guide him. He took Price to what Cole believed were his lies, from both the original statement and what Price had added today, and confirmed that Price stood by each of them as true. What Cole was doing was undramatic but it was also vitally important. It tied Price to his own dishonesty, leaving him no room to manoeuvre when Cole's real cross-examination began.

'Mr Price, you've told this jury that you were disgusted by what your friends Darren O'Driscoll and Simon Kash had done to the Galloway brothers. Correct?'

'Yes, sir.'

'Sick to your stomach, I believe you said.'

'Yes, sir.'

'From the very beginning, Mr Price?'

'Sorry? What d'ya mean?'

'I mean, were you "sick to your stomach", as you say, from the first time you knew what they'd done?'

'Yeah. It was disgusting. Animals don't even do that sorta 'fing.'

'And you told us that this was very shortly after the murder, wasn't it?'

'Yeah.'

'No more than three days after, you said.'

'Yeah. Probably less.'

'So no later than December 18th? Three days after the murder of the Galloway brothers?'

'Like I said. Probably earlier.'

'Was this the first time you had heard about the murder? When Mr O'Driscoll and Mr Kash told you what they had done?'

'Course it weren't. It was all over the bloody news. Everyone'd heard about it. In my area, anyway.'

'So did you already have an opinion on the murder? Before speaking to your friends?'

'Bloody right I did. I fought it was disgusting. You don't do that sorta fing to anyone. Whatever they've done.'

'OK. You already had strong views, then. And then your old school friends suddenly announced that *they* had murdered the Galloway twins.'

'Yeah.'

'Did you tell them there and then how disgusted you were with what they had done?'

'I . . . erm . . . I . . . No. No, I didn't.'

'Why not?'

'Well they'd just bloody murdered two big fellas, hadn't they? What would they do t'me if I'd started going on at 'em about it?'

'But you were their friend, Mr Price. They wouldn't attack you, would they?'

'They would if they thought I was gonna grass on 'em, wouldn't they? They don't like me enough to risk a bloody life sentence, do they?'

'Then why on earth would they have ever told you about it in the first place?'

Price did not answer immediately. Cole's question had clearly not occurred to him.

He glanced towards Epstein, seemingly looking for help. Epstein did not look back. Price was on his own.

'I . . . I . . . look, I don't understand. What d'you mean?'

Cole jumped on the opportunity.

'What I mean, Mr Price, is that apparently Mr O'Driscoll and Mr Kash would not hesitate to kill you if you expressed so much as a little disquiet about what they had done. Which means that they did not feel they could completely trust you. So why, then, Mr Price, would they take the risk of telling a person they could not completely trust all about a crime for which they could be sent to prison for the rest of their lives?'

Price stayed silent. Perhaps realising his error. Cole's question – Cole's speech, really – made perfect sense. And it demanded an answer.

Price finally gave one.

'I guess they just wanted to boast.'

There was no confidence in Price's voice. It sounded as if even *he* did not believe what he was saying.

'That's it, is it, Mr Price?'

Cole had no intention of leaving the answer alone.

'These two men had committed a crime for which they could be imprisoned for life. And they risked that imprisonment just because they felt the need to boast. Is that *really* your answer?'

'I'm not sure this is a fair line of questioning, My Lord.' Epstein had risen to his feet. 'Mr Price cannot be expected to know why the defendants would have chosen to speak to him. He has no insight into their mindsets or motivations.'

'Perhaps not, My Lord,' Cole countered. 'Or perhaps the conversation reported by Mr Price never happened, and the lack of any good reason for the defendants to have spoken to Mr Price is proof of that. But I think the point has been made, so I'll move on.'

Epstein retook his seat. Michael could see his irritation; his interruption had given Cole the chance to make his point in the most direct way possible. A glance across to the jury told Michael that at least they had enjoyed Cole's response.

'OK, Mr Price, let's move on then.'

Cole's Liverpudlian accent was becoming more pronounced.

He's beginning to enjoy himself, Michael thought.

'You're shocked. You're disgusted. No later than December 18th.'

'That's what I said, ain't it?'

Price's mistake had left him rattled. He reacted to that with belligerence.

'It certainly is.' Cole smiled. Another gift. 'And we know why you didn't tell Mr O'Driscoll or Mr Kash how disgusted you were during that conversation. Because you were afraid of what they would do to you.'

'I've already told you that.'

'I know you did, Mr Price. Just bear with me.' The smile widened. 'So you're sick to your stomach, to use your own words. You must have been itching to end that conversation then, right?'

'Right.'

'Because you must have been desperate to get down to the local police station, mustn't you?'

'What?' Price looked confused. 'What are you talking about now?'

'Let's take it in stages. What they had done had disgusted you enough to give a police statement. I mean, you *did give* such a statement, didn't you?'

'You know I did.'

'Yes, I do. And you must have been desperate to give that statement, so disgusted were you. You must have wanted to make it as soon as you could after the 18th of December. Is that right?'

'Yeah. Yeah, that's right. They couldn't be allowed get away wiv it. Not what they done.'

'Exactly, Mr Price. And may I commend your sense of civic duty. Your sense of justice.'

'Er . . . well I . . . er . . . fank you?'

'You're welcome, sir. Now, would you please look at a copy of your original handwritten statement?' Cole looked towards a member of court staff. She was robed like the barristers, but without their wigs and traditional collars. 'Madam Usher, would you be so kind?'

The usher approached Cole and took a small bundle of papers from his outstretched hand. Price's first witness statement. The usher took the copy to Price and placed it on the edge of the witness box.

'Please take a moment to confirm that this statement is yours, Mr Price. That it's the statement you made to the police and signed as being true.'

Price looked at each page closely. Until he was satisfied.

'Yeah. It's mine.'

'Good. Now, please read out the date that appears on the bottom of every page of your statement. You'll find it next to your signature.'

Price just stared at the page without answering. Cole gave him a few moments before insisting.

'The date, Mr Price. What is it?'

'It says March 1st.' The answer stuck in his throat. Its meaning unmistakable.

'I'm sorry, did you say March 1st?' Cole feigned surprise. 'As in, March 1st the following year? Two and a half months after the conversation with Mr O'Driscoll and Mr Kash? That can't be right, can it, Mr Price?'

'You know the date.' The answer was quiet.

'What did you say, Mr Price?'

'I SAID YOU KNOW THE DATE!' This time the answer was shouted. Price's composure had disappeared. 'DON'T PRETEND LIKE YOU DON'T!'

Cole waited for a few moments. For Price's angry outburst to sink in with the jury. Cole met their eyes as it did and shook his head, as if shocked by the reaction.

'So you waited two and a half months to give a witness statement?' he finally continued. 'But you told us how strongly you felt about this, Mr Price. How disgusted you were. Sick to your stomach, you told us.'

'I know what I told you.' The fury was still there. And the volume.

'Mr Price, you are to keep your answers and your demeanour civil.' Judge John Levitt had heard enough. 'Mr Cole is entitled to ask you the questions he is asking. You are to respond to them in a civilised manner.'

'I didn't come 'ere to be treated like shit!' The judge's warning had not worked; Price was still shouting. 'I ain't gotta take this from any of you people.'

'You most certainly have to take it from me.' Levitt's voice was raised. It matched Price's, in volume if not in aggression. When he spoke again it was quieter, but no less authoritative. 'Because if you do not then you will not be leaving this courtroom through the front door. Do I make myself clear?'

Price was not a clever man. That much was apparent. But he knew enough to understand the judge's threat. And to know that Levitt meant it.

Chastened, he turned back to Cole.

'So please explain, Mr Price. Please explain why it took you over two months to go to the police and make a statement.'

''Cause I was scared.' Price's voice was now quiet. Almost nervous. And it might have been convincing, had it not been for the eruption moments before. 'I was afraid what they'd do to me if they found out I was talkin' to the police.'

'And yet you made a statement in the end anyway. What changed, Mr Price? What made you come forward, after being so afraid of the consequences?'

'Because the police arrested Terry Colliver, didn't they? They nicked the wrong fella.'

'You mean you couldn't stand to see that happen? You couldn't stand idly by while an innocent man was tried for murder?'

'Yeah. That's right.'

'So you came forward. Despite Mr O'Driscoll and Mr Kash being your friends, and Mr Colliver being a man you hardly knew?'

'Yeah, I did. Don't make no difference, friends or not. I wasn't gonna let Colliver go to prison for what those bastards done.'

'Are you sure Colliver wasn't a friend of yours, Mr Price?' The smile returned to Cole's face. 'Was he not in reality your great close friend, and Mr O'Driscoll and Mr Kash just people you knew?'

'No.'

Michael could tell from his body language that Price had expected this new line of questions. That he had prepared for it. His indignation was practised.

'I bloody knew you'd say that, didn't I?' Price continued. 'Well it's bullshit. Colliver's no mate of mine. Never 'as been. Never will be. *They* were my friends.' Price pointed at the dock. 'Right 'til I realised what a pair of psychos they are.'

'OK.' Cole was utterly unfazed. 'We'll come back to that in a moment. First though, let's go back to your change of heart.'

'To my what?'

'To the thing that overcame your fear. To Terry Colliver's arrest for a murder you knew he had not committed.'

'What about it?'

'Well, you say that it was his arrest that made you change your mind. That made you go to the police.'

'Yeah.'

'And that arrest was on the 29th of December, wasn't it?'

'Yeah.'

'And you heard about it very soon after that, didn't you?'

'Who says I did?'

'You did, Mr Price. In a manner of speaking. Remember earlier? When I asked when you'd heard about the murder? What did you say? According to my notes you said, "It was all over the bloody news. Everyone had heard about it. In my area, anyway." That *is* what you said, isn't it?'

No answer.

'We can have the tape of your evidence played back if you'd like, Mr Price.'

'Yeah, it's what I said,' Price hissed, his anger once again simmering under the surface. Only Levitt's threat of a cell was keeping him in check.

'Which must mean that just ten days later the murders were still big news. Especially since someone you knew – albeit you say you didn't know him very well – was arrested for them. Correct?'

'Yes.'

'Which means that you knew about Terry Colliver's arrest two months before you gave your statement.'

'So what?'

'So I'd like to know why there was such a delay. Colliver's arrest made you overcome your fears, Mr Price. It made you come forward. Made you cooperate with the police. That's what you've told us. But when we look at the timeline we see that it took *two whole months* to have that incredible effect. *Why*, Mr Price? Why did it take so long?'

Price glared at Cole without answering. Cole met his gaze and held it. A stand-off manufactured for the jury's benefit, Michael knew.

'The jury can draw their own conclusions from your failure to answer,' Cole began. 'I've just got one last subject to ask you about. Something we touched on a moment ago.'

'Yeah? Go on, then.'

'Patience, Mr Price. We're getting to it now.'

Cole smiled again. By now Price must have known the smile's meaning. That there was more damage to come.

'You've said that you were no particular friend of Terry Colliver.'

'That's right.'

'But you *were* aware that between December last year and the beginning of March this year, Terry Colliver was in custody in Wormwood Scrubs Prison in West London? Charged with the murders of the Galloway brothers?'

'Yeah, I knew that. Everyone knew that.' Price seemed more comfortable as they returned to Colliver, the subject for which he had obviously prepared. 'But that don't make us mates though, does it. Like you said, the murder was big news.'

'Yes it was, Mr Price. Yes it was. Now tell me, did you ever visit Mr Colliver in custody?'

'No.' Price answered quickly and with confidence. 'Never. Why would I?'

The poor guy thinks he's back on solid ground, Michael thought, sure of what was still to come. *He couldn't be more wrong.*

'Well, it really isn't for you to be asking questions, Mr Price, but since you have I'll give you the courtesy of an answer. What I am suggesting to you is that if you *had* visited him it would have been so that you could discuss what to say in your witness statement. What lies you could tell to get your friend out of trouble.'

Epstein was on his feet before Cole was even half finished.

'My Lord, Mr Cole knows that such a comment is completely unacceptable. He cannot suggest a motive for a visit which he has not suggested actually occurred. I strongly—'

'I apologise.' Cole interrupted the objection. 'I will approach the matter in a completely different way. One which Mr Epstein will hopefully find less offensive.'

Michael noted Cole's sideways glance at the jury. It left the impression he had intended: a naughty boy who had been caught. And judging by their conspiratorial smiles in response, he had the jury onside.

Cole turned back to the witness box.

'OK then, Mr Price. You did not visit Terry Colliver in prison. Is that right?'

'That's right.' Price was growing more confident. 'Check the prison bloody records.'

'Do you know, that's exactly what we did?' Cole turned to his junior, Billy Taylor. Taylor handed him a large raft of documents. 'In fact, I have them here. Madam Usher, would you be so kind?'

The usher approached Cole for a second time and Cole handed her several sets of papers. She passed them to Price, the judge and finally the jury. In the meantime Cole handed additional sets to Epstein and to Michael.

Once everyone had their papers, Cole continued.

'This, Mr Price, is the complete print out of visits to Terry Colliver during his imprisonment for these offences in Wormwood Scrubs. Will we find your name on here if we look very carefully?'

'Not once. I never visited him. He's not my mate.'

'Well the first part's right, at least.' Cole seemed unfazed. 'You're not on there at all. But let's look at one of the names that we *do* see. Jane Gorr. Recognise that name, Mr Price?'

'Why?'

'Do you recognise the name, Mr Price?'

No response. Price just glared at Cole.

'OK, then. Let's put it another way. Is Jane Gorr the name of your partner, Mr Price?'

No response.

'Is Jane Gorr the name of the woman with whom you live, Mr Price?'

No response.

'Is Jane Gorr the name of the mother of your two children, Mr Price?'

No response.

Cole held up a bundle of papers.

'In my hand, Mr Price, are several of your housing benefit applications that list Jane Gorr as being your co-habitant, your partner and the mother of your children. I also have a copy of your children's birth certificates, listing you as father and Jane Gorr as mother. Do you need to see them to answer my question, Mr Price?'

'Yes.' Price's voice was so low it was almost inaudible. 'Jane's my missus.'

'Is *she* friends with Terry Colliver?'

'I . . . I don't know.'

'Well, she certainly seems to be, doesn't she, Mr Price. Because if we look at the list of visits to Terry Colliver, Jane Gorr visits him once in January, and then five times between February 18th and February 28th. The last visit being the day before you made your statement. With that in mind, can we assume that Jane Gorr – *your* partner – was friends with Terry Colliver?'

'I . . . I . . . well, yeah, I . . . I guess we can.'

'You *guess* we can? Your girlfriend is visiting another man in prison six times in two months and that's all you can say? You don't seem very surprised.'

'Comment, Mr Cole.' Levitt intervened before Epstein could rise.

'I'll put it another way, My Lord.' Cole turned back to Price. '*Are* you not surprised to discover that your girlfriend – your common-law wife, if there were such a thing – was visiting another man in prison?'

'Well . . . yeah . . . I . . . erm . . .'

'Oh come on, Mr Price. Put your back into it. If you're going to tell us a pack of lies at least make some effort.'

'Mr Cole!'

'Sorry, My Lord,' Cole acknowledged Levitt's reprimand before turning back to Price. 'You're not surprised at all, are you Mr Price?'

'I . . . erm . . .'

'You're not surprised at all because Jane Gorr was in Wormwood Scrubs on your behalf, wasn't she?'

'She wasn't.'

'Visiting *your* friend.'

'No.'

'And the reason she was there five times from the 18th of February onwards is because Terry Colliver received his copy of the evidence in this case on the 16th of February. Isn't that right?'

'My Lord,' Epstein protested. 'I fail to see how this witness can answer a question about when Terry Colliver was served with his case papers.'

Cole turned to Epstein.

'Because this witness and Terry Colliver used them to get the details they needed to concoct Mr Price's witness statement.'

'Mr Cole, you know that's going much too far,' Levitt warned, raising his voice again. Cole was pushing his luck. 'This is a cross-examination, *not* a speech.'

'Again, I apologise My Lord.' Another subtle glance at the jury. Another positive reaction. 'But that *is* what is happening, isn't it, Mr Price? You *were* sending your partner to see your friend, in order to get the details you needed for your statement.'

'Bollocks.'

'Details that were only available once Terry Colliver had received the evidence in the case.'

'You 'eard what I said.'

'And you sent your partner there so *your* name wouldn't be on the records. So you could pretend to hardly know your close friend Terry Colliver.'

Price stared at Cole in silent fury.

'Which is why the last visit was the day before your statement, isn't it? Because by then you had all the information you'd need. That's right, isn't it?'

'No.'

'You lied to the police in your witness statement. And you've lied to this jury today. All to get your friend Terry Colliver off of a murder charge.'

'Not true.' Price was desperately sticking to his story.

'Because there was no conversation with you and either of these defendants, was there?'

'There was.'

'There was no confession.'

'There was.'

'It was, is and always will be a pack of lies. Isn't that right?'

Price looked defeated. Exhausted by the hammering succession of questions he had not seen coming.

Cole looked up towards Levitt as he took his seat.

'I have no further questions, My Lord.'

Michael rose to his feet.

'And I very much doubt I can top that. So no questions, My Lord.'

Michael retook his seat and leaned across to Cole.

'Brilliant, Matt. Just excellent.'

He leaned back and put his mouth close to Jenny Draper's ear.

'Didn't I tell you he was bloody good?'

FIFTY-TWO

'Your call has been diverted to the EE voicemail service. Telephone number—'

Frustrated, Michael hit 'disconnect' without leaving a message. Scrolling up, he tapped Sarah's name and put the handset to his ear.

Another voicemail. This time he stayed on the line.

'Sarah, it's me.' Michael's voice was strained. Concerned. 'I've been trying to call Derek but his phone's been diverting to voicemail all day. I'm about to go into the cells at the Bailey but I want to make sure he's OK. Can you try calling for me? Thanks, sweetheart. Speak later.'

Reid had been in Michael's thoughts on and off throughout the day. Ever since Karl Hirst's name had occurred to him that morning. A name which, even now, made Michael's skin crawl.

There was no chance that Hirst could be responsible for Longman and Blunt's deaths. Not while he was still a prisoner. Michael knew that. But for some reason he still felt anxious.

In the few short weeks they had known him, Karl Hirst had played a huge role in their lives. He had almost been a stumbling block to the friendship that had followed, and so his was a name they never discussed. And yet it was a name that Michael would forever connect to his pupil-master, to his own past mistakes, and to the loyalty Reid had shown to Michael all those years ago.

A loyalty that had gone unspoken ever since.

The memory made Michael think of Derek Reid, sitting alone and mourning Phillip Longman. And it made Michael want to be there for his friend, just as his friend had been there for him all those years ago.

For now, however, that would have to wait.

Simon Kash shuffled into the interview room, handcuffed to the same muscular custody officer that had accompanied him from day one. Kash looked as small as ever in comparison, but he also looked engaged. Hope can sometimes be visible in a person. Michael had seen it before, with other clients, but never as clearly as today. It shone from Kash's eyes.

It was barely five minutes since Michael's message to Sarah. The Old Bailey's custody suite was always quieter in the early afternoon. None of the log-jams that blight the mornings. It allowed the lawyers quicker access, and more time with their clients.

Michael intended to waste none of it.

'Did you follow what happened in court this afternoon, Simon?'

'I think so, yeah.' Kash's tone was hesitant. The voice of a man who *hoped* he had understood correctly. 'Mr Cole made it look like Jay had made it up. That he had lied for Colliver to put the blame on us.'

'That's right, Simon.' This time Draper spoke. 'And Mr Cole did it very, very well. The jury were not happy with Price by the end.'

'But Jay stood his ground.' Kash's eyes had shifted to Draper. 'He didn't *admit* he was lying, did he?'

'That's not how it really works, Simon.' Michael again. 'This isn't *Perry Mason.*'

Kash's eyes showed no hint of name recognition. Michael struggled for an alternative. *Rumpole? LA Law? Boston Legal?* None would mean anything to the boy.

Michael took an alternative route.

'What I mean, Simon, is that this isn't TV. It's not a film. This is real life. And in real life witnesses almost never cave in and admit that they're lying.'

'Then how do you beat them?'

'You do exactly what Matt Cole just did to Jay Price. You tie them up in knots. You get them to a place where their only choice is to either break and tell the truth, or to look ridiculous by continuing with their lie. They almost always choose to look ridiculous. Just like Price did.'

'But I don't understand. If they haven't admitted the lie? How has it been proved if they stick to it?'

'The witness isn't the one who decides what has and hasn't been proved, Simon. The *jury* decides that. So if the witness *is* deluding themselves and thinking they've done well by sticking to their guns, that doesn't matter. It's what the *jury* makes of it that counts.'

'And our jury hated Price,' Draper added.

'OK. I get that.' A smile returned to Kash's face. They were clearly the answers he had hoped for. His eyes moved away from Draper and back to Michael. 'And does it mean we don't have to attack Darren now? Now we're on the same side?'

'We're *not* on the same side, Simon.'

Michael leaned forward as he spoke. As if the closeness could emphasise the importance of his words.

'For that one witness – for Price – yes, we had shared interests. But *only* for him. Tomorrow we have Terry Colliver, Simon. And to defend you properly I *have* suggest not only that *he* murdered the Galloways, but that he did it with Darren. It's the only way we win this. The only way.'

Kash sat back into his seat. For once he did not shrink. For once he held Michael's eye.

It's sinking in, Michael thought. *He's finally getting it.*

'Do you understand, Simon?' Draper broke the silence. 'You see what has to be done?'

Kash nodded.

'Does that mean you agree? Or just that you understand?'

'I understand,' Kash clarified. His eyes met Draper's. 'I'm not stupid, Jenny. I know I'm not clever like you guys, but I get it. Darren did this. Darren and Terry. Not me. I don't want to spend my life in prison for them.'

Michael sat upright in his chair.

'That's the first time you've ever said that, Simon. That O'Driscoll really was behind this.'

'I know, Mr Devlin.' Kash seemed as strong as Michael had ever seen him. 'And I know I should have spoken up sooner. But I was scared. I'm still scared. I'm scared of what will happen if I tell the truth. If I let *you* tell the truth.'

'I understand that, Simon. I know what you're worried about and I'm not going to lie to you. I *can't* promise you protection. No one can. So you have to go into this with your eyes wide open. There *might* be consequences if you let me do what I need to do. But you need to have the courage to accept that possibility and let me do it anyway. Because that's all it is. A *possibility*. But if we *don't* do it? If we *don't* go after O'Driscoll? Then you go to prison for the rest of your life. Or a hell of a big part of it, anyway. And that's *not* a possibility, Simon. That's guaranteed.'

Michael watched as tears returned to Kash's eyes. There were less than there had been in the past; he was holding himself together much better than before. But still the decision was a big one. A lot for Kash's weak shoulders to carry.

'When do I need to decide?' Kash's voice was quiet. Faltering.

'Ideally, I'd like to know now.' Michael knew how far to push. And when to stop. 'But tomorrow morning will do. That's when Colliver gives his evidence. So I can give you the night to make up your mind.'

'Thank you, Mr Devlin.' Kash's voice was still soft, but there was a resolve there. A firmness.

'You're welcome, Simon. And I'm sorry to have to press you like this. But it's your life, son. I can help you, but only if you let me. So let me, Simon. Please.'

Kash rose to his feet. As he reached his full height Michael was reminded once again of just how small his client was. How slight. A child in need of Michael's protection.

'I'm going to go now, Mr Devlin. I need to think about all this. But I promise I'll have your answer tomorrow.'

'You need to, Simon.' Draper reiterated the point. 'You really do.'

Kash did not reply. Instead he just nodded his head, turned his back and left the room.

FIFTY-THREE

Michael pulled the phone from his ear and slammed it down with more force than intended. The shelf ahead of him shook with the impact. The mirror above it swayed but the furnishings of the QC's Robing Room had been built to last and were more than a match for the heavy-handed frustration of Michael Devlin.

Twenty minutes had passed since Michael had left the cells. Twenty minutes in which he had called Derek Reid three times, and Sarah twice. The calls to Sarah had diverted directly to voicemail, which meant she was either in a meeting or filming a broadcast. Unavailable either way.

The calls to Reid had connected. A ringtone each time, with voicemail activating only when the call went unanswered.

I don't like it, Michael thought. *Why's his phone not just switched off if he wants to be left alone?*

At first Michael had not been concerned. Just uneasy. But now that unease was becoming something more. Knowing that Hirst could not be responsible was not helping. Two lawyers had been murdered while alone in their homes. Just because it wasn't Hirst or Wisdom Penfold didn't mean Reid was not on *someone's* list.

Shake it off, Michael instructed himself as he stared at his phone's touchscreen, irritated at his own concerns. *What the hell are the odds? And who the hell is getting to him with a police detail parked outside his door? He's probably just too hungover – maybe even still too drunk – to answer.*

But for all of the logic of his reasoning, Michael was growing agitated by the lack of contact.

He shook his head as he placed his silk gown on its hanger. His QC's outfit was still pristine. Michael saw to that each day. He would carefully hang his QC's jacket, buttoned, with his robe positioned above it on the same perfectly sized hanger. But not today. Today his robe was thrust in place. The QC's jacket forgotten entirely.

The phone was back in Michael's hand just moments later. His thumb found the recent calls log. Reid's name sat at the top of the list. The number seven next to it, indicating how many times Michael had called.

Michael pressed Reid's name and waited for the call to connect.

A ringtone. Just like the previous seven calls. And like those calls it went unanswered. Finally, a robotic female voice cut in.

'Your call has been diverted to the EE voicemail—'

'Fuck.'

Michael disconnected. Against everything his brain was telling him, Reid's unavailability was worrying him.

Why the hell is he not answering? Why the hell is he not checking messages.

Michael already had an explanation for exactly that: Reid had told Sarah that he would be out of contact for a few days.

But then why is his phone not switched off?

It was a small thing, probably meaningless. But with so many missed calls now showing, why had Reid not called him back? If only to make sure everything was OK? Michael gazed at the wall, trying to decide what to do next.

Levy.

He did not want to waste her time; God knows she had other pressing concerns. But he could not think of anything else to do and so – with his gut telling him that something was not right – he opened his wallet, found Levy's card and punched her digits into his phone.

'Joelle Levy.' The slightly husky voice was distinctive. Levy's accent was English but it was coloured by a hint of Israeli. Michael had not noticed it before.

'Joelle, it's Michael Devlin. Look, I'm really sorry to call you but I was hoping you could give me some reassurance about Derek Reid.'

'Michael. Hi.' Levy sounded surprised by both the call and the request. 'I, erm, I'm a little confused. What do you mean by reassurance?'

'Just that he's OK. Your guys haven't called in anything out of the ordinary, have they?'

'I'm sorry, Michael. What guys?'

'The guys you stationed to keep an eye on him, Joelle. The protection detail.'

'Yeah, I remember. But that was when we were chasing Wisdom Penfold. When we thought Derek was a potential target. Once Penfold was ruled out the protection was stood down.'

Michael felt the warmth of his body disappear.

'You mean there's no one keeping a watch on Derek?'

'No. Not now we've ruled Penfold out. Why would there be?'

Michael felt himself lose focus for just a moment. His rational mind was trying to keep him on track – trying to reassure him that there was no way Reid was a target – but it was losing to the vivid images of Michael's worst fears.

He forced himself to regain his composure.

'But what about the new suspects? The ones arrested by Blunt. Have none of them brought up Derek's name?'

'We're only just starting that list. I only picked up Sarah's message about an hour ago. So there are no new suspects right now.'

Michael shook his head at the answer. It was not what he wanted to hear.

Levy continued.

'Michael, have you got some reason to think that Derek Reid is in danger?'

'I . . . I don't, no.' Michael felt his blood pressure reduce as he heard his own answer. 'I've just got a bad feeling, that's all. I don't know why.'

'Do you want me to send someone round to his address? To check on him?'

'No. No, there's no need. I'm close by. I'll go myself.'

'Are you sure?'

'I'm sure. Like I said, it's just a feeling based on nothing.'

'OK,' Levy replied. 'Then get yourself there and make yourself feel better.'

FIFTY-FOUR

Lonsdale Square was barely two miles from the Central Criminal Court. A fifteen-minute journey by car, assuming typical London traffic. Twice the time by bus. A good black cab driver could shave another five minutes from the figure by using the back streets and rat-runs learned from the four-year intensive education that was accurately nicknamed 'The Knowledge'.

Michael hailed the first black cab that passed as he rushed from the court building and onto the street outside. It was the right decision. The driver took right and left turns to avoid the traffic, roadworks and dead-ends that blight the route. Paid by distance, he seemed eager to finish the fare and start the next.

Michael watched as the world passed by the window, every inch of it a blur. Nothing his eyes took in could shift the image in his mind. The thought of Derek Reid suffering the same fate as Longman and Blunt. It was ridiculous, he realised. But it would not go away.

The sound of Michael's mobile phone broke through his darkest thoughts. He took the handset from his pocket and lifted it to his ear.

'Is everything OK?' Sarah's voice was worried. 'I've just listened to your messages.'

'I don't know.' Michael could hear how tense he sounded. 'I'm on my way to Derek's. To make sure he's OK.'

'I'm sure he is,' Sarah replied. 'Remember what he told me. He was taking himself off the grid for a few days.'

'Yeah, I know that. But I'm just gonna make sure for myself.'

Sarah was silent for a moment.

'Michael, there's something you need to know.'

The tone of Sarah's voice sent a shiver down Michael's spine.

'It's about Karl Hirst,' she continued. 'Whoever told you that he is still in custody was wrong. Hirst is out. He's been out for three years.'

Michael was silent as his heart rate doubled in an instant. The adrenaline that came with it made everything else seem unreal.

'That's not possible,' Michael finally said, his tone flat. 'I made arrangements. I—'

'It was a political release,' Sarah interrupted. 'A cover-up. Your guy probably couldn't risk telling you. Not with everything else being kept so under wraps.'

Michael tried to think through what Sarah was telling him, but his mind could no longer analyse concepts like politics and cover-ups. All he could see was Karl Hirst and Derek Reid, and the atrocities one could be inflicting upon the other.

The images had awoken the 'other' Michael. The less civilised, more primitive survivor he had long left behind. It was that 'other' Michael who had already taken charge as the cab took the first right-hand turn into Lonsdale Square.

'I'm almost there,' Michael said, his voice flat. 'I have to go.'

'Michael, please. If Derek doesn't answer the door then promise me you won't go inside.'

'I can't do that,' Michael replied. 'If Hirst is out then he's behind all of this. And that means Derek's in danger.'

'But what if you're right?' Sarah's voice was becoming frantic. 'What if it is Hirst? What if he's still in there?'

'Then he won't leave that house alive.' Michael disconnected and turned to the taxi driver. 'Stop here.'

The cab stopped abruptly. Michael stepped out, threw a twenty-pound note through the open window and began to run.

Reid's home was halfway along the left-hand side of the square. Not visible from where the cab had stopped. The greenery of the private garden around which the tall townhouses were built saw to that. It was an obstruction that would last only a few steps.

Michael's eyes stayed fixed ahead as he ran, not blinking in the intense sunlight. In just moments he saw the front of the house, carefully constructed to match the surrounding homes. Rebuilt after an ordeal Michael had thought would be his worst experience in his former home.

Except the worst was perhaps still to come.

It took a few moments to see that the front door was open, revealed by the growing angle as he moved closer. The sight made Michael speed up. Only one thought on his mind.

Hirst.

Michael's fear had passed, replaced by a focused determination to find and to harm whoever had targeted Derek Reid. That was what drove Michael now.

If Hirst is inside, Hirst will pay.

Michael's speed somehow increased as he grew closer. Fast enough that, as he reached the house, he passed through the doorway clumsily, his shoulder colliding with the hallway wall as he banked left. The impact slowed him but it did not stop him.

If only it had.

The door that separated Reid's hallway from his lounge was open, giving a clear view of the room's front half and revealing what Michael had feared the most, visible in all its dreadful glory.

A sight that brought Michael to his knees.

FIFTY-FIVE

'Drink this.'

Sarah's shaking hand placed a crystal glass on the worktop of Derek Reid's kitchen island. Inches from Michael's right hand. The glass was half-filled. Irish whiskey. Two doubles, at least. Reid had not been a whiskey man; he preferred grape over grain. But what he *had* been was an excellent host, and so he always had a supply on hand for his friend.

Sarah had watched Reid pour countless times. She knew where he kept the strong stuff.

'Thanks.' Michael's voice was soft. The voice of a man bereft.

Sarah wiped a tear from her own eye as she watched Michael drink. It was not his first glass of the day. It would not be his last.

She moved away without meeting Michael's eye. She did not want to look at him. Did not want to see his devastation. Reid's death alone was hard to take; Sarah had genuinely loved the man. Combined with Michael's undisguised pain, it became more than Sarah could take.

Worse still, though, was the thought that would not leave Sarah's mind.

I did this. If I had just called Levy. If I had just mentioned Hirst as soon as I knew he was out.

The thought was a crushing mix of abject shame and guilt, on top of her grief. And it was a thought which she feared Michael *must* share.

Sarah was distracted from her own anguish by the sound of Michael placing his glass back onto the worktop. His gaze was fixed upon it, as if fascinated by the now-diminished liquid inside. Sarah knew better. Michael had retreated into himself. Into a dark place she could not hope to understand.

She felt the tears building again, threatening to overwhelm her. She blinked them away, looking around the room for something she could focus on. And as she did so it occurred to her that this was the very room in which she and Michael had first met, almost two years ago. That night it had been Sarah who had lost someone dear to her. Her own friend and mentor.

A shitty damn coincidence, she dully reflected.

'Have Kevin Gilligan and Seth Neil been contacted?'

Michael did not look up from the glass as he spoke.

The names meant nothing to Sarah. She was not sure the question was for her.

'I don't know,' she replied, the otherwise empty room satisfying her that Michael could be speaking to no one else. 'I don't know who those people are.'

'They were the two prosecuting barristers in Hirst's trial. They could be on his list.'

'Right, OK. Yes, Joelle saw to that from Scotland Yard. She said that the prosecutors had been contacted and that their protection officers were on-site.'

Michael did not react to Sarah's mention of protection officers. Instead he wiped the swelling tears from his eyes and spoke again.

'They can't go home. None of us can. Not until Hirst is caught.'

'I don't understand any of this, Michael.' Sarah's voice began to break. The loss of Reid – the whole situation – was hard to take. But combined with the threat to their own lives? It was close to impossible. 'Why is Hirst doing this? To Derek? To us? You guys were on *his* side, for Christ's sake. You *defended* him.'

'You don't need to know, Sarah. You don't *want* to know.'

'Maybe she doesn't.' The distinctive voice came from the kitchen doorway. It carried the slightest accent. One Michael had barely noticed until today. 'But I do.'

Levy strode into Reid's kitchen. It was not the ideal place for a conversation, with his body lying cold in the next room. And she was sure it was the last place either Sarah or Michael wanted to be. But with Michael now a potential target, a house crawling with cops had seemed the safest place for the moment. At least until she could get a protection detail sorted. For now, though, her priority was to get some answers.

She took a seat at the island unit, Michael and Sarah on either side of her. The worktop between them was clear except for Michael's glass. Levy lifted it to her nose and sniffed deeply.

'Bushmills?'

'No idea.' Sarah looked to her right. Towards the bottle on the side worktop. She read the label. 'Actually yeah. Good nose.'

'Good guess, anyway. Do you mind if I join?'

Levy indicated to Michael's glass as she spoke.

'On duty?' Sarah asked.

'Aren't I always?' Levy replied, dispirited.

The death of Derek Reid was a sucker punch. It was bad enough that another innocent man was dead because she had failed to find his killer. But it was made all the worse because the same man had been under police protection until last night.

If there was ever a time I needed a drink . . .

Sarah stood up without another word and poured two more glasses.

'I might as well join you too,' Sarah said as she pushed a glass towards Levy.

Levy drank gratefully, welcoming the comforting burn of the whiskey, all the while aware that Michael was watching her intently.

'Where are you moving Anne Flaherty?' he asked abruptly, as soon as the glass was away from her lips.

Michael had no time for pleasantries. Not today. Levy could understand that. After the devastation of Derek Reid, the priority was the safety of his family.

'We aren't,' Levy replied. 'We are going to keep a protection detail in your home. For all three of you. I assumed that was right?'

'No.' Michael's tone was sure. 'Hirst can't be underestimated. I don't want my family kept anywhere that's been associated with any of us before today.'

'Michael, don't you think—'

'Just trust me, Sarah.' Michael stopped the interruption midstream without a glance. He kept his eyes on Levy. 'It has to be somewhere completely new.'

Levy nodded her assent. It was rare for her to defer to a civilian once she had decided on a course of action. But Michael had been through hell today. And in the last few hours Levy had learned a lot about Michael Devlin that she had not known before. If a man with his experience said extra precautions were needed, Levy was sure as hell going to take them.

'Thomas.' Levy raised her voice as she called out the name, directing it towards the kitchen door and prompting Detective Inspector Thomas Chadwick to enter the room.

'Call the head of the protection detail at Mr Devlin and Miss Truman's home. Tell them that they are to escort Miss Flaherty to Scotland Yard. They're to make sure she's comfortable. And in the meantime I want a suitable safe house sourced, for the family to occupy until this is over.'

Levy turned back to Michael.

'Good enough?'

'Good enough,' Michael replied.

'OK.' Levy returned her attention to Chadwick. 'Get that done as a priority, Thomas. Right now.'

'Ma'am.'

Chadwick left without another word. The MIT chain of command in action.

'Now.' Levy turned her gaze back upon Michael. 'Anne's safe. You're both safe. Which means we have some breathing space. So let's use it. Who the hell is Karl Hirst to you and why did he come for Derek Reid?'

FIFTY-SIX

'Karl Hirst is the closest thing to a pure psychopath I've ever seen.' Michael was retaking his seat as he spoke, his glass again replenished with amber liquid. It was now much more than half full.

'He was also my first real case as Derek's pupil. A hell of an introduction to the job.'

'I know a little of the case, Michael.' Levy was not unprepared. 'I had the files checked. Turns out Hirst was one of the names that came up when Longman was murdered. But he didn't make the cut when we sifted the suspects.'

'Why not?'

'Because we're undermanned and under-resourced and so we had to prioritise the most likely suspects over the less likely,' Levy replied. 'And key details didn't match the MO of this case, so he didn't make the cut. Then Blunt was killed and as far as we saw there was no connection, as Blunt hadn't been Hirst's lawyer.'

'But you didn't look at Blunt's time with the police?'

'We weren't aware of that line of enquiry at that stage.' Michael saw Levy cast a glance at Sarah. 'And once we were? That came too late.'

'How the hell did you not know Blunt had been a cop?' Michael asked.

'Same answer as before,' Levy replied, 'only with added incompetence. I've got half my team split between the Longman case and the gang-killing in Brixton, and that's out of a team that's only at half-capacity already. When we're stretched that far we have to trust our officers to be on the ball. It turns out the one I put onto Blunt's background was less than that. Blunt had no family and no friends, so no one to fill in the blanks, and the idiot DC I put on his background check didn't go any further than "lawyer", as for him it was the obvious conclusion.'

'That's a hell of a mistake,' Michael said.

'And don't think it'll go unpunished,' Levy replied.

Michael drained a mouthful of whiskey as Levy spoke.

'None of which really matters right now,' he finally said. 'Not while Hirst's still out there. What we need to be doing is making sure that anyone else he might be targeting is safe.'

'We've already done that, Michael. We have you and your family under protection, plus the other barristers in the case. We've even put a unit on Adam Blunt's old detective sergeant, just in case. There's no one else left, is there?'

Michael did not answer immediately. His mind was too busy elsewhere. Did he need to tell Levy everything? Could Hirst really find the only other possible target? Michael did not know, and that fact answered the question for him.

'There's one other person,' he finally replied. 'The main witness at Hirst's trial. Tina Barker.'

'There's another target?' Levy exclaimed, startled and angry at the same time. 'Why the *hell* haven't you mentioned her until now, Michael? You were fast enough demanding protection for Derek Reid and telling me how to do my job when it came to Anne Flaherty. But not Tina Barker? She just slipped your mind?'

'She didn't slip anything,' Michael snapped, riled by Levy's tone and overwrought after the trauma of the day. 'And don't lose your temper with me. I'm doing the best I can in the circumstances.'

'Then give me a reason to keep my temper.' Levy met Michael's glare, matched its intensity with her own. 'Because right now it looks like you've left a potential target hanging out to dry.'

'I didn't mention Tina because I didn't think she was in any danger,' Michael replied, still rankled. 'Christ, I *still* don't. She's been safe in witness protection for almost two decades, so I don't see how Hirst could track her down. But you want to know everything and *that's* everything!'

Levy's eyes stayed fixed on Michael's. Neither looked ready to back down from their confrontation. Alpha personalities rarely do.

'How the hell is this helping anyone?' Sarah's voice cut through the angry silence. 'It isn't and it won't. So stop this shit! Both of you!'

Michael did not respond. Levy's suggestion – and her tone – had provoked him. On any normal day he would have risen above it, but today was as far from normal as it could get.

Levy's blood, it seemed, had not risen so high.

'She's right,' she said grudgingly. 'I just don't want to lose anyone else to this sick bastard. And if we're going to achieve that then I need to know what we're dealing with.'

Levy sat back on her stool and took a small sip from her glass.

'Just tell me what I need to know.'

Michael leaned forward and placed both forearms on the worktop, steeling himself. This time he did not touch his drink. He knew it was time to tell his part of the story. He inhaled deeply.

'Tina Barker was eleven years old when Hirst took her. Her brother, Tommy, was eight. Their father was the manager of a high street bank in Guildford. The biggest in the area, but still a local bank. That made it a perfect target. Lower security but still likely a big haul for whoever was willing to take it on a Friday. Which Karl Hirst certainly was.

'Hirst took the children on the Thursday night. In the most brazen way possible. He broke in after the family had gone to sleep. Tied and gagged them all in their beds: both kids, mum and dad. He carried the children one at a time to a van he had waiting on the drive, and drove them away to a disused warehouse five miles away. Once he was there he tied them up again and then went back to their parents.

'He kept the father and mother bound as he gave them their instructions. The father was to make sure that he was the last person in the bank on the Friday evening. He was to work late and make sure everyone else left. Then Hirst would arrive at the rear of the bank in his van, be given access to the safe and time to clear it. Hirst would then leave, head back to the kids and release them at a location he would disclose in a telephone call to their parents.

'Once he had made the arrangements – once he had given the orders – he told them that if the police were called or in any way involved, the kids would die. And just to show them that he was serious, he brought them two fingers from Tina's left hand. Which did exactly the job it was intended to do. The father did as he was ordered, and Hirst drove away with a van full of over seven hundred thousand pounds. A serious haul for one night's work.

'That should have been that. The kids should have been released and he should have escaped with the best part of a million in cash. But for some reason only that sick bastard will ever understand, he didn't let them go as promised. And once they *weren't* released their parents reported the whole thing to the police, who started a manhunt.

'It didn't take too long; Hirst hadn't planned the backend of the job nearly as well as he had the front. After the robbery he stayed put, in the same warehouse where he was keeping the children. He didn't think to move, which was his undoing. Well, that and the time frame from the first night.

'It was Adam Blunt who found him. Blunt worked out the possible driving distances on the night of the kidnap. How far Hirst could have gone in the time it took before he came back to give his instructions to the parents. Using that time frame, Blunt was able to triangulate the furthest distance he could have reached and then identify the most likely hiding places within that distance. Of those possibilities, his gut took him to an old industrial estate. They found the children right there. Little Tommy was already dead. Suffocated, the autopsy said. But Tina was still alive. Badly injured, but alive. Two fingers missing, obviously. But other injuries too. Mental and physical. Not the least of which was that she'd watched her brother die.'

'How was he caught?' It was Sarah who asked. When Michael looked over to answer he saw tears in her eyes. It surprised him. In her job she heard far worse than this. Meaning the heightened emotion was coming from elsewhere.

Derek's death, he thought. But what he did not know was the blame Sarah was placing on herself. Blame for not giving Hirst's name to Levy.

Michael hated to see Sarah cry, but now was not the time to console her. He had to finish what he had started; the most important details were still to come.

He answered Sarah's question.

'Blunt again. With the help of a police helicopter. A figure was spotted two acres away from the warehouse. Hirst had heard the police coming from a distance. Which was when he proved – for me – that he might be a psycho, but he certainly wasn't crazy. A crazy man would waste time on the children. Kill the remaining witnesses. For pleasure, or in some hope it might make a difference. Not Hirst. He didn't go near Tina again. He just ran without a moment of hesitation. The man was always thinking, and he knew that any delay could end with him being caught. So he ran.'

'But he was caught anyway?'

'Yeah. He didn't really stand a chance. Once the police helicopter was overhead it would pick up the body heat of anyone in the area. And on that night it only found one. That was part of the case they built against him. The kidnapper had run, and not ten minutes later there was only one body-heat signature in the vicinity, other than those of the cops. And once they had that bead on him he wasn't going anywhere. They guided Blunt in and he cornered Hirst by a stream. Blunt was armed, Hirst wasn't. A situation like that only ends one way.'

Michael stopped speaking. He had reached the end of part one. The uncontroversial part.

He looked at what was left in his glass. Just under half. *It might see me through*, he thought. *Let's find out.*

The glass was empty when it next touched the worktop.

'Derek had been instructed to defend Hirst from the beginning. The summer before I started my pupillage. So all the case prep had been done before I was on the scene. The trial itself was fixed to begin three weeks into my six months with Derek. That gave me time to read into the case, and to get to know Derek, but not much else.

'Inexperienced as I was, I could still see that Hirst had a good chance of getting off. The case against him just wasn't that strong. Sure, his whereabouts at the time of his arrest was a problem. Plus he had no alibi at all for the thirty-six hours that mattered and he also fit the general description, in terms of height and build. But the kidnapper had worn a mask and gloves throughout the whole thing. From the house to the bank, and the entire time he spent with the kids. So that general description didn't mean too much. In addition to which there were no forensics linking Hirst to the house, to the bank, to the van. Or even to Tina's severed fingers. And no mobile-phone coverage. Cell site evidence was in its infancy then, but it was still useful. And Hirst must have known that, as there was no phone found on him when he was arrested and no calls made on any handset that could have been attributed to him. Like I said, the only mistake he'd made was not leaving the hideout earlier, but even then he wasn't actually found there. It made convicting him a nightmare for the prosecution.

'Which was all good for us, as his defence team. On the first day of the trial I walked into the Old Bailey with a spring in my step. I knew how Derek was going to attack. I knew our strengths outweighed our weaknesses. I was going to be part of a big, high-profile murder trial and we were going to win. So I really thought that this was it. I was starting my career with a bang. And then I met Karl Hirst for the first time.'

Michael paused, thinking back to that first encounter. Those pale, unflinching eyes. It was all coming back to him. All the horrors he had banished from his mind, as he did at the end of every trial so steeped in evil. Forcing himself to forget these things was the only way to survive his job, the only way to sleep at night. But now, as the memory of Hirst's case was flooding back to him, one thought dominated Michael's mind.

I should have known it was Hirst sooner. I should have found out he was no longer inside, and I should have gone to Levy.

The guilt threatened to break him, but he could not let that happen. For now the priority had to be the capture of Hirst. And for that, Michael needed to finish his story. He forced himself to continue.

'Derek and I were in the cells at the Old Bailey at 9.30 a.m. First ones in. It took maybe five minutes for the cell staff to bring Hirst to us. And maybe five minutes more for Hirst to convince me that he was guilty as hell and needed to spend the rest of his life in prison.'

'Five minutes?' Now the questions came. This one from Levy. 'What the hell did he do in five minutes?'

'Everything he needed to.' Michael paused for a beat. Long enough to find the right words. 'I didn't come from the kind of world that produces barristers, Joelle. I grew up around all kinds of people. Plenty of them were decent folk. But plenty weren't. I might have been young but I'd seen enough thugs and psychopaths to recognise one in front of me. And when I met Hirst I could see that he was a whole other level of sick.'

'But what told you that? He must have done or said something specific?'

'He was too smart for it to be something specific. And he didn't tell us anything. You know how it works, Joelle; if Hirst had told us he was guilty we couldn't have defended him properly. Couldn't have gone into court and advanced a version of events we'd been told was untrue. It's against all the rules.'

'Then what?'

'It's impossible to explain. But it was *everything*, I guess. It was *all* off. Don't get me wrong. Hirst stuck to his story. Claimed he had nothing to do with the kidnapping. With Tommy's death. With the robbery. With any of it. He maintained he was just in the wrong place at the wrong time. Out looking for his lost dog when a police helicopter started hovering overhead and he was arrested at gunpoint. If it was anyone else then maybe I could have believed it. But the way he told the story? Smiling the whole time? A smug, superior smile that just didn't slip, no matter how upsetting the detail got.

'Looking back, he was making no effort to have us believe him. No effort to convince us that he was telling the truth. He didn't care. He knew the case against him was crap; he thought he'd be walking if we did our job just half well. And he knew Derek's reputation. "Half-well" wasn't an option. Derek was too good for that. So that was it, really. I walked out of that room knowing Hirst was guilty, and knowing that – in a few weeks – we'd have that piece of shit back on the streets.'

Michael stopped speaking again. He had reached the part of the story he was dreading. The part he and Reid had forced themselves to 'forget' all those years ago. The reason they had never again discussed the case of Karl Hirst.

'What changed in the case?' Levy asked. 'How did Hirst serve fourteen years if he was a dead cert to be acquitted?'

Michael cast his eyes to the floor, knowing that he had no choice but to answer.

'It was me. I'm the reason Hirst was convicted.'

'What do you mean?' Sarah asked. 'What did you do?'

Michael looked up. He felt the burning hint of tears beginning to threaten his eyes.

'I couldn't let him walk away. Not after what he had done to those kids. I couldn't let him do that again, Sarah. And I knew as sure as I've ever known anything in my life; if that bastard was let out, he *would* do it again.

'So I waited. I waited to see how the case went. Whether the prosecution could pull something out of the bag. But when I could see that wasn't going to happen – when I could see he was definitely going to walk – I made a decision.

'I contacted Adam Blunt before Tina Barker was due to give evidence. Said I needed to see him. We met in a pub on the Mile End Road where we knew no one in the case would stumble on us. I told him he was going to lose the case. That was nothing Blunt didn't already know, but he said there was nothing he could do. And so I made a suggestion. I asked him to give me five minutes with Tina Barker the next morning. Before she was due to testify. To let me talk to her and give her some guidance, something that would help in her evidence. At first Blunt refused. He threatened to arrest me there and then; I guess he should have done. But I kept talking, and in the end he caved. Blunt wanted Hirst convicted as much as I did. More, probably. By the time we'd finished he'd agreed to do what needed to be done.

'And so I met with Tina Barker the next morning. Blunt had arranged for her to be at court at 8 a.m., long before Derek or the prosecutor would be there. I was able to speak to her for ten minutes. And in that ten minutes I made her memorise every detail of the small tattoo of a flying bluebird that Hirst had on his right hand. Every single millimetre of the thing. And I coached her on *when* she should say she had seen it. To say it had been a glimpse as he restrained her before removing her fingers. Then a closer look – a longer look – as he smothered her brother. I gave her everything she needed to make an admissible identification from a feature unique to Hirst. An identification which would be enough to convict him.'

'You coached a key witness in a murder trial?' Levy spoke slowly, looking at Michael in disbelief. 'You arranged for Tina Barker to commit perjury, to secure a conviction and a life sentence?'

'Yes.' Michael's answer was emotionless. It was done. He was ready for the consequences.

'Then I . . . I think I have to arrest you.' Levy sounded unsure of herself. As if she was reaching a conclusion that went against every natural instinct. She slowly pushed her whiskey glass away. A sign to Michael that, in that moment, their relationship had changed. 'I don't think you've left me any choice.'

'I know that,' Michael replied. 'I knew that when I started speaking. And I won't deny any of what I just told you when the time comes. But please do me one favour. Please let's deal with Hirst first. Let's not split your resources with another case while that bastard is still out there. Deal with Hirst – catch him – and *then* you can do whatever you have to with me. But *after*. Please.'

Levy did not speak for a moment, and Michael could see her struggling with the decision she now had to make. What he had told her was a confession to a serious criminal offence. It was her duty to arrest him and to do so now, but at the same time he knew she could see the sense in his words. Hirst had to be the priority. Michael's seventeen-year-old crime was a distraction the overstretched MIT One could do without right now.

'After, then,' Levy finally agreed, in a voice that said she would have preferred 'never'. 'But don't think we're not coming back to this, Michael.'

'I don't doubt it.'

'You shouldn't. Now finish the story. Because so far I can see why *you're* a target. And Blunt. And maybe even Tina Barker. But not Derek Reid and Phillip Longman.'

Michael nodded and continued.

'Tina gave her evidence perfectly. To be honest, I think by the time I had finished with her in that room I'd managed to convince her that what she was about to say was true. That she really *had* seen the tattoo. Because she was flawless. Derek and Longman, though? They both knew better.

'Obviously Tina had made no mention of the tattoo in her original statement. Or anywhere else. Otherwise I wouldn't have needed to step in. So when she said it in her evidence almost everyone was shocked. Derek. Longman. And most definitely Hirst. I kept my eyes to the floor and tried hard not to react at all. Too hard, as it turns out. Because I was noticed.

'As soon as Tina's evidence ended, Derek asked for a short adjournment. Longman granted it. And as we stood to leave the court – after the jury had been taken out – Hirst started to go crazy behind the glass. Started demanding that we came straight down to see him in the cells, to go over what had just happened. He was screaming and shouting at Blunt, too. Accusing him of nobbling the witness. Of fitting him up. But Derek ignored him. Instead he took me by the arm and practically ran me out of the courtroom.

'We ended up in an interview room across the way. Just the two of us. And Derek told me then that he knew what I'd done. He said he'd been watching me throughout the trial. That he'd seen my feelings towards Hirst go from distaste to disgust and all the way through to hatred. Derek could tell how desperate I was for Hirst to be convicted. And yet I didn't respond at all when evidence suddenly emerged that could achieve what I so badly wanted. Evidence that could convict Hirst. It was at that moment that I realised for the first time just how much smarter than me Derek really was. He was a million miles ahead. And he knew without question that I'd been involved in the new evidence.'

'What did he do?' Sarah asked.

'He bawled me out. Just like you'd expect. He called me one of the most unprofessional, stupid sons-of-bitches under the sun. And he was *right*. I had no place doing what I did. No place at all.'

Michael felt his voice begin to break as he remembered Derek's fury in that moment, guilt and regret threatening to overwhelm him.

'It's OK, Michael.' Sarah placed her hand on top of Michael's as she spoke.

Michael stood up, taking his hand away. He was not ready for Sarah's touch. For anyone's. Not with the thought of Derek Reid at the very forefront of his mind.

He moved away, back towards the whiskey bottle that had noticeably diminished in the past thirty minutes. He half-filled his glass and sat back down.

'Derek bawled me out,' Michael repeated. 'But when he was done he covered my arse. He didn't have to do that for me – he barely knew me back then – but he did it.'

'How?' Levy asked. 'What did he do?'

'It was what he *didn't* do,' Michael replied. 'He didn't cross-examine Tina on the tattoo. Didn't even mention it. He just acted like she had never said it.'

'Why?' Sarah could not understand. 'Surely he had to challenge it?'

'I guess he felt he couldn't risk it. Tina was a kid, so the chances are she would have opened up about our conversation if cross-examined at all. Which would have cost me my career and God knows how long in prison, for perverting the course of justice. Derek decided to protect me, and so he said nothing.'

'How did Hirst take *that*?' Levy again. 'The only witness against him adds a killer piece of evidence out of nowhere, and his barrister just *leaves* it? Hirst was no fool. How'd he react?'

'He was apoplectic. By the time we got to the custody suite at the end of the day he was already confined to his cell. The security staff wouldn't let him out to see us in the normal way; it had taken seven of them just to get him into his cell in the first place, so no way were they letting him out. Which meant we only got to see him through the wicket in his cell door.'

'And what did he say?'

'He accused Derek of doing exactly what *I'd* done. Said he was in cahoots with the police and the CPS and the judge. Everyone, basically. And he threatened him, said that they were all going to pay.'

Michael's words trailed off once again. A new thought was registering.

'He basically threatened to do *exactly* what he's done. What he's done to everyone *but* me so far. To everyone except the guy who *actually* wronged him.' Michael could not stop the tears from falling as reality hit home. 'They all died for what I did. And Longman? Derek? They had *nothing* to do with it. Jesus, it's my fault. Derek's dead and all he did was cover for me. All he did was protect me from my own stupidity.'

Michael stopped speaking. He had to. His voice had finally broken. Sarah stood up and stepped towards him, but he stopped her with a raised hand.

'I need to finish,' he said, forcing down a sob.

'Yes.' The agreement came from Levy, her tone still professional. 'Yes, you do. I still need to know how Longman fits in to all of this.'

Michael nodded his head in response and took a slow, deep breath to regain his composure. There was no point in wiping his face. It would not stop the tears coming. Instead he took a full gulp of whiskey and continued, his voice faltering throughout.

'That was the last we heard from Hirst. We were fired from the case from that moment. He wanted the trial aborted and a new legal team appointed. To start from scratch. But Longman didn't allow it. Longman didn't believe that Derek or I had anything to do with the new evidence. I mean, he knew Derek, he'd been Derek's pupil-master and Longman knew for sure that he wasn't capable of corrupting evidence, whatever Hirst alleged. And I guess it didn't occur to him that a pupil would do what I had done. So Longman wouldn't let Hirst's decision to fire us – a decision he thought was wrong – derail the trial. Instead he ordered Hirst to either carry on with us or carry on alone. Hirst chose the latter.'

'So Longman didn't think the evidence was suspect?' asked Levy.

'Oh no, he knew something was up,' Michael replied. 'He just got the wrong person. It turned out that when Derek was looking at me as I tried not to react to Tina's evidence of the tattoo, Longman was looking right at Blunt. He saw what Derek saw, just on someone else. So he was convinced that Blunt was behind it.'

'And he didn't stop the trial?' Levy asked, looking perplexed. 'Why?'

'I can hazard a guess. I think it's because Longman *also* thought that Hirst was too dangerous to be on the streets. Longman was a clever man. A very, very clever man. He could see Hirst for what he was and there was no way he was letting him go if he could help it. And he probably thought that Derek had made the same decision when Derek didn't cross-examine Tina on the tattoo. So Longman did nothing. He allowed the evidence to go through, and in doing so he fuelled Hirst's paranoia that we were all in it together. That we'd all conspired to convict him.'

'What makes you think that?' Sarah asked. 'How can you be sure what Longman knew?'

'Longman's final instructions to the jury were a giveaway,' Michael replied. 'So was the sentence. Both cleverly designed to scupper an appeal, which means he must have known there was something *to* appeal.'

'What were the instructions?' Sarah asked.

'They were about the charges. Hirst was on trial for the murder of Tommy Barker, but he was only convicted of manslaughter. That was because of Longman. He directed the jury that they *could* conclude from Tina's evidence that Tommy was smothered by mistake – as Hirst was trying to calm him – and that they might think that a mistake was actually *more* likely from the evidence than an intentional killing. That was bullshit, of course. Hirst meant to kill that boy. I know he did. But Tina's evidence *could* have been read that way as it came out, and so Longman added a little weight to that conclusion. Something which can carry a lot of influence with a jury when it's coming from a judge that senior. It would mean no murder conviction, but manslaughter can still carry a life sentence and if Hirst then appealed the conviction the Court of Appeal would likely say that, if anything, Longman had in fact summed up in Hirst's favour, resulting in the conviction for a lesser offence. Which is exactly what happened.'

'Clever,' Levy observed.

'It was. But that was Longman. And then he did something similar with the sentence. A life sentence was arguably too much for the crime, if Tommy's death was an accident, but giving it a fourteen year minimum made that more reasonable. In reality we all knew the minimum was just that, and that someone as cracked as Hirst would probably act up so much that they might stay inside for ever. But for appeal purposes it was, again, very clever.

And then there was what happened to Blunt.'

'What?' Levy asked. 'What happened with Blunt?'

'There's a reason this was his last case with the police. Longman called Blunt into his chambers at the end of the trial. Told him his suspicions and told him that he expected to hear of his resignation within the week. Otherwise he would contact the Commissioner directly and tell him everything. Blunt took the sensible course.'

'Blunt told you that?'

'He did, Joelle. And he told me at the same time that he had kept my name out of it, for which I was incredibly grateful. He thought we'd done the right thing and didn't see why we should both suffer for it. Over the years that seemed to change. He got more and more bitter at what he'd lost, and it put a real strain on our working relationship. It made him a nasty piece of work in his later years, someone I struggled to be around. But back then? Yeah, he took a bullet for what we had done.'

Silence fell as Michael's account came to an end. It was a lot of information to take in, he knew. A lot for both Sarah and Levy to consider.

'There are still things that don't add up.' It was Levy who spoke first. 'Longman's sentence. Life but with a relatively short minimum. You said Longman probably thought it was safe, as once a guy as violent as Hirst was inside he'd likely behave so badly that he'd never come out.'

'That's right.'

'But he didn't, did he? Which was one of the reasons we had him low on our list of potential suspects. Why others took priority. Hirst got parole on the first application because he had been an exemplary prisoner. He did not have a single act of insubordination on his prison record.

Not a single act of violence. He was seen as the picture of rehabilitation. How does that fit with what we're now seeing?'

'I can't answer that,' Michael replied. 'Because it makes no sense to me at all. The whole parole thing is messed up. I made arrangements to be told immediately if Hirst achieved parole. If he was even close to being released. That's why I thought he was still inside. Yet somehow he's been out for three years.'

Levy opened her mouth to speak. Sarah beat her to it.

'Actually there's even more to it than that.'

Both Michael and Levy turned to look at her in surprise.

'I had Hirst's full prison record looked into today,' Sarah explained. 'Through a source. And just before Michael called me about Derek, I got hold of his Parole Board report.'

'Parole Board reports are strictly confidential,' Levy interrupted. 'What source did that come from?'

'Does that really matter right now?' Sarah sounded exasperated at the interruption. Levy conceded the point and indicated for Sarah to continue. 'My source mentioned some mistreatment of Hirst while he was in Wandsworth Prison. It appeared nowhere on his record, but the Parole Board report filled in the blanks.'

'What sort of mistreatment?'

'The stuff the prison service pretends doesn't happen. Hirst spent a few years as a target to a particular group. A particular guy, really. Just what you'd expect. Beatings. Abuse. Physical. And they suspected sometimes sexual.'

'Horse shit.' Michael had heard enough. 'Karl Hirst never took abuse or punishment from anyone in his entire life. There is no way he was anyone's victim inside.'

'He was, Michael. The report was pretty explicit. Nothing was done because Hirst never complained, but there was a suspicion that it was also ignored because the guy responsible had most of the guards in Wandsworth Prison in his pocket. It was one of the reasons Hirst got parole on the first attempt; to avoid any investigation that would have exposed that corruption within the prison.'

FIFTY-SEVEN

'Show Mr Hale the file, Nathan.'

Sarah indicated towards Detective Inspector Steven Hale with a nod of the head. Nathan Benson's eyes followed. Summoned from the ITV News offices on nearby Grays Inn Road, Benson had travelled to Lonsdale Square with one task. To deliver the confidential parole report of Karl Hirst.

Benson picked up the slim manila folder, walked across the now much busier kitchen and handed it to Hale.

Hale flicked through the file's pages. Too quickly. He could not have been reading the content. Just checking its authenticity.

'Where the hell did you get this?' Hale's voice was sharp, his question directed at Sarah.

The file had passed the test.

Sarah glanced towards Levy.

'We've decided that isn't important right now, Steve,' said Levy. 'That can wait.'

Hale met his DCI's gaze and held it long enough to register his disagreement. Done, he returned to the file. This time he studied the detail.

'It's all there,' he finally said. The room had been silent in anticipation. 'Seems Ferris made Karl Hirst's life hell in every imaginable way when they were in Wandsworth together. And the prison did nothing about it. Unbelievable.'

He stared at the file in silence for a moment while he considered the theory, not quite sure he was convinced yet.

'And you think this makes Hirst good for Ferris and his guys?' he asked, making no attempt to disguise the disbelief in his voice. 'You think that Hirst could have been Ferris's bitch for that long, then suddenly take out a crew of four like it was nothing?'

'I think it's a possibility, that's all.' Levy answered. 'The timing fits. And from what Mr Devlin here has been able to tell us about Hirst, it's pretty clear that he's responsible for Longman, Blunt and now Derek Reid. The only doubt we could have had about that was the three-year gap between his release and the first murder. But if Hirst was also responsible for Ferris, if he was waiting to repay that debt too? Suddenly that gap makes sense.'

'Why?'

'Because let's assume for a moment that Hirst allowed himself to be abused by Leon Ferris when they were in Wandsworth. Let's assume that Hirst could have stopped it, that he could have killed Ferris at any time, but that he knew the act would guarantee a lifetime in custody. Hirst would have known Ferris's sentence. When Ferris would be released. So what if he was willing to take the abuse, in the knowledge that if he waited a while – just three years – then he could have his revenge on Longman, Blunt, Reid *and* on Ferris. All at the same time.'

Hale did not answer but shook his head, still unable to believe it.

'It fills our time gap,' Levy continued. 'It explains why Ferris was killed within twenty-four hours of being released. And it explains why a man as dangerous as Hirst was willing to let himself be a victim in the first place. To best guarantee his early release and allow him to rain down hell on every single person he feels wronged him.'

'OK, I can see how that works,' Hale finally conceded. 'And it helps explain why we haven't been able to identify a single viable suspect since the raid on Ed Burrell's place. But what about the way Ferris and his boys were killed, ma'am? Could Hirst be capable of that?'

'I'm as confident as I can be that he could.' This time Michael spoke. 'Joelle told us what happened to Ferris. To his men, too. Hirst could have done that.'

Hale turned to look towards Michael for the first time since he had arrived.

'I'm sorry, Mr Devlin, but I don't see how we can base an investigation of this importance on your opinion on this subject. Unless there's something we don't know?'

'I fully understand why you'd have your doubts about me on this, Mr Hale,' Michael began. 'But—'

'I can vouch for Mr Devlin on this, Steve,' Levy said.

Hale was surprised by Levy's interruption.

'I'm sorry, ma'am, I don't follow.'

'You don't need to follow. Not yet, anyway. Just trust me on this. I know what I need to know about Mr Devlin and based on all of that information . . .' Levy looked directly at Michael as she continued, '*all* of that information,' back to Hale, 'I am happy that if he says Hirst is capable of what was done to Ferris then Hirst *is* capable. OK?'

'Yes, ma'am.' Hale had heard that tone before. Many times. Further debate would not be welcome. 'And in that case, yes. I can see Hirst being good for the Ferris killings.'

'Good,' Levy said grimly. 'In which case we're joining the investigations. This is now one case. With one suspect. Karl Hirst. And I want every resource we have hunting that bastard down.'

Hale felt a mix of disappointment and relief. The turn of events had taken away his lead role in the Ferris case. A step back professionally. But it was the right decision, he realised. And it might have saved him from a case he could not crack.

'So what do you want me to concentrate on?' he asked. 'Shall I liaise with PR and prepare an announcement on Hirst?'

'No,' Levy replied. 'I've already put Tom Chadwick on that. I've got something else for you.'

'Has any attempt been made to contact her?' Hale asked.

Hale and Levy were still in Derek Reid's kitchen, but now alone. Nathan Benson had left. Thomas Chadwick had returned to Scotland Yard. Michael was in one of Reid's upstairs bathrooms, washing off the emotions of the last few hours. And Sarah was in Reid's garden, speaking to Anne Flaherty on her phone.

The lighter numbers were necessary; the subject was delicate.

'She's been spoken to,' Levy replied. 'And I've arranged for two officers from the Greater Manchester Police to meet her from work and escort her back to her home address.'

'Surely that's enough protection? I mean, do we think Tina Barker is really a likely target?'

'I think she's the *only* target left, other than Michael Devlin. Hirst will have to have pulled off a miracle to find out the new identity she was given after his trial, but it's not beyond the realms of possibility.'

'Where she is, covered by the Manchester Police? They're perfectly good, I'm sure, but they're not *us*, and with how this has gone so far I'm not willing to trust anyone who *isn't* us. Shit, after the miss on Blunt's past, I'm not sure my trust goes even *that* far.'

'That's why I'm sending *you*, Steve. I can't risk a cock-up, not from Manchester and not from any of our team. And I won't be satisfied until we have Tina Barker in a Met safe house where a bloody army couldn't get to her. Do you understand that?'

'Yeah. I get it.' This time Hale was not just submitting to the inevitable. He could see Levy's reasoning. Enough people had died.

'So what do you want me to do?'

'I want you to get yourself up there. Tonight. Meet the Manchester team, take custody of Tina Barker and bring her back to London. I want everyone under our umbrella and, when they are, we're going after the piece of shit with everything we've got.'

FIFTY-EIGHT

'Do you know where we'll be going yet?'

Sarah was sitting on a heavy metal chair. One of the six that matched the intricately decorated iron table at the centre of Derek Reid's garden patio. The garden itself resembled Sarah's own. It was unsurprising considering that Michael had designed them both.

'That's not how safe houses work,' Levy replied. She had taken a chair across the table. The two women were alone. Hale had already left for Manchester. Michael was still upstairs. 'We'll take you back to Scotland Yard with us. Once there we'll connect you with the Close Protection Unit. Tom Chadwick has briefed them and they've already got Anne Flaherty under their care. They'll take custody of you and Michael, too, and it'll be Close Protection who take you to the safe house. No one from my team will know where that is. Not even me.'

'Why not?'

'Chinese walls. It's just safer that way. It means that no one who can be directly linked to your case is capable of finding you. It avoids corruption and coercion, which further guarantees safety.'

Sarah nodded her understanding. The precautions made perfect sense. The fact she now needed them did not.

The two women sat in silence. Both lost in thought. Sarah fingered the glass she had replenished with a further splash of Bushmills. Levy had resorted to water. As comfortable as they had once been, Sarah knew that Michael's confession had changed everything. Any friendship that had been building had to be set aside.

'Do you really think Hirst will come after us, Joelle?' Sarah hesitated as she spoke. Not sure she wanted to hear the honest answer. 'I mean, now that his name is going to be out there and an entire police force is going to be hunting him? Do you really think he'll risk it?'

Levy looked at Sarah without speaking, and Sarah could see that she wanted to reassure her. That she wanted to say 'no'. But lies helped no one in these situations.

Levy reached out and placed her hand onto Sarah's.

'I think he will absolutely risk it, yes.' Levy's tone was sympathetic but certain. 'He *will* come for Michael, for what Michael did to him. The same reason he'll go after Tina Barker if he can.'

Sarah nodded. It was the answer she had expected but not the one she had hoped for. There was little more she could say.

'You sure you don't want one of these?'

Sarah indicated to the pack of cigarettes she had picked up from the table. An uncontroversial effort to break the silence.

'I'm sure,' Levy replied as Sarah lit her own. 'Took me too long to quit last time.'

'I hear you on that.'

Sarah inhaled deeply. The hit of the nicotine was not enough to calm her completely. But it helped. She exhaled a plume of blue smoke before speaking again.

'Tell me truthfully: do you really think you can keep us safe?'

'I was one hundred per cent honest with you a moment ago, Sarah. I knew you wanted to hear something else, but I told you the truth. So please know that what I'm telling you now is *also* what I believe to be the truth.'

'I know that.'

'Good. Because the answer's yes. I *do* think we can keep you and your family safe. It's just a matter of time until we find Hirst. He's got nowhere to run from here. By tomorrow morning his face will be on the front page of every national newspaper. On every news website in Europe. It won't take us long to catch him, and once we do then this is over for you. In the meantime you'll be under the protection of one of the best security teams on the planet, in a location Hirst can't possibly find. You're safe. You, Michael *and* Anne.'

322

Sarah listened carefully. Levy seemed confident, she thought. And Sarah already knew that she was more than capable. Her own research into the case had included looking into Levy, which had told her much about the DCI's meteoric career at Scotland Yard. It had told her far less about Levy's eight years in Israel, but the silence that followed the open record of her first two years in the Israel Defense Forces could mean one of only two things.

Mossad or Shin Bet.

Either way, a different proposition for Hirst to take on than elderly ex-lawyers or, God help him, Derek Reid, Sarah thought.

Levy was right. Hirst *would* come after them. But his chances of reaching them – of getting past Levy, let alone her full team – had fallen to none.

Reassured, Sarah's thoughts turned to the future.

'And what about Michael?' She flicked the ash from her cigarette as she spoke. 'Will you really arrest him when this is all over?'

'I don't see that I have any choice about that.' Levy's voice was quieter now. Almost apologetic. 'Michael's admitted a serious, serious crime. I can't just ignore that.'

'A crime that put a psychopath behind bars for fourteen years,' Sarah argued. She could not accept that their troubles would not end with Hirst's capture. 'And for something the bastard had actually *done*. OK, it's technically perverting the course of justice, but not *real* justice?'

'That makes no difference. What Michael did was an abuse of the system. If we allow that then who knows how many innocent people end up in prison.'

'But if he hadn't done it, who knows how many people – how many kids – Hirst would have murdered?'

'That's not the point, Sarah,' Levy was firm. 'A crime is a crime. Michael knows that. He's accepted that. And once this is all done with he's going to have to pay for that. It's just the way it is.'

Sarah opened her mouth to argue further, but the sound of the opening kitchen door stopped her. She glanced up and saw Michael stepping into the garden.

Sarah took a final draw on her cigarette as Michael approached then stubbed it out as he took the heavy seat at the head of the table.

'Am I interrupting something?' Michael looked between Sarah and Levy. Neither had spoken since noticing his arrival.

'No, nothing,' Sarah answered. Too quickly, she realised.

'Seriously,' Michael asked again. 'What's wrong? What's going on?'

'Really, Michael. It's nothing.'

Michael raised an eyebrow towards Levy in response to her answer. His disbelief was obvious. But he did not push the subject when he spoke again.

'OK. None of my business then, I guess.' Michael turned to fully face Levy. 'How are things coming with the safe house?'

'It's done, Michael. The house has been arranged. The Close Protection Unit are with Anne Flaherty at Scotland Yard. As soon as you and Sarah are with them they'll take you to the location together.'

'Not me.' Michael's response was simple. Just a statement of fact. 'I want you to take Sarah and Anne, but I'm not going with them.'

'You're what?' Sarah could not quite believe what she was hearing, causing panic and anger to flare inside her. 'What do you mean you're not coming with us?'

Michael looked towards her and – for the first time since discovering Derek Reid's body – he placed his hand onto hers.

'I don't know how else to put it, Sarah. I'm not coming. I want you and Anne safe and there's no safer place than with Joelle's people, at least until Hirst is caught. But I can't go with you. I have to stay.'

'What the hell are you talking about?!' Sarah ripped her hand away and sent her chair tumbling against the patio slabs, horrified at what he was saying.

'Is this because of Derek? Because I didn't give Joelle Hirst's name? Michael, please, you can . . . you can . . . blame me for that all you want. God knows *I* do. Leave me if you can't forgive me. But you can't put your life in danger over that. You can't.'

The thought that Michael might be unable to forgive her for not informing Levy of Hirst's release – and for what had happened to Derek Reid as a result – would break her heart. But she would suffer that – she would suffer *anything* – if it kept Michael alive. And so she had meant every painful word she had said.

Michael rose from his seat, but when he spoke his voice was gentle.

'Sarah, believe me, this has nothing to do with you not giving Hirst's name to Joelle. Jesus, what difference would that have made? Derek was dead before I ever mentioned Hirst to you. If anything *I'm* to blame for that; for being too complacent about his imprisonment. Not you.

'And I've no intention of leaving you. I love you, Sarah. Regardless of whatever happened and whatever happens. *Nothing* is going to change that. But I still can't go. I can't sit in a safe house where I can't do any good. You'll be safe whether I'm there or not. Safer, probably; he's after me, not you. Me being there just puts both of you in more danger. But if I go – if I leave now – then Simon Kash's trial *will* collapse. They'll discharge the jury and they'll start again, and if they do that then things will never go so well a second time. I can't do that to Simon. I can't take away an innocent kid's best chance at justice.'

'You're going to put that boy ahead of your own family?' Sarah shouted. Her head was reeling at the thought of losing Michael. 'He can get another lawyer for God's sake. It's not like you're the only one who can save him!'

'You know I didn't say that, Sarah. And you know I'd never do that. I—'

'How the hell else am I supposed to take this?' she shouted again.

'Jesus, Sarah!' Now Michael's voice was raised. 'Would you ever stop hearing what you want to hear and just bloody listen!'

Sarah was taken aback. In almost two years she had very rarely raised her voice in an argument. But it was something Michael had *never* done, and so his shout broke through her anger. It made her consider for the first time how hard this decision must have been for him.

'I'm all that boy has,' he continued, now in a gentler tone. 'I'm all that's standing between him and a life sentence for a murder he didn't commit. There is nothing I can do to add to your safety. Nothing. But if I leave Simon Kash now his trial *will* fall apart, and all the progress we've made on the evidence will be gone and probably never achieved again. How can I run, Sarah? How can I run and hide when I know that's the cost?'

Sarah hated what she was hearing. Both because it left Michael at risk and because she already knew she could not change his mind. One of the traits she most loved about the man was the strength of his convictions. The same strength that was now going to tear him from her.

She sat down heavily as Michael's argument span through her mind. Back and forth. Right and wrong. She reached out for another cigarette. Another attempt to calm herself before speaking.

'OK,' she finally said, having taken time to form her argument. 'I understand that you think you need to do this. And that Anne and I will be safe. But he could get near you. They can't protect you if you insist on putting yourself out there.'

Michael smiled sadly.

'I can't let that stop me from doing what I have to do. Believe me, sweetheart, if you were put in any kind of danger by my decision then I would drop everything and I would run with you. But you're *not*. You're *safe*. *Both* of you are safe. Which just leaves me, and if I'm the only one at risk then I can't abandon Simon Kash. Derek wouldn't have. Derek would have stayed and he would have fought for the boy. But the boy doesn't have Derek anymore. The boy has me. And if I do less than Derek would have done – if I run when he would have stayed – then I wouldn't be the man you thought I was.'

'Oh screw the man I thought you were, Mikey!' Sarah could see that he would not be swayed. That his decision was final. Tears stained her cheeks as she fought the inevitable. 'I'd rather I had a man who hid and lived than one who stayed and died. Screw principles.'

'You don't mean that, Sarah. And if I did it, well, you couldn't live with it any easier than me.'

'Shouldn't I at least get the chance to test that? To see if I *could* live with it? Because it's a whole lot less final than the alternative.'

Michael smiled again. He reached out with his right hand and placed it gently against Sarah's tear-stained cheek.

'Sarah, my mind's made up. My actions have caused this. What I did. Longman and Derek both died for it. Blunt too. I've cost those men their lives. I as good as killed one of the best friends I'll ever have. That's a high enough price for others to pay for what *I* did, isn't it? We can't expect Simon Kash to pay it too. We can't see an innocent kid convicted of murder just so I get to be safe. Can we?'

Sarah was silent.

Michael would do what he felt was right. Sarah knew that. Whether she agreed with it or not was irrelevant. She sat back into her seat and let Michael's words wash over her. Then, for the first time since Michael had entered the garden, she looked back towards Levy.

'What do you think, Joelle?'

Levy met Sarah's gaze. Glanced quickly to Michael. Then back.

'What do I think?' Levy took a moment. 'I think I should have said yes to that cigarette.'

Michael walked into Derek Reid's kitchen, opened the American-style double fridge and took out a cold bottle of Italian Peroni lager. He popped the top and took a swig, immediately noting the refreshing cold weakness of the drink in comparison to the earlier whiskey.

Now that his mind was settled he no longer needed the kick of the stronger liquor. He knew what he had to do.

The explanation Michael had given to Sarah was honest. But it was not complete. The guilt he still felt for Derek Reid's death – for all three deaths – was raw. It was something he might never overcome. Only time would tell. But while it was too late to do anything for them, it was not too late for Simon. Michael could not leave him to his fate. That boy was his lifeline, a chance to do something positive. An act of atonement, however small.

He would stay. He would fight. And he would win.

Because that was what Derek would have done.

All of this was true. But there was something else. Something he could not mention to Sarah or to Levy. A much darker decision he had made that required him to stay in plain sight.

Because then Hirst will *find me*, he thought. *And when he does, that fucker's going to pay for every last thing he's done.*

FIFTY-NINE

Steven Hale reversed his BMW X5 into the space closest to Number 18. It was tight and not exactly where he wanted to be, but it was also the only place left to park. The BMW completed the chain of cars lining the street's kerb.

Hale stepped out of his car, locked the doors and surveyed his surroundings. First the pavements that ran alongside twelve houses on each side of the street. Then the vehicles that lined both kerbs, looking for any hint that a car was occupied.

All seemed empty except for one, parked four cars ahead of his own.

He reached into his pocket for his identification as he walked towards it, before leaning down to speak to the driver through his open window.

'Is she in there?' Hale held open his ID for inspection as he spoke.

'She is.'

'Alone?'

'No, sir.'

'What's the layout?'

Hale looked ahead as he spoke, towards a small terrace house that was one of the narrow homes that lined this side of the cobbled street. None of the properties enjoyed a front garden, each front door opening just feet from the roadside.

'Two bedrooms, sir.'

The speaker was Sergeant Jim Durham of Greater Manchester Police. Durham was sat in the driver's seat of a marked police car, a second officer beside him. It was a tried and tested element of civilian protection; Durham and his colleague were not here to be inconspicuous. Ninety-nine times out of a hundred, their visible presence would be enough.

Durham continued.

'Both upstairs, with a small bathroom in between. There's also a small landing at the top of the stairs. Ground floor, it's the living room, kitchen and a small toilet.'

'Rear access?'

'Same as every street round here. There's a public alleyway that runs at the back of the house. All the gardens have a gate leading into it.'

'Have we got people back there?'

'It's covered, sir.'

'By how many?'

'Just the one, sir.' There was a note of amusement in Durham's voice. A hint of a chuckle. 'Plus two more inside and the two of us right here. All due respect, sir, but I think that's enough.'

Hale stood up straight, putting a few extra feet between his head and the open car window. He looked around, taking in the geography of the street, a quiet, residential road in Salford, a short distance from Manchester. It had taken Hale over four hours to drive here from Derek Reid's Islington address. Durham's security detail had been here even longer. They had secured the address before Hale had left London and had ensured the owner's safety. So far so good, but there was an image that kept returning to Hale.

Four dead men, slaughtered in a Brixton office.

His mind was made up.

'I'm afraid we disagree, Sergeant,' Hale said, his head back level with the open window. 'I want another man in the house and one more at the back. Within the hour. Make it happen.'

Five minutes later, Hale took a seat at the small kitchen table after carrying out a quick sweep of the house.

Like everything else Hale had seen in those five minutes, the kitchen table was tiny. It had to be to fit into the cramped kitchen. Although a reasonably big man, Hale was no giant, but he felt like one here. Especially in comparison to the room's other occupant. The woman who sat on the other side of the table seemed so much smaller than him. And she was clearly terrified.

Hale smiled reassuringly at her. Jessica Boon – as Tina Barker was now known, the identity given to her after Hirst's trial – had been at work when she was visited by Durham and his colleague. They had brought her home in the same police vehicle now parked outside, then left her inside with the three other officers assigned to their team.

Two of those were now in her living room, just a few steps and a sliding door from where she and Hale now sat. The third was in her garden. None had given her a proper explanation for all this, just vague reference to a threat to her safety. Hale could only imagine how frightening that must feel.

'Jessica,' he said gently. 'Have you been told anything about why the other policemen and I are here tonight?'

She gave a slight shake of her head.

'We're here because of the actions of a man you testified against when you were a child, Jessica. Do you remember the name Karl Hirst?'

It did not matter how softly Hale delivered the words. Or how many years had passed. The name still seemed to strike like a bolt of electricity. Jessica immediately looked up. Her eyes bore into Hale's own. Wide and fearful. But she remained silent.

'I'll take that as a "yes", Jessica.' Not that Hale had ever doubted the answer. 'So I don't need to tell you how seriously we take any threat involving that man.'

Jessica opened her mouth to speak. Hale noticed her right hand instinctively cup her left as she did so. Covering her two missing fingers. A subconscious act.

'I . . . I . . . I don't understand.' Jessica's voice was almost inaudible. 'Karl Hirst was sent to prison for life.'

'That's not quite right,' Hale explained. 'He was released three years ago.'

Jessica's eyes widened at Hale's words. Tears had been building in them from the first moment Hale had met her. They now streamed down her cheeks.

'But . . . but . . . that can't be, that can't be right.' The weak voice was now breaking. 'Mr Blunt said that he'd never be released. And Mr Devlin. They both . . . they both . . .'

Jessica's voice trailed off.

Hale watched Jessica place her elbows onto the low table and drop her head into her open hands. Her thin, pale forearms looked barely strong enough to take the weight.

Hale found his gaze drift towards her left hand. A natural human reaction. Somehow Jessica's lank black hair had fallen forward at exactly the right point, obscuring the view of her missing fingers. It could not be a coincidence, he thought; in the height of despair, Jessica was still obscuring her scars.

That one action, more than anything else, revealed to Hale the devastating truth about her life: whether called Tina Barker or Jessica Boon, this poor girl would never stop being Karl Hirst's victim.

Jessica's slight body shook with every sob. Both her physical and emotional weakness painfully evident. As Hale saw the effect of just the name 'Karl Hirst', he felt a combination of anger and sympathy churn within his gut.

For several minutes the only sounds in the undersized kitchen came from Jessica. None of them words, but still they said enough.

Hale did not want to interrupt. He wanted to give Jessica the time she needed. But he knew that he did not have that choice.

'Jessica?' When Hale spoke again his voice was softer than before. 'Jessica, I know how much of a shock this must be to you. I know how you must be feeling. But we're here to protect you. We're here to make sure Hirst can't get anywhere near you. And I'm here to bring you to London. To Scotland Yard. Where you'll be as protected as anyone can be, for as long as it takes us to find him.'

Jessica moved her hands away from her face, cupping her left with her right as she did so. She sat upright, making no attempt to wipe away the tears or mascara that now stained her cheeks.

'Then you really think he's coming for me?' Her voice was stronger now. As if she was becoming resigned to her own recurring nightmare.

'Actually we don't.' Hale slowly reached out and placed his own hand on top of Jessica's right. Careful not to touch her left. 'We don't have any reason to think that he knows where you are. We don't even think he knows your new name, Jessica. We're just not taking any risks.'

Jessica sat back in her chair, took her hands out from under Hale's, placed her left on her lap and used her right to wipe her eyes. For a few moments she was lost in thought while Hale watched. He could see that she was steeling herself for more. Finally she broke the silence.

'What has he done?' Jessica's voice was weak once again. As if asking the question had taken all of her strength. 'Hirst, I mean.'

'I'll tell you, Jessica. But when I do, please remember that he has no way of finding you.'

'I . . . I know that.'

'OK. Then what he seems to have done, Jessica – what he seems to be *doing* – is tracking down everyone involved in his trial. Everyone he blames for sending him to prison for your brother's death.'

'My God!' Jessica's right hand covered her mouth. The tears returned. 'Who . . . who . . . who has he found?'

'Everyone but you and Michael Devlin.'

'And what has he done to them?'

'I, erm, I really don't think you need to know the details of that . . . But I'm afraid they're dead. Hirst killed them all.'

'NO!'

Jessica stood up from her chair. For the first time she made no effort to hide her left hand. Her terror was clear on her face and her tiny body shook as she fought to take a breath. Stepping backwards, she lost her footing and began to fall. Hale – already rising – saw the stumble. With one swipe of his arm he threw the kitchen table aside and caught Jessica before she hit the floor. In a movie the moment would play out as a grand romantic gesture. But not in real life. Jessica was still panicking. She fought to escape Hale's arms, her frail body struggling upright.

'Jessica, please, you have to calm—'

Hale's words were cut short by what sounded like the two beats of a jackhammer. A sound he had heard before.

He wasted no time, placing Jessica onto the kitchen floor and ordering her to stay down. Then he hurried into the small living room at the front of the house.

The two officers were already on their feet as Hale slid open the door that separated the kitchen from the living room. Both looked confused.

'What was that sound?' asked the first. The smaller of the two.

'Suppressed pistol fire.' There was no doubt in Hale's mind as he strode across the room, careful to avoid opening a direct line of sight between himself and the large window that looked out onto the street. The net curtain that hung across it helped, obscuring the view from one side of the window to the other.

The room's other occupants were less sure of themselves. They remained fixed to the spot. Standing in the centre of the living room. If someone was outside and ready to fire, both would already be dead. The fact they were not allowed Hale some comfort.

'A suppressed pistol?' the older officer asked.

'It means a silencer,' said Hale, unsure if the comment had been a question. He reached the window, keeping his back tight to the wall, and glanced through the thinnest gap between glass and curtain. Just for an instant. 'Shit. I can't see from here.'

'A silencer? Then how did we hear it?' The younger officer this time. His voice fearful. Hale had not noticed until now just how inexperienced this guy obviously was.

'Jesus Christ, what is this? A ballistics lesson?' Hale snapped impatiently. 'You heard it because silencers are bullshit. They don't work. Now get that out of your head and get it back on the job. Got that?'

'Yes, sir,' the older, obviously more experienced officer replied. 'What do you need?'

'I need you to get into the kitchen, secure the girl and call this in. We need back-up – armed back-up – and we need it now.'

'Sir.'

'And keep your eye on the front and back doors at all times. Keep out of sight of both of them, and of any windows. We have to assume Hirst is here, so stay away from any point where he could get a bead on you from outside.'

'Shit.'

'Exactly.'

Hale moved to the foot of the staircase, just feet from the front door, and gripped the lowest banister.

'I need to get a glimpse of the car out front. Those two sounds were shots, which means we've probably lost two guys already. The fact they're not banging on the front door right now makes that almost certain. But I need to see, so I need to get upstairs for a better view.'

Hale took the first three steps in one stride. The next two in another. He was upstairs within moments.

The layout of the small house was simple enough. At the top of the stairs was a bedroom that looked to the rear. Next to that a bathroom. And finally a second bedroom that looked outwards onto the street. Which was where Hale needed to be.

He strode through the door, stepping round the small single bed to get to the window. It was dark inside, but there was enough illumination from outside for him to navigate.

The distance from the upstairs window to the street gave Hale a little more security. But not much. The range was still fine for a half-decent marksman. Hale had to assume that Hirst was better than that.

He jerked his head from behind the wall, just for a second. Long enough to get his bearings, short enough to make a clean shot unlikely. It told him little but enough; where the marked police car was, relative to his own position.

Hale slid the full length of his body to the floor, feeling the thin carpet against his fingers. He could smell it as it came close to his face. Clean, but old. It again aroused his pity for the life that Hirst had left for Jessica. For Tina.

Not even a life, in fact. Just a bare existence.

Such thoughts were no help now and so he shook them off, instead concentrating on the job at hand. He crawled to the far end of the window. Once there he slowly lifted his head, so it was just underneath the window ledge. Then he positioned himself where the police car would be directly ahead once he left cover. He knew he could risk just moments. He did not waste a single one.

Hale had positioned himself perfectly. His eyes fixed on the front of the police car the instant his head was raised. Milliseconds later and he saw what he needed to know. What could only be the body of Jim Durham, slumped to his left across the motionless form of his colleague.

'Fu—' Before Hale completed the word, the same jackhammer sound of compressed pistol fire assaulted his ear, twice in quick succession.

The first beat sent Hale diving for cover. The second told him he was still alive. Instinct made Hale search himself for injury. It took just an instant to confirm that there were none.

Hale exhaled in relief. He almost smiled, but the flicker of his mouth was interrupted by two realisations. The first concerned the bedroom window.

Two shots, Hale thought. *Two shots and the window's still there. How the hell did he miss?*

If the first thought had banished Hale's adrenaline and replaced it with confusion, the second brought that adrenaline flooding back.

The shots were louder.

Hale had not moved so quickly in years. The last two shots had come from inside the house. He realised that now. Two shots. Two officers down. The third – the officer outside the back door – most likely taken out silently.

That left Jessica, alone and at the mercy of Karl Hirst. The thought fuelled Hale to an almost superhuman physical effort. It also clouded his judgement.

Hale did not have to question if the next shot – so much closer and therefore so much louder than the others – had hit him. The explosion of blood, bone and ligament at his right knee was his answer.

The impact came as Hale reached the halfway point on the staircase and sent him careening the rest of the way down. The pain as the hard front door abruptly ended his fall should have been debilitating. But the human brain can shut pain off when it needs to. When its continued existence is on the line.

Hale turned himself onto his back, no need to glance at his devastated right leg. Its useless weight told him enough. Instead he looked ahead. At the sight of the other officers, both lying motionless, their lives both ended by a bullet to the forehead.

Despairing, he looked through the hallway that led to the garden. It was open, its frame occupied by the lifeless body of the fifth and final member of Jessica's protective detail.

He could not see how the man had died. Not that it mattered.

Karl Hirst was barely six feet from where Hale had landed. Jessica was slumped at his feet.

Dead? Hale could not tell, but she did not seem to be moving.

His attention was drawn to the suppressed pistol that remained fixed in Hirst's hand.

'No knives this time, then?' Hale asked painfully. He struggled to get the words out as the loss of blood started to hit.

'Do you think I'll fall for that, Steve? Get me talking until the back-up gets here?'

Hale's weakened mind focused on a single word.

'How do you know my name?'

'I know it's what Levy calls you,' Hirst replied. He smiled as he spoke. A soulless, reptilian grin. 'Just like I know she sent you up here to bring Tina Barker into secure custody. To protect her.'

Hirst placed a foot under Jessica/Tina's body and pushed her onto her back. The sound of pain told Hale she was still alive.

'How's that job worked out?' Hirst asked, still grinning.

'How can you know that?' Hale asked again. It was no bluff. No attempt to gain time. There was no back up on the way. Hale just could not understand how this man knew so much.

'How do you think?' Hirst replied. 'Modern technology, Steve. The sort of thing I wish I'd had last time. Surveillance equipment. Bugs so small and so discrete your people would never think to look for them.'

'Bugs?' Hale could feel himself growing weaker. Every beat of his heart was firing more blood from his body, out of his devastated knee. But the pain of Hirst's words was greater. That they had missed something so simple. 'You . . . you bugged us?'

'It's amazing what you can get on the internet, isn't it?' Hirst was enjoying himself. 'Just a few lightbulb bugs at each scene. Perfect place, lightbulbs. The sort of thing your forensic guys would have no reason to check, but good enough to listen in and keep a few steps ahead of you all. That was the plan, anyway. What I didn't expect was *this*.'

Hale could feel himself slipping. He pulled in two lungfuls of oxygen, fighting to clear his head. A glance at Jessica had the desired effect. He was the only thing keeping her alive, and as long as Hirst was talking she would stay that way.

'You didn't expect what?' Hale asked, clinging determinedly to consciousness.

'I didn't think that you'd lead me to Tina. I'd given up on her. I was content with the rest of them. Longman, Blunt, Reid. They were going to be enough. And then I heard you talking about Tina in Reid's kitchen. Heard Levy send you up here. All I had to do was follow you. And you led me straight to her.'

'You . . . you . . .' Hale felt what was left of his adrenaline surge with nowhere to go. The thought that he had brought Hirst here – that he had led him to Jessica – was too much. 'You . . . fucking . . .'

Hirst placed his pistol on the arm of the living room sofa as Hale tried to speak. Then he reached around to the back of his waist.

'That's why it was a gun this time. I had to keep it simple. No time to plan.' Hirst's hand had returned to his side. It was not empty. 'But *you* still get a knife, Steve. You deserve for me to do this right. You deserve to die like a man, for giving me Tina.'

Hirst took a step forward. Slowly. Deliberately.

'Nothing more to say?'

Hale opened his mouth as he fought off the darkness. No sound came out.

'Shame,' said Hirst. 'I was enjoying the chat.'

Hirst lowered himself to a knee as he reached Hale. He placed his left hand on Hale's chest, an eight-inch blade held firm in his right. Then he fixed his pale eyes on to those of his victim.

'I don't know where we go after this, Steve. But wherever it is, enjoy the ride.'

Hirst spoke the final sentence with a broad, lifeless smile as he brought the blade down hard.

SIXTY

Michael Devlin stepped out of the shower and reached for a towel. Warm water dripped from his body as he stepped into the bedroom, wetting the deep-blue carpet with every step. It wouldn't matter. Any damage done would be rectified within hours. One of the few upsides of hotel living.

Michael paid no attention to the increasingly damp floor. Or to much else. Like every waking moment of the past fourteen hours, only two things occupied his mind: Derek Reid and Karl Hirst. The only other thing beginning to break that cycle was his headache. The result of a combination of grief, stress and alcohol.

Michael could not afford to be in this state. Certainly not today. He tried to shake it off, to get his mind moving. He glanced towards the bedside table at the clock face below the wireless Bose iPod dock, as he had done so often during his mainly sleepless night. At least it now read a more acceptable time: 6.23 a.m.

The day had started. It was time for him to join it.

It took just a minute to dry the rest of his body. Done, he threw the towel into the corner of the room, onto a pile of clothes he had dumped there the night before. Michael was usually a tidy man. Meticulous. But not this morning. And certainly not last night.

He had arrived at the Malmaison Hotel in London's Smithfield Market at around 9 p.m. the previous evening. Alone. In the end Joelle Levy had come down on Sarah's side, supporting the demand that Michael should be with his family in the police safe house, but it was an argument neither woman could win. Ultimately the police have no power to force their protection on anyone of sound mind, and so Michael's word was final.

But Levy had at least secured one concession. She had convinced Michael that he could not risk staying alone in the family home. Instead he would stay at a hotel.

Won't make a difference, Michael had thought when accepting Levy's demand. *He'll still find me here. And when he does he'll get the fight of his life.*

A short walk from the Old Bailey, the Malmaison had a large, well-lit and busy reception. A public space that every visitor passed through upon arrival. Levy had seen this as a key defence against Karl Hirst, whose face would soon be as recognisable as any celebrity's.

The fact the hotel was fully occupied was a security bonus. With guests in earshot Hirst would not have the time he had enjoyed in the empty homes of his other victims. It was still far from ideal but Levy had had no choice but to accept that. It was the best she was going to achieve with a man who – unknown to her – *wanted* to be found.

Michael looked around, trying to recall where he had put his belongings the previous night. He found nothing in the bedroom and so he moved to the suite's living area, all the while trying to mentally retrace his steps. It was no easy task. Michael had consumed more than half a bottle of whisky before Levy had let him leave Derek Reid's house. And he had not stopped there. The impressive pile of beer bottles and liquor miniatures strewn across the room's main table evidenced that. Whisky. Brandy. Vodka. There was even a half-finished tequila, a spirit Michael could never usually stomach.

It was an intake that guaranteed hazy memories.

Michael had awoken at 2 a.m. on the sofa nearest the bottle-strewn table, from alcoholic unconsciousness rather than from sleep. He had then struggled to his unsteady feet, moved to the bedroom and collapsed onto the room's king-size bed, where he had drifted in and out for the next four hours. It was nowhere near enough rest to shift the whisky and spirits that still gripped him, but the blast of his hot morning shower had made a difference.

His luggage was on the smaller of the room's two sofas. Across from where he had passed out. Pressing hard on his thumping temple with one hand, he opened the large holdall with the other and pulled out a leather washbag. On any other occasion he would have unpacked as soon as he entered the room. In that, he was a creature of routine, sometimes described as 'a little OCD', a concept he found absurd; how could anyone be 'a little' obsessive? Still, it was unique for Michael to be unpacked a whole night after arrival.

Shows what a damned mess I was, he thought.

The grief of the previous day suddenly washed over him again. It conjured back images Michael did not want to endure. He had seen enough of Derek Reid's crucified body. Had thought enough of the horror of his friend's death. And he had agonised, again and again, over the things *he* had done, all those years ago, to cause it.

Yet he just could not banish the images in his mind.

Michael dropped the washbag into the bathroom, breathing deeply, trying to calm his racing mind.

The music of the Black Eyed Peas suddenly blared out across the room. It seemed out of place, alien to both the time of day and to Michael's own mood. For a moment he did not register the new sound he was hearing; a residual effect of his diminishing hangover. Then it clicked in his mind.

Sarah. Michael panicked. *Why is she calling so early?*

He looked around the room, searching for his smartphone. He could usually follow the sound of a ringtone, but his equilibrium was still suffering a whisky hit. It made a simple task like locating a phone by its sound much more difficult. The prolonged search only increased his panic, which in turn made his hangover worse.

Sarah's favourite song was approaching its chorus by the time Michael saw the illuminated screen, peering from beneath a pillow.

'Is everything OK?' Michael's voice was rushed. Fearful. 'Are you both alright?'

'We're fine.' Sarah's words were reassuring. He heard her take a breath before continuing. 'I'm fine. So is Anne. I . . . I . . . I just want you to reconsider. I don't want you taking this risk. Not now. Not after what happened last night.'

Michael's mind was slowly clearing by the second, but it was Sarah's final sentence that cut through the fog.

'What do you mean, "last night"? What's happened?' He instinctively picked up the television remote control and hit 'power' as Sarah replied.

'Hirst did it again. He killed again.'

'Killed who?'

Michael was confused.

Who else could be on Hirst's list?

The answer came to him before the question was complete.

'Jesus, no, Sarah. It wasn't Tina Barker. Please tell me he—'

'It wasn't Tina, no.' Sarah sounded on the verge of tears again. 'But he *has* her. Maybe he *has* killed her, too. No one knows.'

'Oh no, oh God no.' The knowledge that Hirst had once again taken Tina Barker hit Michael like a kick to the gut. It would be her worst nightmare. 'Then who did he kill?'

'Steven Hale.' Sarah's voice caught on a sob. 'The guy Joelle sent up to Manchester yesterday. The guy who was supposed to bring Tina back.'

'Shit.'

'And five others, Michael. He killed five other cops. The whole of Tina's protection.'

'Jesus Christ.' Every trace of a hangover was gone. Michael's mind was working again, racing to the only logical conclusion. 'That can't be a coincidence. It can't be a coincidence that Hirst got to Tina at the same time Hale did. He must have followed him. He must have found her by tailing Hale.'

'What does that matter?' Sarah's voice was now a mixture of grief and confusion. 'Why are you even thinking about that? What you should be thinking about is five dead cops and what that means. Because what that means is you can't protect yourself against this guy. As long as you're out there and in public, he can get to you. You need to come to us. You need to come to where you'll be safe.'

'I can't do that, Sarah. And we're not going over this again, either. I've made my decision.'

Michael could not face another debate. Not now. The fact that Hirst had Tina Barker – that the sick son of a bitch could be doing God knows what to her – was enough of a blow. Combined with the thought of Hirst massacring a house full of cops, Michael just did not have the capacity for more trauma.

Going another round with Sarah about running and hiding is the last thing I need, he thought.

Michael's eyes flicked to the image on the bedroom's television screen before he had the chance to think again. The sight of Joelle Levy about to address the assembled British press came as a surprise.

He reached for the remote to turn up the volume.

'Sarah? I'm going to have to call you back.'

SIXTY-ONE

'Joelle? Did you hear what I said?'

Levy started at the sound. She had not been listening, instead just staring blankly at the two empty crystal glasses that sat together on her desk. Now she looked up, distracted from her reverie. She wiped her eyes with her fingertips before responding.

'Sir.' Levy's pitch was abnormally high, she noticed. She corrected it with a cough. 'I'm sorry, sir. I was miles away. Can I help you?'

'Don't worry about *me*. What concerns me is *you*. The press conference is due to start in five minutes. Are you sure you're up to it?'

'Yes, sir,' Levy managed, her voice wavering with emotion. 'I'll be . . . I'll be fine.'

'You don't have to be fine.' Chief Superintendent David Rogers' voice was as kind as Levy had ever heard it. 'No one expects that of you. You've just lost a key team member. Not one single copper would think less if you give this one a pass. You're only human.'

'No, sir,' Levy said, her voice suddenly firm. 'I need to do this. Karl Hirst needs to be found and I want to be the one who does it, sir. I'm not walking away from this. Not after what he did to . . . Not after Steve.'

She took a deep breath, preparing herself.

'I need to get the word out on this bastard so we can bring him down before he hurts anyone else. I'm going to make him pay for Hale. And with all due respect, and being genuinely grateful at the compassion you've shown me, doing that is all the TLC I need.'

Rogers did not reply immediately. He just met Levy's eyes and held them.

'OK,' he finally said. 'OK. Then I guess you've been through worse in your past, eh?'

'Worse than losing Steve?' Levy's eyes remained fixed on Rogers' as she replied. She knew what he was referencing. Her past in Israel, 'No, sir. The people I've lost before, I lost them in a war zone. In a place where any one of us could have been killed on any day. You lose someone there, it hurts but it's . . . well . . . it's what you expect. Not like this. Not the way Steve went. I've never experienced anything close to that. And Karl Hirst is going to wish I still hadn't.'

A few minutes later Levy walked into Conference Room Four on the second floor of New Scotland Yard.

The inevitable barrage of camera flashes marked her arrival. They continued as she followed Rogers to the long table positioned ahead of a temporary blue partition wall.

Levy sat in the centre, with Rogers and Chadwick on either side. She looked down at her notes. Aware that video cameras and voice recorders were running. For a moment she was distracted by her own jacket cuffs. By the ornate silver buttons on black fabric. It was rare that Levy wore her formal uniform. It was usually only for press conferences, and she did most of those alongside Steve Hale.

Another reminder of what she had lost.

The slightest touch of Rogers' hand on her own broke through. Levy looked up and began.

'At 10 p.m. yesterday evening five members of the Greater Manchester Constabulary were murdered in and around a residential home in Salford. Ordinarily, jurisdiction over this tragic event would be taken by the Greater Manchester Police. However, I can inform you that the officers were in fact on duty and on location on behalf of Scotland Yard's Major Investigation Team, providing temporary protection for a person we believed to be the likely target of attack: Miss Jessica Boon.

'The individual we believed to be a threat to Miss Boon was convicted killer Karl Hirst. We will be distributing a number of photographs of Karl

Hirst at the conclusion of this press conference and we will request that these be displayed as a matter of urgency on every real and online news resource available to the people in this room, and to the networks that employ you. For now I can offer you this single photograph, taken shortly before Karl Hirst was released from custody three years ago following fourteen years of a life sentence.'

Levy held up a copy of the photograph. There was little that was exceptional about the man it showed. Short – five foot seven according to Levy's records – and slim, with a full head of thick, dirty blonde hair and a messy mouth housing teeth better suited to somewhere bigger. But even from a distance his cold, pale eyes stood out. Their disquieting effect was made worse by those cameras that zoomed in for a closer view.

Those eyes alone made the presence of the man who stared out from the image nothing short of chilling.

'It is absolutely essential that we find Karl Hirst as soon as possible. He is wanted for questioning in connection to the murder of the five Greater Manchester Police officers I have discussed. He is also wanted for questioning in relation to the kidnapping of Jessica Boon, and for the murder . . . for the murder of Detective Inspector Steven Hale from Scotland Yard, who was in the address at the time of the attacks with the intention of bringing Jessica Boon back to London for the purposes of dedicated and specialised police protection. In addition, we wish to speak to Karl Hirst in regard to the recent murders of former Lord Chief Justice of England and Wales Phillip Longman, of London gangland figures Leon Ferris, Kevin Tennant, Harvey Ellis and Tyrone Leach, of retired solicitor Adam Blunt and – just yesterday – of criminal barrister Derek Reid.'

The room came alive at the long list of names. First a murmur. Then a rumble. Finally an outright cacophony. A tsunami of questions poured out from the assembled press, all drowning each other out.

Levy made no attempt to answer. Instead she allowed the assembled reporters to continue until they realised their questions were fruitless. The majority returned to silence and Levy quietened the rest with a lowering of her hands.

Satisfied, she continued.

'No questions will be answered about Karl Hirst at this press conference. So please do not ask them. We are not here today to give you a story. That will no doubt follow in due course, but the purpose of today is to ensure that the public are protected from what we believe to be a very dangerous individual. For that reason we ask that the information and photographs we have given you here are disseminated as widely and as regularly as possible until we have found Karl Hirst. We ask any member of the public who may have any information about him to come forward immediately. It doesn't matter what that information is. No mater how trivial. No matter how tenuous. We want to know it and we want to know it now. Please contact us on the telephone number or the email displayed on the front of this desk, and which we ask the TV networks and internet sites to display also. Finally — and I think this goes without saying in any event — we believe that Karl Hirst is a very real danger to anyone who comes into contact with him, so we ask that no member of the public attempts to engage him. You must stay away and contact the police. For your own safety and the safety of those around you, do not engage this man. Thank you.'

Levy rose to her feet without another word. Turning to her right, she ignored the avalanche of questions thrown at her from the reporters and followed Chadwick from the room.

SIXTY-TWO

Michael Devlin's feet felt heavy beneath him as he took the first creaky wooden step that led from the Old Bailey Robing Rooms to its Bar Mess. On most days he would bound upstairs. Two steps at a time. Three, if he was feeling energetic. Today he took single steps. And he took them slowly.

The Old Bailey Bar Mess held special memories for Michael. Like most successful criminal barristers, he associated it with some of his greatest victories: murder, robbery, kidnap, blackmail. Michael had defended them all in this building, and every morning of every day of every trial began in the cavernous room he was now approaching. A room always filled to capacity with both the greats and the rising stars of his profession. Where barristers would begin their preliminary arguments long before the intervention of any judge; intellectual jousting that as often as not decided the winner before the hearing itself began. And a room where, so many times, Michael had marvelled at Derek Reid's mastery of the art.

But never again, Michael thought as he took the final step. *I'll never see him here again.*

The atmosphere in the Mess was unusually subdued. Derek Reid had been a very popular figure. It was no surprise, then, that every pair of eyes fell on Michael as he walked from the staircase to the head of the Mess. Just a few at first. Just those who had noticed his arrival. But within moments it was everyone. Thirty, maybe forty barristers. All looking with sympathy at the man they knew to be Derek Reid's closest friend.

It was exactly that sympathy that Michael did not want. That he did not think he deserved.

You'd be looking at me differently if you knew what I'd done, Michael thought to himself, the guilt that had tormented him rising again. *If you knew what I'd caused.*

'Michael.'

Jenny Draper had spotted him from across the room and rushed towards him. She was just feet away when she finally said his name. Michael turned in response and found himself engulfed by Draper's arms.

'I'm so sorry. I really am.'

Draper's mouth was close to Michael's ears as she hugged him. It made her low voice seem loud which, for an instant, made Michael suspect that her sympathy was for show; an attempt to pull herself into the attention he was receiving.

Michael shook off the thought. There was every chance that Draper was being sincere. He would not let his grief and his cynicism convince him otherwise.

'Thanks, Jenny.' Michael slipped back from Draper's grasp as he spoke. 'I, erm, I appreciate it. Genuinely.'

'You really didn't need to come today.' Draper reached out and touched Michael's upper arm as she spoke. 'I could have had Levitt adjourn the case to next week without you. No one would have objected. Not in the circumstances.'

Michael nodded his head and offered a weak smile. What Draper was saying was not new; she had told him the same in the four voicemails she had left since 8 a.m.

'I know that. But we're not adjourning the case. Terry Colliver is giving evidence today, and I'm cross-examining him.'

The sympathy evident on Draper's face disappeared as Michael spoke. Replaced by wide-eyed disbelief.

'Michael, you can't do that. You can't take on Colliver so soon after Derek's murder. You won't be up to it. You—'

'I know my limitations.' Michael's voice was firm as he interrupted. 'And I know how to best deal with this sort of thing. We're on a roll in this case. And the Crown are on the ropes. We're not backing off now.'

'But Michael—'

'There are no buts. This is happening and it's happening today. The only thing I'm not going to do is talk to Simon. I just don't have that in me right now. So I need you to go down to him, to let him know I've had some personal issues so I won't be down – do *not* tell him what they are – and reassure him that we're fit and raring to go.'

Draper did not respond; she looked put out at being overruled so abruptly. Colliver was the most important witness in the case and so Michael needed to be at his best. He could understand why – in the circumstances – Draper thought that impossible.

What she thinks is irrelevant, Michael told himself. *Today she'll just have to watch and learn.*

'And Jenny?' he called out as Draper walked away.

Draper turned at the sound of her name.

'Yes?'

'Make sure you get his written permission for us to attack Colliver *and* O'Driscoll. Just like we've discussed.'

SIXTY-THREE

'What I'm suggesting to you, Mr Colliver, is that when the police arrested you, charged you with the murder of the Galloway brothers and remanded you in custody to await trial, they had the right man, didn't they?'

Matthew Cole QC's cross-examination of Terry Colliver was drawing to an end. Cole had been questioning the witness for almost two hours. With little – if any – success. He had taken an approach that Michael found confusing. One which made no attempt to blame Simon Kash for the crime.

Unexpected, Michael thought. *And naive.*

'And what am I supposed to say to that, eh?'

'Mr Cole would like you to either agree or disagree with what he is suggesting, Mr Colliver.'

The intervention of Judge John Levitt – of *any* judge – was not usually necessary when Matthew Cole cross-examined. But today it was justified.

Matt's off his game, Michael thought. *Maybe he's been more affected by what happened to Derek than I expected.*

'Alright then, I disagree. They didn't get the right bloke until they got Darren O'Driscoll 'n Simon Kash. Just like I told Mr Epstein.'

Cole had little choice but to ignore the answer. 'And I'm also going to suggest to you, Mr Colliver, that in order to get away with murder, you named my client – Darren O'Driscoll – because you knew that the police wanted him and his brother much more than they wanted you. Isn't that right?'

'No it ain't bloody right, cos if I thought the police wanted Darren O'Driscoll *and* Patrick O'Driscoll, why'd I only mention Darren? Eh?

Why'd I give them Darren 'n Simon Kash, instead of Darren 'n Pat? Don't make no sense what you're saying, does it? None at all.'

'Mr Colliver, I'm suggesting to you—'

'Wot? Not gonna answer my question then? What's the matter, mate? Got ya stumped, 'ave I?'

'Mr Colliver, I'm not here to answer *your* questions.' Cole resorted to the stock lawyers' response. 'But you *are* here to answer *mine*, so why don't we try and stick to that?'

'Suit yourself,' Colliver replied. 'But I know what I'd think if I was on the jury.'

Michael watched as Colliver folded his arms and sat back into the witness-box chair.

Colliver's winning this, he thought.

The answer and Cole's non-response did exactly what Colliver had said. It undermined Darren O'Driscoll's case in the eyes of the jury. Not least because Colliver's point was a good one. Damaging to both O'Driscoll *and* to Simon Kash.

Yet Cole had dealt with it poorly before just moving on.

What the hell are you playing at, Matt?

Another ten minutes passed before Cole's cross-examination finally ended. It had not gotten worse. Or any better. Cole had made no progress at all; nothing to make the jury believe that Colliver had been involved in the murder of the Galloway brothers.

Now it was Michael's turn.

He rose to his feet, looking directly at the witness box, at Colliver. A man buoyed in confidence by Cole's failure. A man whose arrogance had grown with every success and who was making no effort to hide it.

Michael turned away from the witness pointedly. Almost theatrically. A practised method designed to make the jury do the same.

The turn was towards the dock. To Michael's left. The jury's right. Towards Simon Kash. What they all saw, Michael knew, was the face of a child. Of a boy completely lacking in arrogance. In cockiness.

Of a boy in fear.

Michael knew that the jury would compare the two men and that, when they did, Colliver would be found wanting. But the sight affected Michael, too. It reminded him of why he was here. Of why he was taking this risk. Not for Liam any more, but because Derek had believed in Kash. And so did Michael.

He would not let either one down.

As Michael turned back to the witness box he glanced down at Jenny Draper. Her eyes were cast down towards the old counsel's bench at which they sat. She looked like she was steeling herself for the disaster she expected to follow.

Michael did not care. Because now it was just him and Terry Colliver.

'Mr Colliver, I have some questions to ask you on behalf of Simon Kash.' Michael's voice was strong. No hint of his emotional turmoil. 'Are you happy if we start them now, or could you use a break?'

'Do I look like I need a break?'

'No, Mr Colliver. No you do not. So let's get cracking, shall we?'

'Fire away.'

'I'll do that.'

Michael smiled at Colliver's confidence. Today should not be fun. Michael knew that. But Colliver seemed primed to distract Michael from thoughts of Derek Reid and Karl Hirst. At least for a while.

Michael continued.

'I think it might be best if we start with a little recap. Make sure we're all up to speed on your evidence.'

'Whatever you want.'

'That's very generous of you.'

Michael placed one hand on his wooden lectern and stood up to his full height. He made for an imposing figure from across the courtroom. The gesture was not lost on Colliver, who began to fidget in his seat.

'Now we've all heard that you were originally arrested, questioned and charged with the murder of the Galloway brothers. Correct?'

'I've already been asked that, so you know it's true.'

'Yes, Mr Colliver. We do. That's why it's called a "recap". Now, shall we carry on?'

'You trying to be funny, mate?'

'Not at all, Mr Colliver. Murder is not a laughing matter.' Michael glanced towards the jury as he spoke. To create a connection. Then back to Colliver. 'When you were interviewed by the police – when you were questioned – you said nothing about Darren O'Driscoll's involvement in the murder.'

'No.'

'You made no mention of him at all.'

'You know I didn't.'

'And you certainly made no mention at all of my client, Simon Kash. Did you?'

'I didn't say nuffink about nuffink.' Colliver's arrogance was now joined by a slight belligerence. Michael's questions were beginning to irritate him. 'I went "no comment", didn't I?'

'Indeed you did, Mr Colliver. When first asked about the murder – when under arrest *for* the murder – you essentially said nothing.'

'Yeah.'

'And yet from what you've told this jury today, you could have told the police a hell of a lot.'

'What d'ya mean?'

'What I mean is that you've told this jury today that you were at the scene of the crime very soon after the murder.'

'That's right.'

'That Darren O'Driscoll had called you and had ordered you to collect both him and Simon Kash from the murder scene. To assist in their escape.'

'That's right n'all.'

'Which you could have told the police when you were questioned.'

'S'ppose, yeah.'

'But you didn't.'

'No.'

Michael took a moment to think. He had planned the cross-examination in his mind. An intricate dissection of the evidence. Designed to slowly expose Colliver's lies. But Colliver was already irritated. The one-word answers told Michael that. So did their tone. Perhaps slow and steady was *not* the answer with this one.

It's like questioning a naughty schoolboy, Michael thought. *So let's play it that way.*

'It's right, isn't it, that eventually you *did* mention to the police what you have now told this jury?'

'Yeah.'

'That you told them the same story as you've told today. Naming Darren O'Driscoll. Naming Simon Kash.'

'Yeah.'

'And admitting that you'd driven those men away from the scene of the crime.'

'Well that's what I'd done, innit?'

'Which led to you being charged with an offence of assisting an offender, to which you pleaded guilty.'

'Because I'd done it.'

'And for that you were sentenced to eighteen months' imprisonment, suspended for two years.'

'Look, mate, I've already said all this. Is this goin' somewhere or what?'

'Recap, Mr Colliver. Recap.'

'Listen, mate—'

There was anger in Colliver's voice. Annoyance at Michael's singsong, sarcastic tone. Michael ignored it.

'Now, just so the jury understand, a suspended sentence is when you receive a sentence of imprisonment but don't actually have to serve it, provided you stay out of trouble for a specified period. In your case that was two years. Is that your understanding?'

'You're the lawyer, ain't ya'?'

'Yes, but you're the one giving evidence. And you haven't disagreed with my explanation of a suspended sentence, Mr Colliver. So is that your understanding?'

Colliver glowered silently back at him.

'OK. Then we'll take it that I'm right. So, let's recap a bit of the recap, shall we? You were originally charged with an offence of murder. For which you were remanded in custody, yes?'

'Yeah.'

The belligerence was increasing. Michael's revised, rapid approach had been a good call.

'And if convicted of that murder, you knew you'd receive a sentence of life imprisonment.'

'Yes.'

'Which would *not* be suspended, would it?'

'What?'

'You'd have to actually *serve* that sentence, wouldn't you? Or at least a minimum term of many years.'

'What's this got to do with anything?'

'Quite a lot actually, Mr Colliver.'

Michael always enjoyed a well-placed question from a witness. It was not an opportunity he would miss.

'For one thing, life in a prison is an awful lot worse than a sentence that says "stay out of trouble for a little while and you won't serve another day", isn't it?'

'What?'

'Let me put it more simply.' Michael adopted a more patronising tone, designed to annoy Colliver further. 'Which would you prefer, Mr Colliver? Life in prison or a suspended sentence where you don't get punished provided you keep your nose clean?'

'That's a stupid bloody question.'

'Yes, I suppose it is.' Michael turned to the jury. His smile wider. 'Because I think we all know the answer. But let's move on.'

Michael turned back to Colliver.

'So according to your evidence, at the time of your arrest – when you were facing a charge that could give you life imprisonment – you *already* knew all of the details of the people who had actually committed the offence. Information that could turn that life sentence into a short suspended sentence instead. And yet you chose to say *absolutely nothing?*'

'I'm not a grass, mate.'

Michael smiled. He could not have hoped for a better, more impatient answer. It told him that Colliver was no longer thinking. He was now just reacting. The screws were in place.

It was time to turn them.

'Mr Colliver, you are the main witness for the prosecution in a murder trial against people who you claim were your friends. If what you say is true – and let's just be clear, I'm saying that it is *not* true – then surely you're the very definition of a grass.'

Peter Epstein QC was on his feet in an instant.

'My Lord, it is utterly inappropriate for one of Her Majesty's counsel to be calling a witness in a case of this seriousness a "grass".'

'I agree, Mr Epstein.' Judge Levitt turned towards Michael. 'I believe an apology is in order, Mr Devlin?'

'Of course, My Lord.' Michael's eyes had not left Colliver's. 'I apologise for suggesting that your actions make you a grass, Mr Colliver. What you are and what you are not is, of course, for the jury to decide.'

'Mr Devlin! Mr Colliver is *not* on trial here.'

This time Judge Levitt's intervention was almost a shout. Michael ignored it and continued.

'Mr Colliver, despite telling this jury that you already knew full well who had murdered the Galloway brothers – that you had in fact driven their killers from the scene of the crime – you did not mention *any* of this when arrested and interviewed for that very crime.'

'No. No I didn't.'

'And you say that's because you are not a grass.'

'That's right.'

'But that can't be right, though, can it, Mr Colliver?'

Michael leaned forward onto his wooden lectern. Both arms crossed and supporting his weight. Michael's tone was now almost conversational. He saw the confusion it caused in Colliver's eyes.

'I dunno what you're talking about, mate.'

'Let me explain, Mr Colliver. You were under arrest for murder. So you were in terrible, terrible trouble. Facing a possible life sentence. Still you would not talk. But then, many months later, you *did* tell the police what you knew. Didn't you?'

'Yes.'

'But nothing had changed, had it? When you decided to speak to the police – when you decided to name Darren O'Driscoll and Simon Kash – you were still in exactly the same position. Facing the same allegation of murder. The same life sentence.'

'And?'

'And? And, Mr Colliver? Surely you can follow this? You say you didn't give your account because you're not a grass. But then later, when nothing had changed, you gave it anyway. So your initial silence *cannot* be excused by the fact that, as you say, you're not a grass. Can it? Because you ultimately told. And all that had changed was that your trial was closer.'

'What d'you want me to say?' Colliver seemed genuinely confused.

'I want you to answer my original question. You could have told the police *everything* at the time of your interview. Assuming, of course, that what you've told this jury is true. And yet you answered "no comment". Why, Mr Colliver? And don't say it's because you're not a grass, because we've established that can't be the case.'

Colliver hesitated. The easy ride he'd been given by Cole was long gone. For the first time he thought carefully before he gave his answer.

'I . . . I suppose when I was interviewed I didn't fink I'd be charged, did I?'

Michael saw a smile appear in Colliver's eyes. It betrayed an otherwise perfect poker face. Michael read its meaning. Colliver had hit a home run with his answer.

Or at least he thought he had.

'I'm sorry.' Michael was careful to hide his own amusement. 'Could you explain what that means?'

'I'm sayin' there *was* a difference between my "no comment" interview and when I gave my statement to the police. The difference was

I was charged when I gave up O'Driscoll 'n Kash. Before that I was just *arrested*. For somethin' I'd not done. So I didn't need to put 'em in it then, did I? When I was interviewed. I didn't need t'grass *then*. But once I was charged? Once I was gonna be tried for murder? Different story, mate.'

Colliver's arrogance had returned. He was confident he had delivered a winning argument. Michael could not have asked for more.

'That *is* interesting, Mr Colliver. So the big difference – the thing that made you talk, that made you tell the police everything you knew – was the fact that you had been charged with murder and now faced a trial.'

'That's right. Yeah.'

Colliver sounded less certain. Michael's continued confidence had deflated his own.

'Mr Colliver, do you know what a Plea and Trial Preparation Hearing is?'

'What?'

'You heard me, Mr Colliver. A PTPH. You know what it is, don't you?'

'Why don't you remind me?'

'Happily, Mr Colliver. A PTPH is a hearing at which you are asked whether you plead guilty or not guilty, after which your trial date is fixed and a host of other dates are set down, by which point certain parts of the case preparation must be complete. Ring any bells?'

No response. Michael was sure that Colliver had no idea where this was going.

'OK. Well, unless you correct me – or Mr Epstein does – we'll assume I'm right and that you had a PTPH in this court in January of this year, where you pleaded not guilty to murder and at which a trial date was set for June. Right?'

Michael glanced towards the jury when Colliver did not answer. Just for a moment. Long enough to be sure that they had the point.

'Again, I'm not being corrected. So in January of this year everything had changed, like you said. You *had* been charged. You *had* a trial date. And yet still you had not mentioned Darren O'Driscoll or Simon Kash. Why is that?'

'Because I weren't bloody interviewed again, was I? Where was I supposed to say it?'

This time Michael did not try to hide his smile.

'Have you ever heard of a Defence Statement, Mr Colliver?'

'No.' Colliver's petulant answer suggested a man who had reached his limit.

'Well that is interesting, because I happen to have a Defence Statement that has your name and your signature on it. Would you like to take a look?'

Colliver shot him another angry, silent glare.

'No? Well I'm afraid we're going to do that anyway.'

Michael turned to the court usher.

'Madam Usher, I wonder if this document can be shown to the witness. There's also a copy for His Lordship, one for the court record and six copies for the jury to share. I have additional copies for my learned friends but I can pass those to them myself.'

He handed the documents to the usher before turning back to Colliver.

'Please take a look at the document you're about to be handed, Mr Colliver, and confirm for me that you recognise it.'

The court usher handed Colliver the paperwork, who took a minute or two to read through it. The jury, judge and barristers all did the same. Finally, Colliver nodded his head.

'I'm sorry, Mr Colliver, but we need to hear your answer. For the tape, you understand.'

'Yes.' Colliver's voice was strained. His annoyance barely below the surface. 'I recognise it.'

'Then please confirm for me that this is a Defence Statement, prepared on your instructions to your lawyers and signed by you on the 1st of February of this year.'

'Yes. That's what it is.'

'And please confirm that you were advised by your lawyers that this document should accurately reflect your defence to the charge of murder.'

'Yes.'

'The defence you would advance at trial.'

'Yes.'

'And that anything you did not mention in the document that later formed a part of your defence – or any inconsistencies between the document and your ultimate defence – could be used by a jury to help prove your guilt.'

'Somethin' like that, yeah.'

'So fairly similar to the caution you're given before you're interviewed?'

'Yeah.'

'And you understood that at the time?'

'I ain't thick, mate.'

'Oh, I know that, Mr Colliver. You're far from thick. And yet, despite your intelligence, there is no mention in that document of Darren O'Driscoll, is there?'

Colliver looked like he was already regretting his last answer. Finally he could see what Michael was seeking to achieve. He stayed silent.

'The jury have it,' Michael continued. 'They can see for themselves whether you answer me or not. So we can move on to what concerns me, Mr Colliver. Which is that there is also no mention of Simon Kash, is there?'

Michael paused but still Colliver had no response.

'Or of your supposed presence at the scene of the crime, just minutes after the Galloway brothers had been murdered.'

No response.

'In fact, Mr Colliver, all you *really* say is that you had absolutely nothing to do with the murders. That you knew nothing about them. And that you were elsewhere when they were carried out. Is that not correct?'

From Colliver's hunted look, Michael did not think it would take much more to push him over the edge.

'Is that not what your Defence Statement says, Mr Colliver?'

'THE BLOODY JURY'S GOT IT, AIN'T THEY?' Colliver had reached boiling point. 'THEY CAN READ IT FOR THEMSELVES!'

'Lower your voice.' Judge Levitt did not hesitate to intervene. 'I've said this once in this trial and I'll say it again, Mr Colliver: another outburst and you will be taken downstairs. Do you understand?'

Colliver met Levitt's glare. For a moment it seemed he would try to argue. But with a visible effort he brought himself under control and nodded grudgingly, making no attempt to hide the sneer now etched upon his face. He turned back to Michael, who did not miss a beat.

'So, would you like to explain it?'

'Explain what?'

'The problem with your evidence, Mr Colliver. You see, you've told us that you answered "no comment" because you did not think you would be charged. But that once you were charged you realised you were in serious trouble and so you gave up the names Darren O'Driscoll and Simon Kash. Except that's not true, is it?'

'Yes it bloody well is. I swore an oath.'

'No it isn't, Mr Colliver. We've just seen the signed document that sets out your defence, authorised by you over a month *after* you were charged. Almost a month *after* you pleaded not guilty. *After* you had your trial date fixed.'

'And?'

'Oh come on, Mr Colliver. We're agreed that you're a clever man. You know exactly what I'm pointing out. The problem is that long, long *after* the charge that apparently changed everything – that allowed you to name names – you were *still* telling a different story. You had *still* not blamed Simon Kash. Or Darren O'Driscoll, for that matter. Why *is* that, Mr Colliver?'

Colliver had reverted to silence.

'Come on now, Mr Colliver. That one was an important question. If you don't answer it the jury will surely draw its own conclusions.'

Michael let the pause drag out, as if waiting for an answer he already knew would not come.

'Mr Colliver?'

Finally he turned to the jury.

'So be it then,' he said, shaking his head as if disappointed. 'Let's move on. Tell me, do you recall the date upon which you received your copy of the evidence upon which the Crown intended to rely in your murder trial?'

Colliver glared at Michael. If his arrogance had gone, his rage was now barely contained.

'February 16th.' The answer was almost a growl.

'And that evidence included a detailed case summary, didn't it?'

'You know it did.'

'Good memory, Mr Colliver. You didn't even need to give that answer a moment's thought.'

'So what?'

'So I'm just wondering if there's a reason for that. If there was something in the case summary that made it memorable to you. That made you so sure you'd received it along with the evidence.'

No response.

'Let's not start the silent treatment again, Mr Colliver. It's getting very dull.'

Michael looked down as he spoke, his tone dismissive. This time he did not wait for a response, grabbing a handful of papers from the bench and holding them up for all to see.

'As luck would have it I've a copy of the case summary here. I'm going to pass you page seventeen. Take a look and let me know if it jogs your memory at all.'

Michael turned to the court usher. Handed over copies for the witness, judge and jury, before passing his extras to the other barristers.

He waited while everyone had a chance to read before continuing.

'You agree, do you, that the police summary states that you were suspected of having murdered the Galloway brothers with Darren O'Driscoll. That the police did not believe the murders could be the actions of just one man. But that there was insufficient evidence at that stage to charge Mr O'Driscoll.'

'Yeah, that's what it says. But so what? It's just what the police thought. It ain't evidence.'

'Indeed it's not, Mr Colliver. But what it *is* is the first time anyone

– including *you* – had put in writing or on record any belief of Darren O'Driscoll's involvement.'

'So what?'

'So what? You know "so what", Mr Colliver. It means that before you ever pointed the finger at Darren O'Driscoll, you had in your possession a prosecution document making it quite clear that the police would welcome some direct evidence against him for this crime. In other words, you *knew* the police wanted him before you ever mentioned his name.'

'Oh I've 'ad enough of this, mate. You're talking bollocks.'

'What I'm speaking is the truth and you know it,' Michael said sternly. 'You know it very well. And what's more, at this stage – in this document, which implicates Darren O'Driscoll – there was *still* no mention of Simon Kash. Not from you. Not from the police. Not from anyone. Why is that?'

'I'm not sure this witness can speak for why a police document made no mention of your client, can he, Mr Devlin?'

Michael did not look in Judge Levitt's direction. Just answered the intervention.

'He can if he knows Simon Kash is innocent and is only here because of the lies he has told, My Lord. But I take Your Lordship's point.'

Michael returned his attention to Colliver. The predator was closing in.

'Although I guess, Mr Colliver, that once you had a document naming Darren O'Driscoll, you would *then* be less of a grass if you gave up his name. Since the police already had him in the frame. Is that right?'

Colliver's eyes lit up at Michael's suggestion. A life preserver dangled before a drowning man.

'That's right. That's why I could give my statement then. Darren was already on the hook. So why should I take the fall?'

'Why indeed.' Michael signalled to the jury with a flourish. 'And I'm sure there is not a man or woman here who would think badly of you for doing so. Except for one small factor.'

'What?'

'The date of your witness statement to the police, Mr Colliver.'

'What about it?'

'Your witness statement to the police is dated the 7th of March of this year.'

'And?'

'Well, that's almost three weeks after you first received the evidence. After you first received the police summary that named Darren O'Driscoll, and which therefore allowed you to finally tell the truth.'

'What?' Colliver's anger seemed to have dissipated. Exhausted by Michael's relentless reasoning.

'I want to know why it took you so long? Once you knew you could justifiably give a statement naming Darren O'Driscoll? Because the police already suspected him. Why, then, did it take you so long to do so? Why did it take you three weeks?'

Colliver looked towards Epstein for guidance. The prosecutor's eyes were cast downwards. There was no one else there to help.

'Are you going to answer the question, Mr Colliver?'

Colliver directed a gaze of pure hatred at Michael.

'I just did. OK? I just did.'

'Really? That's the best you're going to do?'

Epstein began to rise to his feet. Slowly. The prosecutor clearly had little enthusiasm left. Michael waved Epstein down before he was fully up.

'I'll move on,' Michael promised. He returned his attention to Colliver. 'The fact is, Mr Colliver, you *couldn't* put the blame on Darren O'Driscoll immediately because Darren O'Driscoll *didn't* act alone, did he?'

'What are you talking about?'

'Darren O'Driscoll acted with *you*. *Exactly* as the police suspected in their summary, but *exactly* as they couldn't prove.'

'Darren O'Driscoll did this with Simon Kash.' The clarity of Colliver's words were overshadowed by his aggressive tone.

'But you knew how badly the police wanted Darren, didn't you?'

'It *was* Darren.'

'You knew that they wanted him so badly that it could be your ticket out if you gave him to them.'

'That ain't right. That's a lie.'

'But the police knew it was two men, didn't they? So to get yourself off the hook someone else had to be that second man. You needed a patsy.'

'All I did was tell the truth.'

'So you took three weeks and you studied the evidence. You looked at everything the police had – all presented to you in the case papers – and you used it to find someone else you could put in your place.'

'That's not true. I've told the truth.' Colliver was sounding increasingly desperate.

'And you found Simon Kash. The bullied kid who did *exactly* what you later claimed to have done yourself.'

'Kash? Bullied? Are you 'aving a laugh?'

'You found that the telephone evidence could be interpreted as placing Simon Kash nearby, and you used it to put him in your place.'

'I didn't put Kash in anyone's place. He's a fuckin' lunatic. I, I—'

'And in turn you put *yourself* in Simon Kash's place.'

'No. Kash did it. Kash n' Darren, but if anything Kash was—'

'You and Darren O'Driscoll killed the Galloway brothers, didn't you?'

'Are you fuckin' mad? Why won't you listen to me?'

'Because you're lying, Mr Colliver,' Michael replied. He was genuinely surprised that Colliver was now trying to make Simon Kash seem so enthusiastic a partner to O'Driscoll. It seemed desperate. 'Because it was the two of you. Big, violent young men. And then when it was done Darren O'Driscoll called Simon Kash – a kid used to being bullied by you all – and ordered him to collect you both from the scene. Isn't that right?'

'You couldn't be more wrong if you tried.' For some reason Colliver was shaking his head and laughing. 'You think Kash is innocent? You think Kash was bullied? If anything he was the reason I didn't bloody come forward earlier, not Darren. And if anyone needs to spend their life in prison—'

'Oh don't go ramping up Simon Kash's role now, Mr Colliver. Not again. Because that's what you did once before, isn't it? To save your own skin, you studied the evidence and you used it to switch your actions – helping Darren O'Driscoll to murder the Galloways – with those of Simon Kash, who did nothing more than drive you both from the scene.'

'NO!'

Colliver's one-word answer was a shout. Not enough to justify an intervention from Levitt. But close. And it told Michael that the time had come.

'You relied on the police's desperation to land Darren O'Driscoll to ensure you'd be believed, didn't you? You knew they'd take anyone remotely connected, provided they got O'Driscoll too.'

'That ain't true. None of that is fuckin' true. I, I don't know where you're getting this . . . this bullshit. You, you don't know what you're talking about. Your client is . . . Simon is . . .'

Colliver seemed close to shouting. Perhaps to rushing from the witness box. But suddenly he deflated. Did not even finish his sentence. Instead he just sat back, looking defeated. It seemed an odd reaction, but Michael did not linger on it. He had reached a critical point.

'Tell me this, Mr Colliver. Who is Jane Gorr?'

'What?' Colliver was bewildered by the sudden change in subject.

'Jane Gorr. She visited you in prison when you were remanded for murder. Six times, I believe. Who is she?'

'She's, she's my mate's bird.' Colliver could not hide his confusion.

'What mate? Jay Price?'

'Yeah.'

'Were you sleeping with her behind Jay Price's back?'

'Christ no.'

'Why not? He's not a close mate, is he?'

'Yes he bloody is. He's the best mate I've got.'

'Really? So if Mr Price were to come to this court, stand in front of this jury and tell them that you and he hardly knew one another, that would be a lie, would it?'

Colliver froze. Michael's shift from murder allegation to Jane Gorr and Jay Price had thrown him. Enough that Colliver had forgotten the content of Price's statement. He remembered it now. And he must have known in that moment that he was lost.

'I . . . I . . .' Colliver's words trailed off.

'If Price had told this jury, for example, that Jane Gorr had *not* visited you six times so you could give her evidential details for Price to put in his statement against Darren O'Driscoll and Simon Kash, that would also be a lie, would it?'

'I . . . I can't say what is and ain't in his statement, can I?' Colliver tried to maintain his belligerence, but the fight had been beaten out of him. 'I didn't write it.'

'At least not in your own hand, no.' Michael smiled one last time. 'But you *did* tell him what to say in it, didn't you, Mr Colliver?'

Colliver stared downwards, dejected.

'And you did that because you needed just a little more evidence to put Simon Kash in your place, right there next to Darren O'Driscoll.'

No response.

'To have Simon Kash accused of the crime *you* committed with Darren O'Driscoll.'

Michael felt a surge of triumph. He expected no answer.

'Your silence says it all, Mr Colliver. I have no more questions.'

Michael took his seat and looked across to Epstein, who was slowly rising to his feet to re-examine. A re-examination that did not come.

A noise from the back of court turned every head.

Darren O'Driscoll was on his feet in the dock. Away from Simon Kash. He appeared calm as he called out across the court.

'Judge. I wanna see my brief. I wanna see him now.'

SIXTY-FOUR

'**M**ichael. I'm very sorry. I shouldn't have doubted you.'

Draper's tone was sincere and maybe a little nervous. The voice of a person proved wrong in the most emphatic manner.

Michael had not spoken to anyone since his final words to Terry Colliver. His determination to save Simon Kash had combined with his usual courtroom adrenaline to see him through the cross-examination. It had allowed him to do his job as effectively as he ever had. Maybe *more* effectively.

But now it was over, he felt utterly drained. He was barely even aware of where they were, having made the silent trip to the Old Bailey cells on autopilot. An unthinking routine. Until this moment, Michael's mind had been somewhere else entirely.

When the sound of Draper's voice broke through, he turned to face her.

'What . . . sorry, what are you apologising for?' Michael asked, forcing himself back into the present.

'For doubting you.' Draper was equally confused. 'I thought I'd annoyed you when I said you shouldn't be cross-examining today. After . . . well, after what happened with Derek.'

'Why would that annoy me? It's your job to second-guess me. It'd be wrong if you *hadn't* asked.'

'Really?' Draper's tone changed from nervous to a mix of hope and relief. A rare moment of vulnerability amid her usual sheen of polished confidence. Draper was keen to explain further. 'I thought that was why you weren't speaking to me. I thought I'd really pissed you off.'

'Then *I'm* the one who should be sorry. You did your job, and you did what I would have done in the circumstances. You must *never* apologise for that. It's what makes you the exceptional barrister you are.'

'I . . . er . . . I . . .' Draper was flustered. And blushing. Two more firsts.

'So I'm sorry if I clammed up. And if I was short with you this morning. It's just . . . it's just there's a lot going on right now.'

'You mean Derek?'

'Yeah. Derek. And other things. It's not anything I can speak about.' Michael did not want to linger on Reid. He changed the subject. 'Interesting outburst at the end there.'

'You mean what he said about Simon? Yeah, absolutely ridiculous. It seemed desperate; there's no way the jury paid any attention to that.'

Michael placed his hands on the table, pushed himself back in his chair and exhaled hard.

'Yeah. Yeah, you're probably right. Except right at the end, you know. He seemed to want to say something else, yet he didn't. He had nothing to lose, so why not say whatever it was?'

'I think maybe you're looking too much into it,' Draper answered, placing her hand on to Michael's. 'You just wiped the floor with him. It was clear to everyone that anything he has said about Simon was a lie designed to save himself. It was a home run, Michael. Don't second-guess it now.'

'I guess you're right,' Michael replied. 'It's . . . it's probably just where my head is at right now. I'm not thinking clearly. Not with, you know, everything.'

Draper squeezed Michael's hand tighter.

'I know you say you can't talk about it. But if you need to? If it would help? I'm here. And I'm a good listener.'

Michael glanced down at his hand. At Draper's. He hesitated for a moment, then slid his own away.

The sounds from the corridor outside of the room caught both barristers' attentions. They looked towards the door just as Simon Kash was brought through. For once he was not dwarfed by his escort. The usual burly guard had been replaced by a stocky woman of average height, no taller than Kash himself.

'That was incredible, Mr Devlin. Incredible!'

Kash was wearing a broad, happy grin. Something Michael had never expected to see. He was also more talkative than he had ever been, with his excited praise starting before the new jailer had uncuffed his wrist from her own.

'That's got to be it, hasn't it?' He was speaking fast, his words falling over each other as they tumbled from his lips. 'You showed everyone that Terry was lying. Everyone saw it.'

'Sit down, Simon.' Michael indicated to the two metal chairs ahead of him. 'Please.'

Kash moved quickly. Climbed across the first chair and into the second, his excitement undiminished. On any other day it would have brought a smile to Michael's face.

'So you think that'll be it?' Kash began speaking again as soon as he was seated. 'I mean, they've got nothing more, have they? There's no more evidence about me?'

'That's right.' Michael lifted the fingertips of his right hand to his right temple. It had been a long day. 'And yes, it went very, very well for us. But it still isn't over. We still have to go through the process.'

'But what about a submission of no case to answer?'

The words felt strange as they hit Michael's ear, catching him off guard. It was not an expression he ever expected Simon Kash to use.

'Where have you heard that term, Simon?'

'Just . . . just in prison. From some of the other inmates.' Kash looked from Michael to Draper. Then back. He seemed suddenly nervous. 'Why?'

'It just isn't something we've spoken about, that's all.' Michael made an effort to smooth his tone. To put Kash back at ease. 'But since you ask, I don't think we have scope to make a submission of no case. They get made when there is *no* evidence against you that a jury could use to convict. Or when the evidence that *did* exist has been so discredited that it can't be believed.

'We're not at that point in your case. There *is* evidence. The phone material and cell-site, for example. OK, one interpretation helps you.

But the other interpretation doesn't. Same as Colliver. He stuck to his guns. He still says that you did it, with O'Driscoll. Now, he *might* be a bad witness. We *might* have made the jury think he's probably lying. If I were a betting man I'd say that we *had* done. And I would be placing a lot of money on you walking out of here at the end of this trial. But that's not the same as a submission of no case to answer. There *is* still evidence for the jury to consider and, although they will probably find in your favour when they do that, the judge can't just *assume* they will. It's for *them* – the *jury* – to do. So no. You don't have a submission of no case.'

Kash sat in silence for a moment as Michael's explanation came to an end. When he spoke again his voice was quiet. Considered.

'So that means there's still a chance the jury *could* convict me. If it gets that far.'

'That's right.'

Michael looked at Kash again, surprised to find him so engaged. He seemed more mature, more able to grasp what he was being told. It was probably natural, Michael thought. Few things would age a person more than facing a murder charge in the Old Bailey.

'And you need to bear in mind, Simon, that things are good now,' Michael continued. 'As good as we could have possibly hoped for. And that there's no more evidence to come from the prosecution. But Darren O'Driscoll still hasn't given *his* evidence, and what he says could still be damaging to you. It could change things. You understand that, right?'

'Darren won't testify,' Kash said.

'What?'

'I mean, I don't *think* Darren will give evidence. It's his temper. He loses it so easy, and after he's seen what you did to Terry? I just don't think he'll risk it, Mr Devlin.'

'Do you know that for sure?' This time it was Draper.

'No. I don't know anything for sure,' Kash sounded less confident now he had been challenged. Michael regretted that Draper had asked so quickly; the new, engaging Kash had been an improvement. 'But you know, I just don't think he'll risk it. If he loses it with Mr Devlin he'll be making himself look like a killer.'

Michael nodded his head. Not entirely sure if Kash was right, but by now too tired to really care. Enough was enough. Michael rose to his feet without warning.

'It's getting late. It's Friday, which means you've got two days now before we see you again. Just remember that things have gone better than we ever thought they would, OK? And you're in a better place than we could have ever expected. It's not the end of the road yet and there are no guarantees, but I want you to head back tonight happy. OK?'

Michael thrust out his hand. Kash got to his feet and took it. A firmer grip than usual. A stronger shake.

'Yes, sir. I'll do that.'

'Good lad. Now sit yourself back down and we'll send a guard back to collect you.'

'Thanks.'

Michael walked out of the door. He turned right and headed towards the metal gates that formed the first of the three sequential secured exit points. Draper was a step behind him, rushing to catch up.

She drew level as they reached the gate.

'Are you OK, Michael?'

'I'm . . . I'm fine.' Michael held his temple as he spoke. As if to press down his growing headache.

'It's just that, well, that seemed a little strained in there. You both seem . . . off.'

'It's nothing,' Michael replied. 'Probably just all this crap that's running around my head. Ignore it, Jenny. Ignore me.'

It really is *nothing*, Michael thought to himself. *My head's all over the place and right now there's only one cure. I need a drink.*

SIXTY-FIVE

T he journey from the Old Bailey to Smithfield Market was not a long one. Even on foot. With his bags and court dress left in the court building, it had taken Michael barely five minutes to reach the block-length warehouse that sat in the centre of the market. Not far enough to qualify as a good stretch of the legs, and certainly too short a distance to shake Draper, who had insisted on joining him for his much-needed post-court drink.

Once the home of London's meat trade, Smithfield had long ago transformed into one of the City's most exclusive districts. The warehouse at its centre held what was left of the butchery shops, while the streets around it now possessed something far more valuable: prime location and late-night alcohol licences. Almost every building housed a bar or a restaurant, each one packed to bursting with big-spending customers. Men and women from the nearby City and stock market. Blowing off steam after another day of playing with the world's billions.

'So, where do you think?' asked Draper.

Michael was leading the way, along the short road that led through the central warehouse and to the busier of Smithfield's two streets beyond.

'The Malmaison at the top of Charterhouse Square,' Michael replied. 'I'm staying there.'

'You're staying there?' Draper was confused. 'Why? What's wrong with home?'

'It's complicated.' Michael did not look across as he spoke. 'Don't worry about it. I've got to stay there and I'd rather drink there too. If that's OK?'

'Hey, you're paying.' Draper's tone was light. The confusion gone. 'Means you choose where you buy them.'

Michael smiled, purely from politeness. His headache was growing. A perfect combination of grief, stress and anxiety, manifesting as physical pain. The conversation Draper was trying to instigate was not welcome. At least not until Michael had managed to medicate with some whisky.

They turned right as they exited the central market warehouse and passed a string of exclusive drinking dens and eateries. Michael had visited most of them in his twenties and early thirties, during his single years. They had probably changed hands time and again in the intervening years. New names. New branding. But basically the same food and drink.

'It's just a little further up ahead,' Michael said as they crossed the junction with St John's Street. 'There's a good bar in the basement, and a—'

Michael stopped speaking abruptly, mid-sentence. The restaurant that sat just north of the junction was new. An expensive, modern design. It included a sheer glass window across its entire front, with a glass door built in. The effect was an impressive statement of the venue's desirability. What it also was – whether intentional or otherwise – was a mirror.

'You OK?' Draper asked.

Michael did not answer. Instead he took Draper by the hand without explanation and increased his pace, Michael could feel Draper's confusion in her grip; first unresponsive, then tightening in enthusiastic agreement.

Hand in hand with him, Draper had no choice but to match Michael's speed, at first without complaint. Then it increased again.

'Michael, slow down. There's no hurry.'

Draper pulled her hand away as she spoke. They had turned left while speed-walking, onto a side street that led to Charterhouse Square and the hotel. It lacked the restaurants, the bars and the traffic of the main road.

A street where they were practically alone.

Michael turned towards Draper as they came to a halt. The intent and passion in her eyes could not have been clearer. It was not a surprise. From the moment he had taken her hand he had known that Draper would misread his action. But he had had no choice. No chance to explain. Even now they had just moments.

'Jenny, get in the doorway.' Michael's voice was firm. Commanding. His words were plainly not what Draper had been expecting and her confusion caused her to hesitate.

'There's no time for this.' Michael grabbed Draper by the upper arms and manhandled her to the nearest recess. 'You need to stay out the way of this.'

As Michael spoke he detected the movement in his peripheral vision. He span round to face it and was confronted by the three men he had seen following them in the restaurant window. Patrick O'Driscoll and two others Michael did not recognise had stopped just feet away.

'What did I warn you about going after my brother in there?' O'Driscoll demanded. He was primed to fight, opening and closing his fists as he eyed Michael.

The men on either side of him were larger than O'Driscoll. Larger than Michael, too. At least width-ways. They seemed more calm, too, showing none of the obvious nerves O'Driscoll was displaying. For them, this was work.

So they're the enforcers, Michael thought. *Less dangerous. They'll do some damage, sure. But that wired bastard's here to kill.*

'What did I tell you, eh?'

Michael looked from man to man. Three against one. Not odds he was fond of. Not back in Belfast in his youth and certainly not now.

But it is what it is.

'Listen, lads. If we're gonna do this then let's get on and do it, eh?'

Michael took two steps back as he spoke. Shrugged his jacket back on his shoulders. As if he were about to remove it.

'But I'm warning you. The week I've had? You've really picked the wrong fucking day.'

The guy on the right moved first. As Michael had expected. Someone had to and he was closest. He moved fast, covering the few feet to Michael in less than a second. There was no hesitation in him. No doubt. Which was exactly what Michael had counted on.

Michael's shoulder shrug had done what he intended. It had brought the attention of all three to his jacket. Made them think he was going to let it drop, where it would momentarily restrict his arm movement.

The perfect time to strike.

At least it would have been, if the impression Michael had given were true. At the same time, the movement had diverted their eyes away from Michael's lower body and so no one saw him carefully place and plant his feet, to allow for as much one-punch power as he could muster.

Michael's two-hundred-pound bodyweight conspired with the first attacker's own two-twenty to shatter the bigger man's jaw with frightening ease. He crumpled at Michael's feet, forming a barrier.

O'Driscoll was less than a step behind as the first punch landed. Over-eager to get to Michael, he had no time to avoid stumbling over his suddenly falling friend, exactly as Michael had intended. O'Driscoll's nerves made him dangerous, but they also made him predictable.

Michael stepped aside and used O'Driscoll's careering momentum against him. Grabbing the flailing man's jacket as he crashed past, Michael span him in a semi-circle, gaining speed and directing him head-first into the oncoming legs of the final man.

The impact with his cohort's right knee stunned O'Driscoll, sending him to the floor and keeping him there. At least for now.

For the last of the three, the collision could have been just an inconvenience. Sufficient to unbalance him for just a moment. But a moment was all Michael would need.

His childhood on the streets of Belfast had taught Michael many things. It had made Michael hungry. Ambitious. And it had made him mentally sharp. Able to spot a con – or a threat – a mile away. But right now only one lesson mattered: never, ever let an advantage pass. No matter how fleeting.

Michael Devlin had learned that lesson over thirty years ago. And he had learned it well.

The distraction of O'Driscoll had lasted no longer than a heartbeat. Nothing more. Yet as that heartbeat passed and his attention returned to Michael, the attacker could do nothing about the blonde head that was now just inches from his face and moving fast. The impact came nanoseconds later, with every ounce of Michael's weight once again brought to bear. This time through his forehead instead of his fist.

Not that it mattered. The result was the same.

Michael heard the sickening crunch as the bone and cartilage in the man's nose crumbled into his face. But the damage did not stop there. Michael's momentum sent his head further forward. The speed and with which Michael's head had connected also shattered the bigger man's cheekbone, with the momentum from the blow sending them both crashing to the floor.

Michael was back on his feet in an instant, fuelled by the massive adrenaline rush that had started just seconds ago. The other man stayed down, as motionless as the guy who had gone first. It had been a while since Michael had last fought. Almost two years. And although he wasn't supposed to admit it – although he was supposed to be civilised – Michael could not deny the truth.

This feels bloody good.

O'Driscoll was not having the same experience. Slightly dazed from the impact with Guy Three's knee, he did not regain his footing as cleanly nor as quickly as Michael. Halfway between horizontal and upright, his head was just beginning to clear when it was impacted by another, much more deliberate knee-strike.

The momentum Michael had built up in just four steps smashed O'Driscoll's front teeth. The impact threw him backwards, into a doorway where he missed Draper by inches. His head landed heavily on the concrete step inside. The thud was sickening.

Michael approached slowly, his heart racing. Something inside – something primal – was hoping that O'Driscoll had some fight left in him. That Michael could be justified in punishing him further. But one glance told him otherwise.

Like his two friends, O'Driscoll was finished.

And Michael's fight was done.

*

For all of Smithfield Market's exclusive bars and restaurants, many butcheries remain. And where there are butcheries there are vans. Parked. Driving. Loading. Unloading.

Karl Hirst's van was parked less than one hundred yards from where Michael Devlin had just dispatched his three attackers in seconds. And, for the first time in a long time, Hirst was impressed.

He had not realised that Michael Devlin was quite so capable. Certainly more of a handful than the others; it might even require him rethinking a few minor details of what would happen between them. Luckily, he knew exactly how to deal with that problem: the woman with whom Michael had been walking hand in hand. The woman who was *not* Sarah Truman.

You dirty bastard, Devlin, Hirst had thought. *You dirty, unlucky bastard.*

She would be the perfect leverage to keep him under control. Of that Hirst was certain.

SIXTY-SIX

'What'll it be?'

Jenny Draper turned to face Michael. Indicated to her hands as she spoke. She had a different miniature bottle between each finger. Six choices. The full selection available in the suite's minibar.

A broad smile told Michael that Draper was at least amusing herself as she wiggled the bottles in his direction.

'Whichever malt whisky looks best.'

Michael could not recall the brand selection from the previous night. And after what had just happened he was past caring. Any alcohol would do.

'Gotcha.'

She was still smiling. Still upbeat. She had been terrified by the fight at the time, Michael knew. But, now it was over, those ten seconds seemed to have excited her more than anything in her life.

Michael had seen the effect before.

For him it was the polar opposite. An intense high during the action. A shuddering low when the deed was done.

The fight had ended as most real fights do; almost as soon as it began. Satisfied that none of the three were moving, Michael had grabbed a shell-shocked Draper and dragged her towards the hotel. He had then called Levy, to ensure that none of the three men would wake up free.

The bar beneath the hotel had been Michael's first destination, until he noticed the blood dripping from his battered knuckles. Those injuries would require immediate attention; he knew that from experience. And with Draper yet to switch from paralysed shock to her current semi-euphoria, Michael had little choice but to bring her with him.

He had not been keen on the idea at the time. Now he was regretting it deeply.

The sound of chinking glass interrupted Michael's thoughts. He looked up to see that the drinks were made and in Draper's hands. She walked towards him and placed a tumbler of amber liquid on the table ahead of him, then placed her own glass next to his. Then she took a seat in the closest chair.

'Sorry there's no ice.' Draper reached for her drink as she spoke. 'But, you know . . .'

She indicated to the ice bucket that sat next to Michael's glass. Michael's right hand – the bleeding stopped – was inside it. The oldest remedy for a swollen fist.

'Whisky doesn't need ice,' Michael replied unenthusiastically. He picked up his own glass with his good hand. 'Only a heathen dilutes this stuff.'

Draper took a sip of her drink. Hers was a long glass, filled with clear liquid. The sip caused the barest grimace.

'Maybe,' Draper placed her drink down again. 'But a gin and tonic definitely needs it.'

Draper reached out and placed her own hand into the ice bucket. Her skin touched against Michael's as she picked out three ice cubes. The contact was not necessary and they both knew that.

'How's the hand?'

Draper dropped the ice cubes into her glass and stirred her drink, all without taking her eyes away from Michael.

'It'll survive,' Michael replied, his eyes drifting to the ice bucket. He was cursing its necessity more with every word Draper spoke. It had become a virtual restraint, holding him in place.

'I've never seen anyone get hit that hard,' Draper said. Her admiration was making Michael increasingly uncomfortable. 'He went down like a ton of bricks.'

'Then you're lucky, Jenny. You don't need to be seeing that sort of thing in your life. It's not . . . it's not attractive.'

'Not sure I agree with that,' Draper said in a low, husky voice. 'Where did you learn to fight like that?'

'It's not something to be proud of.'

Michael took another sip of his whisky.

I don't like where this is going.

'Now I *definitely* don't agree with *that*!' Draper laughed, tapping him lightly on the arm. 'You dictated that fight. Everything that happened. You made it happen on your terms.'

'No I didn't. That wasn't a film, Jenny. It wasn't some choreographed bullshit where they come at you one at a time. It was mostly luck.'

Draper said nothing. She just stared at Michael with the hint of a smile. The fight was playing out in her mind. Michael could see that.

Except it's not, he thought. *Not the real one. In her mind it's already changed. She's already rewritten it.*

'Anyway, let's not dwell on it,' Michael continued. 'It's done. It's over. So let's move on.'

'Where to?'

Draper said the words slowly. Deliberately. It was not a tone Michael had heard her use before. But it was one he recognised.

'Jenny—'

Not waiting for Michael to finish, Draper reached out, took his damaged right hand from the ice bucket and lifted it towards her lips.

Michael pulled his hand away instantly, bashing his injured knuckle on Draper's hand in the process. It sent a jolt of pain up his forearm.

'What do you think you're doing?'

'What we both want.'

Draper moved closer.

'Jenny, stop,' Michael said, his voice firm, but Draper seemed oblivious to his words.

'I said STOP!'

This time Michael almost shouted. He rose to his feet in a hurry, throwing her off balance.

Draper was visibly shocked and confused by the rejection. She steadied herself as she stepped away from him. Michael had done much the same, so by the time Draper spoke they were half a room apart.

'Michael, I . . . I . . . this was what you wanted?'

'No, it wasn't.'

'But asking me for a drink? Bringing me back to your room?'

'Jesus Christ, I didn't ask you for a drink. I wanted to drink alone. You just insisted on joining me. And as for bringing you to my room, what choice did I have? You think I'd have just left you outside in the street, after what just happened?'

'But why else . . .' A look of horror appeared in Draper's eyes. 'Oh God, Michael. I didn't . . . I didn't . . .'

'Look, it's a misunderstanding.' He felt a wave of sympathy towards Draper as he watched the reality of what she had done set in. The moment was suddenly so awkward that it was almost comical. 'We can just forget about this.'

'But I thought it was what you wanted.' Draper sat down heavily onto her original seat. 'I thought you wanted *me*.'

Michael stayed standing.

'There's only one woman I want,' he answered, his tone certain. 'And that's Sarah.'

An uncomfortable silence filled the room. When Draper finally broke it her voice was weaker. Somehow younger.

'Have I ruined this?'

'Ruined what?'

'Us? The work "us", I mean. Have I broken up the team?'

'No. No, not at all.' Michael reached out for Draper's hand. He took it and guided her up from the seat. Ignoring the pain of his injury. 'All you've done is clear the air on something that was building. I should have done it myself a week ago but I was hoping it'd just pass. Now it's done and we can just forget about it and move on. As friends.'

'Still?'

'Still, yeah. But *just* friends. And I think the kind of friends who *don't* drink alone together in a hotel suite for a while.'

Draper smiled awkwardly, wiping away the few tears that had spilled over.

'So time for me to go then?'

'I think so.'

'Do you mind if I clean myself up first?'

'No problem. But I'm going to head down to the bar while you do that. Then you can let yourself out. OK?'

Michael moved away, picked up the room keycard from the table and headed towards the door.

'I'll see you on Monday.'

Draper returned his friendly smile and nodded.

'See you Monday.'

SIXTY-SEVEN

It took Jenny Draper almost twenty minutes to leave Michael's suite. To compose herself, both physically and emotionally.

The first of those had not taken long. Draper had just washed away the tear stains and re-applied her make-up. A quick fix.

It was the emotional fall-out that delayed her. She was not used to rejection. To a man saying 'no'. It was hard to take, and more than a little confusing.

How the hell did I misread his signals so badly, Draper had thought to herself.

By the time the elevator opened into the hotel reception, the lesson had been learned. Humiliating, but valuable. She just hoped Michael's reassurances had been genuine. That it would not make things awkward between them.

Draper walked through the reception and exited the hotel, onto the quiet cobbled street outside. She had not taken in her surroundings on arrival; she had been too jacked up on fear, excitement and adrenaline. Now she did, as she looked around to get her bearings. The large green to her left – Charterhouse Square – and the long, cobbled, antiquated road that led back to the Barbican and the nearest Tube station.

Feeling in need of a drink and some friendly support, she took out her mobile phone from her pocket, scrawled through a list of names and found the person most likely to be drinking locally.

Alyssa Johnson.

The connection was almost instant.

'Where are you guys tonight?'

'You're coming here?' Alyssa sounded surprised, even over the noise of the crowds around her. 'What about your drinks with Michael?'

'Yeah. That didn't go the way I thought it would. And you won't believe what happened before, either. I'll tell you when I see you.'

'What was it?'

'I said I'll tell you when I see you! Patience, Lysh!'

'Okay, can't wait. Love you.'

'Yeah, love you too. See you soon.'

The disconnected call took Draper back to the home screen. A text from Michael had appeared while she had been speaking: *Please don't give what happened in the hotel a second's thought. It doesn't change a thing so don't worry. We're still good.*

Draper smiled, typed 'Thank you' and pressed send. Putting the telephone back in her bag, she began to walk.

Maybe it would *be OK.*

The thought was interrupted and disproved in the same instant.

Draper did not have time to register the sound of a sliding van door. Grabbed by her suit jacket, she was dragged backwards with more force than she had ever experienced and thrown head-first into the darkness of the van.

SIXTY-EIGHT

The screen on Michael's iPhone came to life, displaying a two-word text message: *Thank you.*

Short but complete. Michael smiled when he read it, hopeful that it drew a line under the awkwardness of the past half-hour.

The hotel's small basement bar was dark, despite the long, hot summer nights outside. Michael had taken a tall stool. One of six that lined up against the front of the bar. Four of the other five were occupied. Two couples, it seemed. The stool chair next to Michael was empty.

Otherwise the bar was quiet. There were too many places nearby that were more suited to the good weather.

Michael looked up from his empty glass and caught the barman's attention.

'Same again?'

'Please.'

Within a minute Michael's glass was full. Yamazaki Sherry Cask 2013. No ice. A single drop of water. The barman knew what he was doing. A connoisseur's drink, served the right way.

Not that Michael really cared tonight. Tonight, the alcohol content was all that mattered.

The first mouthful drained half the glass. As it had the previous one.

People drink for a variety of reasons. Some to savour the experience. Some because they must. For Michael it was something else. At least it was right now.

Michael was drinking to forget.

He looked at his right hand as he placed his glass back onto the bar.

The swelling on his knuckles was getting worse. But the pain had gone. Temporarily, at least.

'I'm glad it wasn't you that needed to be mopped up in the street.'

The voice came from behind, the distinctive accent now impossible to miss.

Michael turned to see Joelle Levy as she stepped off the staircase and into the bar. It took her just three or four more steps to reach him. He stood up as she approached and indicated the seat next to him.

'They were still there when your guys arrived then?' Michael asked.

Levy took the seat offered. Michael retook his own.

'They weren't going anywhere quickly,' Levy replied. 'That was an impressive amount of damage you did, Michael.'

'Not like I had a choice. Self-defence, three against one. Everything I did was reasonable.'

'You don't have to defend yourself to me, counsel.' Levy caught the barman's eye and signalled him over. 'No one's going to suggest your actions were anything but legal.'

Levy indicated Michael's glass and asked what it was. Michael told her. She turned to the barman.

'Two more of those, please.'

Then back to Michael.

'What I meant is you're bloody lucky it was O'Driscoll and his stupid friends who came for you. At least you can see that sort coming. What if it had been Hirst?'

'Hirst isn't going to be anywhere public,' Michael replied. 'Not after you've plastered his face all over every news outlet in the country. He could stand next to the Pope and still be the first one recognised.'

Michael did not know if Levy bought his nonchalance. *He* certainly did not; his only regret about the afternoon's violence was that it had *not* involved Hirst.

'That doesn't mean you're safe,' Levy replied. 'He's a ruthless son of a bitch. And he'll still be trying to find a way to come for you. You know that.'

Michael took a gulp of his whisky, emptying what was left in the glass.

Just in time, as the barman returned with two more. Michael turned back to Levy.

'I was sorry to hear about Inspector Hale,' he said, changing the subject. 'I could tell that you were close.'

'Yeah, we were. Steve was a good man. And a great friend.' Levy picked up her glass and held it outwards. Towards Michael. 'What is it you say in Ireland? Sláinte, right?'

'Close enough.' Michael lifted his own glass. Clinked it against Levy's. 'L'chaim. And to Steven Hale, may God rest him.'

'Thanks. Truly.'

Levy took a sip of her drink. Then a second sip – a larger one – before placing her glass on the bar. Levy seemed to be steeling herself to say something, and when she finally spoke she seemed relieved.

'Michael, I'm not going to arrest you for what happened at Hirst's trial.'

'What?' The statement was the last thing Michael had expected to hear. 'Why not?'

'Because no one else knows. No one but you, me and Sarah. And frankly that piece of shit deserved – he *deserves* – everything done to him. So don't worry. Once this is over, it's over.'

'That's kind of you. I appreciate it.'

'Don't appreciate anything. In fact, don't mention it again. Ever.'

'Is that what you came here to tell me?'

'That, and to make sure you're looking after yourself. So I can tell Sarah. She's done nothing but worry about you, but she says you've not been taking her calls.'

Michael felt a pang of guilt at Levy's words.

'It's been a struggle,' he began to explain. 'I can't face her. If I'd only checked on Hirst – if I'd not been complacent that he was inside – then Derek would still be alive. I can't accept that myself, so how can I ask Sarah to? Derek was her friend, too.'

'That's bullshit,' Levy interrupted. 'We had two guys on Derek's house until the Wisdom Penfold theory went south. We wouldn't have increased that number for Hirst if we'd known about him, and after what happened in Manchester do you really think two would have been enough? Because I sure as hell don't. Hirst would have walked through those guys and he would have still got to Derek. All that happened by you not clicking earlier is that two officers got to live.'

Michael tried to find some comfort in her words. What she had said was almost certainly true. That Hirst would have got to Derek regardless; he would have made short work of the two cops assigned to his home. But the guilt remained, and it would take time to fade.

'Call her, Michael,' Levy continued. 'Let her know you're OK.'

Levy looked Michael up and down.

'You *are* OK, aren't you?'

Michael shook his head before speaking.

'I'm separated from my family at the most stressful time of our lives. All I can think about is their safety. That and my best friend's mutilated corpse. So am I OK? No. No, I'm not. But I *can* still look after myself. I can still keep myself safe.'

Levy nodded, taking another sip of her drink.

'I do know you can take care of yourself, Michael. You know that, right?'

'What do you mean?'

'I mean I know who you are. Where you're from. So I know Hirst isn't coming after some ten-stone weakling.'

'How much do you know?'

'I've got the highest possible clearance at Scotland Yard. And anything *they* don't want to tell me, do you think I spent that many years in Shin Bet without picking up a few tricks? I know the lot. Joe Dempsey. Joshua. And Liam.'

Michael leaned back in his seat.

Clearance or no clearance, you don't know everything, he thought. *If you did you'd have put Anthony Haversume at the top of that list.*

'If you know all of that, why are you still so worried about me?'

'Because you're out here on your own this time. I know how much you can handle, but this time you don't have your brother next to you. Or Joe Dempsey backing you up. Hirst is dangerous. Lethal. Look what he did to Hale.'

'We knew that anyway,' Michael replied. 'But I've made my decision. So please tell Sarah I'm fine. And please, no mention of what happened tonight with O'Driscoll.'

'Both of those things go without saying. But you should be telling her yourself.'

'I know. And I will.'

Michael downed what was left of his glass, stood up and indicated to the barman.

'Put all this on my room, would you?'

'Yessir.'

'Thanks.'

Back to Levy.

'I'm going back to my room, Joelle. I need to eat. Why don't you head home to your son? Put this all out of your mind for one night and have some family time?'

'I can't.' Levy got to her feet. 'I wish I could.'

'Then just do it. Life's too short. Go home and spend some time with your boy.'

Levy nodded as Michael took the first step on the staircase.

'And Joelle?' Michael's voice interrupted her thoughts. 'Thank you for the news. About what I did at Hirst's trial, I mean. I really do appreciate that.'

'Forget it. We couldn't try you without Hirst anyway, and that piece of shit won't be seeing the inside of a witness box,' Levy's voice was grim but certain. 'Especially not after what he did to Hale.'

SIXTY-NINE

It was 2 a.m. when Michael awoke. A lot earlier than he had planned. His unconsciousness fought back hard as he tried to open his eyes. It made the world seem unreal for a few seconds. Reality masquerading as a dream. Only the insistent ringing of Michael's mobile phone pulled him through.

Michael's Friday night had not mirrored his Thursday. After parting company with Levy he had returned to his room, where he had undressed and ordered a meal. One look at the menu had reminded him of when he had last eaten. Thursday lunchtime. Far too long.

Michael made up for the unintentional fast. Tempura prawns to start. Followed by a twelve-ounce Hereford rib-eye with fries, grilled tomato, mushrooms and peas. Plus side-orders. Mac and cheese. A half-rack of barbecue ribs. A feast fit for a man who was thirty-six hours late for dinner.

A bottle of Argentinian Malbec had been intended to go with the meal. It now sat on the lounge table, opened but unfinished. Abandoned to a combination of exhaustion and carb overload. Next to the bottle was a small pile of empty plates.

And the mobile phone that had woken Michael from his much-needed sleep.

Michael pushed himself up onto his elbows and tried to shake off the grogginess. He tried to think who could be calling him in the middle of the night until suddenly his mind focused, banishing every trace of sleep in its wake.

Sarah.

He threw the light sheet from his body and leapt from the bed. Within moments he was in the suite's lounge, just feet from his illuminated mobile phone. Two more steps and he would reach it. But still he was too late.

The ringtone stopped as soon as the phone came into sight. The screen, though, remained lit. Michael picked up the handset and read it. Four missed calls. All from the same number.

Jenny?

It was not the name Michael was expecting to see. He looked at his watch, confused. Why on earth had she tried to call him four times in a row at 2 a.m.?

The mixture of relief and concern was a strange one. Jenny could not be calling about Sarah. Michael knew that, but still something was wrong.

He pressed to return the call and it was answered almost immediately.

Michael waited for Draper to speak but there was no sound.

'Jenny?'

Michael felt his heart rate rising again when Draper did not respond. The knot in his stomach returned.

'Jenny? Are you OK?'

Michael's concern was increasing. Fast.

'Listen, Jenny, whatever—'

'I see you haven't lost your accent, Michael.' The voice that interrupted him was one that, until last night, he had never expected to hear again. Emotionless and clinical. Michael recognised it in an instant, knowing in that moment that it could mean only one thing.

'You son of a bitch,' Michael swore loudly. 'If you hurt her—'

'If I hurt her it will be entirely *your* fault, Michael. Just like all the others.' The voice was no louder. It carried no urgency. The words just a statement of fact. 'And if you don't want that to happen you'll do exactly as I say. Understood?'

Michael hesitated. Long enough to think through his options. Long enough to know he had none.

When he answered his voice was flat. Defeated.

'Tell me.'

SEVENTY

3.45 a.m.

It had been a long two hours.

Michael sat at the wheel of an Audi A3. A smaller car than he was used to. One of thousands of Car Club vehicles parked across London. This one was ordinarily parked on St John's Street, just a stone's throw from Michael's hotel. But right now it was forty miles from its base.

The darkness was absolute. A combination of the night and of the setting.

The village of Brookwood was over a mile away. The nearest major town – Guildford – six miles further. Michael was about as far from artificial light as was possible in twenty-first-century England. Natural light was minimal, too, thanks to the overhanging trees of the Surrey countryside.

Michael glanced at the Audi's digital clock. The only illumination visible with the car's battery turned off.

Still 3.45 a.m.

The time matched Michael's watch exactly. Both told him the same thing.

He was fifteen minutes early.

The adrenaline that had gripped Michael in his hotel suite was gone. It would return, Michael was sure. What he was about to face made that inevitable. But for now he had just his nervous energy. His anticipation. His fear.

Brookfield Cemetery was around half a mile from where the Audi was parked. A three-minute drive at night, thanks to the dark country roads. That left Michael with twelve minutes to do what he had to do. To make the necessary arrangements. It was too long. The timing had to be right.

Michael fixed his eyes on his Omega Seamaster wristwatch and focused as the luminous second-hand swept smoothly around the watch's face. Once. Twice. Three times.

Nine minutes, Michael thought. *Good enough.*

Michael's iPhone was logged into the Audi's hands-free system via Bluetooth. He had paired them before setting off. Temporarily dormant, the phone reconnected with the car's electronic brain as soon as Michael turned the key. A single click left the engine off while switching on the electric power.

The central console came alive, displaying a list of options. Michael quickly accessed his address book and found the entry he was seeking.

Joe Dempsey.

Michael tapped the name and waited.

The connection was not instant. Partly because Michael was in the middle of nowhere and partly because it was a long-distance call. Michael rarely knew where he would find his friend, but he knew it would not be nearby. Dempsey was based in New York, but right now he could be could be anywhere in the world.

Finally the ringtone began to chime in his ear. An intermittent single tone. Confirmation that Dempsey was overseas.

Shit. Come on, Joe. Answer the phone, Michael pleaded silently as the phone continued to ring: *four, five, six*, he counted.

Shit. Shit. Shit.

Michael caught his breath as the seventh tone was interrupted. Unsure if it would be a person or a voicemail.

'Mike?' Joe Dempsey's voice sounded concerned. He would have noted the UK time, Michael knew. 'What's happened? Are you OK?'

'Joe, I need your help.' Michael tried to keep his voice calm. To keep it steady. It was no easy task. 'I'm in trouble.'

'Where are you?'

'I'll get to that. First I need you to do something for me.'

'What, Mike?'

'I need you to promise that if anything happens to me, you'll take care of Sarah and Anne. You'll protect them.'

Michael could not disguise the shaking in his voice.

'What the hell are you talking about? What's going on?'

'Promise me, Joe. Please.'

'You know you don't have to ask that. They're family. You all are.' The concern in Dempsey's voice was undisguised. 'Now you tell me what the hell's going on so I can help you.'

'You can't help with this one, Joe. I've got to do it alone.'

'What are you talking about?' Dempsey did not sound impressed. 'Do what alone?'

Michael took a deep breath.

'There's a guy. A guy I defended a long, long time ago. Karl Hirst, he's called. He's been released and now he's come for me. He's come for *everyone* in his case.'

'What do you mean he's come for you? Come for you how?'

'He's killing people. He's killed the judge from the case. The cop. And Derek. He killed Derek.'

'You mean the big guy? Your barrister friend?'

'Yeah,' said Michael, unsurprised that Dempsey had placed Derek so swiftly. 'The bastard killed him. Crucified him.'

'Crucified? Like the judge that was killed. The one in the news? Longman, wasn't it? He was the judge from your trial?'

'Yeah. Hirst got to him too. And to the cop who brought him in.'

Dempsey hesitated again, but when he spoke his reaction was unemotional. Professional. Exactly as Michael would expect.

'What about the police?' Dempsey finally asked. 'What have they done?'

'Everything they can,' Michael replied. 'And they've got Sarah and Anne in protective custody. But he's *still* coming. And now he's got two people – two women – and he's going to kill them if I don't meet him tonight. Alone.'

'Are you serious?' Michael heard a change in Dempsey's tone. A nervous realisation. Something he had never heard before. 'Tell me you're not meeting him, Michael. Tell me you're not going alone.'

'I don't have a choice. Either I do that or they both die. And if that happens he'll come for me anyway.'

'What the hell does that matter? Call the police. Call anyone. Don't go and—'

'I've no choice.' Michael raised his voice to interrupt. 'This bastard knows my every move. I don't know how, but if I risk bringing anyone . . . I can't risk it, in case he knows.'

'Michael, I—'

'I can't risk it, Joe.' Michael cut across Dempsey's plea. 'People have already died. A lot of people. And it's because of *me*. All of it. Because of something *I* did. I can't let any more die. It's been too many already. Far too many. I have to stop this.'

Michael's last words hung in the air. When Dempsey finally spoke his usual calm had returned.

'Tell me where you are and wait there. I can send help. Proper help. *My* kind of help. This Hirst guy will never know they're there. I promise you.'

'I can't wait. There isn't enough time.'

'What do you mean?'

Michael glanced at the dashboard clock. It was now three minutes until he had to begin driving. Exactly as he had planned. Michael had known that Dempsey would try to interfere. That he would not take no for an answer. Michael could not risk that. It was why he had waited before making the call.

Two minutes.

Close enough, Michael thought.

'I mean I have to meet him now. In five minutes.'

'Michael, are you sure—'

'Just listen to me now,' Michael interrupted. 'Please, just listen. I'm meeting Hirst in Brookwood Cemetery in Surrey. Remember that: Brookwood Cemetery. I have to be there at 4 a.m., my time. And I'm doing it. No one else is dying because of me.'

'But—'

Michael ignored the interruption and continued.

'What I need *you* to do is contact Detective Chief Inspector Joelle Levy of Scotland Yard's Major Investigation Team. Tell her where I am. Tell her to get her people here as soon as possible. Because if she gets here soon enough she might find Hirst.'

'But you're not waiting.'

'No. If I turn up with the police, then he'll kill the girls. If I'm there alone then they have a fighting chance, because he'll have to kill me first.'

'How much of a fighting chance?' Dempsey was as blunt as Michael expected. 'Can you take this guy?'

'Who the hell knows,' Michael replied. 'That's why I'm calling *you*. Because if I *don't* get through this and if Hirst gets away, I need you to protect Sarah.'

'Mike—'

'Promise me, Joe. Please.'

Dempsey hesitated one last time before answering.

'I promise. And I promise something else, too.'

'What?'

'I promise that if you don't kill this son of a bitch tonight, I'll kill him for you.'

Michael smiled.

'I know that,' he replied. 'I know you will.'

'And Mike?'

'Yeah?'

'Do me a favour, would you?'

'What?'

'Save me the trouble.'

SEVENTY-ONE

It was not common for Joelle Levy to be at her desk at 4 a.m. But it was not unheard of, either. Even during investigations that had *not* taken such a personal turn.

Levy had taken Michael's advice and had driven from Smithfield Market to her home in Highgate. It seemed like weeks since she had last spent time with her son. Who knew when they would get the chance again? And so Claire Gordon had been relieved of her babysitting duties for a few hours and had gone upstairs to catch up on some sleep, while Levy and Richard had spent the evening together. Fuelled by a pizza, a tub of ice cream and a movie on Amazon Prime.

It was an emotional pit stop that had left Levy reinvigorated.

Shortly after midnight, Richard had fallen asleep on the sofa. Being careful not to wake him, Levy had carried him to his bedroom and placed him in the bed next to his sleeping babysitter.

Refreshed by the rare few hours of rest and the quality time with her son, Levy had then washed, dressed and made her way back to Scotland Yard by 2 a.m.

Two hours had passed since then. Two hours Levy had not wasted.

Steven Hale's long journey to Manchester had taken the most direct route. A journey of that length meant motorways. In turn, motorways meant the Automatic Number Plate Recognition system. The little-known camera network that could trace any vehicle as it travelled throughout the UK.

Levy had made the request in the afternoon. For all system 'hits' made by Hale's own number plate. She had also asked for the 'hits' from all other vehicles in the twenty seconds that followed Hale's.

A vast amount of information. And the only real lead Levy now had.

The material had landed on her desk while she was still at home: 648 'hits' on Hale's plate. Tracing his BMW as it travelled from London to Salford. Alongside those 'hits' were tens of thousands more, made by car after car that passed some of the same ANPR cameras within twenty seconds of Hale.

But Levy wasn't looking for a vehicle that passed *some* of the same cameras. She was looking for the vehicle that passed them *all*.

It had taken almost two hours already.

It was a vast amount of information to go through. Levy had meticulously listed all of the plates registered at the first ANPR camera Hale had passed. Then she had moved onto the second, deleting any entry on the camera-one list that did not pass camera two. Then the same for the third camera. Then the same for the fourth.

By the time Levy's telephone rang at 4 a.m., she was nearing camera five hundred. Her list of other vehicles was now just six plates long.

Levy glanced at her watch. It was early to receive a call.

She picked up the phone and put it to her ear.

'Hello?'

'Is this Joelle Levy?'

The voice was authoritative. It demanded attention.

'Speaking.'

'My name is Joe Dempsey. I'm with the International Security Bureau at the United Nations and I need to speak to you about Michael Devlin.'

SEVENTY-TWO

Michael looked at his watch.

4.15 a.m.

He had arrived at Brookwood Cemetery at exactly 4 a.m. Both his Omega and the Audi's digital clock agreed the time. If both were wrong it would be by less than a minute. A margin of error Karl Hirst had to allow.

Hirst's instructions had gone no further than Michael's arrival. 4 a.m. at the cemetery. Nothing more than that. Michael had obeyed them to the letter and had waited at the gated entrance for ten minutes. In the pitch black of night.

A lamb to the slaughter.

But the slaughter had not come. Nothing had. And so Michael had had no choice but to follow his instincts and to enter the cemetery itself.

Brookwood Cemetery was huge. Over five hundred acres, it was the biggest in the UK and one of the biggest in Europe. Michael knew that now, thanks to a quick Google search.

It was an easy place to get lost. Even in daylight.

And an easy place to get killed.

Michael had been walking for five minutes, but he had no idea where to. He had just stuck to the path, following its twists and its turns.

The darkness was less intense within the grounds. It was an open space, allowing the moon and starlight to do their work. They made a difference; Michael still needed to concentrate to stay on the gravel walkway, but at least it was semi-visible.

He kept moving. Deeper and deeper into the cemetery. Further and further from the road. From the slightest possibility of a passing car.

From any sound but the sound of himself. Of his footsteps. Of his heartbeat.

Michael could not stop his mind from racing as he strode onwards. Every step brought new possibilities. New fears.

Hirst could be anywhere. Behind any of the headstones that Michael could make out in the darkness. Or obscured by any of the larger mausoleums silhouetted in the distance. Wherever Hirst was, he was safe. He was hidden.

Michael was not.

Michael was very aware that he was exposed on the path, the only part of the cemetery that offered no cover. It gave Hirst every advantage. He could take Michael – from a distance – whenever he pleased. With no need to dirty his hands. Michael knew that. And knew he was still breathing for only one reason.

Hirst was enjoying his game.

Michael looked down at his watch. Ten more minutes had passed. Ten minutes of aimless walking. Ten minutes of tortured anticipation. Ten minutes of Hirst's pleasure.

Enough's enough, Michael thought, unwilling to give Hirst a moment's more satisfaction. *Let's just get this done.*

He came to a halt. Without the sound of his footsteps, his heartbeat sounded much louder in his ear. It was rapidly increasing in speed. He could feel the rush of adrenaline starting again.

'HIRST!' Michael's voice broke the silence like a siren. 'STOP HIDING, HIRST! YOU WANT ME, I'M HERE!'

Michael fell quiet. Listened. As intently as he could.

He did not know what he expected to hear. A response, perhaps? The sound of footsteps on grass? Of a bullet being chambered? Michael could not say. All he knew was what he did *not* expect to hear.

'HELP! HELP US!'

The words were faint but they were clear. Whoever screamed them was a distance away. Too far to make out a sex. But that did not matter. It meant that *someone* was alive.

It meant that there was hope.

Michael closed his eyes to block out distractions. To triangulate his position. The voice called out again. It sounded like it came from the right.

Michael did not hesitate for a moment. He began to run.

The direction of the voice took Michael off the path. Onto unsteady ground and unseen grave after unseen grave. They slowed his progress, causing him to stumble time and again and to collide with statues. With headstones. Still Michael pushed on, ignoring his pained lungs and his rampant heart. He concentrated only on the screams.

Until those screams suddenly stopped.

Michael slowed and then came to a standstill when he realised he could no longer hear the sound.

He knew he must be close now. Close enough that he thought he had been able to make out Jenny Draper's voice. Or perhaps that had been wishful thinking.

Michael dropped to one knee, taking advantage of the cover of the headstones. It made him a more difficult target, he hoped. More importantly, it gave him the opportunity to get his breath back. He heaved in lungfuls of air, preparing himself for whatever was going to happen next.

Still catching his breath, Michael looked again at his watch. Ten more minutes had passed. The need to recover quickly would test Michael's fitness.

If they're close then Hirst's close, he reasoned. *I need to be ready*.

Seconds passed. Michael counted them off. Calculating them against his own heart rate. It was falling. Coming back to where it should be. His breathing was doing the same.

He gave himself another minute. Long enough for his legs to feel refreshed. For his head to feel clear. Finally ready, Michael rose to his feet.

'HIRST!' Michael's voice boomed. It echoed off the huge mausoleum he now saw outlined ahead of him. 'I'M HERE, YOU BASTARD. COME AND FACE ME!'

Michael looked all about him as he called out, spinning on his heel.

The attack could come from anywhere. From any direction. Michael would at least *try* to be ready.

But again, no attack came. Nothing disturbed the eerie stillness of the graveyard.

'HIRST!'

Michael waited for the sound to reverberate. For his reflected voice to wash over him. Only when the echo had died did he open his mouth to shout again.

A familiar sound stopped him before he could call out. A sound he had heard many times before. It was unmistakable. Here or anywhere else.

A pistol round being chambered.

Michael turned towards the sound and saw a figure emerging from the darkness. A figure from his past, with a pair of pale eyes that he would recognise anywhere.

SEVENTY-THREE

'You came alone.'

Michael and Hirst had spent hours together in the course of Hirst's trial. In all that time Michael had never heard humour in Hirst's voice.

He heard it now. A cold, vindictive mockery.

'I'm not sure if I'm impressed or disappointed.'

'Where are they, Karl?' Michael glanced at the semi-automatic pistol in Hirst's right hand. 'Jenny and Tina. Where are they?'

Hirst glanced towards the large mausoleum. Just for a moment. Michael could not tell if it was subconscious or if it was an indication. Either way, it answered the question.

'Are they both alive?'

Hirst smiled.

'Wouldn't you like to know.'

'I'm *entitled* to know,' Michael replied. 'Me for them. *Both* of them. That was the deal.'

'You didn't expect me to honour that, did you?' Hirst sneered, a twisted smile on his face. 'You can't be that naive.'

'I don't suppose I did, no.'

'And yet you still did as you were told. You still came alone.'

'I don't see I had much choice.'

'You could have just let them die,' Hirst shrugged.

'No, I couldn't. But I don't expect you to understand that.'

'Ah yes, the famous Devlin chivalry.' A smile grew on Hirst's lips. An unattractive distortion to an already ugly face. It did not extend to his eyes. They remained as pale and as emotionless as ever. 'How did it go again?' "No one else is gonna die for me, Sarah. This is all my fault. They died for something I did."'

Hirst spoke with a bad Belfast accent as he mocked the words spoken by Michael in Reid's kitchen.

Michael stared at him, realisation dawning.

'You bugged the crime scenes. You bugged Derek's house.'

Hirst's smile faded into a malicious grin. It better suited his face.

'And how right I was to do so, eh? Because if I hadn't, I'd have never known about *you*.'

Hirst moved closer as he spoke. Out of reach, but close enough for Michael to see him clearly. He raised the pistol as he came forward and aimed it at Michael.

'And that's the irony, Michael. Because until I killed your fat friend, I assumed *you* had nothing to do with what happened. You were just a kid. I didn't think you even knew.'

'What?'

'I thought it was Reid and Blunt and Longman. I thought *they* were behind it. And the girl. Obviously the girl. But I'd accepted I'd never find her. So after Reid I was done, it was over. And then *you* came stumbling in to Reid's house, confessing everything.'

Michael felt a cold fury growing.

'You piece of—'

'If only you'd kept your mouth shut,' Hirst continued, ignoring the interruption. 'I'd never have known I hadn't finished the job. That there was still one more bastard to kill. The little bastard who was behind the whole thing.'

'And Tina.' Michael was half speaking to himself as he said the name, his rage increasing as the picture came together. 'I told you how to get to Tina, too.'

'Yes, you did.' The ugly smile returned. 'You signed your own death warrant. And you signed Tina's, too. Right there in that house. And now you've done the same to your little barrister girlfriend, too. And just so you know, it doesn't stop there.'

Hirst indicated the large mausoleum as he spoke.

'Because there's one more thing I want you to know before you die. I want you to know that your bitch Sarah Truman is gonna be right behind you. Consider it your special bonus. Just for being you. For being the fucker who put me away.'

The words hit Michael harder than any physical blow. It brought a series of images flashing through his mind. Derek's body, brutally mutilated. Eleven-year-old Tina Barker, traumatised and depending on him. Jenny, with her confident poise. And Sarah. The most important person in Michael's life. His reason for being. Her life threatened by the evil that stood before him.

It was more than Michael could bear.

'You'll get nowhere near my family, you sick fuck.' Michael's voice was low. Almost a growl. The sound of a cornered animal.

'There he is.' The mockery was gone. So was the smile. Only the cruelty remained. 'There's the thing I saw in that alley last night.'

Hirst began to circle Michael, who matched him step for step. A cobra and a mongoose. Both ready to strike. Only in this fight, the cobra carried a pistol.

'I was surprised, Michael,' Hirst continued.

Michael hardly heard the words. Like Hirst, his sole focus was on the man in front of him. And so neither noticed the distant sound that was beginning to break the silence.

'I was surprised to see what you're capable of. Lucky for me, because I *was* gonna just use *this*.'

Hirst pulled an eight-inch hunting knife from the back of his waistband and brandished it in his left hand.

'But when I saw you take those three guys that fast? I thought I'd best bring a little insurance.'

He indicated the pistol. Still held in his right. Still aimed at Michael.

'You don't care whether you're good enough without the gun?' Michael's focus was absolute. He inched closer to Hirst as he asked the question.

'Can't say I'm not intrigued.' Hirst's eyes were fixed. Aware of every move Michael was making. 'But I think I'll stick to the easy way.'

Hirst's words were the perfect signal. They told Michael that Hirst was about to shoot. At this distance he could not miss. And Michael could do nothing to stop him.

But he would at least try.

Hirst must have seen Michael's movement before it began; the telltale muscle tension was impossible to disguise. But even if he did not, the speed difference between a physical rush and a bullet was just too much to overcome.

For Hirst, everything was going to plan.

Right up until the plan fell apart.

SEVENTY-FOUR

The journey from Joelle Levy's desk to the MI6 building in Vauxhall had taken seven minutes. Dempsey had called ahead and pulled rank just as he had promised he would. He had arranged for Levy to bypass security, which allowed her to reach the helipad and board the waiting International Security Bureau chopper with no delay.

Twelve minutes in total, between Dempsey's call and Levy's take-off.

The chopper was unlike anything Levy had ever seen. Which was unsurprising as the RAH-66 Comanche had officially never gone beyond the prototype stage. Designed at a cost of seven billion dollars to be the world's foremost stealth helicopter, the cost per unit had proved too much for even the US military and so the project had been scrapped. The six prototypes, however, had not. Three were on display in specialist flight museums around the world. The other three were now the property of the ISB.

The journey to Brookwood would take just twenty-three minutes more. Far quicker than Michael had managed by car. But long enough for Levy to prepare.

The Comanche came well stocked. All the weaponry Levy could ask for. Certainly more than she would be issued by Scotland Yard.

Levy considered the armoury and selected the L129A1 7.62mm semi-automatic assault rifle. The standard-issue sharpshooter rifle for the British Army's front-line operational units, and the closest to those Levy had used in both the Israel Defense Forces and, later, Shin Bet.

Next Levy selected the weapon's sight. The Trijicon ACOG 6×48 telescope. Again standard-issue. Again, closest to the equipment Levy had used before. She clamped the sight in place before turning to the final piece of essential equipment: the MilSight S135 Magnum Universal Night Sight. Essential if the weapon was to be of any use in the dark of the night.

Levy assembled the weaponry in under a minute. An impressive achievement with an unfamiliar gun. Doubly so in the darkness of a moving chopper. The next five minutes of the journey were spent inspecting the mechanics. Ensuring that nothing would go wrong when the shooting started.

Satisfied, Levy clicked the twenty-round magazine into place and settled back into her seat.

'Two kilometres to the target, ma'am.'

Levy opened her eyes and looked at her watch. Fifteen minutes had passed since she had finished preparing the rifle. She had used that time to make herself as ready as her weapon. Levy had learned the breathing exercises that lowered the heart rate while in Israel. A skill that was essential for a sharpshooter, it was not one she had expected to need again.

'Will they hear us yet?'

'No, ma'am,' the pilot replied. 'We're as close to silent running as these things get. This time of night they'll hear a little something at maybe a kilometre out. But we'll be as close as six hundred metres before we're unmistakable.'

'OK,' Levy replied. 'In that case cover the kilometre, then get us steady.'

Levy returned her attention to her weapon. One last inspection. Just to be sure.

Satisfied, she reached out and slid open the Comanche's side door. Unfastening her safety belt, she replaced it with the side harness. A different kind of body restraint and one which allowed her to safely lean outside of the moving helicopter.

'One kilometre, ma'am.'

The pilot's voice came through Levy's headpiece.

'I know,' Levy replied. 'I can see the cemetery.'

Levy lifted the scope to her right eye. A few inches back, to account for recoil. Then she closed her left, to get the full effect of the night sight.

Levy had used night-vision equipment before, back in Israel. It had been state of the art for the time – the best Shin Bet could obtain – but the technology had moved on. The MilSight S135 was like nothing Levy had ever seen. Its effectiveness was almost distracting, as night had suddenly become day.

Adjusting to it quickly, Levy spotted two lone figures in the middle of the cemetery up ahead. Perhaps a kilometre and a half away from the chopper, they were not in the Comanche's direction of travel.

'Your two o'clock.'

The pilot understood and immediately altered his course, careful to ensure their new flight path would keep them in Levy's line of sight.

Levy's eye returned to the scope. Closer. A better view. But still a kilometre away. Maybe more.

And maybe too late, Levy thought.

The turn of the chopper had changed Levy's angle of vision. In doing so it had revealed the pistol in Karl Hirst's hand. A pistol pointed directly at Michael Devlin.

Shit.

Hirst was ruthless. A killer. He would not hesitate to put a bullet into Michael. Levy knew that. And she knew it could happen any second.

The L129A1 has a kill range of around eight hundred metres. Maybe more with a perfectly placed hit. So Levy had two problems: she was still about a kilometre out, so barely in range. And the likelihood of a hit of *any* kind – a kill or otherwise – from a distant moving chopper was slim to none.

Problems they might have been, but Levy was out of options. Either she took the shot or she watched Michael Devlin die.

She took the shot.

SEVENTY-FIVE

Michael heard two shots ring out, an instant before he felt a bullet tear into his own bicep. As he fell, he saw Hirst spun sideways. A second bullet from somewhere had also found its target. And it was the only reason Hirst's had not hit Michael in the chest.

Michael did not need to see the wound to know he had been shot. It was a feeling unique to that experience, and it was not Michael's first time.

The simultaneous impacts threw both men to the floor. Neither stayed down.

Hirst was up first. Michael – slowed just slightly by his now useless right arm – a moment behind him.

The first thing Michael noticed as he got to his feet was the absence of Hirst's pistol. The second was that Hirst knew exactly where it had fallen.

Michael followed his pale eyes as they locked onto the lethal weapon. A weapon Michael could not let him retrieve.

Hirst scrambled towards the gun. An ordinarily simple task, but less so with a bullet lodged in his shoulder. The injury restricted Hirst's movement. Slowed him.

It is a rare occasion when previous bullet wounds can be called an advantage, but this was one of those times. Hirst seemed surprised by the debilitating effect of the shot. By just how much damage it had done.

Michael was not. *He* had been shot before.

Of the two men, Michael alone knew his sudden limitations. And he knew Hirst's.

He roared as he ran towards Hirst. A roar of pain. Of anger. Of desperation. It distracted Hirst for no more than an instant, but that instant was enough.

The impact of Michael's left shoulder into Hirst's torso was agony for both men. Powerful enough to lift Hirst from the floor and send him crashing into a headstone six feet away. Wild enough to send Michael in the same direction.

Michael lay motionless where he fell, his head thumping from the inside. The pain and effort of his shoulder charge had torn into his energy reserves. Little remained. He could only hope that Hirst had suffered more.

To know for sure, Michael needed to stand.

One glance towards Hirst and the question was answered. He was slowly climbing to his feet. Mirroring Michael's own movement. Sharing Michael's suffering.

They were just feet apart. Each moving with the same exhausted effort. If the bullets they had taken had changed the game, the collision that had followed had assured its imminent end.

Only one question remained. Who wanted it more?

Hirst moved first. A wild lunge towards Michael. Too slow. Too weak.

Michael saw the movement. And he reacted. What was left of his adrenaline surged through his veins. Energised him.

Michael gave no thought to his own wounds as he stepped inside Hirst's blow and slammed his right shoulder into Hirst's nose. Hirst was already unsteady on his feet. Already weak at the knees. And so the force sent him careering backwards. Into the same headstone he had hit just moments before.

The blow sent shockwaves down Michael's right arm. They tore into his bicep, damaging it further and increasing his blood loss. But it did not slow him for a moment. Driven by the knowledge of what Hirst had done – of what he still *planned* to do – Michael leapt forward.

The balance and coordination Michael had enjoyed when fighting Patrick O'Driscoll was absent, sapped by his injury. But Michael did not care.

This was not a street fight. This was a fight to the death.

He thought of nothing but the need to damage as he rammed his head into Hirst's face. The gaping wound that the blow left in Michael's own scalp was meaningless. All that mattered was Hirst, his face a shattered mask of blood.

The headstone at the base of Hirst's spine was the only thing now keeping him upright. Michael neither knew nor cared. His primal rage was all there was left. Directed at the man who had threatened his life. The man who had taken his best friend. The man who would be a danger to Sarah for as long as he still drew breath.

It drove Michael further. Powered him as he delivered blow after blow with his left fist. Four punches. Five. Six. Seven. Michael rained them into Hirst's defenceless head. Striking his face. His neck. His skull. Anywhere.

Michael's hand had broken by the fifth punch. He did not notice.

It was the eighth blow that caught Hirst clean. It slammed into his temple, sending him sideways. The sheer force dislodged him from the supporting headstone. With nothing now holding him up, Hirst slumped to the floor.

And Michael could finally stop.

Hirst was beaten.

No longer a threat.

To Michael.

To Sarah.

To anyone.

Michael stumbled backwards. His eyes fixed on Hirst's slumped, battered body. Suddenly he could feel the cost of his efforts. With no battle left to fight, every step became more difficult than the last. Every second blurred his vision more.

Michael had used every last drop of energy fighting Hirst. He had ignored the blood flowing from the bullet wound in his right bicep. Had pushed himself further than he ever thought possible. Only the combination of fear, instinct and pure adrenaline had kept Michael on his feet. Had kept him conscious.

A combination that now disappeared.

One more step backwards. Two. Three.

By the fourth Michael could no longer focus. Could no longer stay upright. His adrenaline was used up. And so was he.

Stumbling a final time, the world went black as Michael dropped to the floor.

SEVENTY-SIX

Joelle Levy's feet hit the ground before the Comanche had even landed.

The closest open space was at least three hundred metres from Michael and Hirst. Almost a minute on foot, in the dark across uneven ground obstructed by headstones and monuments.

Levy moved out of range of the Comanche's propellers. Twenty metres. Far enough to be sure. She lifted the rifle to her shoulder, placed her right eye back behind the scope and closed her left. It made the world visible once again.

It had been impossible to take a second shot from the chopper. The first had been risky enough. Everything that had followed had happened too fast. Michael and Hirst were either on the floor or on top of one another in the moments that followed. Neither position allowed for a clean shot. Neither guaranteed Michael's safety.

Levy scanned the distance. Both the spot where she knew both men had been and the area nearby. The fight had continued as the Comanche had descended, a necessary movement that had obscured Levy's view.

Neither man had come back into her sight since that moment.

Levy covered the distance fast, fuelled by fear of the unknown. Of what Michael could be suffering at the hands of Hirst. It was a fear that disappeared as she reached the headstone that obscured Hirst's battered body.

Levy had spent her adult life surrounded by violence. And by its results. It took her no more than a glance to know that Hirst was going nowhere. Alive or dead. Levy did not care which. Her concern was elsewhere.

'Michael!' Levy slid to a halt next to Michael's unmoving body. 'Michael, can you hear me?'

Michael was unconscious, but up close he looked in much better condition than Hirst. Levy placed two fingers of her right hand on his neck and felt blood pumping upwards through his artery.

His pulse was strong; it made survival likely.

'Michael?' she asked again. This time more gently. 'Can you hear me, Michael?'

Levy examined Michael as she spoke. From his head downwards. Blood on his forehead made her search for a wound to his skull. She found it quickly. The blood came from a shallow cut close to the hairline. It was easy to find; the presence of Hirst's two front teeth – ripped from his mouth by a collision with Michael's head, where they were now embedded – saw to that.

Michael's other injuries were just as obvious. His left hand was beaten and bloody. The knuckles shattered. Levy did not need to wonder what he had used to leave Hirst in the condition she had observed. The injury to his right arm was more serious. Michael's sleeve was soaked in blood. More than there would be if the blood were not his own.

Levy looked for the injury, found it quickly and concluded that it was not life-threatening.

She turned at the sound of running footsteps. It was the pilot.

'Is he OK?'

'He'll live,' Levy called back. 'But he's been shot. We need bandages and whatever kit you've got in the chopper.'

'And the other guy?' The pilot indicated towards Hirst.

'I'll check him while you get the kit. Now go!'

The pilot turned and ran back towards the Comanche.

Six hundred metres, Levy thought. *There and back. Plus time to collect the gear. Two minutes max.*

She got to her feet, walked over to Hirst and dropped to her knees beside him.

The damage Michael had done to Hirst was severe. But it was not fatal. At least not instantly. Air was inflating and deflating a blood bubble below his right nostril with every breath.

Levy looked up. Towards the Comanche. The pilot was halfway there.

She reached into her inside pocket, found her handkerchief and opened it up fully. So that it covered her entire right hand.

She looked up again. The pilot was nearing the chopper.

Levy looked again at Hirst. For a moment she thought of trying to bring him round. In the hope that he would know what was coming.

There would be justice in that, she thought. But Levy did not need such perfection.

Instead she reached out, placed the handkerchief on Hirst's bloody face and covered his nose and his mouth.

And then she squeezed.

SEVENTY-SEVEN

Michael Devlin wiped through the condensation that clung to the bathroom mirror. His reflection stared back at him. Stripped to the waist, a collection of scars dotted his torso.

Some were old. Some were new. And some – like the bullet wound through his right bicep – were obscured entirely by bandages.

'You ready for me to change that dressing?'

Michael turned at the sound of Sarah's voice. He smiled and reached out with his left arm, careful not to clip her with the plaster cast at its end.

'Best offer I've had all month.'

Using just his left forearm, he pulled Sarah close, tight against his body. The water from his shower soaked her clothes, leaving her white blouse transparent.

'Get off of me, you big injured bear.'

Sarah laughed as she pulled away. She pushed Michael back by pressing her hand against his flat stomach, just about the only spot on his torso not covered in bandages or bruises.

Michael slumped backwards. His spine resting against the sweaty bathroom wall. He forced a disappointed expression.

'Oh, I get it. A few cuts and a few broken bones and suddenly I'm not man enough for you. Is that it?'

'It'll take more than that, Michael Devlin.' Sarah glanced up and down. At the plaster case on Michael's left. And at the wet bandages on his right arm. 'But what use are you to me when your hands aren't working, eh?'

Michael roared with laughter at the answer. A genuine laugh. And a relieved laugh.

The separation from Sarah had been short. Just over twenty-four hours physically, a little more emotionally. Yet it had been the hardest of Michael's life. He had lost. He had suffered. In time he would grieve. But right now – with Sarah beside him – Michael was happy.

As if she could read his mind, Sarah placed her hand on Michael's cheek, raised herself up on to her toes and kissed him softly on his lips.

'Now, come on,' she said as she lowered herself to her normal height. 'Let's look at that dressing.'

SEVENTY-EIGHT

'You didn't have to come to court today, Jenny. Honestly. I'd have understood.'

It was 9 a.m. on Monday morning. Two hours since Sarah had expertly changed the dressing on Michael's bicep. Fifty-two since Michael had confronted and beaten Hirst.

And sixty since Draper had been kidnapped.

Draper and Tina Barker had been found by Levy just moments after Hirst's death. Both were restrained but physically unhurt. Still, it was a near miracle that she had made it to the Old Bailey Bar Mess on the second Monday of Simon Kash's trial. And that Michael was here to meet her.

Draper shook her head as Michael spoke. She took a sip from her coffee cup before replying.

'He didn't hurt me. Just a big old bruise on my head. And my wig covers that.'

'Injuries aren't just physical. What you went through was traumatic. You can't just rush back from something like that. You don't *need* to.'

Draper made a point of looking from Michael's left hand to his right arm, and then to his injured head.

'*You're* telling *me* I shouldn't rush back. What about you? You lost Derek Reid. Your family went into hiding. You came, alone, to rescue me and Tina. And you ended up shot and beaten as a result. And *I'm* rushing back?'

'It's different for me. I have to stick with the case. If I don't, it ends and the trial starts all over again. I *can't* go. But *you* can. Please. Take the time. Take care of yourself.'

Draper smiled and shook her head again. Then she reached out for the bottled water that sat next to her cup. She opened it and held it up to Michael.

'You need a drink?'

'Yes,' Michael replied. 'Yes please.'

Draper lifted the bottle to Michael's mouth, tilted it back and poured the cold water past his lips. Two large gulps. Then she set the bottle down.

'Now tell me, Michael Devlin QC. How do you plan to take a drink after I've gone home to recuperate?'

Michael did not answer.

'Exactly. You've got a broken left hand and a right arm you can't move. You *need* me here, Michael. If only for things like that. And after what you did? For me? What kind of a friend would I be if I left you to fend for yourself?'

Michael opened his mouth to respond. Nothing came out. Draper had him beat. She had turned his own words – his own actions – against him.

Michael smiled. The discussion was over.

'So, what's the news on Hirst?' Draper asked. It was a change of subject. But only just.

'I'm off the hook,' Michael replied. He looked down at his broken hand as he spoke. 'Joelle Levy confirmed it yesterday. He died from the fight, and my actions were deemed reasonable.'

Draper did not speak immediately.

'It's better that way,' she finally offered. 'Can you imagine if we'd all had to go through a trial on this?'

'A trial I could take. But he deserved to die.'

'Then he got what he deserved.' Draper paused before speaking again. 'Thank you, Michael. For coming for me. I don't know any other man who would have done that. Who *could* have done that.'

'You need to thank Levy,' Michael replied. 'If she hadn't shown up Hirst would have killed me. No doubt about it.'

'I have thanked her. And now I'm thanking you.'

'Then don't mention it. Please.'

Draper nodded in agreement. Michael's intent was clear. The conversation was over.

And just in time.

'What the bloody hell happened to you?'

The question came from Peter Epstein QC. Called out as he approached Michael and Draper from the rear of the Bar Mess.

Both looked up, confirming where the question was directed. Michael rose to meet Epstein's approach.

'Way too long a story, Pete,' Michael replied. His tone allowed for no follow-up. 'Are we good to go this morning?'

'Not exactly, Michael, no.'

Epstein stopped as he reached them, giving Michael the once-over.

'What do you mean?' Michael asked. 'What's the problem?'

'Oh, it's far from a problem, old boy,' Epstein replied. 'Not for your chap, anyway. We're dropping the case against Simon Kash. He'll be free to go in a couple of hours.'

Michael took just a moment to process the information. Sure, the case had gone well. Very well. But this was still unexpected.

'Why?' It was all Michael could think to ask.

'The case was getting weaker against him every time you bloody stood up. By the end of Colliver's evidence we were going to need a miracle to get you convicted.'

'But still, Pete. I didn't have enough for a half-time submission. You could have used Darren O'Driscoll against us when he gave evidence.'

'I haven't finished, Michael. You see, O'Driscoll is changing his plea. He's going to plead guilty, and he's doing it on the basis that it was Colliver – *not* Simon Kash – who committed the murders with him.'

'And you're going to accept that?' Michael was confused.

'I don't see why not. O'Driscoll will *only* plead if we let Kash go completely and if we re-open our enquiry into Colliver. And after your cross-examination of the man, well, Colliver seems as likely a suspect as anyone else. So why the hell not?'

Michael tried to think of something to say. It was difficult. Perplexing.

He should have been happy. They had won. Simon Kash would walk free. But something about it did not make sense.

Epstein seemed much less concerned.

'Levitt knows all about it, anyway,' he explained. 'So he wants us in court at 9.45. To get it all sorted before the jury arrives. I'll see you down there.'

He left without another word.

Michael turned to Draper. Still shocked by the turn of events. Draper looked just as surprised.

'Well,' she said. 'That's . . . that's . . . you know. Actually, I don't know *what* that is.'

'Me neither,' Michael replied. 'And I need to get my head around it. Would you go down and give Simon the news? And tell him I'll be down to see him afterwards?'

'And what are you going to do?'

'Me? I'm going to find Matt Cole.'

SEVENTY-NINE

'Mr Devlin. Jenny. I honestly can't thank you enough. I . . . I . . . I just can't believe this has happened. I can't believe I'm going home.'

Simon Kash sat in his usual seat. Across the table from Michael and Draper. His back to the interview room door.

Draper smiled. She seemed genuinely happy that justice had been done.

She reached out and gripped Kash's hand.

'It's the right decision, Simon. The right decision. You should never have been in here in the first place.'

Kash returned the smile before turning to Michael.

'Mr Devlin, you were amazing. This would never have happened without you. It really wouldn't. I'm not sure how I can ever repay you.'

Michael returned Kash's gaze. He stared deep into his eyes, as if seeing them for the first time.

'You could fill in some blanks for me, Simon.'

Michael's voice did not share Draper's good humour. Kash looked surprised.

'Erm, OK. I don't really understand, Mr Devlin. But I'll try. What is it you want to know?'

Michael sat back into his chair.

'What I want to know, Simon, is what the hell happened here? Because this doesn't make sense to me. No sense at all.'

'What doesn't?' Kash sounded confused. And nervous.

'O'Driscoll's decision. At least insofar as it affects you.'

'I still don't understand.'

'It's his basis of plea, Simon. I can understand *why* he would plead guilty. The evidence against him is fairly compelling. And I can understand why he'd want to take Terry Colliver down with him, after the evidence Colliver gave. But what I *can't* understand? It's his insistence that the prosecution stop the trial against *you*. That they let you go. It's his insistence that he would *only* plead guilty on that condition. Why, Simon? Why would he do that?'

'Because I'm innocent, Mr Devlin.'

There was a certainty in Kash's voice. A strength that had never been there before.

'So what?' Michael was not accepting the answer. 'He's a stone-cold killer. A ruthless bastard. *You've* told us that yourself.'

'Yes.'

'*And* he was bullying and manipulating you throughout this whole thing, wasn't he? Right up until I got you moved away from him. Until I had you moved to a different prison?'

'Yes.'

'So why would a person like that suddenly do you a favour? Why would he suddenly do the right thing by you, after you'd let me off the leash? After you'd let me attack him in front of the jury?'

'What does that mean?'

'It means *I* prosecuted him better than Peter Epstein ever did. It was *my* cross-examination that left him with no option but to plead. A cross-examination that was done on *your* behalf and which makes *you* the one that convicted him. And yet he's suddenly doing you a favour. It doesn't make sense.'

'I . . . I . . . I can't explain it if *you* can't, Mr Devlin. You're the smart one. If you don't understand it then—'

'Stop it, Simon.' Michael's voice was firm. An instruction to be obeyed. He had finally had enough. 'Stop the act.'

'What do you mean?'

'You know what I mean. You know *exactly* what I mean. I've spoken to Darren O'Driscoll's barrister. And so I *know* why Darren changed his plea. I *know* why Matt Cole was so ineffective against Colliver on

Friday; why he didn't suggest that it was *you* and Colliver who killed the Galloways. I *know* why you're walking out of here today.'

Kash looked shocked. Shocked and afraid. As nervous as Michael had ever seen him.

Draper stepped in.

'Michael, I don't know what this is about but please. You shouldn't be acting this way to—'

'To little Simon?' Michael interrupted, his voice filled with disdain. He turned back to Kash. 'Come on, Simon. It's over. Whatever happens, you walk. So cut the shit.'

'Mr Devlin, I don't . . . I don't . . .'

Kash did not finish the sentence. He stopped himself. For a moment he was silent. Lost in his own mind. And then he did something that Michael alone had expected.

He broke into a broad, arrogant smile.

Both Michael and Draper looked on as Kash pushed himself back into his chair. As he adjusted his posture. Subtle movements. They made him seem taller. Older.

Kash did not glance towards Draper. Instead he kept Michael's eye.

'When'd it stop, then?' The voice was deeper. The accent more pronounced. 'When'd you stop believing?'

Draper looked from Michael to Kash. Then back to Michael. It was clear she could not understand what she was witnessing.

'Later than I should have,' Michael replied. 'But I've had a lot going on.'

'So it seems.' Kash nodded towards Michael's injuries. 'So what did Darren's brief tell you?'

'He told me everything. No reason not to, not now Darren has pleaded and you're out. He told me that you did it all.'

Kash smirked.

'And he told me that O'Driscoll's terrified of you. That all along he was only willing to fight the case if it didn't hurt *your* chances. That everything was to help *you*, no matter what you said about O'Driscoll or how the evidence would reflect on him.'

Kash shrugged. As if what Michael was describing was only right. Pure arrogance in every movement.

Michael continued.

'And he said that once O'Driscoll had no chance – once he knew he was getting convicted – he instructed his lawyers to do whatever they could to get you out.'

Kash chuckled to himself throughout Michael's answer and laughed aloud when it finished. He nodded his head as he spoke again.

'Yeah. That all sounds about right.'

'Simon, you can't . . .' Draper was lost for words. 'Michael . . .'

'Don't worry yourself about it, love.' Kash mimicked Draper's hand-touch as he spoke. 'Cleverer people than you have bought into that act.'

Kash returned his attention to Michael.

'You know, I thought you'd sussed things on Friday, truth be told.'

'I had my suspicions,' Michael replied. 'But like I said. Distractions. So it wasn't until this morning that it fell into place. Why O'Driscoll would ride you out of this. Why Matt Cole failed to attack Colliver properly, because it would have meant attacking *you*. And why Colliver reacted the way he did when I suggested you were bullied. Why he said for the first time on Friday that it was *you* he was afraid of, and then suddenly clammed up when he was about to say more. That's because he caught your eye, right? You broke the act for a moment and stared him down, didn't you. Just none of us got to see it.'

Kash slowly clapped his hands in response.

'Good guess, Mr Devlin.' Kash said the final two words with as much disrespect as he could manage. 'Yeah, those few months inside gave Colliver the guts to tell the truth, to save his own skin. But I always knew he'd be less brave once he could see me across a courtroom. That he'd be less willing to tell everything. Then you got under that skin and he started blurting things out, so yeah, Little Simon had to take his eyes off the floor for a bit. With all eyes on him, though, none of you lot even noticed.'

'So was that what Friday was, then? Afterwards, in the cells? Were you struggling to get back in character?'

'Something like that, yeah,' Kash replied, still smirking. 'Not that it triggered enough alarm bells for you to work this out for yourself, though. Fine forensic mind my arse. If the tables were turned, let me tell you, I'd have known then.'

'I bet you would,' Michael replied. 'So Colliver was telling the truth. What about Jay Price? He was lying through his teeth. Was that down to you?'

'Me? Nah, that was just a little present Terry gave us. He must have thought his story wouldn't be believed on its own, so he got his mate Price to make up a load of bollocks about a confession to corroborate it. Lucky he did. Without Price telling a load of lies you'd have had a lot less to go after Colliver with.'

'And the phone evidence?'

'It's like you said that day, ain't it?' The smirk again. This time worse than before. 'Just because my phone weren't there, it don't mean I weren't.'

'But . . . but, why?' Draper finally joined the debate. Her shock – her disbelief – was making her falter. 'The Galloways, they did nothing to you.'

'They served a purpose,' Kash replied. 'Just like you two. The Galloways had a reputation in that world. A standing. Now I've got it. It's a big jump up the ladder, all for a couple of hours' work.'

'But O'Driscoll, he just pleaded to the killing?'

'People ain't stupid, love. They might believe the story for a minute or two. But word gets out. I'll get my credit, don't you worry.'

Michael nodded. Everything now made perfect sense.

Little Simon Kash had never existed. The boy for whom he had risked so much was a myth. And all that was left was the smirking sociopath sitting across the table.

He had just one more question:

'If this is all true, why did O'Driscoll's brother come after me?'

Kash laughed again. He seemed to be enjoying himself. Revelling in his deception, in his own cleverness.

'Yeah,' he laughed. 'That one was nearly a spanner in the works. That was Pat trying to stop you cross-examining Darren. They knew I was gonna let you attack him. That I was making out I didn't want to, but that in the end I'd pretend to cave. They couldn't stop *me* doing it – wouldn't dare try – so they thought *you'd* be the weak link; that they could take you out and I'd never be the wiser about who did it. Fucking idiots. It didn't work out too well for them anyway, did it? Not from what I've heard.'

Kash held his hands up at head height and clapped again. A slow, deliberate round of applause.

'So bravo, Mr Devlin. You were the perfect choice all the way round. The perfect little puppet.'

The clapping stopped. Kash placed his hands on the table and pushed down, rising suddenly to his feet.

'And on that note, I'm gonna head back to my cell. Have a little sleep while I wait for my release papers.'

He walked to the door and put his head outside.

'GUARD! I'M DONE!'

Moved his head back in.

'Shame of it is, I've got some things planned. Sort of things where I could have used someone as good as you if they went wrong. But I guess that can't happen now, can it?'

The sound of jangling keys told Michael that a custody officer was coming.

Kash continued.

'Still. I'm sure I'll see you both again. One way or the other.'

Kash looked into Draper's eyes as he said those final words. Draper looked back. Horrified. With a casual wink of the eye, Kash walked away.

Michael and Draper stayed silent as they watched him go. No words. No movements. Both lost in thought.

In the same thought.

What the hell did we just do?

Acknowledgements

In the year since the publication of *Killer Intent* I have been asked a lot of different questions, but one in particular has stood out: 'How does it feel now you're a successful author?'

This question has stuck with me because I don't regard myself as a successful author. Not yet. But the term 'successful author' will always be misleading because it suggests that a book's writer is solely responsible for its creation. This could not be further from the truth. A book, I was amazed to discover, is not purely the product of its author. It is the product of a skilled team. Of a support network. Of experts there to identify and deal with the writer's weaknesses. And of friends and committed readers brave enough to tell the author that his 'baby' isn't as perfect as he thinks. The input from this 'team' is truly invaluable, and so it is my pleasure to now thank them.

For the second time in as many books, I have to begin with the two women who – between them – are the only reason I have a writing career at all.

To my own Sarah Truman, my amazing wife, Victoria. Without your encouragement – and your determined efforts to stop my procrastination and distraction – this book would not have been written. Your patience while I write, your careful reading when I'm done and your ability to make our life work around all of the madness is beyond measure. I cannot imagine my life without you; you mean everything and there are no words that do you justice.

And to my mum: once again you were with me as this book grew from nothing and became *Marked For Death*. Once again you listened to my long, meandering calls as I explained plot points and intricate detail about the lives of people who existed only in my own head. You could have said 'enough' as I set out this imaginary world over the course of months. Instead you humoured me, you encouraged me and you occasionally reined in my more outlandish ideas. You have always been my biggest supporter in everything I do (well, other than boxing . . .) and absolutely none of this would exist without you. Every son owes his mother his life. I somehow owe you more. But 'no charge', right?

Next I need to acknowledge my amazing team at Elliott and Thompson. Where would I be without you? I shudder to think! Jennie Condell, Pippa Crane, Angela McMahon, Anthony Keates, Rob Cox and Marianne Thorndahl. All of you have played your different parts in my career so far, in this book, and in my life. You have become a second family and any success we have with *Marked For Death* is as much yours as it is mine. This is the book it is because of you all. I hope it lives up to your amazing efforts.

Missing from my Elliott and Thompson roll-call is Lorne Forsyth. The boss. The man to whom I owe the greatest thanks. Lorne took an enormous risk on an untested criminal lawyer with aspirations to write, and he has backed that risk to the hilt. Lorne, I've said it before and I'll say it again; my dad aside, I owe more to you than I owe to any other man. Thank you.

To Neil Speight, my friend. It was with Neil's help that I developed any writing style I may have; he knocked off some of the rough edges and those that remain are not for want of him trying. No one has had a greater impact on what I do and a mere 'thank you' will never be enough. Neil is also more responsible than anyone else for *Marked For Death*. It was Neil who advised me to revisit Michael Devlin when all I wanted to do was to follow Joe Dempsey to New York (we'll do that Book Three, for those who wanted to go with me . . .) and it was Neil who, when first reading this book, gave me the confidence that it at least matched *Killer Intent*. Neil, you know how much I owe you and what you mean to me and to my family. Thank you from us all.

To Daniel Gedeon, David Headley, Pavla Safratova and all the team at Goldsboro, for your support and now for your tireless efforts in the launch of the book. It is an absolute privilege for a writer at this stage of his career to find a place at your amazing store. I hope we can make all the hard work worthwhile!

To my brother Derek, who – like Mum – lived and breathed the development of *Marked For Death*, and who provided me with endless encouragement as the story grew into the book you now hold. He might not look much like a cheerleader, but he has been a great one!

To my dad for his wordless encouragement and silent support. Not a demonstrative man by any means, I am still left in no doubt that my dad will do anything I need to make the most of my new career. I could not ask for a stronger foundation upon which my life and the life of my family is built.

And to my sister, Kate, who came to the party a little late but who – once she had read both books – became my most enthusiastic and vocal supporter. And who I am convinced now works for my publishers, as literally no one pesters me quite as often to get Book Three finished! Almost there, Kate.

Next, to the men who provided the inspiration for parts of the storyline. Two of my closest friends, one now a senior barrister (and part basis for the character of Derek Reid) and one now a senior Crown Court Judge. Both were involved in the real-life case from which this story grew. I won't name you for very obvious reasons, but you both know who you are and I hope you both know how much you mean to me, as the writer of this book and as your friend.

To Grant Benjamin, my most annoying friend; for reading the very rough first draft and for being his brutally honest self in his feedback. The fact that he was 90 per cent positive was an incredible boost for me, because we both know he would have loved to pick more holes.

To James Walker, a great barrister and a fine mate who – without going into detail – covered for me professionally when time was tightest, allowing me to kickstart this whole 'writer' thing! I owe you, Jimmy!!

And to everyone at Ewing Law – and particularly my true friend Scott Ewing – for supporting and understanding my drive to write and for bending over backwards to allow me to make this a success. It's easy to say that I could not do this without you but I really couldn't. It is a lucky man who gets to work with his friends, and an even luckier man who can find an office of lawyers as kind, understanding and supportive as they are at Ewing Law.

To the authors who have welcomed me into the crime writing community over the last year, offering support, advice and friendship, and who have made this new career such a pleasure: Ian Rankin, Mason Cross, Imran Mahmood, Angela Clarke, Neil White, Steve Moseby, Mark Lawson and many, many more.

To the many stores – big and small – who got behind *Killer Intent*. It is still a source of amazement when I see a copy on a shelf. I don't think it will ever get old.

And finally I must thank Zoe Ball, Amanda Ross, the team at Cactus TV and everyone at Zoe Ball on Sunday, for selecting *Killer Intent* for the Zoe Ball Book Club and giving me a writing kick-start that money cannot buy. I could not be more grateful.

Which just leaves you, the readers. Ultimately you are what makes a 'successful author'. The reader who enjoys the book. The reader who perhaps reviews the book. And the reader who buys the next in the series. My thanks go to everyone who has read *Killer Intent* and to everyone who has now read *Marked For Death*. Your enjoyment of these books is ultimately all that matters, and I thank you sincerely for your continuing support.

P.S. And thank you to my wonderful son Joseph, who arrived last year; our second big release of 2018! You don't know it, son, but from the moment you were born you became the reason for everything. And who needs sleep anyway?

OUT NOW IN PAPERBACK

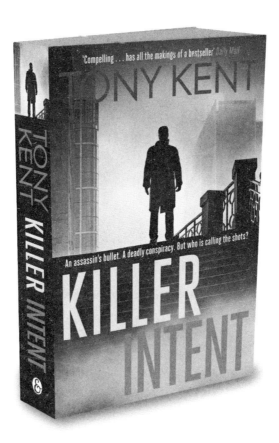

When an attempted assassination sparks a chain
reaction of explosive events across London, Britain's elite
security forces seem powerless to stop the chaos
threatening to overwhelm the government.

As the dark and deadly conspiracy unfolds, three strangers
find their fates entwined: Joe Dempsey, a deadly military
intelligence officer; Sarah Truman, a CNN reporter determined
to get her headline; and Michael Devlin, a Belfast-born
criminal barrister with a secret past.

As the circle of those they can trust grows ever smaller,
Dempsey, Devlin and Truman are forced to work in the
shadows, caught in a life-or-death race against the clock,
before the terrible plot can consume them all.

RRP: £7.99 • ISBN: 978-1-78396-382-9

To hear all the latest news about Tony, his writing and his events, visit **www.tonykent.net** or follow him on Twitter: **@TonyKent_writes**, Instagram: **tonykent_writes**, and Facebook: **Tony Kent – Author**